Where

# Where The Heart Is
## Is
## – Home –

Kate Lock

HEADLINE

Copyright © 1998 Kate Lock and Anglia Television Productions

The right of Kate Lock and Anglia Television Productions
to be identified as the Authors of the Work has been
asserted by them in accordance with the
Copyright, Designs and Patents Act 1988.

Based on the series starring Pam Ferris and Sarah Lancashire,
and created by Ashley Pharoah and Vicky Featherstone.

First published in paperback in 1998
by HEADLINE BOOK PUBLISHING

10 9 8 7 6 5 4 3 2 1

ISBN 0 7472 6023 0

Typeset by
Letterpart Limited, Reigate, Surrey

Printed and bound in Great Britain by
Mackays of Chatham plc, Chatham, Kent

HEADLINE BOOK PUBLISHING
A division of Hodder Headline PLC
338 Euston Road
London NW1 3BH

For Isis

# Chapter 1

Peggy's breath plumed like smoke in the wintry morning air as she jogged flat-footedly along the muddy towpath. Despite the bright sunlight bathing the leafless landscape there was a nip of snow on the breeze. The moors above the small West Yorkshire town were dusted with white and the chill caught at the back of her throat, causing her to stop and cough violently. 'Kill or cure,' she muttered to herself, zipping up the neck of her new tracksuit and pushing on again, wondering why, at forty-four, she was worrying about honing her rather matronly figure. Vic, her husband, loved her ample bosom and well-cushioned buttocks, saying, 'You need summat to get hold of,' whenever she moaned about her bulges (bless him, he was developing pretty good love handles himself). Maybe it would prevent her arteries furring up – they were certainly working overtime at the moment – and at least it gave her precious time to think. Running concentrated her mind, especially when things were bothering her. Like today.

She jogged to the end of the path by the bridge and joined the pavement, pushing damp strands of hair from her eyes. A woman with a shopping basket approached, smiling at her exertions. 'Morning, Peggy.'

'Morning, Doreen, love.' Peggy ploughed on along the road, waving hellos to dog-walkers and early risers. Embarrassingly, a milk float overtook her, George, the milkman, making out he was a jockey, elbows flapping, imaginary whip raised, as he inched the vehicle past. Peggy grinned wryly, acknowledging her slow progress. Her job as a district nurse gave her a visible profile in the community and she knew almost everybody. People trusted her and turned to her with their problems. It frustrated Peggy enormously that she couldn't always provide them with solutions. Particularly when she knew how badly they needed help.

She staggered to a halt and bent over to draw breath, hands on hips, noticing as she stood upright again the Doctor's red car coming towards her. She flagged him down and he stopped, winding down the window impatiently.

'What is it, Peggy?' Dr Frank Underwood said without pleasantries. She leaned into the car, too fagged to speak. 'Peggy,' he snapped, tapping the steering wheel and glaring at her over his glasses.

'I'm sorry to bother you, Doctor. Mrs Hutton . . .' she gasped.

'What about Mrs Hutton?'

'She's in a lot of pain. I wondered—'

He sighed wearily. 'She's in a lot of pain because she's dying. Dying in a damp, depressing house when she should be dying in the hospice where we could look after her.'

Peggy, who had recovered herself, stood her ground. 'She *wanted* to die at home.'

'And you said you could cope.'

'She's in absolute agony.' Miserable, overbearing man. He hadn't been up to the Huttons' hill farm every day like she had and witnessed this woman's suffering.

Dr Underwood continued to patronize. 'Peggy, will you learn something here? You're a district nurse. You put plasters on cuts.'

She ignored the insult. 'Can't you give her anything stronger?'

'There isn't anything stronger. If she wants to go back into the hospice—'

Peggy gritted her teeth and said, stubbornly, 'She doesn't.'

'Then it's her bed, isn't it?' he punned crudely, releasing the clutch without warning and forcing Peggy to jerk her head back out of the car quickly. She watched as he drove away towards the health centre, her heart no longer in her morning run.

Vic Snow, clad in striped pyjama bottoms and a vest, hammered on the bathroom door. Stephen, his seventeen-year-old son, had locked himself in and could be heard singing, 'Say it's only a paper moon, Sailing over a cardboard sea . . .' He appeared to be immune to threats of parental retribution. Vic banged harder. 'Open the door, Stephen! I'm not bloody joking!' Lucy, Stephen's gap-toothed little sister, watched from the safety of her bedroom doorway. She squealed naughtily at her father's exasperated expletive. 'But it wouldn't be make-believe if you believed in me,' Stephen continued to sing blithely.

'I'll knock bloody door down!' Vic was beside himself.

Peggy, who had let herself in and heard the ruckus from the hall, came up the stairs. 'Not again,' she said grimly, still in a black mood about Dr Underwood's remarks.

Vic turned a stubbled chin towards her. 'He's locked himself int bathroom again and I'm going to be late. Again.'

'You could always try getting up earlier,' she said pointedly. Vic liked a lie-in.

'I'd have to be up before I went to bed to get into the bathroom before him,' he responded huffily.

Peggy took charge, as she always did. 'Stephen. Get out of bathroom and let your father in.' There was an edge of menace to her voice.

'What does he *do* in there?' Vic grumbled. 'When I were a lad we tried to stay out of bathroom.' The door opened, a warm rush of aftershave and steam assaulting them, and Stephen appeared, black hair slicked with gel, a bath towel draped like a toga over his fit torso. He looked extraordinarily pleased with himself and wore a huge doggy grin.

3

'About time, you big jesse,' Vic complained.

Stephen – who was playing Stanley Kowalski in the school production of *A Streetcar Named Desire* – merely lounged against the door jamb, still blocking his father, and proclaimed in a mock-Brando accent: ' "I am a one hundred per cent American, born and raised in the greatest country on earth".'

'A big girl's blouse, that's what you are,' retorted Vic.

'Go and get ready for school.' Peggy bundled him out of the doorway.

' "—and proud as hell of it".' Stephen remained in character.

'Stephen!' She gave him a little push. Vic made a 'he's crazy' gesture but Peggy gave him short shrift, too. 'Excuse me. One empty bathroom,' she said, steering him into it. The door closed. Snorts of disgust indicated that Vic thought the bathroom reeked of pretty-boy perfume. Stephen paused, and threw over his shoulder, melodramatically, ' "And that girl calls *me* common".'

Peggy looked strict. 'If I was you I might try behaving myself. Because if I don't like what I hear from your headmaster today—'

'Why can't you just phone like a normal person?' he interrupted.

'—your life won't be worth living.' Stephen disappeared into his room, with a shrug. Peggy sighed. It was only 8.00am and she was feeling wound up already. Lucy, who had been observing with interest throughout, giggled. 'It's not funny,' Peggy said sternly. She felt she should be seen to be keeping the upper hand, but Lucy's laughter was infectious. Peggy's face creased into a rueful smile and she caught herself chuckling.

She went to change into her blue uniform and put her hair up, her thoughts still on her wayward son. It wasn't just Stephen's behaviour at school that was troubling her. Organizing wild parties for the sixth form was one thing, but he was obviously indulging in some pretty wild extra-curricular

4

activities too. She went down to breakfast, pondering how to tackle him about it, but he shot out of the house – wearing her tracksuit top, she noticed – like a scalded cat. Peggy watched as he went up to a pretty, long-haired girl who had apparently been waiting for him outside. Stephen said something and the girl blushed shyly. They walked off up the road close together, bumping schoolbags, and Peggy felt a sudden lump in her throat. Stephen hadn't had any serious girlfriends before, to her knowledge anyway. She recognised her as Deborah Alliss, a classmate of Stephen's, who was playing Stella opposite his Stanley in *Streetcar*. Well, she seemed a nice kid, Peggy comforted herself. If it had to be someone . . . Her musings were rudely interrupted by a shriek from Lucy, who scampered into the kitchen hotly pursued by Vic, still in his vest and covered in shaving foam. 'I'll get you, you little monkey,' he roared, playing monsters. Lucy, mock-scared, ran out again. 'I thought you were late for work?' Peggy shouted above the din, but they were too involved in their game to take any notice.

'Who gave us these?' Ruth Goddard inspected a new tin of Family Assortment for chocolate biscuits. At thirty-four weeks pregnant she had ceased to worry about putting on weight – a few extra pounds were neither here nor there in her condition – and anyway, she was ravenously hungry. Breakfast had, after all, been an hour ago. Junior was obviously a guzzler, she decided. She wore a light blue staff nurse's uniform, let out to accommodate her bump, and her blonde hair was twisted into a neat French pleat. Despite Ruth's advanced pregnancy, her ankles were still enviably slim, her colleague, Patricia Illingworth, noted gloomily. She took off her black shoes, noting her own plump calves, and stood on the medical scales that they kept in their office at the Skelthwaite Health Centre.

'Mrs Wilson. For doing her abscess,' she replied, preoccupied. 'Why can't they give us fruit?' she added, stepping off again.

'How are you doing?' Ruth looked up, munching on a Bourbon.

'Two pounds.'

'That's not bad. It's only been a couple of weeks,' she said encouragingly.

'Two pounds heavier,' confessed Patricia, downcast.

'Oh.' Ruth closed the lid.

Patricia decided to deflect attention from her diet. 'Mr Hutton phoned, said his wife had a bad night.'

'Right. I expect we'll go up and do her first. Poor woman.' Ruth sat down again, one hand supporting her aching back. The door opened and Peggy Snow bustled in, carrying two enormous packs of incontinence pants. 'Morning. Who ordered more pants?' She plonked them down on the floor and opened a cupboard.

'Not me. We've got a pant mountain in there,' replied Ruth. They surveyed the shelves, which were piled high. 'Skelthwaite. Incontinence capital of the world,' joked Peggy.

'Mrs Hutton had a bad night,' Ruth commented, knowing Peggy's feelings about the pain the dying woman was suffering.

'What a surprise.' Peggy, remembering her joyless encounter with Dr Underwood, sounded bitter. 'Who's on with me?'

Ruth got up and put on her cardigan. 'I am.'

'Who else are we doing?' Peggy said briskly.

'Take out the Edrich boy's stitches. Bath for Mrs Perkins.' Ruth pored over the diary and paused. 'And dress Mr Huxley's infected leg.'

Peggy pulled a face. 'You can do that.'

'I did it last time!' she protested, one arm in her coat.

Her sister-in-law winked – Ruth was married to Peggy's brother, Simon – to show she wasn't serious and said, 'Pat, phone stores and tell them where to put their pants.'

'Right.'

Peggy hesitated, weighing the packs in her hands. 'On

second thoughts, don't bother. I'll stick 'em int car and take them round to St Hilda's later. They go through them like a dose of salts.' They got ready to leave. 'Right. Mrs Hutton.' Peggy squared her shoulders.

Ruth gave Patricia a wave and followed Peggy out. 'Mrs Hutton,' she echoed, closing the door behind them. Left alone, Patricia eyed the biscuit tin. It was too bad to have to sit with such temptation. One wouldn't hurt. She crept across the floor, opened the lid and jumped back guiltily as a handwritten message admonished her: 'KEEP OUT FAT PIG!'

Peggy's Ford Fiesta turned out of the health centre and took a route past the towering soot-blackened chimney of the huge nineteenth-century textile mill that had once made Skelthwaite a thriving little town. Nowadays it stood idle, like most of the old mills in that part of the country. Their tall, bleak stacks were testament to the region's industrial past before cheap imports decimated the local economy and left communities locked in historical limbo.

Skelthwaite was not a particularly attractive town. It sprawled in a valley; old, cramped, grimy dwellings at odds with the newer, but equally ugly council houses strung out up the valley's sloping sides. Apart from the mill, a many-arched viaduct was its most notable landmark. Peggy, driving past a parade of dilapidated shops, had never stopped to wonder why she felt so attached to Skelthwaite. She had been born and brought up there. To some extent it defined who she was. She and Vic, for he was a Skelthwaite lad, too. It was only recently, since Stephen had begun to make scathing remarks about it, that she had begun to ask herself what made her spring to the defence of her crumbling home town. Leaving had never occurred to her. Was she so very unambitious – or just easily satisfied? She supposed it was all about having a sense of belonging. Peggy could quite understand why Mrs Hutton wanted to die at home, surrounded by the reassuring, familiar fabric of her life.

The lanes were still clear but the verges and dry-stone walls wore a mantle of snow as the car climbed higher towards the moors. Peggy dropped down a gear and, prompted by thoughts of Stephen, asked, 'Has Mrs Hutton's son turned up?'

Ruth shook her head. 'They can't get hold of him. You can bet your boots that's what she's hanging on for, though.'

'I don't remember him,' Peggy mused.

'He din't hang around. I remember at school, my only ambition was to get a love bite the size of Wales – but all Martin Hutton did was read. He said it were his ticket out of here.'

Ruth glanced out of the window, recalling, briefly, Simon's attempts to deliver said love bite. They were childhood sweethearts and had even been in the same class. Their carefree youth seemed an age ago, she thought. Look at them now: thirty-one years old, married and about to make the biggest commitment of their lives to a tiny human being. She stroked her belly meditatively.

'You know when you were at school. Were you . . .?' Peggy broke into her contemplation.

'What?'

'You know.'

'Was I what?'

'Active,' said Peggy obliquely, not looking at her.

'Active? How d'you mean, active?' Ruth used to hate gym; it ruined her make-up.

Peggy decided to spell it out. 'You *know*. Were you doing it?'

The penny dropped. 'Excuse me! Bit personal, first thing.' Ruth tried to look shocked, wondering where this was leading.

Peggy indicated the glove compartment. 'Have a look in there.'

Curious, Ruth opened it and extracted a small, white, lacy

8

bra. Her jaw dropped. 'Bloody hell! It's never yours?'

Peggy made a 'hrrmph' noise. 'Of course it's not mine.'

'It's like a doll's hammock,' laughed Ruth, stretching the minuscule bra out and examining it closely. 'Where d'you find it?'

'In my bed.'

This time Ruth was genuinely shocked. She stared at Peggy, horrified. 'Not Vic?'

'No, not Vic. If he were going to have an affair he'd have more sense than to do it in his own bed.' That she was sure of.

'Stephen?'

'Must be.'

'In *your* bed?'

Peggy nodded. The car vibrated over a cattle grid. Ruth chortled, her hand over her mouth. 'It's not funny,' Peggy said, for the second time that morning.

'Who's the lucky girl?' Ruth's eyes gleamed.

'I don't know. I haven't had the nerve to ask him.'

Ruth held the fragile garment up to her swollen breasts and sighed. 'I tell you what, though—'

'What?'

'It's not mine.' And, once again, Peggy found herself laughing helplessly.

Vic squatted down, his knees creaking, and squinted at some huge rollers which had jammed up again. He couldn't see what the problem was, but then, he reflected philosophically, that seemed to be his lot in life. Other people got steamed up about things that seemed to him to be quite straightforward. Take Peggy. She would go ballistic when she heard about her brother's latest ploy; Simon, on the other hand, would get irate if Vic didn't do anything about it. Either way, he couldn't win.

Vic felt uncomfortable about being stuck in the middle. Essentially an easy-going man, he was content with his job, working in a toilet-roll factory. It wasn't glamorous, but it

9

paid enough, and with Peggy's income as a district nursing sister, they did quite well – particularly by Skelthwaite standards. Even the fact that his brother-in-law was his employer couldn't throw him, although he professed to hate it. If he was truthful, he was actually rather proud of Simon's achievement, although he would never actually admit it: Simon was quite egotistical and brash enough as it was. Vic suffered his patronage most of the time – out of work they drank together and had a laugh – and he wasn't afraid to take Simon down a peg when he was being obnoxious.

'Oi, Vic,' a voice shouted over the din of the machines. Vic got stiffly to his feet and saw a colleague, Dick, grinning at him. 'I hear we'll be taking orders from Stephen before long.' Dick was a master wind-up merchant.

'Who told you that?' replied Vic crossly, wiping his hands on the seat of his overalls, which were emblazoned with the words, 'Goddard Paper Products' in prominent lettering.

'Little bird. Be odd, taking orders from your own son. I mean, taking orders from your brother-in-law must be odd enough—'

'Dick.' Vic fixed him with a look.

'Yes, Vic?' Dick said innocently.

'Shut up.'

'Yes, Vic.'

'And get on phone to engineers. Tell them number three's buggered again.'

'Yes, Vic.' Dick walked away with smile that could have belonged to the Cheshire Cat.

Vic put down his spanner and climbed the stairs to Simon's office, which had large soundproofed windows overlooking the factory floor. He knocked and popped his head around the door. The office was a haven of quiet after the perpetual racket of the machinery. Simon glanced up. 'Thought you'd like to know – number three's gone again,' Vic said.

'Bloody hell! That paper's got to be up a Texan's bum by next week!' Simon raked a hand through his short red hair.

10

He was a good-looking man and was nattily dressed in a suit and tie, making Vic feel grimy and dishevelled.

'I know, I know.'

'Have you phoned engineers?'

'They're on their way.' Vic turned to leave but Simon was too quick for him.

'Vic?'

'Yes?'

'What did Stephen say?'

Vic squirmed uncomfortably. 'About what?'

'You know about what.'

'I dint get chance to talk to him.'

Simon stood up, placing his hands on the desk in front of him. 'You dint get chance?' His voice rose. 'I'm offering to change your son's life and you dint get chance?' he said incredulously.

'I'll speak to him today,' replied Vic, backing out of the door.

Simon set his mouth in a firm line. 'You'd better, Vic. Because I won't ask again.'

Stephen – still in Brandoesque mode – held Deborah by the arms and looked deep into her eyes. ' "Stell, it's gonna be alright after she goes and after you've had the baby. It's gonna be all right between you and me the way it was. You remember the way it was? Them nights we had together?" ' The other kids in the drama group stopped messing about and watched, impressed by Stephen's convincing performance, his total self-confidence. Stephen Snow burned with an inner light; he was intense, focused, compelling. It was obvious he was going to go far. His teacher, Wendy Atkins, a young woman in her early twenties, studied him carefully as he pulled Deborah close to him. The infatuated Deborah returned Stephen's rapt gaze, turning a deep pink. ' "God, honey, it's gonna be sweet when we can make noise in the night the way we used to and get the coloured lights going with nobody's sister behind the curtains to hear us",' Stephen continued, stroking her hair. Suddenly, he wrapped his arms around the startled Deborah and kissed her long and hard, a mature, sexual kiss. Their smirking classmates began to cheer and clap as Deborah, having no difficulty getting into her part, responded enthusiastically.

'Yes, alright, thank you,' Wendy shouted at the couple. The kiss continued, to whistles and whoops from the cast. 'Thank *you*,' Wendy shouted again crossly, louder this time. Stephen broke away, smiling broadly. Deborah looked at her feet, surreptitiously brushing her lips with the back of her hand. 'I don't remember a kiss in the text. Did I miss something?' Wendy asked sarcastically.

'Sorry Miss.' Stephen looked anything but contrite. 'I just thought that Stanley would want to kiss Stella to remind her of how it used to be.'

'I'm sure if Tennessee Williams had wanted Stanley to kiss Stella that's what he would have written.'

'I know, Miss. But what if—'

'Stephen.' Wendy wasn't going to be shown up in front of the class. It was her first teaching job and she knew how important it was to keep their respect. 'Maybe when you've travelled further than Huddersfield you'll have earned the right to question one of the greatest playwrights of the century. Until then we'll stick to the text. Alright?' Stephen nodded, shame-faced. But only a little.

John Hutton was waiting outside the isolated stone farmhouse for them when Peggy and Ruth arrived. They had seen him from the road below, standing like a lookout and staring down into the valley at Skelthwaite's rooftops in the distance. He was a tough, wiry man in his sixties with a shock of grey hair which seemed whiter every time Peggy visited him. His eyes were sunken and he looked exhausted. She put a hand briefly on his shoulder and followed him inside, to where his wife, Madeleine, lay in a single bed made up in the front room. Her chest rattled rhythmically, seeming to demand every last ounce of energy from her pitifully thin body to draw each new lungful of breath. Peggy smoothed the papery skin of her forehead and took her birdlike hand. She looked at Ruth and saw her face contracted with concern. They both felt so impotent to help her. Yet to see a human being wracked with such pain was almost unbearable. That was why John Hutton had been outside, she realized. He couldn't bear to witness this cruelty.

They washed Madeleine as gently as a baby, sponging her limbs softly and talking to her reassuringly, but even that caused her to shudder and moan. 'Why don't you do something?' demanded John, pacing up and down.

'Mr Hutton—' began Peggy.

'Give her some morphine!' he begged.

'You know we can't do that. We're nurses, not doctors.'

'Get a doctor then!' John's face tightened as Madeleine's fingers clawed at the worn eiderdown, another spasm of pain searing through her.

'I've spoken to Doctor Underwood. He wants her to go back into the hospice.'

'No! She wants to be home,' he howled furiously.

Peggy lead him away from Madeleine's bedside, aware that hearing was often one of the last faculties to decline. 'I know, pet, I know. She knows exactly what she wants. So we just have to be brave for her.'

John looked at Peggy, his eyes pleading, and in a cracked voice said, 'Please do something. You wouldn't let a dog suffer like this. Please.'

She knew what he was really asking her to do, but how could they? The dying woman shuddered again and Peggy knew what her heart told her to do.

Having made Madeleine as comfortable as they could, Peggy made John a cup of hot, sweet tea, despite his protestations that he didn't want anything. 'We should get on. Mrs Edrich'll be on war path,' said Ruth, as they washed up

13

the cups in the Huttons' spartan kitchen.

'I know, I know.' Peggy sighed. 'I don't want to leave her like this.'

'What else can we do?' Ruth meant it rhetorically – they had done all they possibly could – but Peggy answered quietly, 'We could move her.' Ruth's eyes widened. Both of them knew that if Madeleine was moved there was a chance that the fragile thread of her life would snap. 'She's in terrible pain, Ruth. I've never seen anything like it,' Peggy whispered. Ruth had sometimes wondered how she would react in such a situation. It didn't take her long to decide. Faced with such suffering – death could only be hours away now, in any case – her response was instinctive. She folded her tea towel and said decisively, 'We should put her on commode before we go.' Peggy nodded and followed her back into the room.

'Alright, pet, almost there,' Peggy crooned as, one either side of her, they eased the semi-conscious woman into a sitting position on the side of the bed. John hovered behind them, agitated. 'But she dint want to go to toilet.' Suddenly, Ruth winced and clutched her belly, the exertion causing her a dart of pain. Stitch, probably, she thought, exhaling through her mouth. Peggy looked worriedly across at her. 'You alright, Ruth?

'I'm fine. Let's get her on.'

Afterwards they tucked her back into bed and packed up their things, preparing to leave. Madeleine's breathing seemed the same and Peggy felt a stab of regret that they had put the poor woman through such an undignified ordeal for nothing. She glanced at Ruth, who shrugged. Now they really had done all they could. John still dogged their heels, his face a mask of misery. 'You can't just go,' he cried wretchedly.

Peggy tried to be brisk. 'If anything happens, you phone Health Centre, right?'

John was unable to answer, his watery eyes glued to Madeleine's still form on the bed. Peggy squeezed his arm and followed Ruth out into the hall. They opened the front door to find a man in an overcoat standing there, pale-faced and shivering. His arm was raised, as if he were about to knock. 'Hello, Martin,' said Ruth, surprised.

Martin Hutton stared at her, puzzled. He was feeling disoriented after the long drive up the motorway from London, as if he was still in motion. His executive saloon ate up the miles but the traffic had been heavy and he'd got held up in a tailback. Worried by the urgency of the call he'd received, he had not stopped to break the journey, his mind racing through every eventuality. It was a very long time since he'd been home, and coming back to the farmhouse – such a stark, isolated building, stuck out in the middle of nowhere – brought back a lot of memories. Most of them were bad, like the shock of going round the very same bend in the road where Sarah was killed. He noticed there were fresh flowers on the spot.

'It's Ruth. We were at school together.' Ruth stared at Martin and noted that the years had not been kind to him. His lank hair was streaked with grey and his features were pinched.

Martin Hutton barely bothered to acknowledge her. 'How's my mother?' he demanded. He seemed agitated.

Ruth and Peggy exchanged a look. 'We din't know you were coming.' Peggy felt upset. She might have done things differently, had she been told Martin was on his way – she was sure Ruth was right, that Madeleine was hanging on to see her only son.

'I got home to a message saying she wanted to see me. Is she very ill?' he demanded.

'She is, I'm afraid,' Ruth said gently, trying to prepare him. 'Martin—'

There was a wail from inside and he pushed past her. She and Peggy hurried back into the house to find John Hutton on his knees by his wife's bed. 'She's gone! She's gone!' he sobbed, tears of sorrow and relief coursing down his lined cheeks. Peggy took over. 'Let me see, pet.' She felt for a pulse in Madeleine's neck. There was none. She closed the dead woman's eyes, overcome by an emotion she couldn't describe. Ruth picked up the mobile and dialled a number.

'I'm so sorry.' Peggy took in Martin Hutton's shocked face as he stood, white-lipped, in the doorway, realization dawning on him that he was just minutes too late. John Hutton turned around and, seeing his son, snarled unexpectedly, 'Get out of my house.' Martin, transfixed by his mother's gaunt visage, set in death, did not move.

'John?' Peggy was horrified at his reaction.

'Get out of my house!' he roared again, lunging at Martin in a blind fury. Peggy intervened, placing herself between them. 'That's enough, John. Think about Madeleine.'

'I am thinking about her,' he replied bitterly. 'Get him out.'

Martin Hutton, still stunned, turned and went back out into the snow.

# *Chapter 2*

A grandfather clock in the corner ticked rhythmically on, the hollow beat of the pendulum in its dusty casement solemnly measuring time, second by second. The dim parlour, illuminated only by the reflected light from the snow outside the window, seemed different now, as if some vital presence had gone. Madeleine Hutton's body was still there but her spirit had flown, leaving behind a frail husk of a person that was no longer a person at all. Peggy had witnessed this before and was always strangely comforted: if there was any evidence that the soul passed on, the moments after death seemed to show it.

John Hutton had composed himself and sat by the bed, watching over his dead wife until the undertakers arrived, intruding on the meditative silence with the rustle of plastic and a squeaking trolley. Peggy stood beside him giving moral support as they attended to the body. To distract him, she asked, as they left, 'When did you first meet her?'

He smiled then, remembering. 'When I were just a lad. She walked into this dance and I saw her. Every boy in that room held his breath.'

'I'm sorry, pet.' The intensity of the image, of the love that had endured over all those years, moved Peggy deeply. He turned to her, fresh tears in his eyes. 'I wish our lass was here.'

'At least pain's over now.' There was nothing else she could say.

He looked confused. 'No! Our lass. Our daughter.'

'I din't know you had a daughter,' she said, surprised.

'Instead of him!' John indicated his son, who was out in the yard with Ruth. He grew angry again. 'What good is he?'

Peggy glanced at her watch. Half the morning had gone already. She rubbed his arm gently. 'We've got to go now, pet.'

Unexpectedly, he grasped her hand. 'Thank you for what you did.'

'I didn't do a thing.' Peggy was a little taken aback. She would have preferred that John had not made the connection between their moving Madeleine and her death.

'Yes, you did. And Madeleine thanks you, too.' He wrung her hand in both of his. Peggy nodded imperceptibly and left the room.

Ruth's fingers were frozen and she could hardly feel her feet. She stamped in the snow, unable to think of anything that she could say to Martin Hutton that would provide any solace. He bit his lip, blinking furiously as he surveyed the desolate hillside. 'He didn't tell me how ill she was,' he announced suddenly, as if to excuse his belated appearance.

'You knew she was ill, though?' she probed.

'We haven't spoken for a long time. Then he leaves a message saying she wanted to see me . . .'

'She were in a lot of pain. It's for the best,' Ruth said softly. She reached out to touch his shoulder, but he shook her hand off, ramming his fists in his eyes like an anguished child, and stumbled in the direction of the undertakers' van as if he did not want to hear any more. Ruth, feeling overwhelmed, cold and tired, felt hot tears springing to her own eyes. She trod carefully on the slippery cobbles, reaching out for Peggy's gloved hand as she came across the yard to fetch her. 'Come on, love,' Peggy said, taking her elbow. Peggy's eyes were moist, too, she noticed.

'Can you imagine that? Not talking to your parents, not

knowing a thing about them. Not knowing your own mother was dying?' Ruth, having thawed out a little in the warm car, dabbed at her streaked mascara. 'I couldn't bear that,' she added, thinking about the child she was carrying.

'Did you know they've got a daughter?' Peggy was thoughtful.

'They *had* a daughter.' Ruth applied powder to her red nose. 'She died int' road accident when she were about seventeen. She was int' car with a whole lot of others. They came off road near Hotton.'

'Poor man.' The hatred between John and Martin troubled Peggy deeply. She couldn't bear to think of a family being so divided. She was just thanking God for her own moderately contented brood when Ruth gasped and clutched at her belly. 'Ruth?' Ruth was doubled up, her face contorted. 'What's the matter?' Her sister-in-law gulped and looked at her with frightened eyes. Peggy realised, horrified, that Ruth was going into labour. 'You can't be. You've got six weeks yet.' But she obviously was. The fierce contraction subsided, leaving Ruth pale-faced and trembling. 'Bloody hell, Peg.' The hospital was in Huddersfield, almost ten miles away. Peggy put her foot down.

'Alright, pet, alright. You'll be fine. Just remember the breathing they taught you at antenatal class.' Ruth heard Peggy's voice coming through a miasma of pain and fear as another contraction seized her. She gave a long, shaky sigh and tried to lean forward, hampered by her seat belt. This was not how she had envisaged her labour. She and Simon had planned to cope with the first stage at home, Ruth resting on cushions and Simon massaging her back with aromatherapy oils. They were hoping for a water birth – the hospital had just installed a brand-new tub in its birthing suite – and the baby was going to be delivered into a darkened room with some soft classical music playing (Simon wanted Fleetwood Mac but she had put her foot down). It hadn't even occurred to Ruth that the baby might arrive this early. She hadn't packed her hospital bag, she hadn't bought any baby clothes, she hadn't stocked up the freezer ... Mundane considerations jostled with other questions she hardly dared ask herself. Was there something wrong? Would the baby be alright? At thirty-four weeks, the lungs might not be mature enough to allow it to breathe unaided. Would it have to go into special care?

Contractions were coming every four minutes as Peggy swung the car into the hospital entrance and screeched to a halt outside reception, ignoring large signs threatening to clamp her. 'Can we have a bit of help here, please?' she shouted, steering Ruth through the automatic doors.

'Where's Simon?' Ruth moaned, panicking.

'He'll be here,' Peggy, who had phoned him on her mobile, reassured her. Two nurses came over with a wheelchair and eased Ruth into it.

'Will you get bank nurse in?' Ruth said, concerned at how they would manage.

'You just go and worry about yourself,' Peggy smiled, bending down and hugging her.

'Bloody hell, Peg,' Ruth swore again, refusing to let go of her sister-in-law's arm as a contraction took over. Peggy glanced over her shoulder, looking for Simon, mentally revising her plans in case he didn't make it in time and she had to be with Ruth instead, but at that moment he came hurtling in through the door. Spotting Peggy's familiar figure, he rushed over to the wheelchair. 'Hello, love, how are you?' he said anxiously, taking Ruth's hand.

'Oh, I'm fine. Just a touch of agony,' Ruth replied dryly, braver now that her husband was with her. A nurse began pushing the chair towards swing doors where an arrow indicated 'Maternity'. 'This is it,' she thought, adrenalin pumping. 'It's really happening. I'm having a baby.' She twisted round in her seat and waved tremulously to Peggy. Peggy held up crossed fingers, with the knowing smile of a woman who had done it all before.

'Vic? What are you doing home?' Peggy asked, surprised, as she walked into the kitchen to find her husband in his overalls eating his butties. She was still reeling from the events of the morning: one death and a baby on the way, and it was only twelve o'clock.

'Just eating me lunch,' Vic said casually.

'You don't eat your lunch here,' she fished, wondering what was up. He seemed a bit down, which was unlike Vic.

'I do today.' He took a large bite of a cheese and pickle-filled breadcake but did not offer an explanation. She decided not to push it: he would tell her in his own good time.

'Did you hear about Ruth?' she asked, hanging up her coat and scarf.

'Hear about it? Simon was running around factory like a headless chicken.'

Peggy looked fond, thinking about her little brother. 'It seems like only yesterday he was a baby himself.'

'Well, I hope they check behind its ears for numbers,' Vic snapped.

She raised an eyebrow and began buttering herself some bread. 'Who rattled your chain? My brother's having his first child, int' he allowed to be excited?'

'What are you doing here, anyway?' Vic, realizing he'd overstepped the mark a bit – Peg was very protective about Simon – decided to change the subject.

'I've got to change. I'm seeing our Stephen's headmaster, aren't I?'

Vic had forgotten all about it. 'Right,' he said, chomping. He swallowed and fixed serious eyes on his wife. 'Now don't get all het up. If Stephen's out of order let the school sort it out. He's no angel.'

'I know that,' she sighed, thinking about the bra. It was all very well Vic telling her not to meddle; he didn't know the half of it. What Stephen did at school was one thing. What Stephen did in their bed was quite another. The more Peggy

21

thought about it, the more upset she felt. There was something peculiarly Freudian about the whole idea of her son making love in the bed he himself was conceived in. 'Het up' did not begin to describe her emotions.

She dug in her handbag. 'Vic, there's something I think you should see.' He glanced up, butty halfway to his mouth, intrigued. Peggy drew out the lacy bra and laid it on the table. Vic almost choked. Thinking that Peggy was signalling a swift seduction he said, 'Just let me wash my hands and I'll be right with you.'

'Oh, for heaven's sake, Vic,' she snapped, in no mood for jokes. 'I found it in our bed.'

'Our bed?' Vic's eyes came out on stalks. 'What was it doing there?'

'I don't think it's a question of what *it* was doing. More like *who* was doing *it*,' Peggy said acerbically.

Vic looked offended. 'I hope you're not suggesting—'

'Of course not. D'you think I'd be whipping it out as exhibit one if I suspected you? Look at the size of it. It's a young girl's bra.'

'So you're saying I can't pull birds, now, are you?' Vic teased. When Peggy did not crack a smile, he put on a straight face. 'You're saying our Stephen's behind this, aren't you?'

'Well I don't think tooth fairy left it, put it that way.' Peggy, annoyed at Vic's flippant attitude, swept off upstairs to get changed. She returned to find him examining the offending item closely. 'There's not much to it, is there? When I were a lad you had a bit of material to work on,' he said thoughtfully.

'Vic! He's doing it with some little lass in our own bed. You're meant to be cross,' Peggy snorted.

'At least he's doing it with a lass,' he replied with a twinkle. 'He spends so much time int' bathroom he had me worried.' He ignored Peggy's glare. 'Look, he's seventeen. He's sowing a few wild oats.'

This was not the reaction Peggy had envisaged. 'I'll remind you of that when some lad's pawing our Lucy.'

'That's totally different,' he said hastily. No boy was going within a hundred yards of his girl if Vic Snow had any say in it. Which he would have . . .

'Well, this little lass has probably got a father too – just like you. You probably know him. You probably drink int pub with him.' Peggy rammed home her point. Vic felt rattled. He didn't like being accused of double standards. Furthermore, he didn't want to get into a barny with any of his drinking pals because of Stephen's antics. And it would create trouble down rugby club, too. 'Bloody hell! You don't know who it is?'

'I've got an idea.'

'Why don't you just come straight out and ask him?'

'You ask him.' It was, after all, a father-son sort of thing. Peggy got up to leave, smoothing her hair. Vic was toying with the bra again and looking thoughtful. 'You should get one of these, Peg,' he said impishly.

'Me?'

'Why don't you try it on?' Coming back for lunch could have other benefits, too.

Peggy tried to be stern but was secretly rather flattered. 'I couldn't get into that, you silly man.'

Vic grinned broadly. 'I know, but it'd be bloody good fun trying.'

The interview with Mr Pearson, Stephen's headmaster, was not going well. 'I know he's a bright lad. I know his energies need channelling. But I can't let one precocious child disrupt the school community,' he said wearily. Peggy felt as if she was back at school and getting a rap over the knuckles herself. Headmaster's offices must have that effect on everybody, she decided, sitting demurely, her hands in her lap. 'It were just a party,' she answered, feebly.

'Just a party? It was organized mayhem, Mrs Snow.

Organized by your son,' he exploded. She could practically see his ears bristling.

Peggy tried not to smile but, contrarily, she could feel twitching at the corners of her lips. Being told off had always had that effect on her, she recalled. She half expected him to tell her not to smirk. She was taking the matter seriously, and she was going to give Stephen a piece of her mind, but in front of 'Ginger' or 'Dogger' as he was known – she had heard Stephen refer to his head disparagingly by both – she was going to keep the Snow end up. 'There weren't any real harm done,' she said soothingly.

'Apart from the fact that he deliberately flaunted my authority by throwing a party on school property.'

Oh, well then. Peggy eyed the framed certificates hanging behind his desk. 'Apart from that.'

'The place was awash with alcohol,' he trumpeted. 'I've seen enough pools of sick to last me a lifetime.'

'You can't blame Stephen for that,' she said defensively.

'One girl phoned the police and said there were killer vampires under her bed. Another lad – I've taught him, he wouldn't say boo to a goose – danced so much he tore ligaments in his neck. Would you like to hear more?' Dogger was becoming incandescent. A vein at his balding temple bulged.

She raised her chin. 'I'll speak to him.'

'Again?' Mr Pearson cocked an eyebrow, implying that Stephen was beyond her control.

'Again,' she replied firmly.

He twiddled a pencil between his fingers. 'Stephen's not a bad lad, I know that. But I won't let one individual disrupt an entire community. Now if Stephen thinks this pond is too small for him . . .' The statement was left hanging in the air, its meaning clear. Exclusion would be the penalty if he rocked the boat again. Mr Pearson stood up, terminating the interview. Peggy, who did not normally balk at speaking her mind, could think of nothing else to say. 'Thank you for coming in.' Mr Pearson extended his hand and she shook it wordlessly. He opened the door and waved her out as graciously as if she'd come for tea. Peggy found herself standing in an empty corridor, her mind racing. She was so distracted that she barely recognized Stephen's drama teacher as she went past, her arms full of exercise books.

'Mrs Snow.' Wendy Atkins nodded politely.

'Oh, hello, love,' Peggy replied, flustered. At that moment her mobile went off, ringing shrilly in her bag. She delved around trying to find it, embarrassed by its insistent noise – would Dogger think she was being disruptive, too? – and at last retrieved it from a tangle of tissues and Polo mint wrappers. 'Hello, Sister Snow,' she said breathlessly.

'Peggy, you're an auntie,' her brother shouted on the other end.

'She can't have!' Peggy had been so absorbed that she'd momentarily forgotten about Ruth. She glanced at her watch. 'She's only just got there! Are they both alright? What did she have?'

'Bouncing boy, six and a half pounds. He's fine – got a great pair of lungs on him. They don't think he needs a respirator, but they're keeping a close eye on him, just in case,' Simon announced, sounding a little overcome. 'We're going to call him Alfie.' Peggy's face was wreathed in smiles. 'And Ruth? Any problems?' she inquired anxiously.

'Well, she swears she's going to see the vet when she gets home. Either that or she'll send me. In fact she did quite a lot of swearing . . .' Simon paused, trying to take in everything he'd just witnessed, still hearing Ruth's groans as she pushed; weird, primitive noises that seemed to come from the depths of her being. It had frightened and awed him, seeing his wife so transfigured in labour and being unable to help, beyond mopping her brow. But as soon as little Alfie slithered out, purple and screaming, the pain seemed to vanish instantly. 'It's a boy,' the midwife said, and despite his insistence that he didn't mind what sex it turned out to be, Simon had felt a surge of pride. 'Give him to me, give him to me,' Ruth had

25

gabbled, cradling the squalling baby in her arms. Simon could feel himself welling up again. 'Are you still there?' Peggy asked.

It was still lunchbreak and outside in the playground the usual mayhem reigned. This time, however, Stephen Snow wasn't a part of it; instead he was lying on his back on the playing field next to Deborah, watching the clouds as they rolled overhead. 'Have you ever thought what it would be like? America. New York, LA, Las Vegas. Everything that can happen to you in life can happen to you there.' Stephen, buoyed by his role in *Streetcar*, was setting his sights high.

'Is that where you'll go?' Deborah plucked a blade of grass and folded it into a neat little parcel, trying not to appear concerned.

'I'm gonna go everywhere. America. Australia. Africa—'

'Huddersfield.' She laughed uneasily.

'India.'

'Batley.'

'Indonesia.'

'Pudsey.'

He looked sideways at her and smiled that big, wolfish, charming smile that made her stomach flip over. 'You just watch me.' He linked her slender fingers with his and raised their arms to the heavens in a salute.

Deborah asked quietly, 'What's wrong with here?' but never got a reply. Stephen, seeing a football bounce towards them, scrabbled up and caught it, sending it soaring back to the waiting players with an impressive drop kick. He ran to join them, leaving her staring at his retreating back.

He was still showing off with the football, keeping it up in the air without letting it hit the ground, when Peggy marched into the playground. Stephen, who was busy glancing over at Deborah to see if she was watching, did not notice at first. When he heard his mother call his name in her 'battleaxe' voice as he liked to call it, he knew he was in for a drubbing.

26

He let the ball fall to the floor and jogged shamefacedly past a bunch of younger kids who were giggling at the prospect of a senior boy's mother showing him up in public.

'What?' he demanded sullenly, although he knew what was coming.

Peggy folded her arms. 'If you ever pull another stunt like that I'll skin you alive. Is that understood?' He nodded reluctantly. 'I beg your pardon?' Peggy raised her voice. Stephen winced. 'Yes, mother.'

'Thank you.' There was an unexpected twinkle in her eye. He couldn't believe he was going to be let off that lightly, but apparently so. She shooed him away. 'Now you'd better get back to your little friend before she dies of loneliness.' She craned her neck and waved, shouting loudly, 'Hello, Deborah, pet.' Deborah, startled, waved shyly back. Stephen glared at Peggy, feeling humiliated, but she merely smiled brightly back at him. 'Goodbye, Stephen. *Cousin* Stephen,' she added pointedly. Stephen stood, puzzled, as she walked off, and it was several moments before he realized what she was getting at. Then the penny dropped – Auntie Ruth must have had her baby. No wonder Mum was in such a good mood, he thought. 'Nice one,' he shouted, running back to join the other kids, mentally thanking Ruth for her impeccable sense of timing.

Peggy couldn't really get angry with Stephen after hearing about the baby. She was too high. She drove back to the health centre, stopping off to buy a bottle of bubbly to take to the proud parents later, and parked the car, bursting to tell Patricia the news. Just as she was going in, Walter, one of their 'care in the community' cases, came shambling out, trousers half-mast. He was a gentle, amiable, childlike man in his early thirties whom the nurses kept a regular eye on. Innocent and harmless – albeit accident-prone – Walter was an indulged figure in Skelthwaite, where he had been given his own flat. 'Walter! Look at the state of you!' Peggy steered him into the lobby and stooped to pull up his trousers, which

27

were low enough to reveal a pair of bright blue incontinence pants. Walter put his arms around her in a loving hug. 'Can I have badge?' Walter, who had something of a badge fetish – his coat was covered with them – made a play for Peggy's bosom. 'It's not a badge, Walter. It's my watch. How many times have I told you?' she said firmly, straightening his rather stained jumper and zipping up his anorak, which was flapping open.

'Can I have watch?' Walter persisted.

'No, you can't. Now try and keep your trousers up, pet,' she replied, steering him back out of the door. It was only as she watched him go that she realized he had half-inched the champagne. 'Walter,' she called, pointing at the bottle. He returned it with a beatific grin.

She breezed past the waiting room and down a corridor to the nurses' office, catching sight of Patricia's plump form as she came out of the treatment room. 'Peggy,' Patricia began, her face serious.

'Have you heard? Little boy.' Peggy brandished the champagne.

'I know, it's brilliant. Peggy—'

'Six and a half pounds! I wish I could lose six and a half pounds in an hour,' shrieked Peggy jubilantly.

Patricia continued to look grave. 'Peggy. There's someone to see you. I told him to make an appointment, but he were insistent.' Her subdued tone made Peggy stop. Patricia, she suddenly noticed, looked rattled. She opened the office door to find Martin Hutton standing there, glowering at her.

'What can I do for you, Mr Hutton?' she asked calmly, putting down the bottle.

'I think you've already done it, don't you?' he sneered, shaking with fury.

'Why don't you sit down?' She pulled out a chair but he ignored it, coming up so close to her that she could smell his breath. 'I know what you did to my mother,' he spat. He was out of his head on a mixture of grief and anger and Peggy felt vaguely alarmed at the barely contained violence of his body language. 'Please sit down, Mr Hutton,' she said again, moving away.

He followed her across the room. 'What does that feel like? You go to work and . . . you kill someone. Just like that. Like turning off a light.' A muscle in his jaw flickered.

'Your mother was in a lot of pain. More pain than I think I've ever seen. All we did was—'

'I know what you did! My father told me. He was trying to keep your little secret but he let it slip,' Martin Hutton said, savagely triumphant. After the undertakers had gone, the two of them had rowed bitterly. His father's words still taunted him: 'Those nurses did everything for her. They cared about her. They wouldn't let her suffer! Not like you . . .'

'What exactly did Mr Hutton say we'd done?' Peggy asked, trying to keep her composure.

'He said he asked you to stop the pain, that he'd rather she died than . . . carry on like that.' Martin Hutton couldn't bring himself to acknowledge his mother's suffering directly. 'You moved her and a minute later she was dead. *He* thinks you're saints. *I* think you're bloody criminals.'

'We just put her on commode. That's all. She could have gone at any moment—'

'Are you God?' he interrupted.

'No, I'm not God.' But she couldn't meet his burning eyes. She had been so rushed off her feet, what with Ruth and seeing the headmaster, that she'd had no time to reflect on what had happened that morning. Martin Hutton's rantings shook her. Peggy felt a knot tighten in her stomach.

'You had no right to do what you did. No right,' he stormed.

Patricia, who had been standing behind him, broke in angrily, 'And where were you? When Peggy was up at that house day and night, where were you?'

'Ssshhh, Pat,' Peggy warned.

Martin, needled by guilt, exploded. 'As far as I'm

concerned you're a murderer. Do you understand?' He shook his finger under Peggy's nose.

'That's enough. Get out of here.' Patricia tried to bundle him out of the office but he would not budge. He was a miserable sight, upper lip wet with snot, eyes red-rimmed, hair on end. 'I will never, ever, see my mother again because of what you did.' He spoke slowly, spelling it out. 'And I promise you – you will never get the chance to do something like that again.' He pushed roughly past the two nurses and banged through the door, sending the bottle of champagne crashing to the ground, white fizz hissing into the carpet.

# Chapter 3

For the second time that day Peggy found herself sitting behind someone's desk. This time, however, the complaint was about her. Elaine Trafford, the community nursing manager, had called her in to discuss Martin Hutton's accusations and made it clear from the start that she was taking the matter very seriously.

'What happened next, Peggy?' Elaine pursed her lipsticked mouth. She had ceased 'hands on' nursing ten years earlier and had made a seamless transition to power-dressed NHS manager. Normally, Peggy's relationship with her senior was fairly relaxed but today Elaine's demeanour was stiff and formal.

'I told you what happened. We took her on commode and then we put her back to bed,' Peggy insisted tersely.

'Was it your decision to put her on the commode, or Ruth's?' Elaine queried, writing notes on a report pad. Peggy hesitated. 'Mine. Ruth had nothing to do with it.' She wasn't going to drop Ruth in it too, after all that she'd just been through. Besides, it was her suggestion that they move Mrs Hutton, not Ruth's. She was sure she would have thought of commode if Ruth hadn't.

'You knew if you moved her there was a chance she would die? A good chance?'

Peggy gave a deep sigh. 'I knew she were hanging on by a thread, yes. I knew she were in agony, yes.'

Elaine gave her a look that indicated she thought Peggy

31

was being deliberately obtuse and repeated, slowly and precisely, 'Did you move her knowing that it might kill her?'

'How can you sit there and ask me that?' Peggy burst out, trying to appeal to Elaine's own experience as a nurse. To her humanity, God help her, though she seemed to have swapped that for shoulder pads these days. 'I was doing what I thought needed doing,' she cried.

Elaine put down her fountain pen with a grimace. 'Peggy. Please help me. Did Mrs Hutton indicate that she wanted to go to the toilet?'

'Mrs Hutton couldn't indicate anything! She were in agony.'

'You are not helping yourself,' she said frostily.

Peggy bristled. 'I'll not lie, if that's what you mean.'

'He is saying—' Elaine checked her notes, 'that you consciously took the decision to end his mother's life.'

'I put her on commode,' Peggy answered stubbornly.

'Even though she hadn't asked you to and even though you knew it might kill her?'

Peggy folded her arms. 'I'm saying nothing else. If you don't like it you can sack me.' She had had quite enough of being grilled by Mrs Officious Body. If Elaine ever got near enough to a person in pain these days she might remember what the job was about.

'Is that what you think this is about? About being sacked?' Something in Elaine's tone made Peggy's blood run cold. She listened, hardly able to believe what she was hearing, as Elaine spelt it out. 'Peggy. You have been accused of taking another person's life. The police will get involved. If they think you have a case to answer . . .' She didn't need to say any more. Peggy sat, stunned, as a vision of herself in the dock appeared before her eyes. For the first time it sunk in that she could actually be charged with murder.

Elaine got up and showed Peggy out. She was so shocked that she almost cannoned into Dr Underwood, who was pacing nervously up and down the corridor, obviously waiting

32

to talk to Elaine. 'I'm sorry, Peggy. I should have been there,' he muttered, not meeting her eyes. He patted her arm and whispered ineffectually, 'Plasters on cuts. Plasters on cuts,' before switching on a smile for the nursing manager, who was standing at the open doorway.

'Sorry to have kept you waiting, Doctor.' Elaine said crisply, calling after Peggy, 'Just keep a low profile for now, alright?' as if she'd been tried and sentenced already.

Peggy could be relied on to keep cool in a crisis. It was one of the qualities that made her such a good nurse. But even she was beginning to feel desperate at the thought that she was fighting for her professional life. And, perhaps, a lot more. She went outside, hoping the fresh air would clear her head. She needed to think her way through this. Clearly, Martin Hutton was on a crusade to pin the blame on her for his mother's death. Equally clearly, he was doing it to assuage his own feelings of guilt for not being there when it happened, or even being aware that his mother was ill. The bad blood between Martin and John Hutton was palpable. Peggy wondered how long it had been since they last met. What on earth could have engendered such bitterness between them? The wound obviously ran deep: Martin was lashing out in any way he could and she, Peggy, was taking the brunt. If she could only make him see beyond his own obsession, get him to understand how badly Madeleine was suffering, he might change his mind. It was worth a try.

She got in the car and retraced her route back to the farm, formulating a plan as she drove. Martin Hutton answered her knock, but as soon as he saw who it was, went to slam the door in her face. Peggy, too quick for him, wedged a stoutly-shod foot in the way.

'Martin—'

'Do you want me to phone the police?'

'Come with me, Martin. Please.' Peggy pushed hard at the door.

'Move your hand or I'll move it for you,' he ground out through gritted teeth. John Hutton, hearing the commotion, appeared behind him in the hall. 'What's going on?' he called querulously, spotting Peggy.

'It's alright, Mr Hutton. I just want to show your son something—' she puffed, refusing to budge.

'Get inside, Dad.' Martin Hutton tried to shoo his father back. He hadn't told him about his visit to the Skelthwaite Health Centre yet. The older man stood his ground, looking between the two of them, a bewildered expression on his face.

'—*if* he's got the courage,' Peggy continued pointedly. Martin swallowed and opened the door.

It was growing dusk as Vic and Stephen, ruddy cheeked and dishevelled, made their way home together from rugby practise along the tow-path Peggy had jogged along earlier. They did not talk much. Vic was preoccupied – the training session had not been a success – and Stephen's mind was elsewhere, too. Vic's attempts to coach the Skelthwaite Scorpions, the town's ailing rugby league side, were depressing him. The afternoon had been pretty typical, culminating in Dick gashing his head on a tackle bag. If they couldn't hack it with inanimate objects, Vic thought despondently, how on earth were they going to manage to beat a real live team? Apart from his family, the game was his one big love. It was Vic who laundered the shirts and lectured the team. He had even persuaded Simon to stump up sponsorship for them, although that had its drawbacks. He seemed to think he owned them, like he owned every-thing and everyone else. And now he wanted Stephen, too. Vic glanced at his son, who seemed miles away, and sighed. He'd better bite the bullet. It was only fair to give Stephen the option, even if it could result in him bossing his old dad around. Vic cleared his throat. 'Simon wants you to leave school now and join him int business. If you put your head down and learn ropes, I reckon sky's the limit.'

Stephen looked up, his eyebrows quizzical. 'But I want to go to university.'

'Then go to university. I'm just the messenger.' Vic stuffed his cold hands in his windcheater pockets and they walked along in silence for a while. Stephen picked up a flat pebble, skimming it across the water. Alarmed, a duck took off with a clatter of wings. Vic could see that Stephen was tempted. 'You'd be a wealthy young man. You wouldn't have to leave home,' he remarked.

'I want to leave home.'

'Thank you very much,' Vic commented dryly.

'You know what I mean.' Stephen stopped and turned to face his father. 'What would you do if you were me?'

Vic laughed. He had never been academic. 'If I were you? I'd be out of that school like greased lightning. I'd have a big red Porsche and a girlfriend with legs that stretch to Huddersfield.' He paused, working on the fantasy. 'I'd build a bloody big house up on the hill with gold taps and I'd watch daytime telly and eat chocolates 'til I was sick. And I'd see my family on Sundays and I'd die a happy man.' He looked sidelong at his son. 'But I'm not you, am I?'

Stephen picked up another pebble, weighing it in his hand. This time he did not throw it.

A tiny, mewling cry woke Ruth up out of the deepest sleep of her life. Despite her profound tiredness, the little call made her start awake instantly and she was half out of her hospital bed to Alfie's cot before she realized that Simon was still there. 'I think he's hungry,' he said, concerned, scooping Alfie out of his bassinet and bringing him over. The midwife had swaddled him in a sheet marked, 'Property of St Mary's Hospital, Huddersfield', so that he looked as if he'd been wrapped up like a parcel. 'Best present I ever had,' Ruth said softly, taking the baby from Simon and gazing into Alfie's red, screwed-up face. After some fumbling – there was an art to breastfeeding that neither she nor Alfie had perfected yet – Ruth got him latched on and the baby suckled thirstily. She looked up at Simon, who seemed entranced by the sight of mother and child, and smiled. 'What are *you* doing here?'

'What d'you mean?' he asked, sitting down on the side of the bed and stroking Alfie's fluffy baby thatch with one finger.

'I'nt my baby good enough to celebrate?'

Simon dropped a kiss on her head. 'I'm a new man, me. I'll be right by your side every step of the way.' Looking at Alfie, Simon wore an expression that Ruth had never seen before: one of such tenderness and devotion that it took her breath away. This was the Simon she had fallen in love with; the gentle, sweet, caring man that few people ever got to see. Ruth wanted the whole world to know what a wonderful man he was – and what a wonderful baby they had. 'Get down pub, you daft bugger,' she chided, laughing. Besides, for the moment she wanted Alfie all to herself.

The reception area of St Hilda's Hospice was furnished with comfortable chairs and low tables stacked with glossy magazines. Tranquil watercolours hung on the pastel-coloured walls and cheery vases of flowers added splashes of scent and colour. It was not, reflected Peggy, a bad place to die. It was certainly less impersonal than a clinical, white-washed hospital ward, surrounded by drips and tubes and monitors. But it wasn't home, and that's where Madeleine Hutton had wanted to be. Peggy wished Martin Hutton, who had accompanied her there with bad grace, could understand that. Even more importantly, she wanted him to understand the price his mother paid for making that choice.

The Warden, a thin, sprightly woman with cropped, salt-and-pepper hair, spotted them and trotted over. 'Hello, Peggy. How are you?'

'Not too bad. Is it alright if I show a friend around?'

'Course it is,' she replied, smiling at Martin Hutton. He did not smile back.

'Oh, have some blotting paper. We're swimming in them,' Peggy said, handing over the boxes of incontinence pants she had brought in with her from the health centre's 'pant mountain'.

'Thanks.' The Warden received them gratefully. 'I sometimes wish I had shares in these things.'

Peggy glanced into a women's ward. 'Where's Mrs Newton?'

'We had to put her in her own room. End of the corridor, turn right.'

'Yes, I know the one.' Peggy turned round and looked at Martin. 'It's the one your mother was in.'

The sound of ragged, uneven breathing punctuated the stillness in the darkened room. Mrs Newton was heavily sedated with painkillers and, although it was clear that she recognized Peggy when she bent over her, the dying woman was unable to articulate anything other than a few pitiful guttural noises. 'Alright, love, alright,' Peggy soothed, stroking her forehead. She beckoned Martin over. 'Your mother was ten times worse than this woman,' she whispered. 'She made it clear she wanted to go home. To go home to die. Your mother had more courage in her little finger than some people have in their whole bodies. I respected that courage.'

'Is that why you killed her?' He wouldn't let up.

'Martin—'

'What are you trying to tell me? That death isn't nice?' he ranted.

'Keep your voice down, please.'

'Because I know that! I know that! I was on my way to see my mother and you killed her. Nothing you can show me here will ever change that. So what are you trying to tell me?'

Mrs Newton, roused by his harsh voice, moaned softly.

Peggy, contrite at having caused the intrusion, stooped to

reassure her. She twisted round to look at Martin Hutton. 'Thank you for coming,' she said politely, feeling utterly defeated by his intransigence. He stared down at the elderly woman's face, then, without saying anything, left the room abruptly. His expression was unreadable.

Peggy let herself into the house, feeling totally drained. She had called in to see Ruth and the baby on her way home, but even the magic of witnessing a brand-new life couldn't dispel the growing sense of unease gnawing away at her insides. The old saying, 'A death for a birth' occurred to her and she shivered. Peggy had not mentioned Martin Hutton to Ruth and Ruth, who was completely wrapped up in Alfie, did not suspect anything.

'Ah. At last,' Vic greeted her in the hallway, pecking her on the cheek and reaching for his coat simultaneously. 'Simon's standing drinks down pub. You going to join us?'

'Vic—' Peggy didn't know where to begin. She put down her bag and unwound her scarf, wondering how to break the news to him. 'What?'

He was halfway out of the door and gasping for a pint. Clearly, this wasn't the right moment.

'Has Lucy had her tea?' she asked numbly. 'I hope you didn't give her chips again.'

'Daddy cooked his speciality. Lovely, weren't it, pet?' he grinned, as Lucy, hearing her name, popped her head inquisitively around the lounge door.

'He made a mountain of mash with sausages sticking out like rocks and the baked beans were an avalanche,' vouched Lucy, impressed.

Vic winked. 'Creative touch. Either you've got it or you ain't. Am I excused now?'

'Yes, go on then.' Peggy waved him away.

'Right. See you down there.'

'OK.' Peggy needed a stiff drink after the day she'd just had. 'I'll get Sandra to babysit. Where's Stephen?'

'Rehearsing,' said Vic, pulling a smoochy face and going cross-eyed. Lucy giggled.

Peggy gave him a warning look. 'Did you have that little chat?'

'What chat?' asked Vic, momentarily confused. He had put off telling Peggy about Simon's offer to Stephen because he knew how she would react. Perhaps Ruth had mentioned it, he thought.

'You know. About that – that thing I showed you at lunchtime.'

'Oh, that,' Vic said relieved. 'I'll do it later.' Compared with his worries about the future of the rugby team, Stephen's love life was a very low priority.

Judging by the cheering going on, Simon was getting into the party spirit, thought Peggy, as the hubbub from the Skelthwaite Arms grew louder. The lights and music from the pub made it stand out like a welcoming beacon in the town's dark, deserted streets and she quickened her pace. A warm, thick fug of beery bonhomie enveloped her as she opened the door. Word about Simon and Ruth's baby had got round fast and the place was heaving. Simon, his red hair visible at the other end of the bar, was in his shirt sleeves, downing a pint in one. She waved to him and he pushed his way over, beaming. 'Peg! Did you see them?'

'I did.'

'I'nt he amazing?' slurred Simon, as if he were the first man ever to father a child.

'He is.' Peggy embraced her brother fondly. 'He's absolutely beautiful,' she whispered into his ear.

Brushing away a happy tear, Simon turned to the landlady, Sally, and announced, 'Get this woman the biggest gin and tonic int' world.'

Brandishing her drink, Peggy squeezed through the crowd at the bar towards Vic, who was sitting by himself. 'It's mayhem in here,' she commented, perching on a stool beside him.

'Do you remember the night Stephen were born? It was just your step-mum and my mum and a bottle of Tizer int ward,' he muttered morosely.

'What's he done to you now, misery guts? Can't a man wet his own baby's head? Peggy took a large swallow of her gin and tonic and surveyed the room. Patricia shouted across, 'Did you tell Ruth I'd see her int morning?'

'Yes. She said not to eat all the chocolates before you get there,' Peggy shouted back, more cheerily than she felt.

'What kind of afternoon did you have?' asked Vic, remembering her visit to the headmaster.

'The normal,' she replied wearily, taking another big gulp. She would have to tell him, and now was as good a time as any. She drained the glass and added lightly, 'Oh, except that I'm going to be charged with murder.'

Vic stared at Peggy closely as she swirled the ice around in the bottom of her glass. She wasn't smiling. 'You are joking, aren't you?' he said hesitantly.

'No, Vic, I'm not,' she replied.

He shepherded her to a quiet corner with another substantial G&T and listened while she explained the circumstances of Mrs Hutton's death. 'You were just doing your job. Surely he can see that?' he burst out, when she told him of Martin Hutton's intervention.

'He's upset.'

'I don't care if he is bloody upset.' Vic's cheeks flushed angrily.

'What if he's right?' said Peggy, voicing for the first time the fear that had been going round and round in her head since Martin Hutton's visit. 'I knew what I was doing. I knew there was every chance it would kill her. That's why we did it.'

Vic covered her hand with a broad, blunt paw. 'Not kill her – help her to die.'

Peggy looked at him, her eyes troubled. 'He asked me if I were God.'

'If you saw a dying dog you wouldn't sit there and watch it die in agony, would you?'

She sighed. 'That's what John Hutton said.'

Vic gave her hand a squeeze. 'And he were her husband.'

'But what if they take my job away?' Peggy began shakily.

'They won't.'

'I mean, I know I moan about it, but . . . I can't imagine life without this job.' Vic wasn't used to seeing his indomitable wife looking so vulnerable and upset. His Peggy was, above all, a fighter. 'The people in this town won't let them take your job away,' Vic insisted gruffly. '*I* won't let them.'

Another loud cheer rang out as Simon, who was now standing on a table, sprayed the throng around him with champagne. 'Look at him.' Peggy smiled, despite herself. 'He's like a kid at Christmas.'

'A kid with a bank account,' Vic said sourly. 'He thinks he can buy and sell anything.'

'He does not.' Peggy sprang to her brother's defence, glad of the change of subject.

'He bought me, dint he? I'm forty-four years old and I wear stupid bloody overalls and work int bog paper factory.'

'There's no shame in that.' Peggy studied Vic's grumpy face. 'What's wrong with you today?' she asked. He was scoring far higher than usual on the Simon Goddard needle rating.

Vic, who knew he wasn't doing a good job of breaking his own piece of news tactfully, decided to take the bull by the horns. 'Would you want our Stephen working there?'

Peggy looked uncomfortable. 'Stephen's different.'

'Let's hope so.' Vic took a draught of his pint. 'Simon's offered him a job.'

'He's done what?' Peggy was, predictably, aghast.

'Not just any job. He wants Stephen—'

'Stephen's going to university. Everybody knows that.'

'I know, I know.' Vic tried to placate her, but Peggy was on a roll.

'Why the hell wasn't I told about this?'

'It's not cut and dried,' he said quickly.

She snorted. 'Bloody right, it isn't.'

Before the argument could ensue any further Patricia trotted over and nudged Peggy warningly, pointing in the direction of the door. Peggy looked across and saw Martin Hutton standing there. 'Vic, you stay here,' she said, getting up.

'What is it?' He followed her gaze and spotted a stranger scanning the room. 'Just sit there, Vic,' Peggy ordered. She seemed perturbed. All at once, the penny dropped. Vic leapt to his feet and pushed his way through the crowd. Peggy tried to restrain him but he got to Martin Hutton first. 'You've got a bloody nerve coming in here. You threaten my wife again and I'll bloody have you,' he roared, shaking his fist at him. Dick – sporting a large plaster above his eye, courtesy of the tackle bag – grabbed Vic's arm and hauled him away.

The rowdy bar fell silent as Peggy stepped forward and looked Martin straight in the eye. 'What do you want?' she said, regaining her old composure.

He cleared his throat nervously. 'To talk to you.'

Peggy took Martin into the deserted lounge bar to hear him out, Vic hovering anxiously the other side of the smoked-glass door. Martin was still pale but his anger seemed to have evaporated. He looked as if a great weight had fallen off his shoulders. 'Dad and I have made it up,' he announced unexpectedly. Peggy said nothing, letting him talk. 'I have you to thank for that. You made me see beyond my own frustration and – and guilt.' He hung his head, tracing a knot-hole in the wooden table where they were sitting. 'You made me see what my mother went through. And what really matters is that she's free now, she's not suffering any more. Not my own hang-ups.' What he couldn't say was that after the visit to the hospice he had driven home, deeply disturbed, to find his father sitting in the dark. The old man's face was wet with tears. Martin had sat down next to him and felt for his hand, and in that simple contact the bitterness of years gave way to a shared grief, his father holding him tight as

Martin allowed himself to let go at last and sob wretchedly.

'You must think very badly of me,' he continued quietly. 'You must wonder what kind of a son I am. I didn't even know she was ill, so when I got the message she wanted to see me . . . I knew something was wrong.'

'How come you didn't know she was ill?' Peggy coaxed.

'We had a row a few years ago. I wasn't speaking to them; they weren't speaking to me.'

'That's a big row,' she agreed.

'I grew up here, you know. But it never felt like home. It was dull and drab,' he said, looking around the unpretentious room. A gas fire flickered over mock coals in the grate, illuminating one side of his face and throwing the other into deep shadow. 'London was so exciting – that's where I felt at home. I was running around with all these new friends having the time of my life. I hardly gave Skelthwaite a thought. Then one night I got this phone call. My little sister had been killed in a crash.' He took a shaky breath and continued. 'Sarah was . . . she was fantastic. Pretty and bright. I loved her to bits. But I didn't love her half as much as Mum and Dad did.'

'Of course they loved her,' Peggy said soothingly.

'No. They adored her. I was always arguing with them, battling them, trying to get away. Ridiculing them, half the time. She just had to smile at them and they melted like snow.'

'I still don't understand why you weren't speaking,' Peggy prompted.

'When Sarah died . . . I was hammered by it,' he said slowly. 'I was only young, I'd never known misery before. I didn't know what to say or who to say it to.'

'Couldn't you talk to your mother?' Peggy was horrified at the thought of a son being so estranged.

'I came up from London for the funeral. Mum, she was . . . I looked into her eyes and I could see that something had died for her. I felt ashamed I was still alive. They'd lost this life and love and been left with me.' He stifled a sob. Peggy

43

stroked his hand, genuinely moved by his story.

'I had a few drinks after the funeral, said a few things I shouldn't have. And Dad said a few back. It was terrible. I rushed back to London as quick as I could.'

Vic put his head round the door and mouthed, 'Are you alright?' to Peggy, who waved him away.

Martin Hutton didn't even notice. 'First I missed my mother's birthday. Quite intentionally, let them see I didn't care. Then they missed mine. Then a Christmas . . .'

Peggy shook her head, shocked at this catalogue of hurts. Martin Hutton ploughed on: 'About two years went by, we hadn't spoken. I was about to graduate – the first person ever from our family to get a degree. I sent them an invitation. I was searching the seats of all the parents, proud as punch. They didn't come.' He laid his hands flat on the table and looked Peggy full in the eyes for the first time. 'I loved my mother and I'm angry I didn't see her before she died. I'm angry with myself and I'm angry with Dad . . . But I've no right to be angry with you.'

'I am so sorry, Martin,' Peggy said, meaning it.

He stood up and held out his hand. 'I'll tell them in the morning. I was upset, I misunderstood what my Dad was saying . . .'

She shook it, relief at her own reprieve mingled with concern for him. 'You've still got your father. He'll need you to be strong now.'

Martin looked dubious at this, as if the fragile bond that had recently been restored might not be enough. 'What do you think your sister would want you to do?' Peggy asked gently.

They had been in there an awful long time, thought Vic, who was keeping one eye glued to the lounge-bar door. If Peggy was any longer he was tempted to go in and break it up, sling that Martin Hutton out on his ear. He didn't deserve Peg's sympathy, not after what he'd put her through today. Vic

44

supped the remainder of his pint and wiped his foamy moustache with the back of his hand. He was about to go and rescue Peggy when Stephen pushed his way through the boisterous crowd. 'Alright?' shouted Vic (the volume level had risen by several notches). 'Can I buy you a pint with your Uncle Simon's money?'

'I'm not stopping,' grinned Stephen, who was on a promise. His skin prickled with anticipation. He glanced around. 'Where's Mum?'

Just then Peggy and Martin Hutton reappeared. Vic saw her show him to the door and pat him on the arm. 'Everything alright, love?' he enquired, concerned, as she squeezed her way through the sea of shiny-faced drinkers to his side.

'No thanks to you, hero,' she laughed fondly. 'And as for you, young man,' she began, addressing Stephen, 'If you think I'm going to stand by and let you throw your—'

'Peggy,' warned Vic.

She carried on, unheeding him. 'You are not going to go and work for your Uncle Simon.'

'He's only thinking about it.'

'There's nothing to think about,' she said adamantly.

'It's up to him, love.'

'He doesn't want to work in a toilet paper factory all his life,' Peggy blurted out unthinkingly.

Vic looked as if he'd got the hump. 'Thank you very much.'

'That's not what I mean.'

Stephen watched the two of them bat the argument back and forth with an amused expression on his face, as if he were spectating at a tennis match. Then, when he could get a word in edgeways – they seemed to have forgotten he was there – he announced, 'I'm not going to take job.'

There was a pause as this sunk in. 'Right. Good.' Peggy was caught out mid-lob.

'Will you tell him, Dad? You know, thank you but . . .' Stephen was eager to get away.

Vic raised his glass. 'I'll tell him.' He peered down the bar at Simon, who was chucking another pint down his neck – literally; most of it was soaking his shirt – to the accompaniment of more drunken egging-on. 'Maybe not just now, though.'

'Right. I'm off home. You gonna be here all night?'

Peggy winked. 'Someone's going to have to carry your Uncle Simon home.' She delved in her bag for money. 'Give this to babysitter. You can put Lucy to bed, can't you?' Watching him go, she said wistfully to Vic, 'I only want what's best for him'.

'I know.'

'Why can't they have a university in Skelthwaite?' Peggy felt suddenly weepy. He put his arm round her and they sat a while without talking. Then she asked, 'Did you ever want to leave here?'

'Skelthwaite? No, never.'

'It's funny, int it? It never crossed my mind, either.'

Vic squeezed her plump shoulders. 'If he stays, he stays. If he goes to university he'll be back here before you know it.'

Martin Hutton's tear-ravaged face came back to Peggy. 'No, once he goes he won't come back,' she said fatalistically. Catching herself being uncharacteristically self-pitying, she gave a weak smile. One way and another it had been a very long, very traumatic day. Bed. That was what she needed now. 'I'm tired, Vic. I think I might go soon. Make sure he gets home.' She pointed at Simon, who was leading a rousing chorus of 'Swing Low, Sweet Chariot', with all the rude actions.

'Come on, have another drink.' Vic wanted to cheer her up. Visions of Peggy's generous breasts in a skimpy lacy bra had been torturing him since lunch and he was beginning to feel romantic.

Peggy allowed herself one more G&T before setting off into the night. She had spotted the glint in her husband's eye and wasn't feeling up to it at all. Better to crash out under the covers before he got home and hope that deterred him. Her shadow overtook her and grew longer as she went under a streetlamp by the church. Hurrying past the dark yew trees overhanging the pavement, a bobbing torchlight in the churchyard caught her attention. She froze, straining to listen, wondering if it was someone about to steal lead from the church roof. It wouldn't be the first time. She could make out two people. They sounded familiar. Then she realized: it was John and Martin Hutton. A thin beam picked out a grave stone. It was too far away for Peggy to read but she hazarded a guess that it was where Sarah Hutton was buried. 'Your mother will go there and I'll go here. Will you see to that?' John Hutton's cracked voice carried distinctly on the frosty air.

'Of course I will, Dad. And where will I go?' she heard Martin Hutton reply. Peggy felt a lump in her throat and walked briskly on. Madeleine Hutton could rest easy now.

The first thing Peggy noticed when she let herself in to the house was Stephen's shirt, which he had left lying on the floor. The second thing she noticed, as she stooped, tutting, to pick it up, was the faint, but nonetheless perceptible squeak of bedsprings. Thinking it must be Lucy mucking around – she was fond of treating her bed as a trampoline – Peggy prowled stealthily upstairs to catch the little culprit at it. But it wasn't Lucy who was misbehaving. There was a light coming from her and Vic's bedroom and, as she stole closer, she heard soft laughter. The door had been left slightly ajar and, even before she peered through the crack, she knew with a sinking heart what she would find. But not, as it turned out, who. Peggy thought she recognised the slim figure and long, brown hair of the girl lying naked in her bed, but when she turned over, Peggy saw her face clearly. Clapping her hand to her mouth, Peggy bobbed out of sight, totally thrown.

Making love to her son was Wendy Atkins, Stephen's teacher.

# Chapter 4

Had it been Vic she had caught with a mistress, Peggy would have stormed right in and confronted the pair of them. But this was her son, *her baby*, in a new incarnation – adult lover – and, for once, she was too thrown to do anything. Seeing Stephen as another woman might see him was a shock. Peggy had always been proud of her handsome lad; she used to tell him he'd be a heartbreaker when he grew up, but she had postponed indefinitely contemplating him as a sexual being. As far as she was concerned, he was not so very long out of short trousers. Innocent kisses behind the bike sheds with a nice girl like Deborah she could handle, even indulge. He should have friends of his own age. But full-on sex with an experienced older woman . . . that was taking things far too far, too fast. He was young and vulnerable; easy prey for some nympho after a toyboy. Wendy Atkins had obviously seduced him, Peggy decided.

Even after she'd heard the front door open and Stephen bidding Wendy a whispered goodnight, Peggy said nothing. She sat downstairs in the dark, seized by indecision, listening to the floorboards creaking in the room above as he straightened the sheets. For once, she had no idea what to do next. Even when Vic got home, pissed and singing, 'Like a rolling stone,' she said nothing. He was too drunk to talk about it sensibly, and by the next morning the moment had passed. Peggy left her secret stewing away in the back of her mind. She would come up with an answer, eventually.

In the meantime, there was work to keep her busy. She accepted a stilted apology from Elaine Trafford, the nursing manager, following Martin Hutton's withdrawal of complaint, and discovered a more attentive side to Dr Underwood. Peggy would have been amused had she not been so busy. With Ruth on maternity leave they were reliant on bank nurses and things were more than a little hectic. Having to keep tabs on Walter did not help, either.

'How did you do this, pet?' she asked, examining Walter's burnt hand. They had been called out to his flat by one of Walter's neighbours, who had noticed his raw, blistered skin. Walter, however, seemed not to be bothered by the injury. He was much more interested in watching daytime TV and merely laughed in response to Peggy's question.

'He's burnt every pan,' shouted Patricia from Walter's tiny, filthy kitchen. She was trying to clean it up a bit – not part of their job, but the place was a health hazard – and was finding it hard to know where to start.

'He shouldn't be here on his own, should you Walter?' Peggy chided gently. Walter was becoming a bit of a liability. 'I'm going to have words with that social worker. He's going to burn this place to ground one day.'

'What's that smell?' Patricia emerged from the kitchen, holding her nose. 'Can't you smell it? It's terrible. It smells like something died.' She glanced around the room, which was piled with both opened and unopened cans – Walter only ate convenience food – and a horrifying thought suddenly crossed her mind. 'Peg. Have you seen his cat?'

Peggy knew what Patricia was thinking. 'Walter, where's your cat, love?'

'Can I have badge?' Walter said, unconcerned.

'I think it's coming from here,' Patricia called. Peggy followed her into the kitchen, to find Patricia squatting down beside the oven. She gulped and reached tentatively for the handle. Just as she was about to turn it, a loud 'miaow' hailed the sudden arrival of Walter's tabby cat, who jumped in through the kitchen window, landed neatly on the draining board and sauntered into the sitting room to rub herself against her master's legs. 'Phew.' Patricia, relieved, opened the door, only to recoil with a scream. Seething in the reeking remains of a very ancient takeaway was a mass of fat, white maggots.

Peggy's bleeper going off gave her, at least, the opportunity to escape the hell-hole that was Walter's kitchen. She left Patricia scrubbing – she was obsessive about cleanliness – and headed for Skelthwaite Junior School where Billy Bevan, a classmate of Lucy's, had fallen on a slide and hurt himself.

'He's in there.' Mrs Shelley, Billy's teacher, indicated an empty classroom. 'I'll join you in a minute. I'm just having a chat with Mrs Bevan in my office.'

Billy's chin was oozing sticky blood, but once she'd cleaned up the wound Peggy could see the damage was superficial. She talked as she dabbed to distract the child.

'What a brave lad! You know it's much easier if you go down slide on your bum.' Billy, she gathered from his disjointed explanation – he had a slight speech impediment – had slipped going down on his tummy and had banged his jaw. 'Right, all done,' she said, standing back and smiling at him. Billy smiled back. 'Thank you.'

'My pleasure, love. Now, arms up! Let's get you out of these bloody clothes.' She pulled a funny face. 'Hey, I think I just swore.'

'Bloody clothes!' repeated Billy, delighted. He lifted his arms obediently, allowing her to pull his shirt and jumper up over his head. Peggy drew in her breath sharply. Billy's pale little body was covered with bruises, some old, some obviously recent.

'You have been int wars, haven't you. Where d'you get these from, Billy?' she asked, very concerned, examining a graze on his shoulder.

'I fell down.'

At that moment, Billy's mother, Carol Bevan, appeared. 'Hello, Peggy,' she said wearily. She ruffled Billy's hair. 'Look at the sight of you.'

'Mmm. I was just admiring his war wounds. How did he do these?' Peggy tried to sound offhand.

'He fell down stairs last week. And yesterday he fell down int car park.' Carol Bevan eyed Peggy, suddenly suspicious. 'Why d'you ask?'

'Just interested.'

Carol straightened up, her face furious. 'Just interested? We may not be the perfect family—'

'I never said a thing, love,' Peggy returned quickly.

'We would never hurt Billy.'

'I know you wouldn't. I dint mean—' She stopped. That was a lie. It was exactly what she did mean. Carol Bevan could tell, too. 'Come on love, let's get you home.' She zipped Billy, minus his shirt and jumper, into his coat and hurried him out of the classroom, half-dragging him across the playground in her haste to get away. Peggy decided she needed a chat with Mrs Shelley.

'I think we should tell Social Services,' Mrs Shelley said, after Peggy had described Billy's bruises.

'Just because he's been a bit naughty?'

'He's not a 'bit naughty'. He's a very disturbed little boy with serious behavioural problems. And now these marks on his body . . .' Mrs Shelley felt guilty about that. She had been sure something was up – Billy was always causing trouble and had fallen behind in his classwork – but even she hadn't suspected physical abuse. When she'd questioned his mother, she had defended him as 'dreamy and clumsy', but the problem ran deeper than that.

Peggy shifted uncomfortably. Warning bells had gone off in her mind, too, but she found it hard to believe that Carol Bevan could have inflicted the bruises. She was, as far as

Peggy could tell, a devoted mother. 'She explained marks. I know Carol, she would never hurt Billy.'

'What about Mr Bevan?'

Joe Bevan was a different kettle of fish altogether. He wasn't local and didn't seem to go out much. Was he abusing Billy? Surely Carol would know, though? 'Give me a couple of days, see if I can't get to the bottom of it,' Peggy said, compromising.

'No Peggy. If anything should happen to Billy . . .'

'This sort of thing can ruin a family. Chances are it's all completely innocent.'

Mrs Shelley considered for a minute. It meant putting her reputation – her job – on the line, not to mention Billy's wellbeing. But Peggy had a point. 'Alright. I'll give you weekend. Then we phone Social Services.'

Ruth, having spent a week in hospital with Alfie, was itching to get out and about again. The staff had kept them in longer than usual to keep an eye on the baby, but Alfie was his father's son, a lusty, bonny lad who tipped the scales at an impressive weight for an early baby, and he was never in any danger. Like most babies, he'd lost a little of his birth weight, but was more than making up for it by demonstrating a voracious appetite. Ruth spent most of her first few days at home in her dressing gown, locked into an endless cycle of feeding, winding, nappy changing and feeding again. Simon, who was not one for delegating, had returned to take charge of things at the factory, leaving the usually capable Ruth feeling housebound and frumpy. Even her nurse's training hadn't prepared her for the total change of lifestyle that having a baby brought about. The interior of their home, a luxurious barn conversion which used to look as if it had been lifted straight from the pages of a glossy magazine, was overrun with piles of laundry and drying babygros and the once-pristine fitted kitchen was a mess.

'I don't feel like me any more – just a sort of zombie-like

milking machine,' she moaned to Peggy on the phone.

'It gets better, really.'

'That's what everyone says. But it dunt feel like it when he's crying three hours every night with colic.'

'I know, love, but it'll soon be a distant memory, believe me. He'll be going to school in his little uniform and you'll wonder where your baby went,' Peggy said, heartfelt. 'Enjoy it while you can.'

'Ha!'

'You need a change of scenery, that's all. I've got to pop out to supermarket in my lunchbreak. Why don't you come along?'

The thought of the rigmarole involved in getting herself and Alfie washed, dressed and into the car – let alone round a supermarket – nearly put Ruth off, but Peggy was firm. 'It'll do you good. You're going stir-crazy cooped up at home.'

Other mothers managed it, Ruth told her reflection, as she applied mascara, for the first time in a fortnight, dug out a sweater that had not been decorated with regurgitated milk and squeezed herself into a pair of pre-maternity trousers. The simple pleasure of being able to do up the zip again gave her an instant lift. 'Come on then, young man,' she said, sweeping into the room and scooping Alfie from his carrycot. 'Now all we have to do is figure out how to strap you int car seat and we're laughing.'

Peggy had another motive for getting Ruth out. She wanted her advice – and she needed to confide in her. As they strolled along the aisles, Alfie snoozing contentedly in Ruth's trolley, Peggy told her about the incident with Billy Bevan, and Mrs Shelley's suspicions. 'She thinks his father might be involved. Joe Bevan. He's a comer-in, isn't he?'

Ruth nodded. 'From Leeds. Came here when he was about sixteen. I remember cos Carol was in our class and she fell head over heels in about five minutes.'

'What's he like? I mean, I know him but I've never really talked to him.'

Ruth paused by the pasta. 'He keeps himself to himself. I know he's been out of work for a couple of months.' She surveyed the packets. 'I'd better get a lot of this, and sauces. It's about the limit of Simon's cooking. Oh, and I need oven chips. We're living out of freezer at moment.' She peered across the aisle and spotted Patricia in frozen foods, inspecting tubs of ice-cream. Ruth, her sense of mischief restored, crept up behind the unsuspecting Pat and made loud snorting noises. Patricia, who had been comparing the calorific value of Belgian Chocolate and Pralines and Cream, squealed, 'I were only looking! I were only looking!' while Ruth, who was enjoying herself hugely, continued to make pig-like sounds.

Peggy, who was chuckling at Ruth's antics, heard someone clear their throat and looked round. It was Carol Bevan. She looked drawn and tired, as if she hadn't slept well. Billy, dreamy as ever, tagged along behind.

'Hello, love. How are you?' Peggy inquired carefully.

'I'm fine. I'm sorry about yesterday. You were only doing your job,' she replied haltingly.

Peggy patted her arm. 'I know you'd never hurt Billy.' She followed Carol's eyes and saw him raiding a promotional counter of cheese samples on cocktail sticks. 'He says he has to eat a lot now because he won't eat snails on the school trip to France.' Carol smiled fondly. Ruth, who had left off teasing Patricia, joined them. She popped a cube of cheese in her mouth and grimaced.

'It's disgusting, i'nt it?' whispered the cheese lady, confidentially. 'How's Alfie?'

'He's fine. Sleeping right through.' Ruth tickled the baby under the chin.

Peggy, spying an opportunity to talk to Billy on his own, said to Carol, 'Listen, love. I'm taking our Lucy out on rounds this afternoon. Why don't I take Billy along?' Home visiting with children wasn't protocol but the patients never minded – most of them welcomed kiddies with open arms, especially the old folks – and it saved paying for a babysitter. 'It'd give you a break and keep Lucy occupied,' she pressed.

'I don't know.' Carol Bevan obviously doubted her motives.

'Don't tell me you and Joe couldn't do with an afternoon on your own?'

Peggy scored a bullseye. Carol Bevan's face relaxed into a smile. 'No, I wouldn't tell you that.'

'That's sorted then,' she said briskly, turning to Billy. '*Doctor* Bevan.'

Ruth and Peggy, with Billy in tow, continued their leisurely shop, frequently getting waylaid by people who wanted to coo at Alfie. Alfie, bundled up in his pramsuit and hat, remained impervious to all this attention and continued to doze peacefully. 'Is Stephen nervous about play tonight?' Ruth asked, eager to catch up on all the news.

'If I ever saw him, I'd ask him,' Peggy said tartly.

In the toiletries aisle they discovered Walter, bandage still intact (but rather grubby), filling his basket with boxes of tampons. Peggy groaned. 'What are you doing, Walter?' Walter looked nonplussed. 'You don't want these, pet,' she said, putting them back on the shelf. 'What are you looking for?

'Biscuits.'

'Put one of those in your tea and you'll crack cup,' Ruth laughed, helping Peggy. Henry, a friend of Stephen's who had a Saturday job stacking shelves, dawdled past. He had three crates of baked beans to arrange and was putting it off for as long as possible. Peggy, spotting an opportunity to check on her son's whereabouts, collared him. 'Have you seen our Stephen this morning?' she asked casually.

'No.' Too late, Henry realized that he might have been Stephen's alibi for something. 'I don't think so. I might have done. I can't remember.' He blushed to the roots of his lank hair.

'Thank you, Henry.' There was a touch of steel in Peggy's voice. Henry escaped to his baked beans.

'What was all that about?' Ruth's ever-inquisitive nose was twitching.

'Stephen dint come home last night because he was "rehearsing play with Henry".'

Ruth's eyes gleamed. 'You think he spent night with Deborah?'

'He wasn't with Deborah.' Peggy set her jaw.

'Where was he, then?'

Peggy glanced around and hissed, 'Can you keep a secret?'

'Of course I can't.' Ruth waited while Peggy considered. This was obviously Major Gossip. 'Peggy, if you don't tell me I'm gonna wet myself int aisle.'

Peggy leaned over and whispered her news in Ruth's ear. Gobsmacked, Ruth clapped her hands together and shrieked long and loud, her laughter echoing around the store. 'I'll have what she's having,' a nearby shopper joked, looking at Ruth in amusement. For once, Peggy could not see the joke.

'I don't want to get her sacked but it's not right, is it? I mean, she's his teacher,' she grumbled, as they loaded carrier bags into Ruth's car. 'It'd be like us taking advantage of a patient.'

'Please!' Ruth said, horrified at the thought. Most of them were far too wrinkly. Unlike Stephen . . . She could see why Wendy Atkins was tempted. 'I'm not saying she's right or anything. But she's probably really lonely, int she? I mean, it's her first job, miles away from home—'

'So it's alright for her to seduce her pupils?' Peggy said crossly. At that moment, her bleeper went off again. She groaned. 'Time to go. Billy, love, come here.' Billy, who had been throwing stones at a pile of cans, trotted over and was almost flattened by Stephen careening across the car park. 'Stephen?' Peggy called, as he shot past, shirt-tails flying. He waved but carried on running, vaulting a low wall and heading off down the road, a kit bag bumping on his shoulder. Peggy sighed.

There was no way Stephen was going to stop for an interrogation by his mother. He was late, very late, for that afternoon's match and whatever mood she was in – not a good one, judging by her expression – he had the prospect of his dad's wrath to contend with first, especially if he let the team down. Stephen galloped towards the rugby ground, wondering if Wendy was miffed by his sudden departure. They had spent all night and all morning at her place – the first time they had done so – and he was so intoxicated by his desire for her that he had completely lost track of the time. Being with Wendy, looking deep into her eyes as they made love, or simply lying by her side, stroking her hair, made Stephen feel charged with an almost superhuman strength. It was as if he could conquer anything. Her gravitas, her intensity, her physicality bowled him over. To see her at once so emotionally exposed, so needy of him, gave him a high that no drug could match. The fact that she was his teacher and five years older than him made it even more potent. He could tease her by snogging Deborah in rehearsals or staring at her in a certain way in class and she would get flustered, turning a delicate pink and going all strict with the class. Afterwards she would try and tell him off, and end up instead melting in his arms.

It had been after she cast him in the school play that they'd got together. 'That was good but you need some voice coaching,' she said, after he'd read Stanley's 'Polack' speech for the audition. He'd stayed behind after school with her, working on his American accent, and one evening it had just happened. Maybe it was Stanley's swagger, his bravado, that had given him the courage. Maybe it was the fact that she was reading the part of Blanche Dubois and not the strict teacher. Maybe they were just destined to be together. Whatever the trigger had been, Stephen had found himself kissing her. More importantly, she had kissed him back.

Finding opportunities to meet had been difficult – he couldn't overuse the 'rehearsing at Henry's' excuse – which was why they'd resorted to doing it at his house. The risk involved in making love in his parents' bed had given Stephen an almighty thrill, but Wendy wasn't so happy. This morning she'd realized that she'd mislaid a bra and was worrying about having left it behind, although he had reassured her by saying that if his mum had found it they'd both be dead. Stephen knew she was uncomfortable about meeting Peggy and Vic at the play that evening – 'It feels like we're flaunting it,' she'd said – but he had no such qualms. 'Of course it's right,' he'd insisted, kissing her gently. After all, how could anything so perfect be wrong?

Vic had already started his pep talk when Stephen staggered into the downstairs room of the Skelthwaite Arms which was the Scorpions' changing room. He was breathless and scarcely in any shape to talk, let alone play. 'Sorry I'm late,' he gasped, grabbing the shirt that Vic had left hanging on his peg. He stripped off, to wolf whistles from the rest of the team, who were already changed and sitting on the bench.

'Nice of you to come,' Vic replied acidly, with an 'I'll deal with you later' look. 'Right, lads! Start concentrating,' he continued, eyeing them one by one. 'I don't want a repeat of last week's shambles.'

'Here, here,' chipped in Simon, who was there in his sponsor capacity (or 'overlord' as Vic called it).

'We'll hit them so bloody hard in tackle they'll wish they'd never been born,' said Vic, glaring at Simon.

Terry, a local plasterer, nudged Stephen. 'What do they look like?' Stephen stretched out his arms wide. Terry sucked in his breath. 'It's the white shirts, makes 'em look bigger.'

'They're not wearing white shirts this year,' Stephen

informed him, as he bent down to lace up his boots. A pall of gloom settled over the dispirited team.

Peggy and Patricia had been called out on a delicate mission. Billy and Lucy, who had gone with them, were dispatched to play outside while the two nurses attended to Grace Buckley, a farmer's wife in her sixties, who was stuck in the bath. She was a woman of vast proportions and her overweight body had created a vacuum in the old metal tub. In an attempt to preserve her dignity, they covered her with a towel while they baled out the bathwater with a pair of saucepans. Her husband, John, spectated from the doorway.

'Feel free to help if you want,' said Peggy crossly, as John lit up a cigarette.

'There's Members of Parliament would pay hundreds of pounds to watch situation like this,' he replied, laconic.

A whimper escaped from the embarrassed Grace. 'I'm so ashamed.'

Peggy patted her plump arm. 'Don't be silly, pet. It's not your fault, it's these old baths. They were made when people were smaller, weren't they? We're always having to get people out of these things.'

'Really?' she looked up, encouraged.

'We must have problems with these at least once a month. Don't we, Pat?'

Patricia nodded vigorously. 'At least.'

'Right. Let's try again.' Peggy rolled up her sleeves. 'OK, Grace? You push and we'll pull.' Much heaving and grunting ensued, while John Buckley continued to watch, amused. All at once there was a 'pop' as the vacuum broke and Grace was freed. Peggy and Patricia, taken by surprise, almost fell into the bath with her. They looked at each other and spluttered with laughter, Grace Buckley, the towel barely covering her elephantine form, joining in, relieved. 'Like parting bloody atom,' her husband commented, turning to go now the fun was over.

Suddenly, a scream of pain from outside brought them all up short. Peggy recognized her daughter's wail instantly. She scrambled to her feet and ran to the window. Lucy, who had been clambering on bales in the barn with Billy, was standing in the farmyard, blood pouring from a gash on her forehead and trickling down her anguished face.

# Chapter 5

'How did this happen?' Peggy asked Lucy, hugging her daughter to her chest as she staunched the bleeding with a gauze pad. Lucy, who was perched on the kitchen table in the Buckley's kitchen, stared accusingly at Billy through wet eyelashes. 'We were up on the bales, talking French. I said the school trip was going to be brilliant and I was going to eat snails and drink wine and stuff and *he* started making his stupid face. He knows I don't like it and he does it on purpose—'

'I don't!' protested Billy, who was skulking at a safe distance behind Patricia.

'—and I asked him to stop and I just gave him a little shove and he pushed me off.'

'I never!'

'You did!' Lucy started crying again. Peggy folded her arms and looked at Billy, who dropped his head, ashamed. Given his record of misbehaviour, it wasn't difficult to know who to believe.

John Buckley, who was, as before, propped in the doorway observing all of this, drew on his cigarette and said, 'Shall I string him up, then, missus?' Billy shot back out into the yard smartly.

Despite the fact that her protective instinct had gone into overdrive, Peggy decided to take the 'softly softly' approach with Billy. (She did, anyway, feel a nagging sense of guilt for leaving the children to play in a potentially hazardous farm-yard.) 'You sit in the back so that Pat can look after your poorly head,' she told Lucy as they bade goodbye to the Buckleys. 'Billy, you come int front with me.' A subdued Billy buckled himself in beside her. He looked very pale, she noticed. Shock, probably. 'I bet you're looking forward to going to France,' she said, once they were under way. He shook his head. 'No? Why not? I would be,' Peggy quizzed.

'Cos they'll all gang up on me.'

'If they gang up on you, tell Mrs Shelley. She'll soon sort 'em out, won't she?' Billy did not reply. Peggy tried again. 'How's your dad?' Patricia caught her eye in the rearview mirror but Peggy pretended she hadn't spotted her warning expression.

'Alright,' Billy said indifferently.

'It must be nice having him home all the time.' Silence. She ploughed on. 'But I expect he'd rather be working, wouldn't he?' Still Billy said nothing. Peggy arched an eyebrow – 'See!' – at Patricia, feeling her worst suspicions might just be right.

Carol Bevan, predictably, stuck up for her son when Peggy dropped Billy off back home. 'I'm sorry if Lucy hurt herself but if Billy says he dint do it, he dint do it,' she said defensively.

'I'm not having a go at Billy— ,' Peggy began.

'He gets blame for everything.' She glanced over her shoulder through the lounge window at Billy, who was kicking a football around in the back garden with his father.

'Carol,' Peggy said, sticking to her guns, 'the boy's got behavioural problems. You know he has.'

'He's just going through phase.'

'I know what it's like. I know how naughty they can be. You're tired, you're at the end of your tether—'

'No.'

'Or maybe you're frustrated cos you can't get work, can't do your bit for family.'

'No!'

'Look,' Peggy tried to calm her down. 'Let's sit down, have a talk about this.' Carol Bevan sank onto the sofa, as if it was suddenly all too much for her. 'I would never lay a finger on Billy, no matter how naughty he was. And he *is* difficult sometimes,' she admitted. 'It worries me so much . . . his dad had similar problem. When Joe was a lad – not much older than Billy – he started doing badly at school. The more he fell behind the others, the more stupid he felt. He started showing off like kids do. Silly little things – fighting with other boys, cheeking teacher. Then they decided he was a bad penny and he needed taking out. They took him away from all his friends and put him int Special School.'

'I dint know that. But it changes nothing. If Billy is—'

'There were nothing wrong with him!' Carol Bevan said fiercely. 'All it did was isolate and humiliate Joe. When I met him he was a shadow of the man he is now.'

Mindful of Mrs Shelley's deadline, Peggy continued to push. 'All I ask is that you let a child psychologist take a look at Billy.'

'No.'

'Either you take him voluntarily, pet, or they'll come and get him.' Peggy laid it on the line. 'If you've got nothing to hide—'

'I haven't!'

'Then take him.'

She hesitated. 'If I do it, will you leave us alone?' Peggy nodded. 'Alright, I'll do it,' she agreed. 'Waste of time though it is.'

'No you won't,' snarled Joe Bevan, who had just come in through the back door. Both women jumped. 'Billy's going nowhere unless I say so. And I don't say so.'

'Joe. Listen to what Peggy's got to say,' his wife pleaded.

He looked witheringly at her. 'I don't discuss my family

with people like this. Leave, please,' he said to Peggy.

'I know a child psychologist in Huddersfield. He's a lovely man—' she began, as Joe Bevan seized her by the arm and yanked her up.

'I said "leave",' he shouted, frogmarching her into the hall.

'Joe!' Carol Bevan tried, without success, to restrain him.

'You keep your bloody nose out of my family.' He opened the front door and bundled Peggy outside. 'Come near us again and . . .'

'What will you do? More of this?' Peggy touched the tender spot on her upper arm where he had gripped her with iron fingers. She looked pointedly at Carol. Joe Bevan slammed the door in her face.

The rugby ball sailed high into the sky, arching in a perfect parabola. Stephen, running backwards, shouted 'Mine!', confident that he could intercept the pass, but somehow it didn't work out quite like that. The ball plummeted like a meteor landing, falling through his outstretched arms and hitting him in the groin with such force that he dropped to the ground with a grunt, the wind knocked out of him completely. While he was still lying in the mud, curled up in agony, the ball trickled across the goal line, giving an opposition player the easiest touchdown of his rugby league career.

'Bloody hell,' swore Vic – and it wasn't in sympathy with his son's injury. If the Skelthwaite Scorpions played any more farcically, they'd be up for panto next Christmas. He spat on the chewed-up turf, trying to ignore Simon's shouted comments of 'What a shambles!' and 'Good job I bought you yellow shirts!' from his position on the touchline with Alfie.

'Shame!' yelled Ruth, who was enjoying herself acting as physio. Two outings in one day – however ordinary – had made a new woman of her.

Vic, feigning deafness, turned to his team. 'Come on, now, lads, bit of pride,' he said, with a cheerfulness he did not feel.

Stephen picked himself up and limped behind the goalposts, half bent over. 'Stephen! D'you want magic sponge?' Ruth called, holding up a bucket. He grimaced, wondering whether his injury would affect his performance that night – on and off the stage. Just as he was contemplating playing Stanley Kowalski in falsetto, the conversion flew through the uprights. Vic groaned so loudly Stephen thought for a second that he'd been hit where it hurt too.

As far as Vic was concerned, that was exactly what it felt like. Like being thumped in the goolies, hard. He wanted so much for the team. Playing rugby wasn't just a hobby to him; it was a chance to grab at glory. It wasn't as if manufacturing loo paper gave you anything to boast about, he thought despondently as they trooped off the pitch. Witness Peggy's offhand rejection of it the other day. She hadn't meant to hurt him, he knew, but he sometimes felt as if what he did didn't matter. And Vic wanted to matter: to his family and to himself. Captaining the rugby team defined him differently. As much as anything, he wanted it for his town, which, like the team, had taken a severe beating over the years. People said that Skelthwaite had had the stuffing knocked right out of it, what with the mills closing and the lay-offs. And in some ways, they were right. But the spirit was still there, despite the hardship. It just needed igniting. That was what Vic always contended, but on present form even he was having a tough time believing it. *Who am I kidding*, he thought sourly.

The rest of the team, infected by Vic's mood, trudged into the changing room and slumped on the benches, too dispirited to undress even. 'There's always next week,' Terry said eventually, trying to brighten things up. The others turned mud-streaked faces towards him and glared.

There were few compensations for being involved in such a crushing defeat – the Scorpions had lost by an embarrassing twenty-nine points to six – but soaking his aching body in a really hot bath at least made Vic feel that life was bearable again. He submerged himself beneath a sea of pine-scented bubbles and let the heat envelope him. Bliss. Peggy knelt on the floor beside the bath, seeing to a nasty graze on his elbow. She was going on about some lad who had hurt Lucy, and seemed more worried about the boy than her own daughter. Reassured that Lucy's injury was minor, Vic was only half listening. Peggy was in her dressing gown, her splendid cleavage brushing tantalisingly close to his face. If he wasn't so knackered . . . Vic leaned his head back and closed his eyes, snapping them open again suddenly with a wince as she applied stinging antiseptic. 'Bloody hell! Is this what you do to your patients?'

'Only the complaining ones. There. You'll do.'

Vic reached for the soap and began lathering his sore limbs. 'Do you really have to get involved?' he asked, apropros the Bevans. It was something he said to Peggy quite often.

She never took any notice. 'You'd rather I did nothing? Little lad like that?' she replied predictably.

'I'd rather you scratched my back.'

Peggy complied. Vic, loving it, made happy, doggy noises and wallowed.

'Int it about time you hung up your shorts?' Peggy said, spoiling his reverie. Vic did not like being reminded that he would be forty-five next birthday.

'Boots,' he corrected. 'Over a bit, down . . . I said I'd make Skelthwaite a power again and I will. There! Oh, that's goo-ood.'

'Obviously.' Peggy looked down at the evidence for this, which was poking proudly above the bubbles. Vic smiled in anticipation, but before he could give her any more explicit instructions there was a knock on the door. He seized a flannel and covered up just in time as Lucy burst into the bathroom. 'It's stopped bleeding,' she announced, brandishing the plaster from her forehead.

'That's my girl,' said Vic, flustered, sinking lower into the water. Stephen, queasy with first night nerves – the dress rehearsal had been a disaster – stuck his head round the door. 'Can I get in here, please? I have to get ready.'

'Excuse me.' Vic was indignant. 'Man having bath here.'

'Please,' Stephen begged. He looked unusually pale.

Peggy got up and dried her hands. 'Come on, Lucy, let's leave your Dad to it.'

Vic's face fell. 'I thought you were going to . . . scratch my back.'

'I'm sure you can finish yourself off,' she said pointedly. The door closed. Vic glanced down at the flannel, which was floating flat on the water. The moment had passed.

Peggy drew back her lips in a semi-snarl and applied a fierce, red lipstick. She pouted at herself in the mirror, decided, regretfully, that she couldn't really get away with such a vivid colour at her age, and wiped it off. She would deal with Wendy Atkins barefaced.

The decision to go and see Stephen's teacher had been brewing for a while and she couldn't put it off any longer. Vic was not privvy to Peggy's plans because she knew he might try and stop her. He always said she charged into things like a bull in a china shop. Besides, she was going to have to be brutal and, when it came to the crunch, Vic was a big softie. Better to sort it out by herself. In a curious way, Peggy was looking forward to it.

Vic and Simon had gone out for a drink to get themselves into the mood for the evening's entertainment, so Peggy was able to go via Wendy's flat undetected. She pressed the doorbell and waited. A flustered Wendy, who was obviously in the middle of getting ready – curtain up was in less than an hour – answered, hairbrush in hand. 'Come in, Mrs Snow,' she said, taken aback. Peggy stepped into the kitchen, taking in a pair of coffee mugs on the table. 'It's a bit of a mess, I'm afraid,' Wendy apologised, noticing them too and dumping them in the sink. 'Please sit down.'

Peggy sat. Wendy, nervous, sat opposite her. Peggy fixed her with a level stare. She said nothing but her look said everything.

'What can I do for you?' Wendy asked haltingly.

'I think you know, don't you?'

She swallowed. 'No.'

Peggy opened her handbag and produced Wendy's bra. She laid it on the table between them, her trump card. 'Yours, I believe.' Wendy flushed crimson. 'Don't bother to deny it. I saw you both,' Peggy said coldly. 'I know you're a long way from home and it's your first job and everything. But I trusted you with my child and you've abused that trust. Not only did you sleep with my son – your pupil – but you did it in *my* bed. Is that what they taught you at teacher college?'

'No.' Wendy hung her head. 'What are you going to do?' she asked finally in a tremulous voice.

'What are *you* going to do?'

Wendy looked up at this, confused. Peggy's face was stern. 'As I see it, you've got two choices. You can either go to Headmaster and hand in your resignation and no one will be any the wiser. Or—'

'But I've only just got here!'

'—Or you can make me do it. In which case, everyone will know about this whole sorry business. Do you like teaching, Wendy?' Peggy inquired menacingly. Wendy, too terrified to reply, merely nodded.

'I'm not expert in these things but seducing the kids can't look too good on CV, can it?' Peggy was on a roll, so when Wendy choked, 'But I love him, Mrs Snow', she was taken totally by surprise. 'I don't want to know about that.'

'What about Stephen? Doesn't he get a say in this?'

'No, he doesn't. Because I know him. He's loyal, affectionate and he'll stand by you, no matter what he really thinks.'

'He loves me, too,' Wendy sobbed in a small voice.

'If he gets hurt now he'll put it down to experience and get on with his life. Perhaps he'll even be the richer for having known you,' Peggy said, softening for a fraction. 'But if you pull this scandal down on his head and frighten him and humiliate him . . . I won't let that happen. So you end it now or I'll end it for you.' She stood up and picked up her bag, leaving Wendy in no doubt about the options open to her. 'Good luck tonight,' she added. 'I'll let myself out.'

It was 7.00pm and temporarily quiet in the Skelthwaite Arms. Sally, the landlady, took advantage of the lull between the after-work crowd and the evening drinkers to empty ashtrays and clear away glasses. Only three customers occupied the public bar: Vic and Simon, and Joe Bevan. Joe was drinking by himself and didn't even seem to notice when Sally asked, 'Thirsty, Joe?' as he drained his pint in one long draught. The other two, in their 'best' clothes, were conducting a post-mortem on the afternoon's fiasco in an attempt to postpone the bum-numbing prospect of the play to the last minute.

'It's a recipe for disaster, int it – ageing forwards and schoolboy backs,' Simon said, not mincing his words.

*There he goes again*, thought Vic. *I'd like to see him getting muddy for a change. Preferably flat on his face int middle of pitch*. 'Just cos you bought set of shirts dunt give you right to slag team off,' he replied crossly.

'Yes, it does.'

Vic thought better of continuing this conversation and downed the rest of his ale. 'Come on, let's go and see play.'

'Do we have to?'

'Yes, we do. Sup up.'

Just then, Joe Bevan walked past. He stopped in front of Vic and put his face threateningly close. 'Do you want a bit of advice, Vic?'

'Not really.'

'Keep your wife's nose out of other people's affairs.'

'I'll certainly try, Joe, if that's what you advise,' Vic said,

71

trying not to look intimidated. Joe Bevan had a reputation as a bit of a wild card, especially since he'd lost his job.

'Or someone might just do it for you.' Joe Bevan stalked out of the pub. Simon's sandy eyebrows were practically in his hair. 'What's *that* all about?' He'd been out of his head when Martin Hutton came in and regretted not being there for Peggy. Now it seemed his sister had been stirring things up again. She always had liked bossing people about, he reflected.

'I promise you, you don't want to know. See you later, Sally.' Vic saluted her.

'Tell Stephen to break a leg,' she replied.

'That's not very nice,' Vic hissed at Simon as they walked towards the door.

'It's what theatre people say to each other. It means "good luck".' Simon shook his head at Vic's ignorance.

'How would you know?'

'I've been to theatre.'

'When?'

'Last year. Theatre Royal, Huddersfield.'

Vic snorted. '*Mother Goose*!'

'It was a theatre.'

They stepped out into the night, drawing their coat collars up to keep out the chill wind. Suddenly, Vic stopped. Beyond the streetlamp he could just make out the dark form of a body. 'Look, there.' They hurried over. Lying slumped on the ground in a pool of vomit was Joe Bevan. He was out cold.

# *Chapter 6*

Peggy, watching Stephen on the stage, could hardly believe the young man up there was her son. His performance was utterly compelling. From the moment he appeared, he had captivated the audience and, proud mother that she was, Peggy had no doubt that they were witnessing something special: the debut of a future star. Lucy, beside her, was equally transfixed (although Peggy could foretell a lot of 'why?' questions coming on afterwards). She glanced along the row at Vic, who was fidgeting – Tennessee Williams wasn't his cup of tea, no matter how spellbinding Stephen was – and noticed Wendy sitting next to the headmaster. She was blinking rapidly and once or twice brushed her cheek with the back of her hand. Peggy almost felt sorry for her. That was, until Stephen, as Stanley, made a speech to Deborah's Stella that stunned her with its irony.

' "She's not going back to teach school! In fact, I am willing to bet you that she never had no idea of returning to Laurel! She didn't resign temporarily from the high school because of her nerves! No siree, Bob! She didn't. They kicked her out of that high school before the spring term ended – and I hate to tell you the reason that step was taken! A seventeen-year-old boy – she'd gotten mixed up with".'

*Life really does imitate art*, Peggy thought. *I'm surprised that Miss Atkins didn't see the writing on wall. It's not as if she doesn't know how the play turns out*. She leaned forward

73

and caught Wendy's eye deliberately. Wendy bit her lip and looked away.

The curtain fell on Deborah and Stephen to rapturous applause. Peggy leapt to her feet, face shiny with tears, clapping madly. Ruth, she noticed, was standing too, and, judging by her glistening eyes, equally moved. (Simon, who was signing 'Drink?' to Vic, was obviously more moved to return to the pub.) Peggy looked behind her and saw other parents joining in the standing ovation until the entire school hall was on its feet. The company took three curtain calls and on the third, Stephen stepped forward and held out his arm, beckoning Wendy, the director, up onto the stage. Wendy looked unsure but Mr Pearson waved her out of her seat magnanimously and she had no choice but to comply. Watching her join the line-up and raise Stephen's hand in a victory salute suddenly soured Peggy's evening.

The backstage party was not of the calibre of the illicit one Stephen had been disciplined for organising (Mr Pearson was only allowing crisps and Coke) but there was a disco and everybody involved in the play was letting off steam on the dance floor. Stephen, who was the centre of attention, was being hugged and congratulated by a stream of (mostly female) admirers – Wendy stayed in the background – and even 'Dogger' shook his hand warmly. 'What did he say to you?' asked Peggy afterwards, observing this thawing of relations.

'He said he hoped I'd remember that I had my formative experience at Skelthwaite School when I'm famous. I said there was no way I could ever forget it.'

'Hmmn.' Peggy, reading the innuendo in Stephen's wide grin, was not amused.

Patricia spotted them both and bustled over, beaming. 'That was excellent, Stephen. Really good.'

'Thanks.' Stephen was enjoying lapping up all the attention.

Peggy nudged her colleague. 'We're going to have to carry his big head home int wheelbarrow.'

'Take no notice, love. She's as proud as punch,' Patricia laughed.

'Did you really like it?' Stephen asked bashfully when Patricia had gone. Peggy's heart swelled. Her opinion still mattered to him. *She* mattered to him. 'It were brilliant. And so were you.'

Stephen was swift to press home his advantage. 'We're having a bit of a party later – a proper party, not this kids' stuff,' he added, glancing around disdainfully at the juniors and teachers bopping about. 'I thought I might—'

'No.' He looked up at her stern voice. The smile had vanished from Peggy's face. 'No rehearsing-at-Henry's, no revising-at-Deborah's. I want you home.' Stephen opened his mouth to frame a question, then thought better of it. He was saved by Deborah, who bounced up to them and grabbed his hand. 'Can I borrow him, Mrs Snow?' Not waiting for an answer, she dragged him off to dance. 'He's all yours, pet,' Peggy replied, half to herself. If only it were true.

She scanned the room to check on her other offspring and spotted Lucy sitting on her own making gargoyle-like faces at Stephen, who was jiving with Deborah. 'What are you doing?' Peggy asked, amused, plonking herself down next to her gurning daughter. 'Bonjour Mama. Trying to make Stephen laugh. Is he in love with Deborah?' Lucy replied, swinging her legs.

'Ssshhh. You shouldn't make faces like that. Wind'll change.'

Lucy pouted. 'Billy does it.'

Peggy put an arm round her. 'Billy's not you, is he? Did you enjoy play?'

'It was alright. Don't they have adverts in plays?'

'Obviously not,' Peggy smiled. Vic and Simon, who had decamped to the Skelthwaite Arms, had probably wished the same thing. She got up. 'Come on, let's get you home.'

'Will Billy come with us on rounds again?' Lucy inquired, slipping her hand into Peggy's.

'Would you like him to?'

'No.'

This was very unlike Lucy. 'I thought you two got on?'

'He's gone all horrible and funny.'

'What d'you mean, "funny"?'

'He knows I don't like his horrible faces but he does them anyway and he falls down and frightens me.'

Peggy stopped walking. Something was definitely going on with Billy Bevan. 'He always makes faces before he falls down?' she asked, thoughtfully.

Lucy, solemn, nodded. 'Then he says he dunt remember.'

Stephen, clowning around on the dance floor, was only too aware of the woman he really wanted to be with standing in the shadows. Wendy had let go of his hand as if she'd been stung the minute the curtain fell. He could understand that, but ever since she seemed to be avoiding him. Considering he was the star of the show, she ought, at least, to have congratulated him. Maybe she was saving it up for later. Once or twice he had managed to catch her eye but she shied away nervously. *She's taking these precautions a bit too far*, he thought. Still, he liked the idea of having a double life: it appealed to the actor in him and the secrecy gave him a heightened awareness. 'It's as if I had whiskers, like a cat. I can sense when you're around, even if I can't see you,' he had told her once. Like now. He knew she had been collared by Ruth, that she was uneasy, desperate to escape. Stephen spotted Henry, hovering by a table of soft drinks, and waved him over. Henry fancied Deborah like mad but was too shy to make a move. 'Look, Debs, I've gotta go. Mum's giving me grief,' he said, winking at Henry. Her face fell. Stephen pretended not to notice. 'Henry'll give you a dance – won't you?' He clapped Henry on the back and, satisfied with his attempt at playing Cupid, went to find Wendy. But Wendy had gone.

He found her walking hurriedly across the car park, pulling her coat tightly round her slim frame. 'Excuse me, Miss,' he shouted, keeping up the schoolboy protocol in case anybody else could hear.

Wendy started. 'What is it, Stephen?' She looked harassed.

'Can I come and see you later?' he asked, lowering his voice.

She glanced around. 'No. Not tonight.'

A gang of pupils, chattering and larking, emerged from the school's front entrance and headed in their direction. 'Why not?' Stephen whispered urgently.

'Because I said so.' Her tone was cold and hard and she wore a cross expression. The rejection hit Stephen like a slap in the face. She had never spoken to him like that before. He looked at her for a long second, realizing she meant it. Hurt, he turned and walked away. 'Stephen!' she called after him, but he ignored her. Tonight, of all nights, he had wanted to be with Wendy, to celebrate. Suddenly, the wave of energy he had been riding all night broke, sending him crashing to the floor.

Ruth was pushing Alfie's pram across the playground – it was way past his bedtime but, fortunately, he was out for the count – when she saw, ahead of her, Wendy Atkins and Stephen engaged in intense conversation. Not wanting to barge past she loitered, waiting until they'd finished. Besides, her curiosity was piqued: ever since Peggy had divulged her news in the supermarket she had been dying to see this teacher of Stephen's. They'd had a brief exchange inside, during which Ruth had remarked, naughtily, 'Stephen's good, int he?' just to see how Wendy would react. A confused look had passed across Wendy's face. 'At acting,' Ruth continued, innocently. Wendy, flustered, had agreed.

Wendy and Stephen appeared to be having some kind of lovers' tiff. Ruth watched as Stephen stormed off across the car park and disappeared into an alley. It was too cold to hang around any longer and, anyway, Wendy had obviously seen her because she gave a half-hearted smile as Ruth and Alfie approached. 'Your nephew. He just won't be told.' Wendy gave an exasperated sigh. 'I'm assuming you know?'

'About you and Stephen? Yes, Peg told me this morning.'

'Oh, God.' Wendy fell in beside Ruth as she wheeled the pram. 'Who else knows?'

'Just me. She hasn't even told Vic.'

'She came to see me,' Wendy confided. She hadn't made many friends during the few months she'd been in Skelthwaite. Ruth was near enough to her in age for Wendy to feel able to talk to her. And she needed to talk to someone badly.

'I know.' Peggy had updated Ruth during the interval.

'Hands off the beloved son or else.'

*I would love to have been a fly on the wall for that one*, thought Ruth. Peggy could be very impressive when she was breathing fire. All the same, she felt for Wendy. She was a young, inexperienced girl who'd got in over her head with Stephen. And Stephen was a good-looking lad, there was no denying that; a right charmer. But there were family loyalties to consider. 'There's one thing you have to know about Peggy,' she explained, in defence of her sister-in-law. 'I mean, she loves Vic, she loves Lucy. But Stephen . . . she adores Stephen.'

'So do I,' Wendy replied simply. 'I've never met anyone like him. I've never met anyone so . . . alive and exciting. I've never met anyone who loved me like he does.'

'What will you do?' asked Ruth, genuinely sympathetic.

'I haven't got much choice, have I?'

'I'm sorry, pet.'

'I'm not running away,' Wendy announced defiantly. She gathered herself up. 'If I really thought Stephen and I had a snowball's chance in hell of staying together, I'd fight her every inch of the way. I'd get the sack, I'd take the gossip, I'd live in shame in a cardboard box if I had to.' She fell silent for a moment and then added, sadly, 'But I know I'd lose him anyway. He'll grow out of me.'

'You don't *know* that,' Ruth chided.

'Yes, I do.' Wendy's face was serious. 'People like Stephen don't end up with people like me.'

They parted at the end of her road, and Ruth carried on, mulling over Wendy's words. There had been, briefly, someone else in her life once; someone glamorous and going places. Places beyond Skelthwaite. Ruth had thought the same thing: we're not in the same league. She'd made the safe choice, Simon, and she was happy with that. Most of the time. But the passion that shone in Wendy's eyes when she talked about Stephen made Ruth feel vaguely let down, as if she'd been cheated out of something. She shook her head in silent reprimand at such self-indulgence and wondered when Simon would get home from the pub.

Peggy was still mulling over Lucy's words when they met up with Vic and her brother in the Skelthwaite Arms. 'What was Stephen like?' Sally asked her, pulling pints for the men.

'He were brilliant, thanks pet. Not that I'm biased,' Peggy said, glowing. Vic chucked Lucy under the chin – the pub took a relaxed attitude towards children, so long as they were accompanied – and ordered her a lemonade. 'Oh, and a vodka and tonic for Modest One here,' he added, indicating Peggy with his thumb.

'I'll tell you what, if he could play rugby as well as he prances about on stage we'd be in business,' Simon chipped in.

'Give it a rest,' Vic said, testily.

'Pass to me! Pass to me!' Simon squealed in an effeminate voice. Others around the bar started laughing. Vic scowled. To change the subject, Peggy said to Sally, 'I hear Joe Bevan had a bit of a skinful earlier.'

Sally looked surprised. 'Joe? No. A couple of pints.'

Vic snorted disbelievingly. 'Couple of pints? We found him face down int car park counting diced carrots. He were in hell of a state. Me and Simon were going to take him home but he got up and staggered off saying he dint want no help from likes of me.'

'He weren't drunk when he left here,' Sally said, reaching up to pour a measure of vodka. 'Not exactly life and soul, but not drunk.'

'Are you sure, pet?' enquired Peggy.

'I don't know much—'

'True,' butted in Simon.

'—but I know a drunk when I see one – don't I, Simon? – and Joe Bevan wasn't drunk,' Sally stated firmly.

That made up Peggy's mind. 'Give Pat that vodka. I'm going to see Bevans again,' she said, getting up.

'Peggy,' Vic laid a restraining hand on her. 'He don't want you interfering. You'd best stay out of it.'

She shook him off. 'No. I think I know what's wrong with Billy.'

Peggy hesitated in front of the Bevans' house, wondering whether to leave it until the next day, then remembered Mrs Shelley's deadline. She took a deep breath and lifted the latch of the garden gate.

Joe and Carol Bevan's raised voices were audible as she walked down the path. They were having a major row. Carol Bevan was almost hysterical. 'You're the one who said they'd take him away. And now you want to do the same!'

'It's not the same. He'd be with us.'

'There are people who care about him—'

'Interfering people.'

'He knows them! He trusts them.'

'You don't get it, do you?' Joe Bevan's voice said roughly.

'No, I don't. All I know is he's in trouble and he's staying here.'

'I won't let them ruin his life like they ruined mine!'

Peggy stopped. She didn't dare disturb them now. Joe Bevan already saw her as the enemy and, with his unpredictable temper, there was no knowing what he might do. She turned and was about to retrace her steps when she heard a tapping noise coming from the other side of a frosted glass panel in the front door. Something was knocking against it but she couldn't tell what it was. From the living room, the row had intensified.

'I hate this town! It's done nothing for me! There's no work, there's nothing here. What's Billy going to do in a dead-end hole like this?' Joe Bevan ranted.

'Billy will be alright. He'll go to a good school with good teachers—'

'Good teachers! They want to take him to Social Services!'

'Because they care!'

'They don't care. They just want to feel good, to look good in front of their teacher friends. They don't care about Billy.'

'Of course they do. You're just too bitter to see it! I'm sorry about what happened to you but it's left you twisted, Joe. You don't see straight.'

'I see straight enough, woman.'

Peggy was torn. She didn't want to be caught eavesdropping but the tapping was becoming wilder. She squatted down and peered closely through the glass. It was difficult to make out anything clearly but she thought she could see a foot thrashing about. Suddenly, there was a sharp crack as the foot thumped the glass door so hard that it splintered into a jagged jigsaw of white-edged fragments. 'Billy?' she called, alarmed. 'Billy?' The foot struck the door again, hard, and the glass shattered with explosive force, shards flying outwards and only just missing Peggy's face. From inside, Carol Bevan screamed. Now Peggy could see Billy lying on the floor, his little body jerking convulsively. Calmly, she reached up through the hole in the door and undid the bolt, letting herself in as his parents rushed into the hall. Billy's eyes were rolled back under half-open lids and he was unconscious, legs and arms twitching disjointedly. Peggy knelt down beside him and checked his airway. 'Phone for an ambulance,' she instructed Carol, who was standing white-faced beside her. 'Alright, Billy, alright,' she soothed, as the fit gradually subsided. She rolled him into the recovery position and glanced up. The Bevans were still rooted to the spot, too shocked to move. 'Joe! Ambulance! Tell them he's having an epileptic seizure,' she repeated. Joe, appalled, stumbled to the phone.

It took the ambulance almost twenty minutes to get there, twenty minutes during which Peggy went back over and over the signs and kicked herself for not having spotted Billy's condition earlier. Everything fitted: Billy's dreamy, faraway look, his peculiar faces, unusual behaviour, the falling over, not remembering what had happened. They were classic signs of a grand mal, a type of epileptic seizure. Joe Bevan hadn't been drunk, he'd had a seizure too, and, from Vic's description – Joe had gashed his head but was otherwise OK – he was lucky not to have been more badly hurt. But why hadn't he said something? Clearly, Carol Bevan hadn't known anything about it, until this evening, anyway. 'He told me when he came back from pub,' she said to Peggy after her husband had been dispatched upstairs to fetch a blanket to cover Billy. 'He just caved in, started crying. Said he dint tell me before cos he thought I'd think less of him.' Her voice started to break. 'He knew all that time what Billy was going through and he dint say owt. He wanted us to leave here, move to Leeds, run away from it, like he's bin running away from it all his life. He said—,' she took a shuddering breath, '—he said Billy would grow out of it. Like *he* has, obviously,' she shot angrily at Joe, who had come back down the stairs with the blanket. She stroked her son's hair. Billy was conscious now, but con-fused and drowsy. Joe Bevan draped the blanket over him

82

where he lay in the hall. Peggy looked up questioningly at him. He turned away. 'I'll get his things,' he mumbled, and disappeared upstairs again.

Joe Bevan remained silent all the way to the hospital – Billy had requested that Peggy go with them – and disappeared into Accident and Emergency with his family leaving Peggy to ponder her own part in the chain of events. She got herself a cup of instant coffee from a vending machine and took it out onto the balcony overlooking the hospital gardens. Leaning against the iron railings she looked up at the night sky, noticing that the orange glow of the urban sprawl made the stars appear fainter and dimmer than they did over Skelthwaite. Beyond the dark trees lining the grounds, set after set of headlights swept past on the main road; people still moving about the town even though it was now past midnight. *They're probably on their way home*, she thought, feeling overwhelmingly tired and a little out of her depth. The coffee was hot and she curled her fingers around the cardboard cup, appreciating its warmth, and took a scalding mouthful.

'You're still here, then?' The inquiry made Peggy start out of her reverie. She turned round to see Joe Bevan framed in the doorway behind her. He sounded tentative rather than angry, and his shoulders sagged wearily.

'Is he going to be alright?' she asked, concerned about Billy.

Joe Bevan ran a hand through his hair. 'So they say. He's an epileptic – like I am.'

Peggy knew what it had taken for him to finally admit that. 'It's different now, I promise you,' she reassured. 'They've got pinpoint medication and all the support you can think of. He'll be no different from any other child.'

He joined her on the balcony, leaning his forearms on the railings. 'I tell you what, Peggy, I feel that stupid.'

'How d'you think I feel? Trained nurse not spotting something in front of her eyes.'

83

At that, he looked up. 'Thanks for sticking your nose in.'

Peggy smiled at the apology. 'My pleasure, love.'

Stephen, scrambling up the steep path out of Skelthwaite onto the moors, turned his face to the same giddying panorama of stars and was energised by their age-old light. From his vantage point on the hillside, the constellations looked so vivid and close he felt as if he could gather the glittering sky and cloak himself in it, like a king. He raised his arms in salute to Orion, abandoning himself to the mercy of the gods. A chill breeze tautened his skin and he closed his eyes, feeling once again Wendy's breath on his cheek, her lips parting to receive his. Despite her rejection of him after the play he had gone round to her flat, buoyed up by a couple of drinks at the unofficial cast party. She was cross at first, telling him to go home, but this time he refused to listen to her stern teacher voice. Taking Wendy in his arms he had kissed her and immediately her body melted against his without the slightest show of protest. Hungry for her, he pulled her into the bedroom and tore off her dressing gown, revelling in her total nakedness. It was only after they had made love – twice – that she dropped the bombshell. He noticed that she seemed withdrawn and asked what the matter was. 'It's over, Stephen,' was all she said.

'What d'you mean?'

She had turned her face away then. 'Please don't make this any harder than it has to be.'

He was rocked to the core. 'If we love each other, nothing else matters.' Love conquered all, didn't it? Stephen would take on the world if he had to. Anything to be with her.

'That's just it. I don't love you.' She wouldn't meet his eyes.

He lifted her chin so that she was forced to look at him. 'I don't believe you.'

'Believe me.'

'Say it again, then,' he faltered, thinking this was a joke, some sort of test of his maturity she had stored up. Wendy gazed at him dully, unblinking. 'I don't love you,' she repeated. She handed him his clothes. 'You'd better go home to Mummy.'

Stephen opened his eyes and found himself staring not into Wendy's pale face but the wan countenance of the moon, which had slid out from behind an inky cloud. He tipped back his head and let out a roar, a throat-searing cry of frustration and anger and despair that welled up from his guts and bellowed around the bleak landscape, bouncing off the rooftops of the houses far below.

# Chapter 7

Monday morning assembly: the lowlight of the week, Stephen thought, only half listening to the Headmaster droning on about graffiti from the raised platform in the school hall. He was so tired, his eyelids kept drooping – he'd hardly slept that weekend, thinking about Wendy – and the prospect of a history lesson first thing didn't do much for his flagging spirits either. He stifled a yawn and looked about him at the serried rows of uniformed pupils, the younger ones down at the front where the teachers on the platform could keep an eye on them, and thought, *The sooner I'm off to university, the better. I'm too old to be with these kids. They don't know anything. I've already been through more than some of those uptight old fogies sitting up there.* Except that they weren't all old and uptight. Wendy, who he had last seen naked in his arms, was also there, expressionless. Stephen glanced at his watch and wondered how he would get through the day, especially the English class he had with her later. Henry, sitting next to him, nudged Stephen in the ribs and cocked his head at the stage, indicating that Dogger had said something that was vaguely interesting. 'Miss Atkins is leaving,' he hissed. Stephen mouthed 'What?' as the Head continued, 'Miss Atkins has been with us for less than a year but in that time we have all come to appreciate her tremendous energy and commitment to this school and this community. In particular, her magnificent production of *A Streetcar Named Desire* will be remembered for many years to come.'

Wendy's expression did not alter, but her eyes, flickering across the packed hall, briefly sought Stephen's. He stared back, angry and confused. What was she playing at? 'Unfortunately, an illness in Miss Atkins's family has forced her to seek a position nearer her parental home,' Mr Pearson explained. 'So it only remains for me to thank Miss Atkins for her work at Skelthwaite High School and to wish her every success in her future career.' He started clapping and the rest of the school joined in, with a few cheers and whoops from the cast of *Streetcar* – all except Stephen, who sat as if turned to stone. Henry leaned over and said, 'Did you know she was going?' but Stephen appeared not to hear him.

By the end of history – during which he was told off twice for inattentiveness – Stephen resolved that he had to have some answers from Wendy, there and then. He cut the next class and went to look for her, peering through classroom doors at lessons in progress. Eventually, he found her, teaching a group of eleven-year-olds. They were sitting attentively as she read to them from a book, gesticulating enthusiastically with her characteristic immersion in a subject. Stephen watched as she got up from her desk and wrote something on the board. At last he could bear it no longer and rapped on the door. 'Come in,' she called, before turning round. He entered, creating a buzz of excitement among the pigtailed young girls, who had elevated him to the status of school sex god after his charismatic performance on Saturday night.

Wendy's eyebrows shot up. 'Yes, Stephen?'

'Can I see you for a minute, Miss?'

'I'm in the middle of a class,' she snapped, momentarily rattled. She took a deep breath. 'Come to the Staff Room at lunchtime.'

Stephen remained where he was. 'It's important,' he insisted, remembering, just, to observe formalities. 'Miss.' He fixed her with a stare that brooked no argument. One of the girls pursed her lips at him and the rest of the class giggled. Wendy, worried about what Stephen might say next, put down the blackboard rubber. 'I'm right outside the door,' she warned the class. 'I don't want to hear a sound from any of you.'

She shut the door behind them and turned on Stephen in the empty corridor. 'What do you think you're doing?' she whispered furiously.

'Why dint you tell me you were going?' he demanded, ignoring her question. 'I have to hear it in assembly with all the other kids? How d'you think that makes me feel?'

'I'm sorry, but—'

'Sorry?' he snorted bitterly.

Behind them, the volume level from the classroom began to rise. Wendy glanced back, distracted. 'I can't talk now.'

'Then I'll see you at lunchtime.'

'No, Stephen, I've got things to do.'

'At your place,' he said firmly, turning and walking away.

Ruth had decided that it was time she put in an appearance at work, just to check how they were all managing without her while she was on maternity leave. *If* they were managing without her, which she doubted very much. She took Patricia by surprise, Hob Nob in hand, when she turned up with Alfie. 'Here, you show him ropes,' Ruth said, swapping the biscuit for the baby.

Patricia jiggled Alfie on her knee. 'He's definitely his father's son, int he?' she laughed as he stared stonily at her.

'Hmmn,' Ruth replied through a mouthful of crumbs. 'Tried to sell me a second-hand breast pump yesterday.'

'Don't you listen to her,' Patricia said to Alfie, holding him up in front of her and making big eyes at him. 'You're lovely, you are.'

Ruth sat down at the communal desk and surveyed the paperwork spread all over it. 'I bet it's been chaos here without me.'

'No, we've been fine,' Patricia returned airily.

Ruth pulled a disbelieving face as she surveyed the mess. The phone rang and she reached for it automatically. 'Staff Nurse Goddard . . . oh, hello, Mrs Byas, how are you? . . . sorry to hear that. What's problem?'

At that moment, Peggy bustled into the room, pink-cheeked and puffing. 'Sorry I'm late. Mr Ellins's boil went up like Mount Vesuvius.' Patricia waved one of Alfie's tiny mittened hands at her. Peggy gave a broad smile. 'Look who it is! Hello, Alfie, what are you doing here?' She glanced at Ruth, who had the phone tucked under her chin and was reaching for the appointments diary. 'I could have sworn she were on leave.'

Ruth cupped her hand over the receiver. 'Mrs Byas. Can you come and look at her stitches only she thinks she burst them doing garden,' she said to Peggy.

'And what d'you think you're doing?' Peggy greeted her.

Ruth looked put out. 'I'm ont phone to Mrs Byas.'

'You're on maternity leave. Feet up. Sore nips. Daytime telly.' Peggy reached out her hand for the phone.

Ruth relinquished it reluctantly. 'I bet it is,' she said ruefully to Patricia.

'What?'

'Chaos.' She flicked a paperclip at Peggy, who flapped her hand at her, annoyed. 'Hello, Mrs Byas, Peggy here. What's happened, love? . . . Is it looking bad? . . . It is? Well, I can squeeze you in now if I hurry. Would that be alright? OK, I'll be round in ten minutes. See you then.' She put the phone down and picked up her bag. 'Come on, you two,' she ordered, scooping up Alfie, who was sprawled on Patricia's capacious bosom. 'You can walk me to the car.'

'I don't mind doing a bit of paperwork. I can do that at home,' offered Ruth, trotting along beside her.

'Int your mother stubborn?' Peggy nuzzled Alfie's downy head, inhaling soft baby smells.

'I give you another week. You'll be on your knees, begging,' Ruth retorted. They had reached the car before she remembered her prime piece of gossip. 'Did you hear about Wendy Atkins?'

'What about her?' Peggy got out her keys. 'Don't tell me – she's robbed school safe and run off with a handsome six-year-old.'

'She's leaving. Says her mother's sick and she's going home.'

Peggy looked surprised. Despite her ultimatum, she wasn't sure whether Wendy Atkins would take any notice. 'When's she going?'

'Today, I think.' Ruth eyed her sister-in-law closely. If she didn't know her better, she would have said Peggy looked just a little bit shamefaced. 'So, it worked, then, your little chat,' she teased.

Peggy had the grace to colour slightly. 'I think she should count her blessings. I mean, I could have gone straight to the headmaster.'

'You don't mess with Old Ma Snow.' Ruth was enjoying winding her sister-in-law up.

'I could have had her struck off.'

Ruth took Alfie back, whispering into his neck, 'She don't like strangers round here.'

Peggy got into the car. 'You'll not make me feel guilty,' she said firmly. Ruth laughed, knowing that she did. 'I assume you'll be vetting her replacement?'

'Very funny. I've got to go, there's Mrs Byas's stitches to see to.'

'Best make sure she's well stitched up, then.'

Peggy shook her head, fed up with all this. 'You wait till Alfie's Stephen's age. Then you'll feel differently.'

Alfie blew her a stream of bubbles. 'See you soon, Ma,' Ruth joked. Peggy revved the car and drove off. She wasn't smiling.

Vic was enjoying a day off from the factory – 'It's research,' he told Simon, 'Part of my rescue plan,' – and had name-dropped his way into the Huddersfield Rugby League Club, where he knew the assistant coach, Dougie Walford. He sat high up in the main stand, surrounded by a sea of empty seats, looking down at the pitch below where the team were being put through their paces in the bright winter sunshine. The difference between the fit, fast Huddersfield players and the Skelthwaite Scorpions was embarrassing, to say the least. He scribbled notes on training techniques, drawing sketches and diagrams in a notebook, but it was with a sinking heart. *We can't hope to play like this, ever*, he thought, observing the seamless running and passing, dodging and tackling. Compared to his lot, he could only gaze in wonderment. Part of the trouble was, he acknowledged privately, that he didn't have enough experience himself to pass on to the lads. What they needed was someone who'd been there, who'd played the big boys. Someone who would knock them into shape. For free.

He heard his name being shouted and he glanced around to see Dougie making his way down the aisle to greet him. Vic rose to say hello and clap him on the back and they sat down together, watching the team. 'They look a good bunch of lads,' Vic commented casually.

'Not too bad,' Dougie said, pleased.

'It must be frustrating for ones who don't make team.' Dougie nodded. Vic fished a bit more. 'Like race horses, aren't they? Need to have gallop every now and then . . .' He paused, letting this sink in. 'I mean, a real game is always better than training, int it?'

'Don't even think about it,' said Dougie, twigging. 'These boys are insured from head to toe – we'd not get a penny if they hurt themselves playing for likes of you.'

'Just a thought.' Vic slumped back into his gloom.

'Problems with Scorpions?'

'Nothing thirteen decent players wouldn't solve.'

Dougie, returning his eyes to the pitch, noticed that training had broken down and one of the players was lying on the ground, injured. 'What's he done now? Excuse me, Vic,' he said, leaping up and hurrying off. Vic sighed, his last chance extinguished. He was about to call it a day when a dark shadow loomed over him, as if a mighty giant had materialized from behind. He turned and saw that it was a giant, albeit a benign one, judging by his good-natured smile. The thick-set young man, a Maori, was dressed in a tracksuit and had a kit bag over his shoulder. He extended a meaty hand. 'Kenny.'

'Vic Snow.'

'Pleased to meet you.'

'Likewise, son. Take a pew.'

Kenny sat down next to Vic, causing the plastic bucket seat to creak alarmingly. Below them, training had started up again. A whistle blew shrilly and Dougie, who was now down on the pitch, could be heard bawling out a recalcitrant player.

'You with this lot?' asked Vic.

Kenny shook his head. 'Nah.' He looked disappointed. 'I was doing the whole Europe thing. Ran out of money. Thought they might give me a go here. But . . .'

'Nothing doing?'

'Nada.'

Vic was intrigued. 'Where's home?'

'Paekakariki.'

'Oh, yes, I know it. Up Pudsey way, int it?' Vic said dryly. Kenny grinned. 'New Zealand.'

'Long way from home.'

'Yeah.' Kenny looked wistful. 'I just wanna make a few bucks and get back there.' A miskicked rugby ball whizzed past Vic's ear and Kenny reached up with one hand and caught it as easily as if a ripe fruit had dropped into his palm. With one smooth, elegant movement he spin-passed it back with a speed and accuracy that took the waiting player below by surprise.

'Nice one,' said Vic, with a glint in his eye.

93

Stephen arrived at Wendy's flat just after noon, ready to demand answers. How could she say she loved him one minute and not the next? Why was she going? Where was she going? Why hadn't she told him? Wendy let him in and he stood, beetle-browed, in the kitchen, arms folded. 'I'm not leaving until you tell me what's going on.'

'Oh, Stephen,' she wailed, her face unexpectedly crumpling. 'I'm so sorry.'

'Hey.' He softened immediately, stepping forward to hold her. 'I didn't mean to upset you. It's just that I don't know where I am with you any more. And I can't bear thought of losing you.'

She looked up into his face with a tremulous smile – 'Let's not waste our last hour together talking' – and pushed open the bedroom door. The room was almost bare, dressing table cleared of make-up and clutter, pictures gone, clothes packed, but Stephen didn't register any of this. All he knew was that he needed to make love to her as if his life depended on it.

Afterwards they lay curled up in bed together, Stephen tracing her features, trying to sear her image into his brain. She took his fingers and kissed them, one by one. 'I didn't expect it to happen so quickly,' she whispered softly. 'My Mum got ill – she rang Sunday morning – and I managed to get hold of Mr Pearson at home and tell him. As it happened, he knew someone who he thought could step in at short notice and they confirmed this morning, just before assembly. I didn't even see you, so how could I tell you? It all happened so fast.'

'What's wrong with your mum?'

'They're not sure. But she wants me there and that's where I'm going.'

His arms tightened around her. 'I'll come with you, then.'

'Don't be silly,' she said wearily.

'I'm not being silly. I love you.'

Wendy swallowed. 'No, Stephen. You've got your resits coming up – maybe university. You've got your whole life ahead of you.'

He started to cry, then, helpless tears that he'd dammed up all weekend spilling down his cheeks. 'I don't want it unless I'm with you.'

Wendy nursed his head on her breast, holding him while he wept, feeling his body shake. At last, she said, 'Can I tell you something?'

'No,' he replied gruffly, embarrassed at breaking down.

She tipped his wet face up to hers. 'One day, when you're a little wizened old man looking back over your life, I hope you'll remember me.'

'Of course I'll remember you.'

'Maybe a little footnote in "Stephen – The Teenage Years". Because you're going to have a fantastic life.' She stared deep into his eyes and wiped away a tear with her thumb. 'But me . . . I'll be an old lady and I'll remember every line in your face and every thing you ever said or did.'

For a moment, the world seemed to Stephen to have stopped. 'You love me, don't you?'

'Of course I love you.' She took in his delighted smile and added, quietly, 'I'm still leaving, though.'

The remainder of the hour stole away all too quickly. Stephen tried to persuade her to bunk off for the rest of the afternoon – 'It's not as if it's going to matter, now, is it?' – but Wendy was steadfast. 'I'm not letting the other children and teachers down. And you can't afford to cut any more classes. Come on, you'll be late.' Dressed but dishevelled, he stood in the kitchen once more, all the old Stephen Snow self-confidence gone. 'Is this it?' he said miserably. 'Is this how it ends?' All the romantic books, films and songs he'd ever read or watched or listened to couldn't give him a point of reference for the pain he was feeling. There had been times, when, revelling in their secret liaison, he had felt as if he were playing a part, almost as if he knew what his lines were.

But there was no script for this; this was for real. Reality was Wendy physically pushing him away, saying, 'Have a brilliant life,' practically bundling him out of the door. He stumbled down the road, ignoring the left turn he normally took to the school, and kept on walking. He couldn't go back there, not today. He might bump into her again.

Having seen to Mrs Byas, Peggy decided to call in on St Margaret's nursing home on the way back to the health centre. She and Patricia had been trying to track down Walter, who was not at his flat, and St Margaret's was a favourite hang-out of his. The old folks indulged him and played riotous games of snap with him, and he usually managed to cadge tea and cake into the bargain.

David White, the warden, greeted Peggy as she stepped into the guests' lounge. A gentle, unassuming man in his early forties, he insisted on the term 'guests' rather than 'residents' and encouraged them to be as independent and active as possible. Peggy admired his attitude. She had been in other nursing homes where the old people were treated like imbeciles, divested of their dignity and parked in overheated rooms to wait to die. The St Margaret's crowd were frail and infirm but they maintained a robust spirit and, as a consequence, the atmosphere was happy and relaxed.

'Peggy! What can we do for you? Don't tell me – you couldn't resist the tempting aroma of lunch cooking,' he joked.

Peggy sniffed. 'Steak and kidney? Makes a change from boiled cabbage. What is this love affair institutions have with it?'

The Warden laughed. 'Just trying to keep them all regular.'

She pulled a face. 'It were the first thing used to hit me every time I went up to Merson Hall. But that's going back a bit.'

'Just as well they closed it down, a draughty old asylum like that. It was crumbling around their ears. And as for what it did to the people there . . .' He glanced around the room and indicated a woman in her late-sixties, who was peering into the tropical fish tank in the corner. 'Well, Martha Travis copes quite well, actually. No concept of the outside world, but what can you expect when someone's spent most of their life cooped up in a mental hospital? Martha – you going to have a nice cup of tea?' he called. The woman, who was haphazardly dressed in a long green cardigan and patterned skirt, looked up. 'Seven,' she said.

'Sorry?' David White gave Peggy a wry smile.

'Seven guppies,' explained Martha, pointing at the fish.

'Oh, right. That's nice.'

'Should be eight.'

'Should there?' He went over and squinted into the tank, trying to count them. 'You're right, Martha. Where's number eight?'

'Eight's been ate.' Martha cackled with pleasure at her little joke.

He rejoined Peggy. 'There you are. Bright as a button. If only she'd been rehabilitated earlier . . .'

'Not that they're much better off being slung out into the community when we don't have the resources to help adequately,' Peggy said, with feeling. 'Talking of which, have you seen Walter on your travels?'

'Yes, he's around somewhere. Probably snaffled that fish for his cat.'

On cue, Walter shuffled in, this time minus his trousers altogether. Fortunately, his incontinence pants were still in place, although even these were slipping down. Oblivious to the tittering from the old ladies he helped himself to a biscuit from the tea trolley. 'Walter! What are you like?' Peggy grabbed a rug from the back of one of the armchairs and wrapped it round his waist.

'I expect he's left them in the toilet again,' David White said, sending an auxiliary to find them.

'I'm sorry about this. It's enough to put anyone off their

food.' The missing trousers were handed back and she got him presentable again. 'Come on Walter, let's get you home.'

'Spoilsport!' called one of the ladies. 'We were enjoying the floor show.'

'Come and have a look. You've got nothing to lose,' Vic said to Kenny, after telling him about the Skelthwaite Scorpions.

Kenny shrugged his broad shoulders. 'OK.'

'It's a good town. I'll fix you up with some work, provide you with board and lodgings. In return, you train us up and turn out for us. How does that sound?'

'Sounds good, Mr Snow.'

They caught a bus back and Vic took him straight to the rugby club. Surveying the scruffy, waterlogged pitch, ill-marked touchline and leaning uprights, even he had to admit that, compared with the smooth green turf and 18,000-seater stands at Huddersfield, the Skelthwaite Scorpions Rugby League Club was a bit of a comedown. A stray dog wandered onto the pitch and cocked its leg against one of the posts. Kenny viewed it all impassively, then placed the ball down carefully in front of him. His kick sent it high and true through the posts. He brushed his hands together and turned round to Vic, who was beaming from ear to ear. The smile left his face when he saw Kenny's obvious disappointment. 'I told you it weren't Wembley.'

'You weren't lying, Mr Snow.'

'Think of it as a challenge. Something to really get your teeth into while you earn your passage. And you'll be home before you know it.'

Kenny looked thoughtful. 'Are they keen?'

Vic coughed guiltily. 'As mustard.'

'Alright, Mr Snow, let's give it a go.' Kenny held out his hand. Vic wrung it gratefully. He was sure Simon could find the saviour of the Skelthwaite Scorpions a job. After all, it would do big things for his sponsorship image.

They walked back through the centre of the town alongside

the murky river that fed the now-defunct mills dominating the landscape in the valley. Overhead, dark clouds were drawing in, blotting out the sickly afternoon light. 'If you can see hills they say it's about to rain. If you can't, it already is,' joked Vic. Kenny looked about him. 'They say the same sort of thing about the rainforests in New Zealand.'

'It used to be a manufacturing town. Textiles, mostly.' They stopped outside a dilapidated mill, its tall stack blackened with soot. 'My father worked in there,' Vic said, sadly. 'Now we manufacture teenagers and toilet paper,' he added, spotting Stephen approaching, head down. He presumed his son must have finished school early to do some revising. 'Stephen, I'd like you to meet—' he began, but Stephen, barely bothering to look up, much less halt, cut him short. 'Not now, Dad.'

'It's a friendly place, mind,' Vic continued dryly, ushering Kenny towards the pub. 'Let me show you the club house.'

A hastily convened meeting of the Scorpions was arranged in the public bar for 8.00pm that evening. Dick, who arrived first, was initially sceptical. 'How do you know he's genuine?' he murmured to Vic, who was getting in another round at the bar. The fact that Kenny was drinking orange juice did nothing to evince Dick's faith in his abilities. As far as he was concerned, real rugby players downed pints. Lots of them.

'You wait till you see him kick,' Vic replied, tapping his nose with a knowing finger. 'He says he's tried out for the All Blacks.'

'Let's see him prove it, then. Alright, mate?' Dick approached Kenny, who was sitting at a table with some of the others. 'What's that war dance thing you fellas do at start of match?'

'The *haka*,' Kenny enunciated, baring a lot of white teeth.

'Do it for us, then. Give us a laugh.'

Kenny stared at him for a few, long seconds, during which time Vic wondered whether he was going to grind Dick to mincemeat, then said mildly, 'Good idea, mate. It can be part of your training. You learn to act fierce, you learn to play fierce.'

'Us?'

'Some hope,' snorted Simon, who had just come in.

'You gotta believe it first, Mr Goddard. Think positive. Winning is about attitude,' Kenny interjected politely. Simon, disarmed, muttered, 'Couldn't agree more,' and took a long swallow of his pint. Vic, grinning broadly, banged an empty glass on the table to summon the others' attention. 'Kenny's coaching us, lads, so let's do what he says. Everybody up.' Pushing chairs out of the way, he made space in the middle of the room. Drinkers at the bar looked on in amusement as the men formed two lines behind Kenny. Kenny shook out his legs and flexed his arms, then dropped into a straight-backed half-squat, stamping out a rhythm as he slapped his bulging thighs. '*Ka mate, Ka mate, Ka ora, Ka ora! Tenei te Tangata Puhuruhuru! Nana I tiki mai whakawhiti te re! Upane! Upane! . . .*' The men floundered hopelessly behind, stamping out of time and barging into each other, reducing Peggy and Patricia, who were watching from the other side of the room, to hysterics, along with the rest of the observers. 'Who's big lad?' Patricia spluttered into her gin and slimline tonic.

'Kenny. Vic says he's future of Skelthwaite rugby,' Peggy returned.

Patricia ogled him speculatively. 'Handsome, int he? Is he staying with you?'

'The future of Skelthwaite rugby is going to have to sleep on sofa cos I'm not turfing Stephen out of his room,' Peggy said decisively. She was still feeling slightly guilty about her part in Miss Atkins's sudden departure. It had been bothering her all day. Ruth's comments, although said in jest, had stung, and she knew that, with Wendy gone, Stephen would be hurting. Still, it was best in the long run, she consoled herself.

'I've got spare room,' Patricia broke into her reverie, her eyes still glued to Kenny.

'Can't risk future of Skelthwaite rugby. We don't want any creaking floorboards.'

'Behave yourself,' Patricia giggled, as the team, on their second run-through, leapt into the air with a ragged shout, thoroughly enjoying themselves. 'I'm only talking home comforts.'

Peggy raised an eyebrow. 'That depends on what he's used to.'

'Well, you don't get that big, and I should know,' Patricia stretched out her plump calves, 'without having a very healthy appetite.'

Stephen had pounded the streets of Skelthwaite all afternoon, trying to sort out his head. Wendy's behaviour just didn't add up. Even when it started to rain, slicking down his black hair and drenching his school clothes, he merely turned up the collar of his jacket and trudged on. There was a harsh, masochistic pleasure to be had in the soaking. It grew dark and he went into a run-down pub the other side of town that wasn't so fussy about under-age drinking. After a couple of bottles of strong cider, he came to a decision and set off for Wendy's flat. He had to do something to stop her.

She was piling her cases into a taxi as he turned up, shivering now with the cold and the wet. He heard her say, 'Huddersfield Station, please,' and stepped out of the shadows. 'No, Stephen,' she said in a choking voice as she spotted him.

He grabbed hold of the taxi door, holding it shut. 'This is not right.' She went round to the other side. 'When will I see you again?' he shouted as she opened the passenger door.

'I don't know.'

Stephen dodged round there too and caught her by the wrist before she could get in. 'I'll come down to London and see you.'

'No.'

'Why not?'

'Stephen! Because I said not!' she said angrily, trying to pull away.

'But after your mother's better—'

'For God's sake, Stephen,' Wendy screamed, losing control. 'There's nothing wrong with her! Don't you see what's happened?'

He looked at her, shocked, the rain dripping off his hair and sliding down his face in great, fat drops. 'No.'

Wendy, already regretting what she had let slip, said more quietly, 'I have to go. That's all there is to it.' She kissed him on the cheek and got into the car, leaving him standing on the pavement, bedraggled and miserable. Only when the taxi had pulled away did she allow her own tears to come.

Stephen was making himself a hot cup of coffee when Peggy returned from the pub. She noticed his hair was damp and supposed he'd just had a bath. 'Hello, pet,' she said gingerly. 'What sort of day have you had?'

He shrugged. 'Usual. I'm going to bed to read.'

She glanced at him, but his face gave nothing away. 'Did your teacher get off alright?' she probed casually.

'What teacher?' He headed for the kitchen door.

'Miss Atkins. She were leaving today, weren't she?'

'I don't know.' His voice sounded bored.

'I wanted to see her before she went.'

'I'm sure she'll get over it. Night,' he said, pecking her on the cheek. Peggy listened to his heavy tread on the stairs, wondering what was going on in his head. Outside, the wind buffeted the trees, hurling handfuls of rain against the windowpane with a sudden splatter. The weather had turned so bad she couldn't tell whether the moaning noise was the wind in the chimney or what.

# Chapter 8

The alarm clock went off at 6.30am, resounding in Vic's sore head like a set of kettle drums. He clapped the bell on the top and peered at it blearily. *Ten more minutes*, he told himself, and was awoken again at 7.00 by Peggy digging her elbow in his side. 'What time are you two supposed to be going running with Kenny?' Vic groaned. He had been all fired up about Kenny's training regime when he outlined it to him, exhorting the lads with, 'No pain, no gain'. This morning, however, just getting out of bed felt like a major achievement. He pottered to the bathroom and tried to focus on his reflection in the mirror. *How difficult can it be? Peggy does it*, he thought. Slightly comforted, he pulled on his tracksuit and banged loudly on Stephen's door. 'Are you up yet?' The muffled response indicated that Stephen was still under the duvet. 'I'm not going soft on you because you're family. Do it Kenny's way, or you won't play, simple as that. I'll see you downstairs.' Drawing the curtains in the living room, he saw that it was still dark. Vic shivered. The future of Skelthwaite Rugby looked like being a long, hard, cold one for the next few months.

'I don't care what you call this in New Zealand, it's pure bloody torture,' Dick panted, trailing behind Kenny with the rest of the team. Kenny, ignoring their insults, ran ahead, eating up the ground in long, easy strides.

'Tell him to stop, Vic. He'll kill us all,' puffed Terry, who was no fitter than Dick, but Vic had no breath left to tell their new coach anything. Stephen, whey-faced, brought up the rear. His mind was on other things. What had Wendy meant about her mother not being ill? Why go then? Especially as she admitted she loved him. None of it made any sense. The blood pounded in his head as he forced his aching legs on and his chest rasped painfully. As if distilled by the physical exertion, the solution suddenly became clear. He would have to go and see her. His pocket money wouldn't cover the train fare, but he could make it to the M1, then hitch. Wendy had told him that she lived in Chiswick High Road. Once he got down to London he could look up her mother's house number in the phone book. Then he'd turn up on the doorstep and Wendy would have to listen to him. The plan gave him renewed energy and he sprinted to catch up with the others, almost cannoning into them as Kenny brought the ragged bunch of men to an abrupt stop. 'Keep moving! Jog on the spot!' he shouted, as they bent over, gasping and coughing. Dick, who had turned the colour of a boiled lobster, right to the top of his balding head, propped himself up on Vic's shoulder. 'Let's raid social fund and buy him next bloody plane ticket home.'

'It'll get better,' spluttered Vic.

'It'll have to. Or you won't have a team left.'


'Peggy. I'm going nuts sitting here at home. I've made a decision – I'm coming back early, part-time,' Ruth said into the phone. Simon hadn't been particularly keen on the idea, but then he wasn't the one climbing the walls with boredom and frustration every day. As much as she loved seeing Alfie's darling little face – no matter that it seemed to be screwed up, snotty and red half the time – she missed work terribly. Staff Nurse Goddard was beginning to feel like another person; someone her daily routine of changing, feeding and burping the baby seemed to have eclipsed. It was as if she was only living half her life. And the entertainment value of her current job was dire. At least when she was out with Peg and Pat they had a laugh. 'If I have to spend another day watching cookery programmes and quiz shows I'll go stark, staring mad,' she threatened.

Recognizing the note of desperation in her voice, Peggy held off lecturing. 'Alright, love. If you're sure you're ready. Have you cleared it with Elaine Trafford?'

'Yes. We agreed three mornings a week.'

'What about Alfie?'

'I'll get babysitter for now.'

'When were you planning to start? I'll have to rearrange rosta.'

'Monday morning?'

The first thing Ruth did when she returned to the office was to vet the appointments diary. 'What's this?' she asked, running her finger down the page. 'Mrs Fowles/WS?'

'My shorthand,' answered Patricia, 'stands for Won't Say. As in won't say what problem is. She were very mysterious on phone.'

'Oooh.' Ruth's eyes lit up. 'Can I come?'

'It's up to Peg,' Patricia replied. 'I don't mind taking the calls and dealing with paperwork. I've got a couple of care plan sheets to do and record cards to fill in.'

Peggy hesitated. 'Well . . .'

'Please, please?' Ruth begged, crouching down with her tongue hanging out, pretending to paw Peggy's leg.

'She has gone loony. For goodness sake, take her with you,' Patricia laughed.

'Come on, then. Fetch,' Peggy tossed the car keys at her. 'Let's go walkies.'

On the way, Peggy updated her about work. 'Have you heard any more from Martin Hutton?' asked Ruth.

'He faxed me a letter the other day saying he were going to get a transfer to Leeds to be nearer his father. Funny how that all worked out.'

Ruth pursed her lips. 'Not so funny at the time, for you, though.' She paused. 'I still feel bad about that, Peg. You should have told Elaine that it was my decision as much as yours, putting Madeleine on commode. I suggested it.'

'And I suggested moving her. Dunt matter now; it's all blown over – though it were worrying at time,' admitted Peggy. 'I didn't fancy prison food much.'

Ruth looked at her, her face serious. 'It wouldn't have come to that.'

'What about doctors that get prosecuted for mercy killing? A few more ccs of morphine to put someone out of misery. It's a fine line.'

'I suppose you're right.' Ruth stared out at the moors, which were spread out either side of the motorway. The road cut straight over the top of the Pennines, the eastbound lanes separated from the higher westbound lanes by a narrow strip of land.

'Anyway, it's given me an idea for the Nursing Conference in Scarborough,' Peggy continued. 'I've been asked to speak. We deal with death all the time. I want to say something about that.'

'I'm looking forward to it.'

'My speech? Or the conference?'

'Letting my hair down with you and Pat. Girls' night out. Having a drink again.'

'Watch out Scarborough,' Peggy said dryly.


The Fowles's farm was well-known to the motorists of Yorkshire, sandwiched incongruously in the middle of the stretch of green between the two carriageways. 'Have you been here before?' shouted Ruth, above the noise of the traffic thundering past. Peggy surveyed the ramshackle out-buildings and overgrown farmyard, which was strewn with rubbish – old fertilizer sacks, oil drums, bits of rusting machinery – and pulled a face. 'No, never.' They picked their way through the mud towards a gate which opened into the

106

yard. At the sound of the latch there was a ferocious barking and a large Alsation came tearing round the side of the house. They retreated hurriedly, closing the gate again just in time as the dog jumped up at it, snapping and snarling. 'Nice doggy,' Peggy said cautiously.

'Sod off, nice doggy,' Ruth corrected her. 'Now what do we do?'

A man emerged from a pig sty across the yard to see what the commotion was all about. Ruth and Peggy recoiled slightly at the sight of him. His clothes were filthy, his unshaven face was red and shiny – what could be seen of it, beneath the splashes of dried-on muck – and his nose dripped like a melting icicle. 'What do you want?' he growled.

'Mr Fowles?' asked Peggy, politely.

'What?' He wiped his nose with his sleeve and stuck a rolled up cigarette in his mouth. It hung on his wet bottom lip, as if glued. Ruth stared, fascinated.

'We've come to see your wife,' Peggy persisted.

'What for?'

'She dint say.'

'Nowt wrong wi' her.' He glared at them suspiciously with rheumy eyes.

'All the same, she called us, so we'd like to speak to her. *If* you don't mind.' He yanked hold of the straining dog by the collar and hauled it into a shed, slamming the door. 'Better come int house,' he said grudgingly, leading the way. They followed him into the most squalid kitchen either of them had ever seen. Ruth nudged Peggy and held her nose at the stench of rotting food. There were unwashed pots and pans every-where, the walls were growing mould and the pattern on the threadbare carpet had disappeared under a layer of trodden-in mud. Peggy nodded, appalled, as they followed the farmer along a passageway.

'She's in there,' he wheezed, indicating a door.

'Thank you,' Peggy said, breathing through her mouth.

'D'you want tea?' he asked reluctantly, wiping his snivelling nose with his sleeve again.

'No!' they chorused, rather too quickly.

'Suit yourselves.' He turned to go.

Peggy cleared her throat. 'You've really no idea what this is about?'

Mr Fowles merely sniffed fruitily and clumped back off up the passage in his dirty boots. Peggy glanced at Ruth and knocked tentatively on the bedroom door. 'Mrs Fowles? It's Sister Snow here. Can I come in?' There was no reply. She tried the handle and opened the creaking door slowly. An even worse smell assaulted their nostrils. 'Oh my God,' breathed Ruth as they stared into the stinking, darkened room.

Patricia leant back in her chair and kicked her shoes off under the desk. She put her pen down, yawning, and wondered what to get Kenny for his tea that evening. The novelty of having a man about the house again meant that Kenny was extremely well-fed. Patricia's late husband had died of cancer after five, short years together and their marriage had been childless. She was forty-seven years old, overweight and frequently lonely, though she put on a brave face. Having Kenny as her lodger (she had offered him the room after three G&T's in the pub and he had accepted) was like a gift from the gods. He was certainly as handsome as one, she reflected – a taut, tanned, muscular Adonis – as well as being polite, tidy and handy around the house. Every girl's dream, in fact . . . Patricia, carried away by her fantasies, nearly jumped out of her skin as the telephone on the desk rang loudly. 'Staff Nurse Illingworth.'

'Hello? It's Mrs Herrington speaking.'

'Hello, love, how are you? Feeling any better?' Mrs Herrington, a genteel widow in her early fifties, had been very down in the mouth recently.

'I'm very well, thank you very much for asking. Actually,

it's not me I was ringing about, it's my friend.' Mrs Herrington hesitated slightly. 'He's become very tired and I think he needs a boost.'

'Can't he see doctor?'

'He can't get out, my dear.'

'What's his name?'

'Percy.'

'Percy who?'

'Oh, I just know him as Percy.'

'And he couldn't phone himself?'

'No, dear. To tell you the truth, he's not All There,' she whispered hoarsely.

'Is he staying with you?'

'Yes, that's it. He's been with me a few weeks now. Fit as a fiddle until recently.'

'But you don't know what problem is?'

'It's delicate, my dear. Better if you come round and take a look.'

Patricia sighed. Another mystery call. She made an appointment, put down the phone and scribbled Mrs Herrington/WS in the diary.


'Stephen. Are you OK?' Deborah looked at him, concerned. He had frozen her out over the past couple of days, which was unlike him. Normally they were good friends. Doing the play together had brought them even closer and, ever since he had kissed her in front of the drama group, she thought he wanted her to be more than just a friend. At the disco, she had waited for him to kiss her again, not as Stanley Kowalski but as Stephen Snow. She had prayed they would put on a slow number, but Stephen, riding high on success, was more interested in being the life and soul of the party. Then he had suddenly dumped her on Henry and rushed off into the night. When he reappeared at Sonia's party later he was in a foul mood, downed a few drinks, and disappeared again without any explanation.

They had just had an English class with Miss Atkins's replacement, Mrs McCormack, a peculiar little Scots woman with wild grey hair and a faintly witchy look, when Deborah caught up with Stephen in the corridor. 'Stephen.' She twitched his sleeve. 'I said, "Are you OK?" You look terrible.'

'Thanks for that. Dad made me go for another training run with our new coach at first light. I'm completely knackered.'

'Poor you.'

An awkward silence followed, during which Deborah waited for him to say something funny or tease her or chat like he normally did, and Stephen slipped back into morose self-absorption. 'Is something bothering you? You haven't been the same recently,' she said hesitantly.

'I'm fine.'

'Because if you did want to talk . . .' Deborah paused, then took the plunge. 'Maybe we could go out somewhere. You could tell me what's up. We could have a laugh—'

'I told you, I'm fine,' he snapped. 'It's the revising, that's all. I've got behind.'

'So . . . you don't fancy going for a drink, then?' she blurted, instantly wishing she hadn't said that.

'Look, Debs, I'm busy. I've got a lot riding on these exams. I'd love to, but I just can't afford the time.' He glanced at his watch – 'Gotta run, sorry,' – and strode off down the corridor, leaving Deborah feeling distinctly as if she'd been given the cold shoulder.

'Mrs Fowles?' called Peggy, dubiously. The curtains were drawn and she could barely make out anything but the shapes of a wardrobe and a bed. The smell almost made her gag. Beside her, Ruth covered her nose and mouth with her hand. News stories about discoveries of decomposing corpses passed briefly through her mind, until an unpleasant cough alerted her to the fact that Mrs Fowles was, at least, alive. 'I'm just going to open curtains, love, get a bit of light on situation. Alright?' she said bravely. There was no reply. Peggy nodded at Ruth, who ripped the curtains back, revealing a cluttered, chaotic room, the heavy furniture thick with dust and the floor littered with encrusted plates and decaying food. Both of them drew in their breath sharply. Lying in the fetid bed was a creature out of some Dickensian novel, her long grey hair matted and tangled, her skin grimy and her nightdress stained and soiled. The bedclothes were in a similar state.

'Hello, pet. What seems to be trouble?' Peggy faltered. The woman moaned. Peggy signalled to Ruth and they edged forward. 'Leg,' Mrs Fowles pointed.

'Your leg hurts? Have you been seeing doctor?'

'Don't like doctors.'

Peggy braced herself. 'Right, let's have a look at you.'

Ruth picked her way round the other side of the bed and together they folded back the disgusting sheets. 'Can you not get to bathroom?' she asked, appalled at the state of her.

'If I want to.'

'You have to keep yourself clean, love,' Peggy said briskly. A dirty bandage was tied around the woman's leg. She started to unwind it gently, expecting at least a putrefying ulcer. But there was nothing. 'You're sure it was this leg, love?' she queried. Mrs Fowles did not reply. Puzzled, Peggy asked, 'It was *you* who called for nurses?'

'Or was there something else?' Ruth suggested, thinking no-one let themselves go like this if they weren't incapacitated. Suddenly, Mrs Fowles burst into tears, sobbing inconsolably. 'Here, love, take this.' Ruth offered her a handkerchief. She blew her nose loudly and handed it back to Ruth, who pocketed it trying not to show her distaste.

'Come on, Mrs Fowles, tell us what's upsetting you. Maybe we can help,' said Peggy, feeling desperately sorry for the pathetic creature.

'I want you to stop him wanting it,' she gulped through her tears.

'Sorry?'

'Stop him wanting it!' she said, suddenly forceful.

'Wanting what, love?' Peggy was completely baffled. Mr Fowles stumped past the window outside and at last the penny dropped. She hardly dare look at Ruth. Surely even the repulsive old farmer would be hard-pressed to fancy this? Then again, he obviously wasn't fussy about minor details like personal appearance, hygiene, conversation . . .

'If you don't want sex with your husband, you just say 'no'.' Ruth said impatiently.

'Give him pill! Like int War!' Mrs Fowles demanded.

'Like bromide, you mean?' said Peggy. Ruth, baffled, mouthed 'What?'

'Int War they used to give soldiers bromide to . . . well, to . . .'

'Stop them wanting it,' obliged Mrs Fowles.

'Exactly.'

Ruth folded her arms. 'So you want us to speak to your husband about his . . . needs?'

Mrs Fowles did not answer. '*Is* that why you asked to see us?' Peggy prompted. She nodded. Peggy sucked in her cheeks. This went way beyond their job description.

The Fowles's bathroom was just as unpleasant and, judging by the cobwebs and dead spiders in the bath, infrequently used. 'There's nothing here – no soap, no shampoo, nothing,' exclaimed Peggy, peering into cupboards.

'Just a lot of testosterone,' Ruth giggled.

'Can you imagine!'

'I'm trying not to. Stop him wanting it!'

'It's not funny,' Peggy said, grinning.

Ruth wiped her nose on her sleeve with a juicy sniff and came at Peggy with outstretched hands. 'I want it. I want it,' she grunted. Peggy exploded with laughter.

'What are we going to do? I mean, poor woman is really unhappy,' Ruth said at last, when they'd both calmed down.

'I'll pop into town and get some soap and stuff – the least we can do is clean her up a bit. I mean, that's no way to keep him away. She could go down with something really nasty if she dunt take care.'

'What about me?'

'I thought you could stay here and have a word with Mr Fowles.'

'Me? No way!' A look of horror crossed Ruth's face.

'Someone has to.'

'*You* do it. You're the boss. I'm supposed to breaking myself back in gently.'

'Pah! You were itching to get back to work.'

'I'm sorry, I'm not doing it. "Excuse me, Mr Fowles, you don't know me, but would you mind curbing your sexual appetite?".'

Peggy conceded. 'Alright, alright – we'll both do it.'

'Might need two of us anyway, if he's that rampant.' Ruth did her impersonation again, lurching at her sister-in-law with a lopsided leer. 'I want it, I want it.'

It took Vic longer than usual to climb the stairs to Simon's office because his legs had stiffened up so much. He winced as he pulled himself up by the handrail, praying that Kenny's advice about a hot bath and a muscle rub would sort it out. Until the next morning, anyway. Vic didn't even want to think about that. The team was already threatening to mutiny. 'He in?' Vic asked Denise, Simon's secretary, motioning towards the office door.

'Yes.'

'Good mood?'

'Fair, I'd say.'

'Fair to good? Or fair to middling?'

'Just fair.'

'Oh.' Vic knocked briefly and stuck his head round the door. 'Can I see you for a minute, Simon?'

'I'm busy, Vic. Can't it wait?' Simon scowled.

'Not if you want to snap up bargain of century.'

'You'd better not be trying to sell me domestic cleaning products.'

'I'm offering you a two-in-one deal,' Vic said, his patter well rehearsed. 'A worker who can keep your clapped-out old machinery going. And chance to see your logo on backs of a winning rugby team. Now that can't be bad, can it?'

Simon looked thoughtful. 'Kenny?'

'Yes.'

'He's had engineering training?'

'Studied in Auckland. That's when he got involved in rugby, at university.'

'And you really think he can turn the Scorpions around?'

'Yes.' Behind his back, Vic crossed his fingers. 'He's a real motivator.'

Simon leaned back in his chair, putting his hands behind his head. 'Tell him if he can halve my bill to engineers, he's on.'


'Mr Fowles?' Peggy leaned over the pigsty wall, where a herd of large, white-haired pigs were squealing and shoving in the quagmire, eager to get at the bucket of feed he was emptying into a trough. The farmer came over reluctantly, tipping his greasy cap back and scratching his head with grimy hands. 'The thing is,' Peggy continued, 'we've been having a chat with your wife and she seems a little – well, a little agitated . . .' Her voice trailed off. Mr Fowles took out a tin of tobacco and started making another roll-up. He seemed entirely unconcerned. She looked at Ruth for inspiration. Ruth took a deep breath and tried a different tack. 'What would you do if one of your female pigs was resisting charms of one of your male pigs?'

'Sow.'

'Excuse me?'

'Female pig – sow. I'd kill her and then I'd have her for breakfast,' he growled, lighting up. Ruth rolled her eyes at

114

Peggy: your turn. Peggy cleared her throat and waded in. 'Mrs Fowles thinks you're being a little bit . . . pushy. Int bedroom.'

'Pushy?'

'She's concerned that there is a disparity in your physical . . . drives.'

He glared at her. 'What are you talking about, woman?'

Ruth decided to lay in on the line. ' "No" means "no", Mr Fowles. Dunt matter if you've just met or you've been married fifty years. Buy a magazine, love.'

'Ruth,' Peggy admonished her. 'I hope you don't think we've spoken out of turn, Mr Fowles, but your wife seemed quite concerned about it.'

He looked from one to the other of them, wiped his nose on his sleeve and spat in the muck for good measure, before walking away without commenting.

'I think we made our point,' Peggy said.

'I think we did,' Ruth agreed.

# Chapter 9

'That's better, int it? I knew there'd be skin under there somewhere,' Ruth said cheerfully, soaping Mrs Fowles, who was sitting glumly but co-operatively in a hot bath.

Peggy, who was rinsing shampoo from her hair with a jug of clean water, added, 'We had a word with Mr Fowles.'

'Did you stop him wanting it?'

'I think he got message.'

'Did he not say anything to you?' Ruth asked, a mischievous twinkle in her eye. Mrs Fowles shook her head.

'Did he bring you anything? Flowers, anything like that?' Peggy hinted. They had spotted Mr Fowles in town when they went to the chemist to buy toiletries. Dressed in his market-day best, he looked positively dapper – for him, anyway – and was making his way along the road with a sprightly step, clutching a large bouquet.

'Flowers? He hasn't brought me flowers in forty years. He's that tight he squeaks.'

Ruth winked at her. 'People change.' Mrs Fowles looked instantly suspicious.

'You saw him with flowers?'

'I couldn't possibly comment. I'm not spoiling anyone's surprise.'

'Where did you see him?'

'We saw him in town,' Peggy said. 'They were lovely! Biggest bunch of red carnations you've ever seen.'

At that, Mrs Fowles let out a banshee wail, making them both jump out of their skins.

'He's still at it,' she cried. 'He's still at it!' Peggy looked at Ruth, more confused that ever.

'Come on, pet, better tell us whole story.' Having calmed her down, dried her off and bundled her into a dressing gown, Peggy decided it was time for some explanations. Mrs Fowles, however, refused to sit still, darting round the living room, emptying vases and overturning cushions, as if looking for something. 'We used to be alright, me and him,' she said, scrabbling around at the back of a cupboard. 'I mean, it weren't no fairy tale, but it were alright. He were out of my hair, working all day, and I kept house. I kept it alright, too. Kept myself alright, and all,' she added quietly.

'What happened?'

'They built that bloody road, that's what happened,' she snarled.

Ruth glanced out at the incessant motorway traffic thundering past the window. 'It is a bit noisy, I suppose.'

'It's not the noise! They gave us money for noise.'

'Compensation?' Peggy inquired.

'Compensation. Yes. That's when it started.' Mrs Fowles found what she was hunting for – a small key – underneath a dingy-looking doilly and moved over to a chest of drawers. She unlocked the top one and pulled it open. It was empty. 'See that? It were full of money, once. And that one,' she said, opening a second. The third drawer she opened was still half-full. Peggy and Ruth's eyes widened at the thick wads of bank notes – at least several thousand pounds' worth – stashed in the drawer. Neither of them had ever seen so much money. 'I'll give him a year,' Mrs Fowles pronounced grimly.

'Where's rest of money gone?' Peggy said, reeling.

'He sat around here, too much time on his hands, thinking. Men like him aren't built to think. They're meant to get on with things.'

'Is he spending it all on himself?' Ruth asked, dubious. She couldn't imagine what on.

'Not on himself. On *her*.' She rifled through another drawer, producing a stack of invoices and receipts. 'Colour television, three-piece suite, new carpet. What's this one?' She handed it to Peggy.

'Microwave.'

'Holiday in Disneyland,' Ruth read, picking up another pile.

'Paris?' queried Peggy.

Ruth shook her head. 'Florida. New boiler. New bed . . . sorry,' she added, realizing she was rubbing salt into the wound.

Peggy sat back, amazed. 'When did this start?'

'Three months ago he started spending money.'

'Have you talked to him about it?'

'We're not the talking type.'

'Three months!' Ruth was horrified. 'You've been lying unwashed in that bed for three months?'

'I wanted him to notice! To worry about me! But he dunt care about me, he dunt care about farm. Just that woman,' Mrs Fowles sobbed, breaking down again.

'Hey, hey, enough of that,' Peggy soothed. 'Do you know who she is?'

'No. But I've got address.' She passed it to Peggy.

'Dunt ring a bell.' She gave it to Ruth, who shook her head.

Mrs Fowles, distressed, grabbed Peggy's hand. 'Go and see her! Tell her to leave us alone!'

Peggy was taken aback. 'I don't think we can do that, love. It's not really our business, is it?'

'You're meant to make people better, aren't you?'

'Well, yes, but—'

'Please. Go and see her. I've got no-one else to turn to.'

Normally, Stephen would have gone for lunch with Deborah and Henry and the others, but today he couldn't face them,

119

Deborah especially. He knew he'd been insensitive, rejecting her offer so brusquely, but he hadn't known how else to handle it. If they'd gone out together, she would have been kind and sympathetic and understanding and he might have dropped his guard, spilled his guts about Wendy. He couldn't risk that happening. Wendy was a precious secret; too special to be shared with anyone.

Shoving his hands deep in his pockets, he mooched round the school grounds, brooding on his plan for going down to London, which involved waiting for a time when his mother was not around. She was going to a nursing conference in Scarborough soon, stopping overnight. That seemed like the best option. His dad wouldn't be a problem: he was much more easy-going. With any luck, he wouldn't even realize he'd gone.

The scuffed turf behind the science block was littered with dog-ends, testament to its popularity with Skelthwaite High School's miscreant sixth-form smokers. Stephen, rounding the corner, spotted Robbie Johnson sheltering in the lee of the wall, his hand cupped around a glowing cigarette. Robbie, like Stephen, had retakes coming up, though expectations of him passing were not quite as high. There wasn't much love lost between them: Robbie, a hulking, acned lad, resented Stephen's flair and popularity, especially with girls, while Stephen and Henry took the mickey out of Robbie for being thick.

'Snow flake! Wotcha doing?' he called gruffly, trying to wind Stephen up. He didn't like his school nickname.

'Not a lot.' Stephen kicked a stone against the wall. Robbie grinned. 'Come for a fag?'

'No.'

'Have you had one before?'

'Of course.'

'Go on, then.' Robbie held out a packet of cigarettes. 'Prove it.'

It wasn't the first time he'd had one – Stephen had smoked

120

once at a party, although he hadn't enjoyed the experience – but now, all of a sudden, they suited his dark and dangerous mood. The fact that, if he was caught, he was likely to be excluded from school – Mr Pearson was sticking to his 'three strikes and you're out' policy on misbehaviour, and Stephen had used up all of his chances – merely added to their allure.

He lit up and drew on it, coughing and hacking. 'Ha!' Robbie said scornfully, 'I knew you hadn't. You're all mouth, you are.' Contemptuously, he ground his own cigarette butt into the grass and left. Stephen was still staring at the smoke trailing between his fingers, wondering what on earth the appeal was, when he heard Deborah's voice.

'Stephen! I didn't know you smoked.'

'What are you doing here?' he asked, taken by surprise.

'I could ask you same question,' she replied stiffly, 'but I suppose answer's pretty obvious.'

'Robbie gave it to me.'

'You have sunk low.' Her voice dripped with sarcasm.

'Look, about this morning . . .' Stephen began haltingly. 'I'm sorry I was so off. It wasn't personal. It's just – I've got a lot on my mind at the moment.'

She was silent for a while, as if trying to make up her mind about something. They stood, listening to the cries of children in the playground, wheeling and swooping like gulls on the wing. 'That's OK,' she said.

They smiled at each other and he knew he was forgiven.

Deborah reached for the cigarette. 'Here, let me have a try'. She took a surreptious puff and spluttered. Neither of them noticed Mr Pearson bearing down on them until it was too late. 'You. Put that thing out. Now,' he ordered, glaring ferociously at her. 'I want both of you in my office after school. I hope you appreciate just how much trouble you're in.'

The address Mrs Fowles had given Ruth and Peggy was of a small, modern house on a newish estate on the outskirts of

Skelthwaite. They stopped the car and looked at it, unsure, now, about their mission. 'We can't just barge in and accuse some woman of having an affair,' Peggy said.

'I'm not sure Wendy Atkins would agree,' teased Ruth.

'That was completely different,' she blustered. 'I don't know about this.' But Ruth, ever-impulsive, was already halfway out of the car. 'Come on, think about Elsa Fowles,' she cajoled. Ruth started up the path, beckoning Peggy, who followed reluctantly.

'Yes?' A woman in her forties answered Ruth's bell. She was neatly dressed, but had deep crow's feet and a sagging mouth, as if life had been hard. She looked between the two of them and suddenly brightened. 'Oh, hello! It's Lucy's mum.'

'Er, yes. Mrs . . . Figgis, int it?' Peggy stammered, realization slowly dawning.

'That's right,' the woman said, smiling.

'Mrs Figgis is dinner lady at Lucy's school,' Peggy explained to Ruth.

'Oh.'

'What can I do for you?' she asked sociably. 'Won't you come in?'

The living room was small and cramped, which made the huge, black, state-of-the-art television dominating it look even more out of place. A new-looking three-piece suite took up the rest of the space. Two small boys in tracksuits and socks were sprawled on the sofa, gazing fixedly at the screen. 'Would you like cup of tea?' Mrs Figgis said, fussing and straightening cushions.

'If it's no trouble.' For once, Peggy was not keen to get straight to the point.

'No trouble at all.'

The two boys glanced up at the visitors and, with the absence of social graces that small boys have, returned to the television without speaking. 'Hello,' Ruth said, bending down, assuming they were shy.

'That's Daniel, he's six, and Callum, he's eight. But you won't get a word out of them when they're in front of that thing.'

'Mmn. Nice telly,' Ruth commented, with a sideways look at Peggy.

'Thank you.' She dusted her hands together and said, 'You wanted to talk to me about one of your patients?'

Peggy opened her mouth to speak, but was cut off by yet another small boy, this one aged about five, who emerged from the kitchen with his arms full of red carnations. 'Mum, do I have to cut stems off them all?' he complained. Presented with the evidence, Peggy had no alternative. 'Can we go somewhere a bit quieter?'

Mrs Figgis put the kettle on and listened, first with amazement, then with anger, as between them, Peggy and Ruth described Elsa Fowles and the state she was in and her odd request. 'I dint know he had a wife! I promise you. I thought he were a widower!' she exclaimed.

'He's got a wife alright,' Peggy said.

'Not a very happy one,' Ruth added.

'I had no idea. I met him at bus stop in Huddersfield. It were raining and we got talking. He said he were a wealthy widower. He paid for us to get a taxi all the way back to Skelthwaite.' She stared at them both, her expression grim. 'I know what you're thinking. How could she? A horrible old man like that?' Daniel, the middle boy, burst into the kitchen and demanded, 'Mum, can I go and play at Michael's?' Mrs Figgis gave him a weak smile. 'Alright love. Be home for your tea.' He slammed the kitchen door and scampered off round the back of the house. She watched him go. 'Three boys I had, one after the other,' she said, still gazing out of the window. 'Then one night their father tells me he's had enough, he's moving out. He'd found a younger model – even his infidelity was unoriginal. And that was that. I worked where I could, I scrimped and saved where I could. We moved here to try and make a fresh start.'

'I'm sorry,' Peggy sympathized.

'My relationship with Mr Harris . . . is that his real name?' she broke off.

'No, love, it's not.'

Her face hardened. 'My relationship with . . . whoever the hell he is . . . is purely business. He provides me and my family with some of the good things in life and I provide him . . .' Her eyes darted between them. 'I know. There's a name for women like me, int there? But you haven't been where I've been so you don't know what you'd do to help your kids.'

Peggy shifted uncomfortably. 'We haven't come here to judge anyone.'

'Why have you come here? To laugh at me? To see who it could be who could stoop so low?' The two nurses exchanged complicit glances. Mrs Figgis noticed. 'Well, now you know,' she said harshly.

Ruth coloured faintly. 'We came because an unhappy woman asked us to.'

'I knew nothing about her, I swear!'

'We believe you.'

Mrs Figgis wrung out a dishcloth as if she wished it were Mr Fowles-cum-Harris's neck. 'Bloody men.'

An awkward silence descended. Peggy looked at her watch. 'We ought to get back, love. We'll not stop for tea.'

'Yes, Alfie'll be wanting his,' Ruth said, suddenly aware of how long they'd been away. The fact that she'd been so caught up with her job she hadn't thought about her baby for several hours gave her a sharp stab of guilt.

Mrs Figgis showed them to the door. 'You can tell Mrs Fowles that I'll not be seeing her husband again.' She paused. 'And *you* can tell *me* something. I like it here, my kids like it here. Are we going to have to move on?'

Peggy patted her shoulder. 'Not because of us, love. As far

as I'm concerned, today never happened.' They turned to go, only to see Mr Fowles himself on the other side of the street. He was about to cross when he caught sight of them, too, and stopped dead in his tracks. 'I'll deal with him,' Mrs Figgis said resolutely. She beckoned him towards her, a severe expression on her face. 'Mr "Harris" . . .'

'Vic!' Simon materialized from behind a pastel-coloured mountain of toilet rolls, waiting to be packed. In contrast with the dark, oily machinery, their rainbow hues – pink, green, apricot, pale blue, primrose – gave the factory floor a fey touch, a promise of puppies and kittens and fairyland, where everything was bouncy and squeezy and soft. Not that Simon saw it that way. He only saw an order that should have been out of the door yesterday. 'Vic!' he shouted again. Vic appeared, wiping greasy hands on a rag. 'What's up?'

'Why hasn't this lot been shifted yet?'

'Because the lads have been working overtime trying to keep up production after number three went down again and buggered things up. You can't have it both ways.'

'If we don't flog it, there's no point in making it, is there? Get them over here right away. I want it on road tomorrow morning.'

'Whatever you say. Just decide what it is you want.' Vic tugged at an imaginary forelock.

Simon was peeved. 'It would, of course, be a lot easier for me to run this place if I had someone I could rely on. Someone young and go-getting, hungry for a challenge. School-leavers these days, they don't know they're born . . .' Vic rolled his eyes. He was well aware of what Simon was implying. Stephen's rejection of a job at the factory had miffed Simon. Simon had left school at sixteen and reached his current position by dint of hard work and pushiness. He had no time for graduates.

'. . . Instead, they've got pie-in-the-sky ideas about

'poncing around on stage and going to uni-ver-sit-y,' Simon continued, spelling out the latter in a posh voice.

'Now just you hold your horses.' Vic had had enough of Simon's goading. Their relationship was a finely balanced one at the best of times. Simon was the boss, he provided Vic with a living wage and financed his beloved rugby team, and on all those counts he was beholden to him. But Simon was also family and, most of the time, a friend. Vic put up with a great deal more from him because he was Peggy's brother than he would have done from anyone else, and it was something Simon had begun to take for granted. There were times, though, when Vic wanted to thump him, and today was one of them.

'You saw our Stephen in play. I know it weren't your cup of tea – it weren't my cup of tea, either – but we both of us know enough to recognize talent when we see it. And that boy's got a future. You'll be glad to welcome him home when he's made a name for himself. And he won't do that making bog paper.'

'Well, I hope you're right, Vic. And I hope you *can* spot talent,' Simon said viciously, 'because I'm not giving any more folks jobs just when you want them. Remember who pays the piper round here.'

Many years' worth of resentments over Simon's crassness came boiling to a head. 'Are you reneging on our agreement this morning about Kenny?' Vic shouted. 'Call yourself a man of your word!'

'I'll give that Kiwi a job,' Simon snarled. 'But he'd better deliver goods, Vic. On the pitch and off. Cos if he dunt come up to scratch, I'll take it out of your bonus. And if we dunt beat Hoxton this time, I'll drop sponsorship of team.'

'I will not tolerate smoking on school property. Both of you know that. So what have you got to say for yourselves?' Mr Pearson said curtly. Stephen opened his mouth to answer, then realized the Headmaster obviously meant the question rhetorically, because he swept on, barely pausing to draw breath. 'I'm especially surprised at you, Deborah, though I put it down to Stephen's pernicious influence. I assume that was his cigarette? You do realize, don't you Stephen, that you've overstepped the mark very seriously this time? I've given you more than enough chances already. I will consult with the board of governors but you are facing permanent exclusion.'

Stephen, who was sure Robbie Johnson had tipped off Dogger, felt no compunction to cover for him. 'Look, it wasn't—' he began.

'Sir, that was my cigarette, not his. Stephen didn't smoke it,' Deborah interrupted. She hung her head, studying the pattern on the carpet. Stephen stared at her, astonished that she would take the rap for him.

'Are you quite sure about that?' the Head asked, icily. Deborah Alliss had never been in trouble for anything before. As far as he was aware, she was a model pupil.

'Yes, Sir,' she replied, subdued.

'Is that the truth, Stephen?'

Deborah kicked him hard on the shin below Mr Pearson's line of sight.

'Er, yes, Sir.'

'Really? Well, I'm astonished.' He looked between the two of them keenly but they kept their faces blank. 'Well, Miss Alliss, you will be in detention for two hours every night for a week, since this is your first offence. But I warn you, I will not go so easy on you a second time.'

Once outside his office, in the playground, Deborah earned her kiss. 'You're a lifesaver,' Stephen said, enveloping her in a bear hug. He took her face between both hands and kissed her gently, sweetly, on the lips, making her tingle all over. 'Thank you, thank you, Debs. I owe you one.'

'So you'll take me out for that drink, then?' she said, smiling.

'It's incredible, int it? Two intelligent women like that made miserable by an unwashed pig farmer with a bit of brass,' Peggy said, as she parked the car outside the Skelthwaite Health Centre once more.

'Men always find that one female in trouble, don't they? Then just home in on her,' Ruth agreed.

'Like an instinct.'

'They have their little dreams and desires and somehow they find women to make them happen. Quite a trick, really.'

'It's a good job we're wise to it, int it? Peggy joked.

'The *real* trick is,' Ruth added, 'to let them *think* they're in control . . .' Laughing, they walked in to the office, to find Patricia looking slightly frazzled.

'Another good deed done by the dynamic duo,' Ruth announced, dusting her hands together.

'And it's only your first day back. Is there no stopping this woman?' Patricia feigned amazement. 'When do you return full-time, Ruth?'

'After Nursing Conference at Scarborough.'

'For which,' Peggy reminded them, 'I'll need your support, both of you. I've never given a speech before. Not to big crowd, anyway.' She took off her coat. 'Any interesting calls?'

'The phone's been red-hot. Mrs Herrington rang. I'm seeing her tomorrow. Mr Jones. His leg's playing up again. Walter. Wanted to know why his biscuits were swelling up when he dunked them—' At this, Peggy and Ruth screamed with laughter.

'What?' asked Patricia, who wasn't in on the joke.

'He insisted on buying tampons at supermarket. We tried to tell him they weren't Rich Tea.'

Patricia giggled. 'He said they were chewy.' She recovered herself and continued, 'Oh, and Carol Bevan called in. She wanted you to know Billy's out of hospital and on the right medication. Joe's being treated, too. She brought you these.'

Patricia indicated a box of Quality Street. 'Don't bother looking for the soft centres,' she added, as Ruth grabbed the box. 'I needed something to keep me going while you were both out saving the world.'

# Chapter 10

' "Palliative Care in the Community – A Worm's Eye View". What do you reckon?' asked Peggy, keeping her eyes on the road. They had borrowed the Skelthwaite Scorpions' minibus to go to Scarborough, a cumbersome vehicle with leaden steering which felt like a tank after her nippy hatchback. Ruth, who wasn't paying attention, exclaimed, 'This is hopeless. I can't get a signal,' as she held her mobile up to her ear.

'It's these hills. Wait til it flattens out a bit. You've only been gone five minutes.'

'A lot can happen in five minutes. Especially when you've left your baby in a factory,' Ruth said darkly. Simon was looking after Alfie – no babysitters were available and a permanent childminder had yet to be appointed – while she attended the conference with Patricia and Peggy. Despite his oft-protested 'new man' credentials, a few minutes was all it took for Ruth to start worrying about Simon's baby-care proficiency.

'What do you think of my title?' Peggy persisted.

'What is it?' Patiently, Peggy reeled off her title again.

'A Worms Eye view?' Ruth queried, pulling a face.

'It's good that bit, int it?' Peggy said proudly. 'I want to emphasize how hands-on we are.'

'I know, but . . . I mean, you're talking about death, aren't you?'

'So?'

'People don't like to think about worms when they think about death, do they?'

Peggy's smile faded rapidly. 'It dint even cross my mind.'

'They'll all be asleep, anyway, won't matter what you say.'

As an attempt to buck Peggy up, this did not go down too well. 'Thanks very much,' she replied, bristling.

Ruth sighed. 'I dint mean it like that.'

Peggy gripped the wheel tightly. 'I'm the first District Nurse they've ever asked to speak and I'm not going to let myself down.' This had become her mantra, but she wondered who she was trying to kid. She had been preparing her speech for weeks and was still undecided about it. Beside her, Ruth, fretting, punched out a number again. Peggy glanced in her rearview mirror at Patricia, who was sitting silently in the back. It occurred to her that Patricia was not her usual jolly self – on a junket like this, she would normally cajole them into singing a few rousing choruses and pass a tin of sweets around. 'Alright back there?' Peggy asked. Patricia, preoccupied, merely nodded.

'Damn.' Ruth snapped the mobile shut. 'If you see a phone, can we stop?'

'They'll be alright. Stop worrying.'

'How old was Stephen before you left him on his own with Vic?'

'Stephen? This is the first time.' Ruth gawped at Peggy, alarmed. 'I'm joking, I'm joking,' Peggy chuckled, seeing her wide eyes. Suddenly, Patricia broke her silence, leaning forward between the two of them. 'Mrs Herrington,' she announced, apropos nothing.

'What about her?' Peggy asked.

'You know how happy she's been?'

'I said that to Ruth only yesterday, didn't I, Ruth? She went from being the most miserable widow int world to Laughing Cavalier in about a week.'

'I know why.'

'Why?'

Patricia hesitated. 'She says it's broken and I have to get it fixed.'

'What's broken?' Patricia, Peggy noted, looked deeply embarrassed. 'Come on, out with it.' Reluctantly, Patricia delved into the bag she had been nursing on her knees. 'Meet Mrs Herrington's friend,' she said. There was a split-second's silence as they regarded the object on Patricia's lap, then Ruth and Peggy squawked with laughter, their raucous screams ricocheting around the van. 'That's above and beyond call of duty, int it? Ruth gasped, mopping her eyes.

'She insisted he were vital to her continued emotional and physical wellbeing. What could I do?'

'Tell her to buy magazine an' all.' Ruth turned to Peggy. 'D'you think it worked for Mr Fowles?'

'Well, Mrs Fowles seemed happy enough when I saw her int butchers.'

'She were up?'

'Up, washed, dressed – a different woman. She were glowing! Said she were going to make him something special. I think she were planning a candlelit dinner.'

'So she dint want him to stop wanting it with her?'

'Apparently not.'

'Ugh.' Ruth shuddered at the thought. 'Letting herself go like that. And Mrs Figgis, doing it for a microwave.'

'Human sexuality is a complicated business,' Peggy said, philosophically.

'Especially when your motor's bust,' Patricia added, waving Mrs Herrington's friend under her nose.

Simon, trying to change a wriggling Alfie, was grateful he didn't have any appointments that day. His executive image was lying in tatters, along with half the contents of his office. Papers, memos, order forms and balance sheets had all been knocked flying when Alfie kicked his 'In' tray off the desk, scattering them on the floor. Not only that, but the place reeked of dirty nappies. 'Bloody hell, lad, what have you

133

been eating? Lie still!' he yelled, as Alfie stuck a wayward foot in the soiled nappy he was in the process of removing. Alfie shrieked joyfully and yanked his tie, which, Simon realized, too late, was also trailing in the mucky nappy. 'God!' he shouted, exasperated. Denise, Simon's secretary, came into the room, trying to keep a straight face. 'I've got Mr Hunt from Florida on phone.'

'Tell him I'll speak to him later.'

'He said it was important.'

Simon squinted at her from under his arm as he brandished baby wipes. 'Does it look like I can speak to him now?' Alfie, liberated, celebrated his Pampers-free state by squirting a jet of pee at Simon, catching him full in the face. Urine dripping down his nose, Simon ground out, 'If you so much as grin, you are sacked. Alright?' Denise backed out of the room and shut the door. Simon could hear her peals of laughter all the way down the corridor.

A bottle of milk and a snooze later, Alfie woke up red in the face and screaming. Simon, loathe to go to anyone for advice, put up with it for ten minutes, during which the cries intensified to a level comparable with his outmoded machinery and Alfie went from puce to purple. Eventually he could stand it no longer and carted the baby down to the factory floor to seek help from his brother-in-law. He found Vic watching Kenny, muscles bulging under his 'Goddard Paper Products' overalls, as he worked on one of the broken-down rollers.

'What's up?' Vic said, coming over.

'I think he's ill!' There was real panic in Simon's voice.

Vic examined the white ring around Alfie's mouth. 'Have you fed him?'

'He's been eating like a horse all morning.'

'Give him here.' Vic took Alfie gently from Simon and laid him over his shoulder, patting his back firmly.

'Don't hit him!' Simon said, concerned. Vic ignored him and continued patting, until Alfie produced a magnificent burp. 'Poor bugger's got wind, that's all,' he remarked.

Simon look sheepish. 'I thought that's what it was.'

'Have you heard from women?'

'Only every five minutes. Give us him back.'

Vic handed the baby over and gestured behind him. 'I think Kenny's got this one sorted. I told him you'd give him keys to town if he fixed it.'

But Simon didn't seem to be listening. He sniffed Alfie's nappy, an expression of disgust on his face. 'Bloody hell! You just get him cleaned off and he does it again!' He disappeared back upstairs, leaving Vic shaking his head.

There was something wonderfully romantic about seaside resorts in winter, thought Ruth, feeling her spirits rise with the first bracing breath of sea air. They had made good time to Scarborough, arriving well ahead of the first lecture, giving them a chance to settle in to their hotel first. The twin-bedded room Ruth and Patricia had been allocated was cramped but cosy, with tea-making equipment, TV and a basket of complimentary toiletries, which they squabbled over instantly. 'You can have sewing kit; I'll have shower gel,' Ruth decided.

'Only if I can have body lotion and bluebell soap as well.'

'But that just leaves me with shampoo.'

'And a shower cap.' Patricia opened the window and leaned out, surveying the view. 'It's alright, int it?'

'Can you see sea?' asked Ruth, through a mouthful of shortbread, which she had discovered with the sachets of hot chocolate. She switched on the television and reclined on a bed, channel-hopping with the remote.

'I can see something. Not sure if it's the sea or the car park. Ooh, biscuits,' added Patricia. She raided the basket and sat down on the opposite bed.

'No snoring – I can reach you from here,' Ruth said, swatting at her. She watched as Patricia bounced up and down, testing the softness of the mattress. 'If you want me to make myself scarce later, you will say, won't you?'

'Why would I want you to do that?'

'I don't know. Why does Mrs Herrington want you to fix her friend?'

Patricia grabbed a pillow and walloped her with it. 'You are so crude!'

'I dint say a thing!' laughed Ruth, keeling over on the duvet in hysterics.

Rehearsing her speech in a spacious single room further along the corridor, Peggy felt much less lighthearted. 'Ladies and gentlemen, thank you so much for coming this morning – and I'd like to thank the committee for inviting me,' she addressed her reflection in the wardrobe mirror in a soft, modulated tone. 'The title of my talk is, "Palliative Care in the Community – a Nurse's Eye View". I have been a district nurse in the town of Skelthwaite in West Yorkshire for twenty years . . .' The paper trembled in her fingers and she gulped unhappily, '. . . 'and I would just like to say . . . my hands are shaking. I am absolutely terrified and I wish I could wake up and it'd all be over.' The last bit wasn't part of her speech, but it was from the heart. She drew a deep breath and was about to try again when there was a knock on the door and Patricia and Ruth entered, dressed for the off. 'Come on, get your coat on! That funny man's lecture starts in twenty minutes,' Ruth said. Patricia glanced about, taking in the large room and the sea view. 'This is a nice room, Peg.'

'The trappings of power,' Ruth said in a stage whisper, rubbing her gloved hands together.

Peggy looked guilty. 'I had to have single room to prepare my speech.'

'Well, I'm not complaining – rather you than me.' Ruth could see Peggy was eaten up with nerves and wasn't surprised when she announced she that couldn't face the lecture – 'He's always so brilliant, that man, and I'll get intimidated'. She said she was going for a run instead, so they set off without her, going via the fudge shop for some

rum 'n' raisin to fortify themselves until their eagerly antici-
pated fish-and-chip lunch.

The wind blew Peggy's hair into her eyes, hampering her
progress as she struggled to run along the massive headland
high above the town, which was dominated by the thick
buttressed walls of Scarborough Castle reaching out along
the cliff edge. Eventually she gave up her unequal battle with
the elements and took refuge in the ruins of the ancient walls,
panting heavily. Far below, the boats in the old harbour
looked like children's toys, and from her lofty vantage point
she could see along the coast and inland to the North York
moors. She unfolded her speech from the pocket of her
tracksuit top, the pages flapping in the breeze. Up here, she
felt less intimidated. She cleared her throat and declaimed,
'We think of our own death as . . . well, it's ours, int it? It
belongs to us. It's private. I have been involved with many,
many deaths in my own community—' No, that didn't sound
right. It sounded as if she was a mass murderer! Peggy got
out a pencil and altered 'involved with' to 'seen', and
continued, 'Not one of them, not the loneliest man in the
loneliest farmhouse, died without sending ripples out into the
community beyond.' She sighed. It still didn't sound right.
Inside her, she knew what she wanted to say, but putting that
across in a lecture hall was another matter. Her brain felt as if
it had seized up. 'Vic, what am I doing here?' she murmured,
a sinking feeling in the pit of her stomach.

  Deciding to have another go at it in the evening, she
returned back down the steep winding path and eventually
joined the esplanade. The place was almost deserted, except
for the odd dog-walker, patrolling the sand head down
against the wind. Salt spray stung her lips as she pounded
the beach, making her eyes water, so that at first she didn't
recognize the wet-suited figure jogging towards her, a surf-
board under his arm. The surfer, a rugged, good-looking
man in his early thirties with cropped, George Clooney-style

hair, was accompanied by another, younger man, similarly kitted out. As they got closer, something in the older man's face made her glance at him again, and this time she realized who it was. Peggy dropped her eyes quickly, averting her face, and they ran past her without stopping. She followed their athletic bodies as they raced whooping down to the shoreline and ran into the foaming water, paddling their boards out towards the big breakers. Charlie, she reminded herself, had always been keen on making waves. It was best not to tell the others.

Stephen had told Deborah this much: he had been seeing an older woman who he was mad about, but that he couldn't tell his family because they wouldn't approve of the age difference.

'So you're a toy boy,' she'd giggled, her head swimmy. They had gone to The Drayhorse, the pub on the other side of town that wasn't fussy about asking for ID. Deborah had downed an alcoholic lemonade, as befitted a bad girl who had been given detention for smoking. She was rather enjoying her reckless new image.

'Yes. No. It's not like that. We're equals,' Stephen said slowly. 'It's not some exploitation thing. She loves me. And I love her.'

Deborah's eyes widened. 'Seriously?'

'Yeah. Seriously.'

'What are you going to do?'

'That's the killer. She's moved away. Her employers wanted her to relocate. So she's in London and I'm stuck up here.'

She took another swig from the colourful bottle in front of her. 'And you want to go on seeing her?'

'Want to? I've got to, Debs. I miss her so much. Sometimes it makes me feel desperate.'

'Wow.'

'What?'

'Strong stuff.'

'I know. I feel as if I've grown up overnight.'

'No, I mean the lemonade. Can I have another?' Deborah said, being deliberately blasé. All she'd dreamed about for the past few months was having Stephen Snow to herself, and the kiss in the playground had revived her hopes. Now she had him, and all he wanted to do was talk about this other, older woman who she couldn't possibly hope to compete with. She needed a drink to deaden the pain.

'OK, but don't get drunk. I need to go through my plan with you.'

That was two days ago, and Stephen, waiting on the slip road to the M1 southbound, was confident he had Deborah on side now. She had agreed to make his excuses at registration, telling his form teacher that he had flu but would carry on revising at home. Stephen hitched up his shoulder bag and held out a handwritten sign, which read 'LONDON' in large letters. He was full of hope, imbued with the spirit of adventure. Down in London, where no-one knew them, he and Wendy could be together openly, without pretending. Freed from the constraints of having to creep around keeping things secret, their relationship would flourish again. She would see how mature he really was and they could start afresh. He'd apply for places at London universities, then, as soon as he'd finished school, he could come down and join her for good. If she loved him – and she said she did – the plan was sure to succeed. A lorry flashed its lights at him, jolting Stephen out of his reverie. He saw it indicate and slow down, and bounded joyfully along the muddy verge to the cab.

'Here she is! I ordered you a Knickerbocker Glory,' Patricia greeted Peggy. She had arranged to meet them after the lecture at a 1950s-style café round the corner and got there to find them already installed behind two very large, very creamy milkshakes. Peggy joined them at the chrome counter and perched precariously on a high stool. A waitress in a dinky yellow uniform, her hair caught up in a swinging ponytail, placed a gigantic ice-cream confection in a tall glass in front of her. 'How was it?' she asked, digging in with a long-handled spoon.

'It was excellent,' Ruth enthused. 'He should be on stage, that man, he's so funny. He had these slides—'

'Slides?' Peggy hadn't thought of that.

'Mmm, he had slides and sound effects and—'

'Not that you need slides to give a good speech,' Patricia jumped in, sensing Peggy's growing discomfort.

'I know, but—' Ruth continued, until she spotted Patricia's warning look. 'It wasn't so funny,' she tailed off.

Peggy sighed. 'It's alright. I'm not pretending to be something I'm not.'

'Come on! Let's finish these and go down arcade. It'll take your mind off it,' Ruth said brightly.

Patricia leaned forward and whispered conspiratorially, 'Can we see to Mrs Herrington's friend first? It'll be such a weight off my mind.'

'Did she say "we"?' Peggy asked Ruth innocently.

'Can't think why. It's not as if Mrs Herrington has formally introduced us.'

'True. She left him in your capable hands, Pat. It's nothing to do with us.'

'Beasts!'

They deposited Patricia outside an electrical shop and watched from across the road as she dithered by the door. 'Look at her,' Ruth laughed, as Patricia, bag tucked protectively under her arm, pretended to be fascinated by the window display of power tools. She turned and looked back at them helplessly. 'Go on!' Peggy mouthed, waving her forward. Patricia squared her shoulders and opened the door, which broadcast the arrival of the new customer with a jangle of bells so loud that any further attempt at remaining inconspicuous was now superfluous. 'There goes one brave woman,' said Ruth.

Ten minutes later there was still no sign of Patricia returning, so they decided to go for a stroll to ward off the cold. 'I remember coming here with my best friend and her mum and dad – I must have been all of thirteen. D'you remember Tracey Hardcastle?' Ruth said, looking about her at the shops and winkle stalls and souvenir stands, which looked drab and tawdry in the grey afternoon light.

'I do. Pretty girl with pigtails. Whatever happened to her?'

'She married a plumber in Sheffield. We used to stagger around arcades on our heels, enough make-up to sink a battleship.' Ruth smiled a little sadly at the memory of her giddy former self.

Peggy looked back over her shoulder, wondering about Patricia. 'Why do you think she's taking so long?' she asked, but Ruth was miles away.

'One night we lit a little fire ont beach. We lay on our backs and looked up at the stars and imagined what we'd be when we grew up. Tracey was going to be a model. She'd marry an incredibly handsome photographer called Sebastian and go and live in a villa in Rome.'

'What about you?' Peggy said, pulling her scarf up around her face to stop her nose turning red.

'Me? I was going to be a vet.'

'A vet?' Peggy was surprised. She'd never associated Ruth with small cuddly animals.

'Not hamsters and things – thoroughbred horses,' Ruth replied dreamily. 'I'd travel the world performing miraculous operations and be showered with gifts by beautiful young sheikhs.'

Peggy glanced back again, concerned. 'D'you think we should have gone with her?' Perhaps the shop-owner had got the wrong idea about Patricia.

'That's the funny thing about having Alfie,' Ruth continued. 'I mean, I love him to bits . . .' She stopped and looked wistfully out towards the sea. Peggy stared at her, worried. Ruth sounded regretful, almost. 'What's the matter?' she asked.

'Nothing.' Ruth laughed it off. 'My hormones are all over the place, that's all.'

'Tell me.'

They turned round and began retracing their steps. 'I feel like all the dreams are over now – d'you know what I mean? I am what I am. I've been given my place in the world. I'm a district nurse in the town I was born in. I'm a mother and a wife.'

'I think that's quite a lot,' Peggy said indignantly.

'I know it is. All I'm saying—'

'A lot of women would give their eye-teeth for what you've got. Think of Carol Bevan. She were born in Skelthwaite and she can't even get a job, let alone a good one like yours.'

'I know, I know, I'm being silly,' Ruth placated her, realizing that her sister-in-law didn't understand what she meant.

'I think you are,' Peggy replied, terse. She was fiercely protective of her little brother. After all, Ruth had only gone and married Skelthwaite's self-made man. Simon Goddard was considered quite a catch. And she had a wonderful new baby . . . She was about to deliver a little homily to this effect when Patricia came panting down the beach towards them. 'Thank you for your support,' she said sarcastically.

'How d'you get on? I was getting quite worried.'

Patricia brandished her bag triumphantly. 'Mrs Herrington's friend has made a full recovery!'

The lorry driver, a middle-aged man who had pictures of his wife and three kids stuck up around the cab, took a parental interest in Stephen when he found out how old he was. 'I hope you're not running away from home, cos you can get out at the next services and go right back again,' he lectured him. 'Streets of London aren't paved wi' gold like you young lads seem to think. You'll end up sleeping rough, destitute, and getting into trouble. It's not worth it.'

Stephen grinned. He had a grand view of the road, a wintry sun was shining and he was going to see Wendy at last. 'No, but she is,' he replied happily.

The driver shot him a sidelong look. 'Got a girl down there?'

'Sure have.'

'Ah well, now love's a different matter. You got an impulse, act on it. Might not get the chance second time around.' He clapped him on the shoulder. 'In that case, son, you have my blessing. How far do you want to go?'

'You heading into London?'

'Yup.'

'All the way.'

Which was how, some four hours later, Stephen found himself at Piccadilly Circus in the heart of London's West End, his senses reeling as taxis, buses, cars and motorbike couriers streamed past and people came at him from every direction. It was as if he were in a speeded-up film, he thought. Bemused, he found a space on the steps of the fountain of Eros that wasn't already occupied by Australian backpackers and Japanese tourists, and looked about. High above him, massive electronic billboards flashed advertisements and messages and further along, the names of famous theatres beckoned in neon. '*I've arrived*,' he told himself, breathless with excitement. He spotted a London Underground sign and got out his pocket diary, which had a Tube map in the back. It looked like a horribly complicated wiring diagram. '*Focus*,' he repeated. '*Focus*.'

At one point he realized he was travelling the wrong way on the District Line, but after that getting to Chiswick proved easy. Londoners, he noticed, had tight, tense, closed faces. He tried smiling at a few people on the Tube but no-one would meet his eyes, apart from a guy with a moustache wearing a leather jacket, who smiled back, rather too welcomingly. When he changed at Earl's Court, Stephen melted into the crowd, realizing why people kept themselves to themselves.

He got off at Turnham Green and consulted his newly acquired *A-Z of London*. Chiswick High Road had wide pavements and a well-heeled ambience and he followed it past trendy cafés and shops, taking a right into a tree-lined avenue. Outside number fifteen, a three-storey Victorian villa, he paused and checked the address he had written down on a scrap of paper. This was the one. He took a moment to compose himself and then knocked on the door.

'Yes?' A woman in her early fifties, iron-grey hair neatly coiffed, opened it and goggled at him suspiciously.

'Mrs Atkins?'

'Who are you?' He supposed he did look a bit suss, dressed as he was in black bomber jacket, jeans, trainers and woollen hat, with a kit bag over his shoulder.

'Is Wendy in?' He smiled reassuringly.

'Who are you?' she repeated nervously.

At that moment, Wendy shouted from inside the house, 'Who is it, Mum?' She came into the hall and stopped dead when she saw him. 'Stephen!' He smiled weakly, unsure of his reception, but she ran out of the door and threw her arms around him. 'Oh, Stephen,' she whispered, her lips brushing his neck. 'Stephen.'

'Who wants to do what?' said Peggy briskly, as the three of them walked arm-in-arm along the beach. Ruth voted for the arcade but Patricia wanted to shop, causing Ruth to complain she could shop in Skelthwaite.

'You can't get Scarborough rock in Skelthwaite,' Patricia pointed out.

'What do you want that stuff for? It'll take your teeth out,' Peggy pretended to scold.

'Presents.'

'Who for? We're both here.'

'I don't know,' Patricia fibbed, looking flustered.

'I do!' Ruth laughed wickedly. 'It's the lodger.' She put on a bad New Zealand accent. ' "What d'you do with it, Mrs Illingworth, mate?" '

Patricia looked mulish. 'He happened to mention that they don't have sticks of rock in New Zealand.'

Peggy decided for them. 'We'll go to shops and buy rock. Go to arcade and lose money. Then we'll go back to hotel for a drink.' The others nodded approvingly and they were about to turn round when a lone surfer, his head as slick as a seal, came towards them. Peggy, spotting who it was, tried to steer them in a different direction, exhorting, 'Come on! Last one there's a sissy!' but the stranger, who had seen their faces, called out wonderingly, 'Ruth?'

Ruth stopped and stared at the wet-suited figure, puzzled, then, suddenly, her face lit up with an incandescent smile. 'Charlie!'

Peggy's heart sank like a stone.

# Chapter 11

Wendy and Stephen walked and walked, saying nothing. They headed west, at first letting the roar of the traffic fill the vacuum between them, eventually turning back via the towpath along the Grand Union Canal. By this time it was growing dusk, and their conversation, though stilted, was at least friendly. Stephen was relieved. Wendy's behaviour before she left had been so erratic and unpredictable he didn't know where he was with her. He still couldn't tell what she was thinking. So far, they had kept to neutral subjects, but there was an undercurrent of uncertainty between them. Neither wanted to be the first to open up, and it wasn't until Stephen took advantage of the growing darkness to slip his hand into hers that she finally acknowledged their intimacy.

'I'm meant to be furious with you. What am I going to say to my mother? "It's alright, Mum, it's just one of my pupils I slept with up in Yorkshire"?'

He grinned, pleased that she was opening up at last. 'She's made a fantastic recovery.'

'More than I have,' she confessed, her serious face illuminated by the pale shimmer of street lights on the oily black water. He stopped and drew her close to him. 'I missed you,' he breathed, holding her tight. She looked up at him, her eyes gleaming. 'I thought you'd be on to the next one by now.'

'You thought wrong.' He kissed her, feeling longing surge through his body. 'For a teacher, you can be really stupid.'

They resumed their stroll, arms around each other, happy

just to be in each other's company. 'How's the revision going?' she asked.

'Alright.'

'Don't just cram it all in and spew it all out on the day. *Learn* it,' Wendy said, going into teacher mode.

'It's not easy when I'm always thinking of you.'

'Don't you dare blame it on me! If you don't pass that exam—'

'I was joking!'

'How do you think that would make me feel?'

Stephen smiled, his teeth flashing in the dark. He was sure her lecture was not a disinterested one. So she did want him to be with her in London! 'You want me to pass, I'll pass,' he replied coolly.

'You'd better.' Suddenly, Wendy grabbed hold of Stephen's wrist, holding it up and squinting at his watch. 'What's the time?'

'Why?' he asked, surprised.

'I'm supposed to be meeting some friends.'

'Good – I'd like to meet your friends.'

'No you wouldn't,' she said hurriedly. 'I'll just pop in and out. I'll be one minute.'

He didn't like the implication in her words. 'You haven't told them about me.'

'Yes, I have. They're my friends.'

'So you're ashamed of me?'

'No, I'm not.' For a moment they were both tense again, then she relented. 'You'll be bored silly, but if that's what you want . . .'

'It is,' he said firmly. At last, they could be a proper couple.


For the first time since she'd had Alfie, Ruth felt like a sexy woman. Her figure had returned to (almost) its former size – one of the advantages of breastfeeding, as she'd told Patricia, although Patricia deemed it a very roundabout way to lose

148

weight. Another advantage was that she possessed the finest cleavage she'd ever had, or was likely to have, in her life. Ruth smoothed her chic black dress over her hips and regarded herself sideways in the mirror. 'You'll do,' she said to herself, satisfied with her appearance. After their encounter on the beach, Charlie had invited her out to dinner and Ruth, refusing to catch Peggy's eye, had accepted. She had arranged to meet up with him in the hotel bar and was feeling pleasantly fizzy inside at the prospect.

'So tell me all about Charlie,' Patricia insisted when Ruth finally joined her colleagues in the crowded bar, face carefully made up and blonde hair elegantly styled. Peggy and Patricia had gone down earlier and bagged a table, knowing seats would be hard to come by later. The delegates were gearing themselves up for a riotous evening and the hubbub was growing noisier by the minute.

'He was a wild lad at school. You know the sort, always at the centre of everything.'

' "Nasty little boy" is the expression you're looking for,' interjected Peggy waspishly.

Ruth considered this. 'Not nasty, mischievous.'

'I remember one year, he burnt down every bonfire in Skelthwaite – on November fourth. He was a wicked little so-and-so,' Peggy continued, her memories clearly very different from Ruth's.

Ruth sighed. 'He was handsome, though.'

'Still is,' Patricia said, impressed.

'In a crude sort of way,' Peggy offered.

'And romantic!' Ruth ignored her sister-in-law. 'He was going to travel world and write poetry.'

Peggy looked dour. 'Well, he got to Scarborough.'

'Peggy never liked him because when I split up with Simon, I—'

'You and Simon split up!' Patricia's jaw dropped.

'Only for a couple of weeks when I was sixteen. Anyway, I went out with Charlie,' Ruth explained.

'You never!' Patricia's tongue was virtually hanging out. 'Did you sleep with him?'

'Please!' Peggy groaned.

'I'm not telling you that!' Ruth said coquettishly. Her eyes sparkled. 'But he could kiss like an angel.'

'So how come you ended up with Simon? No offence, Peggy,' Patricia added hastily.

Ruth took a long swallow of her gin and tonic. 'Simon . . . he showed me how much he loved me.'

'Aaaaahhh. How did he do that?'

'He hit Charlie over the head with a hammer.'

'He never did!' Peggy said crossly.

'He did! You know he did!'

'Speak of the devil,' said Patricia, glancing up and seeing Charlie coming towards them. Charlie was fashionably dressed in a slim-fitting, obviously designer suit with a casual top underneath, unbuttoned at the neck to reveal a tiny shell pendant on a leather thong He was deeply tanned, his firm jaw flecked with golden stubble, and he wore a single earring, all of which combined to give an off-duty film-star effect. 'Yum, yum,' Patricia slavered.

'Ruth. You look fantastic,' he exclaimed, holding out his hands. She rose and took them, blushing faintly. 'I was going to wear this tonight, anyway,' she replied, mostly for Peggy's benefit.

He helped her on with her coat. 'All set?'

She looked back at the others, feeling guilty. 'Are you sure you don't mind?' Not that she needed to ask Peggy's permission, but she could see her nose had been put out of joint . . .

'No, you run along. We'll be fine,' Peggy replied jauntily.

'OK. I won't be long. Perhaps I can hear your speech when I get in.'

'It's alright – Patricia can hear it.' At this, Patricia's face dropped. She had been looking forward to letting her hair down in the hotel disco with all the other conference-goers.

'Don't worry, Peggy, I'll look after her,' Charlie said,

putting a protective arm around Ruth.

'It's nothing to do with me. I'm not her keeper.' She turned to Ruth and said, offhand, 'D'you want me to speak to Simon?'

'I've just called him. They're both fine.' Ruth picked up her bag. 'Bye.'

The two of them disappeared into the hotel lobby. They made a glamorous couple, both of them turning heads as they made their way out. Peggy watched them go, annoyed, and noticed Patricia following Charlie with saucer-shaped eyes. 'Don't dribble, Pat,' she snapped, and stomped back upstairs to rethink her speech about death.


Simon took advantage of his wife's absence to have a lads' night in, complete with beer, pizza and football. The Goddards had the sports channel on satellite and a massive, widescreen television, so the opportunity to watch a big international match live was snapped up by Dick, Kenny and Vic. Lucy, who had been dragged along by Vic to save on babysitting expenses, was less enthusiastic, complaining that football was boring and she wanted to watch cartoons. She had her eyes glued to the remote control by Dick's elbow and was biding her time. Dick, comfortably ensconced on the sofa, was filling his face with a huge slab of pizza, while beside him Kenny crunched on a crisp, green apple. 'Here, have some of this.' Dick proffered a wedge of deep-pan pepperoni, dripping with mozzarella.

'No thanks, mate,' Kenny replied mildly, taking another bite with his whiter-than-white teeth.

Dick scowled, riled by Kenny's dedication to healthy living. 'Get a life, Kenny. You take this thing too far. We're not professional sportsmen.'

'I noticed that, mate.'

'We play for the love of the game.'

'Me too. I just love it more if we win.' Kenny hurled the core accurately into the wastebin on the other side of the room.

'Dad always misses when he does that,' Lucy piped up, coming round the side of the sofa, her quarry in sight.

'Thanks, Luce. Grass me up,' Vic spluttered, getting up to make hot drinks. The Goddards' spacious, farmhouse-style fitted kitchen was a mess, empty pizza cartons and crumpled lager cans cluttering the large pine table, in the middle of which Simon had cleared a space to lay Alfie out on his changing mat. 'I think I'll just pop a cork in him till Ruth comes home,' he said, wrinkling his nose as he examined the baby's nappy.

Vic sniffed. 'He is a bit whiffy, int he?'

'Sign of virility. I'd better stick him int bath.'

'Not too hot.'

'I know "not too hot",' Simon replied, peeved. 'You just make the coffees, Doctor Spock. Two sugars for me.'

At that moment, Lucy burst in screaming, hotly pursued by Dick. 'Little terror's pinched remote and left us with Bugs Bunny,' he explained, prowling round the kitchen. 'Grrrr. You can run but you can't hide, Luce. Pizza monster's coming to get you.'

'Sugar?'

'Just the one.'

'She's behind door,' Vic revealed disloyally. After a short spell of tickling, Lucy relinquished her prize and they settled down to watch the match.

'Look at him! Four million quid and he wears gloves! It's a disgrace.' Dick jabbed his finger at the screen.

'He's from Africa. It'd be like you playing football in Antarctica,' Vic said mildly.

Kenny took a sip of his drink. 'Good coffee, Vic.'

Simon nodded his agreement. 'Ruth's had me on that semi-skimmed stuff – dunt taste the same at all.'

'It just sends wrong signals to opposition, dunt it?' Dick continued to rant.

'What does?'

'Wearing gloves.'

Simon peered into his mug. 'Vic. Where d'you get milk from?'

'From fridge.'

'In a little plastic bottle?'

'Yes.'

'That's Ruth's breast milk.'

There was a pause while the four men absorbed this information and its ambiguous connotations, then the sound of unanimous spitting.

Charlie had booked a table at an expensive fish restaurant on the waterfront which looked out over the bobbing lights of the harbour. A dinner-jacketed pianist played discreetly in a far corner of the softly lit room as the head waiter ushered them to their table by the window. Charlie smiled at Ruth from over his menu. 'They do a good Chablis here.'

'Fine by me.'

'And the mullet is always excellent.'

'Sounds good.' She looked at him across the candlelit table, so relaxed, worldly, a far cry from the wild youth she had once dated, and felt suddenly shy. 'Where did you go to after we left school? I always wondered.'

'Oh, I lived in Australia for a couple of years. Went surfing in South Africa. Had a look at Nepal and Goa.'

Ruth gazed at him with new respect. 'You said you'd do it and you have – that's brilliant, Charlie.'

'I don't know about that,' he said, staring deep into her eyes. Ruth ducked her head and fiddled distractedly with the stem of her wine glass. 'I'm still right where you left me. I haven't done anything you wouldn't have put money on me doing.' There was a note of frustration in her voice.

Charlie took a bread roll, tearing it methodically into small pieces as he spoke. 'Sometimes I'd be on a bus or in a car and I'd go by some little-known town or other. Lights on, dinner in the oven, kids waiting for the sound of his key in the door . . . I really wanted that sort of life.'

'The whole world has that sort of life.'

'Once I was so envious I got off the bus and tried it for myself,' he admitted.

'You met someone?'

He nodded. 'After a while I'd be lying in bed at night, listening to the trains going by, wondering what it's like around the next corner, over the next hill. So I got back on the bus.'

'How did you end up in Scarborough?' she asked, fascinated.

'I didn't want to be in my forties and fifties, still drifting. I had a few dollars saved up. I'd always liked it here. I've got a little surf shop in North Bay. I like it, it keeps me busy.'

The waiter brought their starters, a crab salad for Ruth and bouillabaisse for Charlie, interrupting their conversation. When he had gone, she said, curiously, 'Have you ever been back to Skelthwaite?' Charlie shook his head and continued to eat his soup. 'Why not?'

'Because . . . it doesn't matter. Have some more wine.' He refilled her glass. Intrigued at why he was avoiding the question, she persisted. 'Why not, Charlie?' He took a sip of his own wine and paused, looking uncomfortable. Eventually, he said, quietly, 'Because you were there'.

'Me?' Ruth sat back in astonishment.

'I'd heard you'd married Simon – I knew you would. I just didn't want to bump into you and talk about the weather and where I'd been and who was doing what.'

'I wasn't even sure you'd remember me,' she gasped.

A shadow passed across his features. 'Yes, I remember you. When you went back to Simon that time, I was . . .' He let the sentence hang in the air between them, and for the first time Ruth realized how much she'd meant to him.

'But we were just kids.'

He sighed and ran a hand over his cropped hair. 'That's what I kept saying to myself – you're just a kid. It can't be her, she can't be The One, you haven't even left bloody

Skelthwaite yet. But I didn't believe it then—' He looked her straight in the eye and drew a deep breath, '—and I don't believe it now.'

'He's amazing, isn't he? He's seventeen, never been to London before. Just look at him!' Wendy said, watching Stephen play pool, wielding his cue confidently and laughing with her mates. She was sharing a corner table in the pub with her best friend, Sophie, who did not seem to be as enamoured with Stephen as she was.

'Until he goes home to mummy and we start all over again,' Sophie interjected acidly.

Wendy blinked rapidly. She did not want to think about that. Stephen turning up on her doorstep out of the blue had made her so happy. In one moment, the empty feeling she'd been nursing in her guts ever since she'd left Skelthwaite was gone and she felt whole again. She had realized, walking alongside the canal with him, that this wasn't just some schoolboy crush on his part. The thought that they actually might have a future together started to crystallize then, and the more she watched him talking and joking with her friends, the more the prospect became a reality. If he could be accepted by successful young professionals like Ryan and Barney, surely there was hope for the two of them? Not wanting to be lectured by Sophie, she got up and went over to the pool table and stood next to Stephen as he played a masterly shot.

He put an arm around her shoulders and, nodding at Ryan, said, laughingly, 'Let's see you get out of that one, then'. Joking to her to watch Ryan didn't cheat, he headed off to the loos. Wendy noticed Sophie button-holing him as he passed her table, and sighed. She hoped her friend wasn't giving him grief. She had half a mind to intervene, and then thought better of it. If they were going to be together, Stephen would have to prove himself on her territory, fight his own battles. Anyway, she reassured herself, he had done pretty well so far.

Ryan gave a shout of triumph and she turned back to the game. It was some time before she realized that Stephen had not returned.

Charlie's confession had a curiously liberating effect on Ruth. To be seen as someone other than a wife and mother – someone desirable, even – reconnected her with a part of herself that she was beginning to feel she had lost. The fact that this handsome, eligible man had travelled the world and yet still wanted her, the girl he had dated for two weeks as a teenager, both disturbed and excited her. More than that, though, it confirmed something that she'd always known in her heart, even if she did have cause to question it sometimes: she loved Simon. Faced with a choice – and from his intense expression, Ruth knew that Charlie was serious – there was no choice to be made.

'I always knew I was going to marry Simon. When I was eight and he put that frog in my knickers – I think I knew then,' she explained, as they walked back along the esplanade after the meal. 'I know some people don't like him – I mean, he can be a bit brash and a bit rude sometimes. He demands a lot of people. But they don't see what I see – he's kind and funny and he makes me feel strong.' She stopped, feeling suddenly self-conscious. 'I've had too much wine,' she said ruefully.

'No, go on.'

'Sometimes I watch him when he doesn't know I am – when he's fixing a plug or watching telly or something – and I get this feeling, right here, an actual, physical feeling.' She pressed her hands against her chest. 'I was always going to be with Simon. And I always will be.' They were silent for a while, both of them listening to the slapping of breaking waves and the rattling backwash of pebbles. 'Int it beautiful?' Ruth whispered softly, her face tipped up to the velvety black sky. A nearby church clock struck midnight and, as the last stroke died away, the two of them seemed to be trembling on the edge of a moment; a moment that Ruth, secure in her

156

marriage, hadn't experienced since she was sixteen and had never imagined happening again. 'Ruth, what would you do if I kissed you?' Charlie asked tentatively.

'I don't know,' Ruth answered honestly. She gave him an embarrassed grin. 'I hope you don't.' However intrigued she was – and the thought of being kissed by Charlie was not unpleasant – Ruth was sensible enough to resist. She wasn't about to betray Simon's trust for a moment's mad impulse.

Charlie gave an imperceptible shrug. He didn't share Ruth's high opinion of Simon, but this wasn't about settling old scores. He cared for her too much to do that. 'Well, this is me.' He indicated a narrow, quirky, three-storey house built like a tower.

'Is this where you live? It's lovely.'

'Come in and have a nightcap.'

Ruth looked apprehensive. 'I don't think so, Charlie. I should get back.'

'Come on,' he coaxed. 'I might not see you for another twenty years.'

'I'm so tired. I've had about three minutes' sleep since Alfie arrived.' She smiled apologetically.

His face fell. 'Sure. I understand.' He looked so hangdog that Ruth capitulated.

'Come on, then. One little drink.'

If a house described its owner, Ruth thought, taking in the eclectic interior of Charlie's bachelor abode, this one spoke volumes. It was decorated in Californian beach-house style and crammed with a hotchpotch of souvenirs, surfboards, ornaments, pictures and *objets trouvés* from his travels. She collapsed on a comfortable, rug-covered sofa while Charlie busied himself pouring brandies. He also, she noticed, lit some candles, which threw pools of warm, flickering light on the walls, casting the exotic wall hangings into deep shadow. A sinister carved wooden mask stared down at her and, for a second, it crossed her mind that she had placed herself in a vulnerable situation with Charlie, that he might try and seduce her. He sat down beside her and lifted his glass. 'Here's to . . .?' He looked at her questioningly.

'Friendship,' she said softly, 'and . . . finding your place in the world.'

'Have you found yours?' he asked, leaning forward, his eyes burning.

Ruth smiled to herself. 'Yes, I have. I dint think I was happy with it, to be honest, but now . . .' She glanced up at him shyly. 'Being away from Simon and Alfie, talking to you – it's made me really appreciate it.'

'Some people spend their whole lives looking for what you've got.'

'I know.'

She took a sip of brandy. 'I've got some photos – d'you want to see Alfie?' Without waiting for Charlie to reply, Ruth dug in her handbag. She hadn't seen her baby since early that morning and suddenly found she was missing him intensely. 'Here he is at a week old. And this is him at two weeks. Dunt he look like his dad?'

Charlie peered at the photos in the dim light. 'He does. Poor little mite. Only joking,' he added quickly.

Ruth passed him another. 'Here's Simon, celebrating Alfie's arrival.' The photo showed Simon in the bar, grinning from ear to ear. Charlie stared at it for a long time. 'One happy man,' he said at last, returning it to her.

She yawned hugely, overwhelmed with tiredness. 'I'm sorry. Here I am, boring the pants off you with my pictures and I'm the one yawning.'

'You're not boring me.' He studied her face, searching for a clue, a hint, anything to give him hope, but it was clear Ruth had only come in out of kindness and was dead on her feet. He took her hand and held it for a second, caressing the palm, then released it and stood up. 'I'll phone a taxi.' By the time he returned, she was fast asleep, still clutching the picture. 'Ruth?' He tried to wake her but she was out cold. Gently, he swung her legs onto the sofa and covered her with a rug, easing the photo out of her fingers. Simon, his old rival, beamed up at him, triumphant. 'You lucky bugger,' he murmured, blowing out the candles.

'Oi! Watch where you're going.' Stephen muttered an apology to the young couple he had just barged in to and stumbled on, hardly able to see where he was going for the tears in his eyes. His conversation in the pub with Sophie churned round and round in his brain, the same phrases sticking every time. 'Do you know what she's been like, since she's been back? I've never seen her so miserable.' Sophie's ambush had shattered him. 'Wendy was desperate to be a teacher. She could have done anything she wanted to but she wanted to teach. She loved that job and now she's lost it. Because of you.' Baffled, he had denied it, but then Sophie stuck the knife in. 'She's your mother, isn't she? She knew about you. She threatened to end Wendy's career.' When he said he didn't believe her, she'd poured scorn on his protestations, saying viciously, 'Why don't you go home and ask her? Better still, why don't you just go home? I've spent ages picking up the pieces of my best friend and I don't like it. It's never going to end happily, so it has to just end.'

Stephen rubbed his eyes furiously as he ran along the pavement, dodging pedestrians, barely aware of what he was doing or where he was going. All he could hear in his head was Sophie's parting words: 'If you really care about her you'll leave her alone and let her start again. That is, if you *really* care . . .'

# Chapter 12

'How am I going to look Simon int face after this?' Peggy, dressed in her best suit and pearls, paced up and down the hotel lobby, seething. When Patricia came down to breakfast by herself and timidly admitted that Ruth had not returned, there was only one conclusion she could draw. And in her mind's eye, she was drawing it vividly. *After all that rubbish Ruth came out with yesterday. I should have known! I should have known something were up and I shouldn't have let her go.*

'I'm sure nothing happened,' Patricia said soothingly.

'Her husband, my brother's at home with baby and she's off gallivanting around town with another man!'

Patricia glanced at her watch. 'Peggy, we should be there by now.'

'How can I give a speech when I don't even know where she is? She might be lying dead in a ditch somewhere.' Peggy's anger, notched up by nerves, was threatening to boil over. At that moment the door swung open and Ruth rushed in, still wearing her glamorous, but wholly inappropriate, little black dress, which now looked distinctly rumpled. 'I am so sorry,' she gabbled, heading for the stairs.

'Where the hell have you been?' Peggy waylaid her in a booming voice, causing the receptionist, a scrawny young lad with a prominent Adam's apple, to eavesdrop openly. 'I fell asleep at Charlie's.' Ruth had a huge ladder in her tights, her hair was uncombed and she had smudgy mascara all round her eyes.

161

'After doing what?'

'Not now, Peggy, please. I have to—'

'Is that what you're going to tell Simon? "I fell asleep at Charlie's"?' Peggy demanding, scathing. Several hotel guests who were signing out looked round at the outburst.

Ruth swung round, eyes blazing. 'Yes, it is, if it's any business of yours!'

Patricia, who had been trying to intervene, said anxiously, 'We really should be going.'

'You go, I'll catch up with you.' Ruth started towards the stairs again. A taxi driver put his head around the hotel door and called, 'Do you want this cab or not?', to which Patricia, attempting to propel Peggy outside, answered firmly, 'Yes, we do.' Peggy, however, would not budge. 'Once in my life I get to do something like this. I dint think it was too much to ask for a bit of support from my friends.'

'I said I was sorry,' Ruth snapped. 'I have to—'

'I might as well not bother now.'

The taxi driver sighed impatiently. 'Do you want this cab?'

'No!' Peggy replied sullenly.

Patricia got hold of her arm. 'Yes!'

'I'll see you there,' Ruth repeated, a look of desperation on her face.

'No, you won't!' Peggy stalled again. 'We'll all go together if we're going.'

'I can't.'

'Why not?'

'Because—' Ruth lowered her voice.

'You're not even going to bother to come?'

Ruth, losing her temper completely, grabbed her chest and shrieked, 'Because if I don't get these to a breast pump soon I am going to bloody explode!' She crashed off up the stairs, leaving the receptionist gaping. 'I thought that only happened in aeroplanes,' the taxi driver muttered, scratching his head as he escorted Peggy and Patricia to the waiting car.

162

Stephen woke up in paradise. Tall, exotic plants with bright, spiky flowers greeted his bleary eyes in the pale daylight filtering through a lush canopy of greenery. His clothes stuck clammily to his body in the humid atmosphere, which was cloying with the perfume of the almost obscene stamens. Unfamiliar birdsong clamoured in his ears, along with the harmonious bubbling of a fountain. Stretching his stiff neck, he gazed around the tropical glasshouse. He had managed to get in last night – the old, rusty locks had proved easy to force – and had spent a fitful few hours curled up on a wooden bench. The only money he had was a pocketful of loose change, and with nowhere to go – contacting Wendy was not an option – the Victorian hot-house had seemed a lucky find. At least he had stayed warm and dry, even if he was hungry and dying for a cup of tea, he comforted himself, and it was better than spending a night on the street. Stephen had been shocked by the number of homeless people he had passed sleeping in shop doorways. He was just getting his stuff together when he heard the door open. Brisk, heavy footsteps rang out on the concrete floor. He looked up nervously to see three beefy security guards bearing down on him. 'Hi. Sorry. I had nowhere else to go. I – I haven't touched anything,' he stammered.

Their unsmiling expressions did not alter. 'You little bastard,' snarled one, lunging at him. Stephen tried to get away but the others had spread out and were blocking off other escape routes. 'I've had enough of you lot,' the man hissed, advancing towards him. 'It's time you were taught a lesson you won't forget.'

'But I haven't been here before! I'm not with anyone. Honest.' Stephen tried to retreat but the bench was in the way. He collapsed onto it, his heart hammering. The man loomed over him, his face menacingly close, breath reeking of stale cigarettes and coffee. 'Look, I'll pay for lock – I've got money back home, I'll send it. This is my first night sleeping rough. I didn't know—'

'Better make it your last then.' Stephen had a fleeting impression of cold blue eyes and a stubbled jaw before a fist smashed into his face, knocking him sideways. He felt sticky wetness on his cheek and noticed, almost objectively, the metallic taste of blood trickling down the back of his throat. 'Now get out.' The man hauled him up by his jacket and frogmarched him to the door, sending him sprawling onto the gravel outside.

'My stuff,' Stephen croaked through swollen lips, but the guard just grunted, 'Think yourself lucky you still got teeth' and slammed the door. Stephen got slowly to his feet, feeling sick and dizzy. One eye was closing rapidly. He limped off down the path, trying not to cry. Suddenly, Skelthwaite seemed a million miles away.

Stephen's absence was noted by Simon, who was watching – and gloating – from the sidelines as Kenny supervised the rugby team's Saturday-morning training session. 'Come on boys! Last ten minutes of a game's where it's won and lost,' Kenny exhorted as the Scorpions staggered up and down the pitch. 'First ten in our case,' remarked Simon, chipper. He hitched Alfie up on his shoulder. 'So where's Stephen?'

'Don't know. Didn't come home last night,' Kenny replied, his eyes glued to the playing field. He noticed Dick stumble and drop the ball and blew his whistle shrilly.

'His mother will kill him – *after* she's killed Vic.' Simon sounded delighted at the prospect. Kenny beckoned Dick over. 'On the ground, Dick! Give me ten!'

'I can't, man. I'm absolutely bloody knackered,' he complained, drooping.

'Don't talk! On the ground! Ten press-ups!' Kenny was brooking no argument. Dick, glowering, got down on his hands in the mud just as Vic wheezed by. 'He's a nutter, Vic. He's going to kill someone,' Dick panted.

'It'll be worth it. You want to win, don't you?'

'I think I'd rather live.'

Kenny frowned. 'I said no talking! Ten more, Dick!' This was a bit much, even for Vic, who was puce in the face himself from the exertion. He went to have a word with the over-zealous Kenny and was buttonholed by Simon. 'How's it going, Vic? You look like Alfie did when he came out.'

Vic ignored his taunt. 'I know you're keen, Kenny, but don't you think we're running before we've learned to crawl?'

'No, look at Dick!' Simon cackled, pointing. 'He's crawling.' Dick, belly-down in the mud, merely groaned.

Peggy blinked out into the darkened auditorium. The lights on the platform were dazzling and she couldn't see much, although she could make out enough rows of empty seats to realise that most of the conference-goers were probably still in bed nursing hangovers from the previous evening's boozy shenanigans. She rustled her papers with nervous fingers. The moment of truth had arrived. 'Good morning, ladies and gentlemen,' she said, leaning forwards towards the mike. The sound system shrieked with feedback. Flummoxed, she paused, clinging on to the lectern as if her life depended on it, then straightened up. 'Thank you for coming this morning – and I'd like to thank committee for inviting me to address you today. The title of my talk is "Palliative Care in the Community – A Nurse's Eye View",' she read from her notes. Peggy had learned this bit off by heart, but now that she was actually there, her mind had gone a complete blank. Moreover, her tongue felt like some unwilling creature that was refusing to co-operate with her teeth and her mouth was parched. With a shaking hand she picked up the water glass provided for speakers and took a large gulp, which was amplified around the lecture theatre. Someone in the audience giggled. Peggy cleared her throat. 'I have been a District Nurse in the town of Skelthwaite in West Yorkshire for twenty years. In that time I have seen a lot of people die.' She forced herself to look up and spotted Patricia sitting by herself near the front. Patricia smiled encouragingly. Falteringly, Peggy carried on.

'Each person's death affects so many people. Relatives, friends. And us – the carers – who have seen that person in their last weeks and with whom we have shared the most intimate moments of their lives. Even if we start as strangers we often end up as friends. And not one of those deaths happened without sending . . .' She turned the page and discovered, to her horror, that the next one did not follow on. Shuffling through the pages, trying desperately to remember what came next, she dropped some of them on the floor and, in stooping to pick them up, clouted the microphone. An almighty thud boomed out. 'Excuse me. Not one of those deaths . . .' she reread, trying to jog her memory. A mist was forming in front of her eyes, blurring the dancing words in front of her.

'Ripples,' hissed Patricia, who, having listened to numerous revisions the previous evening, could quote chunks of Peggy's speech verbatim.

'Each person's death . . .' Peggy floundered, not hearing her.

'Ripples!' Patricia called again, louder this time. Peggy looked up, bewildered.

'Ripples?' The audience began to titter and stir. Peggy wanted the earth to open up and swallow her. This was fast becoming the most terrible moment of her life. By now she had shuffled all her pages completely out of sequence and was hopelessly lost. She stared out into the auditorium, frozen with fear. Just as she was about to apologise and scurry off, there was a clatter at the back, causing everyone to swivel round. 'Sorry,' Ruth apologised, hurrying down to the front and sitting down next to Patricia. 'How's it going?' she whispered. Patricia's face said it all.

Stephen counted out the coins in his pocket with trembling fingers. He had just enough for the Tube fare up to Brent

Cross in North London, where the M1 began. From there he ought to be able to cadge a lift back. He shuffled along the pavement in a daze, the sea of besuited, briefcase-carrying office workers parting round him as people noticed his bruised and battered face and hurried on, not wanting to get involved. Washing his face in a Gents toilet, he saw why. His blood-encrusted upper lip, black eye, and torn and dirty clothing made him a intimidating sight, marking him out as someone to be avoided. On the Tube, commuters sat apart from him, as if he had an exclusion zone around him. Stephen realized that he probably smelled, too, but by then he didn't care. All he wanted to do was to get back to safety, to the place that he knew. He wasn't sure if he could call it home any more. Not after his mother's betrayal.

Peggy found the right place in her speech at last and ploughed on with it, her voice quivering. 'The thing I always try to teach my new nurses is that each and every person int world is going to die. There's no shame in that and there's no point in pretending we're going to be the first human being to live for ever. Because – and I hate to be the one to tell you this – we're not.' Her pause was punctuated by a loud snore from a less-than-captivated member of the audience who had fallen asleep. Two girls sitting behind Ruth and Patricia snorted with laughter, causing Ruth to swivel round and look daggers at them. 'Looks like that one's gone already,' Peggy said, trying to make a joke of it. This time, no-one laughed. She cleared her throat and returned to her notes, tracing each line with a finger to avoid losing her place.

'What I'm trying to say is that palliative care needn't be a depressing subject. I can honestly say I've learnt as much about life dealing with the dying than I have anywhere else. We should be proud of what we do. We should cry when we feel like crying and get cross when we feel like getting cross. We're not computers, we're people.'

A group at the back, who were paying no attention to

Peggy, started talking among themselves, hardly bothering to lower their voices. Ruth turned round again and glared. 'Excuse me! I'm trying to listen to this.'

'You must be dead already, then,' one of the men joshed.

'You little—' A furious Ruth had to be forcibly restrained by Patricia, who hauled her back into her seat by her coat. Peggy, who heard the exchange, was suddenly stung into retaliating. Her anger swelled up inside her, swamping her earlier nerves, and she put down her speech and addressed the audience directly. 'I'm very sorry. You want to get on and enjoy yourselves and I'm blathering on about dead people. Which has got nothing to do with us, has it?' she added sarcastically. 'We're never going to be lying on that bed in terror, are we? We're never going to be squeezing a stranger's hand int middle of night wondering if we'll ever wake up again if we go to sleep. We're never going to be surrounded by the people we love, seeing them grieving in front of us. Oh no, not us.' She took a deep breath, composing herself, and suddenly knew what she wanted to say. What she should have told them all along. The simple, unvarnished truth . . .

'I'm going to tell you one little story and then you can go and I'll feel like I haven't completely let myself down.' She stared out at the audience, challenging them now. People, she noticed, were sitting upright, listening, and the group at the back had fallen silent. Even the snorer had been prodded awake. Ruth smiled encouragingly.

'When I was fifteen years old, my mother died. I loved my mother and this was the most terrible thing that had ever happened to me – it still is. I couldn't believe life could be so horrible. She were in hospital a long time. Twice a day – every day – I'd go and talk to her and watch her trying to hide the pain from me. The nurses were lovely but they dint know my mum from Adam and sometimes they talked to her as if she was stupid. Like she must be stupid if she's dying. What a stupid thing to do – die. "Hello, Mrs Goddard",' she mimicked in a sing-song voice. ' "How are you this morning? Has your daughter been to see you? Has she?".'

Patricia and Ruth sat riveted. This was the return of the battling Peggy they knew and loved, but they had never heard her speak about her mother before. To open up to an auditorium full of people about something so intensely private stunned them both with her honesty and her courage.

'My mother and I tried to get a lifetime's living into those last weeks,' Peggy continued. 'We talked about practical things – how I would manage when she were gone – and we talked about big things. My father refused to believe it was happening and only talked about how she was looking better, how the doctors might be wrong. He brought her glossy holiday brochures for places that she knew she would never see. That was his way of coping with it, but it dint help my mother. She dint want her life to end in a lie like that.' Peggy was there, by her mother's bedside, reliving the experience, and the words poured out of her as if inspired. 'So we talked in this scrubbed, clean little ward, all starched sheets and jolliness and scary doctors who knew about everything. Everything, that is, except the only thing that really mattered – they knew nothing about my mother or where she was about to go and they were helpless to help her. And as each white-washed, hygienic day passed, the great, terrible thing that was her death got nearer and nearer until her fear started to obliterate her courage.

'One day, she turned to me and said she wanted to die in her own bed, surrounded by the people and things she cared about. So I went to see this big, scary doctor. He said, "No", how could they look after her away from the hospital? And I spoke to Dad, and Dad said "No" because doctors always know best, don't they? They've got qualifications and big houses – they must know best.' The memory was almost too much for her and Peggy stopped for a second and shut her eyes, holding on to the lectern to steady herself. The auditorium was so quiet that for a brief moment she wondered whether anyone was out there at all – perhaps they had all crept off to the bar – but when she reopened them she saw the rows of people sitting absolutely still, waiting for her to carry on with her story.

'I was only fifteen, but I kicked up such a fuss! I made them think about Mum – about the way she wanted to die, not about the way they wanted her to die. In the end they let me take her home if I promised to look after her.

'She lay in her bed – her lumpy old bed in this chilly little bedroom – with the sound of the television coming up from downstairs and my little brother shouting in the hallway and my dad making the most disgusting meals you can imagine – and she smiled. I promise you, she smiled. She wanted to die in the middle of her life. That's all. I sat with her at night and turned her so she could see the moon through the window and hear the drunks coming back from pub and smell the bread van first thing. And that's how she died that morning, with me holding her hand. It was so little to do with death and so much to do with life.'

Peggy surfaced from her memory like an underwater diver coming up, looking about her, almost disoriented. She saw Ruth and Patricia gazing at her, their faces wet with tears, and knew then how she was going to finish. 'A friend said to me yesterday that she had found her place in the world. I found mine that morning – my place int world. It's good there, I like it. Thank you very much for coming.'

There was a few seconds' silence, during which she assumed she'd bombed again, then warm applause lead by Ruth and Patricia, who were on their feet, clapping enthusiastically. Peggy, surprised and delighted, bowed her head as the applause swept through the auditorium and other people stood up. She had touched them. She had made a difference.

Afterwards, Peggy, Ruth and Patricia headed for the bar, where Peggy downed a large gin and tonic in record time. 'I will never, ever, do that again,' she announced breathlessly.

170

'Look at me.' She held out her shaking hands.

'I thought you were fantastic,' beamed Patricia.

Ruth caught hold of Peggy's hands. 'So did I,' she said softly.

Peggy laughed. 'Do you know what I'm going to do now?' They shook their heads. 'I'm going to have another one.' While another round was being ordered, Patricia nipped to the Ladies, leaving Peggy and Ruth alone. An unusual awkwardness – things said, things unsaid – hung in the air between them. 'What a day!' Peggy exclaimed brightly.

'That was . . . I never thought you could surprise me again, Peggy. I am so proud of you,' Ruth said, sounding choked.

'It's not so bad when you just say what you feel.'

Ruth knew what Peggy was really saying. 'Nothing happened last night, between me and Charlie,' she repeated, calm now.

'It's none of my business.'

'Of course it is. I'm inquisitive about the world, that's all. I sometimes wonder what might have happened to me if I'd made other choices, but . . . I love Simon and I love Alfie and I'm happy with the choice I made.'

Peggy nodded. 'I know that, pet.' They smiled at each other, the row forgotten, and clinked glasses. Peggy took another large swallow and said, 'I feel like letting my hair down a bit! What shall we do? Go to arcade? Or that ghost train – that'd be a giggle. Or we could have our palms read!'

Ruth put down her drink. 'I know what I'd like to do.'

'What, love?'

'I'd like to go home.'

Patricia, returning from the loo, concurred readily – 'She's dying to check on the lodger,' Ruth teased – so they went back to the hotel and packed up. The van was loaded and ready to go when Ruth suddenly said, 'Hang on a moment. I hope that Alfie's hungry,' and dashed off with her breast pump, just missing Charlie, who turned up two minutes later.

'Peggy,' he greeted her guardedly.

'Charlie,' she nodded.

'You're off then?'

'We are.'

'Will you give Ruth this?' He handed her some photographs. Peggy shuffled through them and saw they were all of Alfie and Simon. 'Imagine that,' Charlie said wistfully, 'To be loved so much she takes your photograph away with her for one night. Tell her thanks for the evening.'

'She won't be long. Tell her yourself.' Peggy turned round to see where Ruth had got to. When she turned back, Charlie had already left. Watching him lope away, a tall, lithe figure in snug-fitting jeans, even Peggy had to admit that Charlie was drop-dead gorgeous. Now if Vic only had a bum like that . . .

'Did you?' she grilled Ruth later, as they drove back across the Pennines in the dark.

'Did I what?' asked Ruth, who was behind the wheel this time.

'Sleep with Charlie when you split up with Simon?'

'Peggy,' Ruth remonstrated.

'I won't tell him.'

'Well . . . no, I didn't, as a matter of fact, although I won't say I wasn't tempted.'

'Right.' Peggy looked straight ahead, stony-faced. From behind them, Patricia snored gently. Peggy was silent for a few seconds and then gave her sister-in-law a naughty grin. 'Why ever not?'

After almost two days and a night of looking after Alfie by himself, Simon was so nonchalant about nappy-changing that he was doing it in the pub. Alfie, who was laying on a table surrounded by pints of bitter and overflowing ashtrays, was equally relaxed about it, although Terry, who was nearest to the business end, was less comfortable. 'Should you be doing that here, Simon?' he inquired, wrinkling his nose.

'Alfie doesn't mind.'

'It wasn't Alfie I was thinking about.' Terry wafted a beer mat in front of him.

'That's not Alfie you can smell.' Simon nodded in Dick's direction. Dick was determined to introduce Kenny to the delights of English pub food, with little success. 'Go on. One pickled egg's not going to hurt you,' he insisted, waving it in Kenny's face. Kenny wore an expression of distaste. 'My body is a temple, mate. You wouldn't understand.'

Vic was also at the table, staring gloomily into his pint. Stephen had still not made an appearance, and although his son's absence hadn't particularly bothered him until now – Stephen was old enough to look after himself – he knew Peggy would go into a major spin. Besides, he was getting just a little bit concerned himself. Vic beckoned Sally, who was clearing away empties, and handed her some change. 'Stick another half in there for Walter.' Walter, who was sitting on a bench nearby, grinned happily and waved his glass. Beside him, Lucy, taking everything in with beady eyes, was sucking orange juice through a straw noisily. 'Have you seen our Stephen today?' Vic added casually.

'No, Vic, sorry.' Sally disappeared with her tray.

Simon looked up from cleaning Alfie and said cheerfully, 'You're a dead man, Vic Snow.' He returned to the job in hand, just in time to catch Alfie peeing up into the air. 'Missed!' Simon dodged the stream of urine skilfully, only to see it fall as a shower into a fresh round of pints. The group was rendered momentarily speechless.

'I've had beer that tasted of cat's piss before, but even I'm not drinking that,' Dick said.

Kenny raised his eyebrows. 'You surprise me.'

'Your round, I think, Simon.' Terry fixed him with an 'I told you so' look. 'I'll have a clean glass.'

The conversation progressed to the Scorpions' forthcoming match against Hoxton and Kenny's training timetable for it, which Dick continued to protest about. 'You take out what you put in,' Kenny said unsympathetically. 'The harder you work, the better you get.'

'He dunt know what hard work is,' chipped in Simon, returning with the fresh pints.

Dick scowled. 'You get your money's worth out of me, thank you very much.'

'Imagine it, though, beating Hoxton!' Vic's face wore a faraway look. 'That would be worth every tired muscle, every drop of sweat.' There was a brief pause while they all considered this unlikely glory.

'We did it once in this dream I had. Fifty-seven–three we won,' Terry mused. 'Then I noticed referee was Jenny Agutter int *Railway Children* and I woke up.'

Kenny pushed aside the matchboxes he had been using to demonstrate a manoeuvre and asked seriously, 'How good *are* they, Vic?'

'Good.'

'It's like tackling trucks ont M1,' Dick confirmed.

Alfie added his own succinct comment by possetting curdled milk on Simon's shoulder. 'Can't hold his drink, can he?' Terry commented.

At that moment, the door opened with a rush of cold air and Peggy, Ruth and Patricia burst in to the pub, rubbing their hands and stamping their cold feet to revive their circulation. 'Three gin and tonics, please Sally,' ordered Peggy. 'That strange man there with moustache will pay.'

Vic leapt to his feet. 'Hello, love, how was speech?'

Peggy ducked the question, hugging Lucy and demanding to know what she was doing in the pub. 'Dad says it's cheaper than a babysitter,' Lucy chirped, 'And I've been having burping contests with Walter.' Peggy raised an eyebrow at Vic, who squirmed slightly. 'Come on – how was speech?' he insisted, changing the subject.

'I don't want to talk about it,' she replied wearily.

'Oh, you,' Patricia gave Peggy a little push. 'It were fantastic, Vic. We were that proud of her.' She glanced round

174

to look for Kenny, who had tried to hide his hulking form between Dick and Terry. 'There you are, Kenny.' She zoomed in on him, causing the others to grin at each other knowingly. 'Did you have those chops I left out?'

'Yes, Mrs Illingworth, thank you,' he said meekly.

Lucy jumped up and down in front of Peggy. 'Have you got present?'

Patricia pointed to their luggage by the door. 'Get my bag, love. There's sticks of rock for you and Walter. And there's one for you, Kenny,' she added shyly. Dick and Terry nudged him, sniggering rather obviously, and Patricia blushed.

'How's Stephen?' Peggy asked, settling herself down next to Vic. Ruth and Patricia slipped in on the bench beside them, Ruth cradling Alfie close, oblivious to everyone and everything else.

'Stephen?'

'Our son,' she said sarcastically.

Vic shifted in his seat. 'I'm sure he's fine.'

Peggy immediately smelt a rat. 'What d'you mean by that? Where is he?' Vic swallowed and was about to admit he didn't know when the pub door opened and Stephen entered.

'He's behind you, where d'you think he'd be?' he said, initially relieved and then horrified when he saw the state of him. Stephen's clothes were stained and ripped, his lip was swollen, his cheek was badly grazed and he had a livid black eye. In true saloon-bar style, the pub fell silent as everyone else caught sight of him.

'Stephen, what on earth have you done to your face?' Peggy said, aghast.

He came up to her, his expression grim, and suddenly she hardly recognized him any more. And not just because of his bruises. 'Never, ever, interfere in my life again' he shouted angrily. He stood there, breathing heavily. 'Is that clear?' Peggy's jaw dropped and for the second time that day she was speechless as Stephen turned on his heel and stormed out of the pub.

'What's all that about?' Vic asked, concerned.

'I'll tell you later.' Stephen had obviously found out the truth about Wendy's departure, Peggy realized. What else had happened she was too fogged with tiredness to attempt to work out. 'Is this day never going to end?' she sighed, exhausted.

Patricia rummaged around in her bag for the sticks of rock and drew out something long and pink. A split second before Lucy saw it she stuffed it back in again with a shriek of horror. 'What is it?' Peggy said, as Patricia collapsed, convulsed with giggles.

'Mrs Herrington's friend,' she spluttered. 'A present from swinging Scarborough.'

# Chapter 13

Peggy had got little out of Stephen about where he disappeared to or what had happened to him while she was away. He retreated into his room like a crab into its shell and only came out to make coffee and raid the fridge. Whenever he reappeared in the kitchen she chipped away at his stony carapace asking questions, until one evening he flung at her, 'I went to London, right? I saw Wendy. And I found out what you did. Satisfied? You should be – you ruined her career.'

'Look, love, I didn't mean to—' Peggy, who was washing up, turned round, hands dripping with suds.

'Of course you did,' he spat. 'You knew exactly what you were doing. I didn't know you could be so cold and calculating. My own mother.'

'I'm sorry. I just wanted the best for you.'

'Oh, sure,' Stephen leered. He pointed at his rainbow-hued eye. 'Like this, I suppose?'

'She never hit you?' Peggy gasped.

'I got – bloody – mugged!' he shouted. He slammed down his cup, slopping coffee all over the work surface.

'Shouldn't we report it?' she asked anxiously.

'No!' he bellowed. 'Just stop nagging and leave me alone.'

After Stephen's outburst in the pub, Peggy had been forced to tell Vic about her hand in Miss Atkins's sudden departure. She had not felt particularly proud of herself recounting it. Vic had sucked in his cheeks and whistled, but all he said was, 'That were a bit drastic, weren't it, Peg?' Nonetheless, she couldn't help feeling that she had let herself down. What she hadn't been able to work out was why. Any mother, she reasoned, would have done exactly the same.

Later that evening she went up to check on Lucy and couldn't resist the urge to pop her head around Stephen's door. The bad blood between them was making Peggy feel wretched: the atmosphere had infected the whole house. He was hunched over his desk, revising, his books illuminated by a pool of yellow light from an anglepoise lamp. 'You still up?' she said unnecessarily.

He did not turn round. 'Looks like it,' he muttered, continuing to scribble notes.

'You've got an exam int morning.'

'Is that right?' he replied sarcastically. 'I thought I was doing this for fun.'

'You'd be better off getting a decent night's sleep. What you don't know now—'

Stephen looked up at her at last. 'Will you shut door when you go?'

Peggy, getting angry herself, stepped right inside and pushed the door to behind her. 'How long is this going to go on?' she demanded.

'What?'

'I said I was sorry about your little teacher friend. I should have spoken to you. But I was only doing what I thought was right.'

'No, you weren't!' he blazed. 'You had to stick your nose in because it was something I had that had nothing to do with you.'

'Don't be so ridiculous.'

'It's true. I'm not a kid any more—'

'Stop acting like one, then.' Any attempt at peacemaking had evaporated as Peggy's rage built up a head of steam.

'I'm going to pass this exam.' He said it quietly, menacingly.

'I hope you do – you should have passed it first time around.'

'D'you know why?' Stephen continued, ignoring her. 'Because it's my ticket out of here, that's why.'

'Good,' Peggy hurled back. 'Tell me when you're going and I'll pack your bag.'

'You don't need to pack my bag! You don't need to do anything for me any more.' Having made his total rejection of her clear, Stephen returned to his books. Out on the landing, Peggy found she was shaking.

His two days of father-son bonding with Alfie had given Simon cause to rethink his stance on child-rearing, a view he had been expounding to Vic over several pints in the safety of the Skelthwaite Arms. 'I'm not shaying every woman should be at home chained to kitchen sink—' he slurred.

'I should hope not,' Vic interrupted, taking a large bite out of a toasted cheese-and-ham sandwich. 'Half your employees are working mothers.'

'I know, I know.' Simon batted his hand at him. 'What I'm shaying is . . .' A befuddled look passed across his face as he lost the thread of his argument.

'What *are* you saying?' Vic asked, chewing hungrily. He had had no tea and he strongly suspected that Peggy would have packed up catering for the night.

'She dunt need to do it, does she? She dunt need to work at all yet she's back full-time now. You tell me why she spends her days up to her elbows in other people's blood and pus—'

'Excuse me! Man eating sandwich here.'

'—when she could be home all day int warm with Alfie. Give me the choice and I wouldn't think twice.'

'Hmmn.' Given the state of the kitchen when he and Lucy went over, Simon-as-househusband was a concept that Vic had a little trouble with. 'I remember when our Stephen was born,' he said, by way of a cautionary tale. 'I just mentioned to Peggy that maybe she could – you know – knock nursing on the head for a while and concentrate on being a mum.'

'What did she say?'

Vic made a play of untucking his shirt. 'Have I ever shown you those scars?'

But Simon was not to be deflected. The thought had been growing in him for some time that the answer to their chaotic lifestyle was for Ruth to give up work. It wasn't as if he couldn't provide for them, after all. If Ruth was less hassled, he reasoned, everything would be better. Alfie would be looked after properly, by his mother rather than a stranger. Their life would be less disrupted, they might have proper meals together again – even sex might be possible. Ruth had been more affectionate since their night apart, telling him she loved him and she'd missed him, but now she had started work full-time again she was always dog-tired. Simon was beginning to feel he came rather low on her priorities.

'Sally – here a minute,' he said, waylaying her as she passed, collecting up glasses. 'If I said to you, you could have anything you wanted, lovely house, lovely baby—'

'Simon, I never knew you cared,' she replied, hand on heart.

'—you'd jump at chance, wouldn't you? I mean, no woman really wants to work, do they, not when they could be at home with their baby?'

'Have you talked to Ruth about this?' Sally asked tactfully.

'Not yet.'

'He's going to tell her to give up job,' Vic explained.

'Why don't you have a little word with Ruth, before you decide her future?' Sally began mopping their table, emptying crisp packets and ashtrays into a bin-liner. 'You're a good customer, Simon, and I'd hate you to die and leave a hole in my profits.' She took in his glazed expression and added wearily, 'Take him home, Vic'.

Outside, lurching along pavements glistening with newly formed frost, Simon continued to expand on his theme. 'The thing is, it's a major life change when you have children, int it? You have to make adjustments.'

'No more drinking int pub every night,' Vic said dryly.

'Kid has to come first,' Simon agreed.

'So you are now going to go home and tell Ruth she has to give up work?'

'No, no, no.' Simon shook his head in an exaggerated fashion at his brother-in-law's naivety. 'Not "tell". You've got to use psychology. She has to think she's made decision for herself.'

Vic snorted. 'What kind of flowers would you like at your funeral?'

'You'll see.' Simon tapped his nose. 'That is why I am a Chief and you, Vic, will always be an Indian.' So saying, he slipped on the icy surface and slithered into someone's privet hedge, yelping. Vic, extracting him from the bushes, tutted, 'Someone's going to be in heap-big trouble when they get home.'

Ruth, glancing at the kitchen clock, saw that it was gone eleven. Simon had promised to be home by nine o'clock. She carried on folding baby clothes, trying not to feel resentful. She had a busy day scheduled for tomorrow. The last thing she needed was Simon rolling in drunk and waking up Alfie at midnight. The doorbell rang and she peered cautiously out of the hall window, wondering who on earth it was calling at that time of night. It was Walter. He was wearing nothing but a T-shirt and his usual half-mast trousers, but seemed impervious to the cold. 'Have you got key?' he said, when she opened the door.

'Come in, Walter, you'll catch your death.' Ruth hustled him inside. Walter immediately pounced on a scarf clip she had left lying on the hall table. 'Can I have badge?'

'No, Walter, you can't.' She removed it gently from his fingers. 'Now, what have you done? Have you locked yourself out again?'

Walter nodded vigorously. 'Feed birds. Birds asleep. Door locked.'

181

Walter had a habit of shutting himself out of his ground-floor flat, which was why Ruth held a spare key. Tonight, however, she was feeling less charitable than usual about dealing with him, and when he repeated his request for the key, she snapped, 'I'm looking, aren't I? I'm sick of this, Walter', feeling close to breaking point inside. The baby monitor crackled and Alfie's start-up wail sounded like a siren going off. 'Oh, Alfie,' Ruth said, frustrated, still scrabbling about in a drawer. 'Alfie,' Walter echoed, delighted at hearing his little friend in full voice.

'Here it is.' Ruth retrieved the key. 'Don't lose it – this is the last one we've got.' She placed it in his palm and closed his fingers around it, then looked at him and sighed and fetched him an old jacket of Simon's. 'There you go, put this on. What are we going to do with you, Walter?' she said, relenting. She did up the zip, pulling the collar up around his neck.

'Don't know,' Walter laughed good-naturedly.

'I'll come and see you int morning, alright?' Ruth propelled him towards the door. Walter stopped suddenly, a bemused look on his face. 'Have you got key?' he repeated. Ruth grabbed his clenched fist, exasperated, and opened it to reveal the offending item. 'Here. I just gave it to you.' She stood back and looked at him. This was not going to work. At this rate, Walter was certain to lose the key before he'd even got back. She would have to take him home herself, which meant getting Alfie up again because Simon, her caring, sharing husband, still wasn't back from the pub. 'Stay right where you are,' she said crossly, running upstairs to placate the now-screaming baby. Walter grinned happily.

The minute Ruth unlocked the door to Walter's flat, she knew something was wrong. An acrid smell, stronger than the pong of catfood that normally prevailed, assaulted her nostrils. Only too aware of Walter's history of domestic accidents, she followed him inside, Alfie cradled in one arm. 'Walter, have you left something on?' she asked, sniffing. Hearing a crackling noise, she pushed past Walter, who was standing, transfixed, in the doorway to the living room, and saw flames leaping from an armchair which had obviously been left too close to the electric heater. 'Oh, my God.' Ruth took in the scenario at a glance, bundling Alfie into Walter's arms. 'Take Alfie outside!' she ordered, looking for something to quench the fire. She beat ineffectually at the flames with a cushion, but the fire had a good hold and was starting to roar. Casting around for a blanket or rug, Ruth looked over her shoulder and realized Walter was still in the doorway, eyes goggling. Alfie's little face was bright with the reflected orange glow of the flames, which were climbing higher and higher, licking towards the ceiling. 'Walter! Outside! *Now.*' Ruth shouted, coughing, as thick black smoke curled from the upholstery and began to envelope the room. Startled, Walter finally began to move, just as the stuffing of the chair ignited with an explosive whoosh, turning it into a fireball. Ruth, caught unawares, staggered backwards and almost fell. The heat on her skin was intense and her eyes were streaming, making it difficult to see what was happening in the smoke. Panic started to bubble up inside her. Had Walter got Alfie out safely? Giving up on the chair, she blundered towards the door, just as a dark male figure materialized in front of her. 'Walter, get back!' she screamed, terrified for her baby.

'Ruth?' An arm stretched out towards her, pulling her into the hallway. It was Simon, with Vic close behind him. 'I'm alright! Where's Alfie?' she said, looking around wildly.

'He's outside, he's alright,' reassured Simon, suddenly sober.

'Bloody hell,' said Vic, ripping a fire extinguisher Ruth had failed to notice from the wall. Walter's shouts of 'On fire! On fire!' had attracted their attention as he and Simon were wending their way home. The last person they had expected to find in the blazing flat was Ruth.

'Go and get the Crosses out!' Ruth spluttered, pointing to the flat above.

'And get fire brigade,' Vic added, aiming the extinguisher at the flames.

'For Christ's sake, Ruth, you're not staying here!' Simon hauled her into the fresh air by her sleeve. Neighbours were beginning to gather outside, some of them wearing coats over their dressing gowns, bare legs conspicuous in slippers. Jenny Cross, a single mother who lived in the upstairs flat, leaned out of the window, a crying toddler in her arms. Her tousle-headed young son, Richard, was visible beside her in his pyjamas. 'What is it?' she shouted, alarmed.

Simon cupped his hands. 'Fire! Get yourselves out!'

Shivering on the pavement, confused by the people running about and shouting, Walter recognized the clamour of an approaching fire engine and hugged the startled baby closer. 'Bloody hell, Alfie.'

By the time the flames had been doused and Walter's charred armchair removed, most of the street was milling about outside his flat. Feelings were running high; residents who had initially tolerated Walter's ineptitude were angry at having their lives put in danger. Peggy, who Ruth had called up on her mobile, had her hands full dealing with the battery of complaints.

'He's a danger to himself and a danger to everyone else. He's flooded house, he's burnt pans—' Mr Hobbs, Walter's elderly next-door neighbour began in a quavery voice. He was interrupted by an agitated Jenny Cross. 'I feel sorry for him, Peggy, I really do – but I live above him, I've got two kids to worry about.' She clutched the childrens' hands tightly.

'I know, love,' Peggy said sympathetically.

'We'll talk to someone int morning,' Ruth added.

'No! I'm sick of talk! He has to go, Peggy. It's not fair on rest of us,' Jenny insisted. Mr Hobbs nodded vigorously. Ruth opened her mouth to speak but was distracted by Simon, who barked irritably, 'Ruth! Come on!' to her from the car.

'I'd better go,' she said, embarrassed and annoyed at being shouted in public. 'I'll see you tomorrow.'

'Alright, love,' Peggy replied. Now the excitement was over and the firemen were packing up, people were starting to drift back to their beds. Walter, sitting in the blackened remains of his chair on the pavement, surveyed the scene like a deposed monarch, his cat on his knee.

'You're sure you don't want to come home with us, Walter? Just for tonight?' Vic asked.

Walter shook his head violently. 'My house.'

'I know it's your house, Walter – but just for one night.'

'My house,' Walter repeated, gripping the arms of the chair.

'So. Would you like to tell me what the hell you thought you were doing?' Simon confronted Ruth after she'd put Alfie to bed. Ruth knew this was coming. Simon had been simmering with tight-lipped anger ever since the immediate threat of the fire had passed and they had driven home in strained silence. 'Not now, Simon,' she said wearily. She had no reserves left for a row.

'Yes, now. I want to know. What were you doing there? It's middle of night, you're not on duty—'

'Keep your voice down!' Ruth hissed. 'I've just put him down.'

'—next thing I know you're taking a baby into a burning building!'

'Don't exaggerate – one armchair caught fire.'

'The whole house could have gone up! And you and Alfie in it!'

Ruth took a deep breath and said, as patiently as she could, 'Alfie was outside with Walter. He was completely safe.'

'Completely safe!' Simon's skin had flushed almost as red as his hair. 'Walter's the one who set fire to chair int first place! You don't mix Alfie with your job, it's not safe!'

There was no talking to Simon in this mood, thought Ruth.

He would keep bludgeoning the point without listening to a word she had to say. If she was honest, the incident had frightened her, too, but she trusted Walter with Alfie. It wasn't as if he was going to run off with him. 'I'm tired and I'm going to bed,' she said, turning on her heel.

'I'm not having it.'

Ruth swung round. 'I *beg* your pardon?' she said, enraged.

'If you want a bloody job so badly I'll find you a bloody job int factory.'

'I've got a job, thank you very much.'

'It's not a job, it's an obsession,' he shouted, banging the kitchen table with his fist. 'You spend more time with Peggy and your patients than you do with me and Alfie.'

Stung by the accusation, Ruth felt herself snap. 'That is not true! Alfie wants for nothing!'

'Alfie wants *you*! Not some childminder!' As if on cue, Alfie began to cry again from upstairs, coughing, whimpering sobs that had Ruth starting towards the stairs again in an instant. Shaking with fury at Simon's heavy-handedness, she turned in the doorway and said, 'You – be – very – careful,' wagging her finger for emphasis, before slamming the door behind her.

The following morning, the atmosphere at breakfast was still tense. Ruth and Simon had slept back to back, not speaking, something that rarely happened – they made a pact when they married never to go to sleep with cross words between them. Ruth, in her uniform, was flying around the kitchen trying to dress Alfie, pack his changing bag and eat toast, all at the same time, while Simon sat at the table, drinking coffee. 'I can do that,' he volunteered at last, breaking the frosty silence.

'No, no, you sit there. I've only got the childminder coming in a minute and a job to get to and dips to make for Peggy's birthday do tonight.'

'Then let me see to Alfie.'

'And have you accuse me of not looking after my baby?

No, I'm alright, thank you,' she replied coldly.

Simon put down his cup. 'Ruth—' he began, trying to make peace. The doorbell rang and he went to get up, but Ruth was too quick for him. Tucking Alfie under one arm, she swept out of the kitchen saying loudly, 'Come on, Alfie. Let's go and let in the evil childminder.' Simon, realizing he should have stuck to the psychological approach, sighed. He had not handled this well at all.

In the Snow household, Peggy had woken to an altogether warmer reception: breakfast in bed, courtesy of Lucy, along with a stack of birthday cards, which Lucy had brought up on the tray. 'Thanks, love. Is this for me?' Peggy opened a gaudily wrapped present. 'Look at that! My favourites!' she exclaimed, holding up a box of chocolates and putting off her healthy eating plan for another few days.

Vic, who had been woken abruptly by Lucy pinching his nose, reared up from under the duvet, his grey hair wild. 'Happy birthday, Peg. You don't look a day over seventy-two,' he joked, leaning over and kissing her.

'Thank you very much.'

There was a knock on the door and Stephen entered. 'Happy birthday,' he said, as insincerely as he could get away with. Vic glanced at Peggy and took a sip of the tea Lucy had brewed. He winced and put his mug down. 'I haven't got you anything yet,' Stephen added, in tones that suggested he might not, either.

Peggy, who deeply regretted what she had said the night before, said brightly, 'That's alright, you've had a lot on'.

'Stephen's tight,' commented Lucy, who had clambered over Vic and was sandwiched safely between her parents.

'Come in and sit down.' Peggy patted the side of the bed.

'No, I'd better get ready.' A curt Stephen left without saying goodbye, leaving Peggy feeling suddenly deflated. *I am forty-five years old and my son hates me*, she thought. She and Vic exchanged a look.

'Exam nerves,' he said, putting an arm round her shoulder. 'He'll be OK later.'

An emergency meeting about Walter was hastily convened that morning in the nurses' office at Skelthwaite Health Centre. Louise Winters, the occupational therapist who was one of the team responsible for overseeing Walter's case, had driven over at once and was listening intently as Peggy described what had happened. 'He's always been borderline, we knew that when his mother died,' she commented. 'We thought he was better off on his own than in an institution – you said that yourself, Peggy.'

'I know.'

'Now you're saying his circumstances have changed?' Louise, an intense, dark-haired young woman, started scribbling notes on a pad.

'Not so much Walter, although he's not getting any easier. But in the early days the neighbours helped out a lot more. Cooking, shopping – just keeping an eye on him.'

'That was one of the reasons we kept him in the community.'

'I think the novelty's worn off,' Ruth said bitterly.

Peggy explained, 'He's had a few accidents over the years.'

'Nothing too serious, though,' Ruth chipped in, trying to soften Peggy's words. Despite everything, she felt guilty, as if they were telling tales out of school.

'I'm not blaming anyone. His neighbours have got kids and mortgages, they've got their own lives to worry about,' Peggy continued.

'It's very disappointing.' Louise made another note.

'We could go round a bit more, Peg.'

'No, we couldn't.' Peggy was decided on that score. 'We've got other patients, we've got our own families to look after. We did our best, we gave him every chance.' She turned to Louise and said, firmly, 'He needs sheltered accommodation.'

Louise looked doubtful. 'It's not that easy.'

'I think Walter would thrive in a place where he had his own space but where there were people to look after him.'

'What will Walter think?'

'He'll hate it. He loves that little flat,' Ruth said.

Peggy was brisk. 'He just hates change, that's all. We'll make a fuss of him, we'll make it seem like an adventure. As long as he's around people he trusts . . .' She glanced at Ruth, who nodded reluctantly, knowing in her heart that Peggy was right. 'I heard Mrs Pentland died up at St Stephen's. I thought if there was a room available there—'

'Hang on, Peggy.' Louise stood up. 'Let's go and see Walter first.'

Walter's flat was a depressing scene. It smelt like a day-old bonfire: the walls and ceiling were scorched, wallpaper hung off in strips and there were huge bubbles in the plaster. Louise stepped into the living room and the soggy carpet squelched under foot. 'I see what you mean.'

'It looks a bit worse than it is,' Ruth said defensively.

'It's freezing in here.' Louise drew her coat tighter around her.

'The electrics shorted. Has that electrician not come yet, Walter?' Peggy asked. Walter shook his head.

Louise turned to Walter, who was hovering in the background. 'I hear you had a bit of an accident last night, Walter.'

'Fire.' He hopped from foot to foot.

'I bet that was a bit frightening.'

Walter grinned. 'Got new chair.' He displayed an ancient, mouldering armchair that he had retrieved from the town dump that morning and brought home on a supermarket trolley.

'It's very nice.' Peggy admired it, noticing the huge hole in the seat and the springs falling out underneath.

'How have you been, Walter, apart from last night?' Louise continued.

'Fantastic.'

Peggy grimaced. 'We've had a few little adventures, haven't we, Walter?' She lowered her voice. 'Those marks there are where a firework went off.'

'A firework?'

'Fantastic!' Walter repeated happily.

'And we've had a couple of floods from bathroom. Couple of kitchen fires.'

Louise had seen and heard all she needed to. 'Alright Peggy, I'll speak to the team, see what we can come up with.'

As they went to go, Ruth noticed Walter had a white envelope in his hand which he had produced from a drawer. 'Peggy,' she said, stopping them. Peggy turned round. 'Happy birthday,' Walter said, beaming innocently at her.

'Thank you, Walter.' Peggy took it and gave him a kiss. She felt like Judas.

# *Chapter 14*

'Roll out the bar-rel,' Vic sang, pushing a metal barrel of beer into the living room in preparation for Peggy's birthday party that evening. Peggy, who was cleaning the french windows, gawked at it and said, 'How much beer do you intend drinking?'

'It's not for me, love, it's for guests.'

Peggy continued to polish the same bit of window, her thoughts elsewhere. A robin in the garden cocked his head and looked back at her, bright-eyed. Snow was beginning to fall in big, fluffy flakes, drifting down like white feathers and settling on the top of the fence. 'Where's Stephen?' she asked. Dealing with Walter had put him temporarily out of her mind, but since she'd got home at lunchtime she had been able to think of nothing else but the bitter words they'd exchanged. She and Stephen had argued before, but never like this, never nastily. Usually, things blew over quickly, but judging by the expression on Stephen's face that morning, it would be a long time before he forgave her. If ever.

'He's probably with friends,' Vic said reassuringly. He heaved the barrel up onto a table with a groan. 'Careful!' Peggy warned. She looked at him anxiously. 'He always runs home and tells me how he got on.'

'Don't worry about him.'

'I *do* worry about him.'

Vic began tapping the keg of beer. 'He's still sulking about that teacher business, that's all – he's punishing you.'

It was more than that, Peggy knew. She had – or used to have – an emotional connection with Stephen, her first-born, that was as intimate as if they were still linked by an invisible cord. She could always tell what he was thinking. They did not have the kind of antagonistic relationship that most teenage sons had with their mothers. Stephen confided in her. They were friends. Until Wendy Atkins came along. Since then, he had shut her out completely, severing their special bond as brutally as . . . Peggy couldn't quite bring herself to draw the comparison. What she had done was a different kettle of fish altogether.

'I feel like I'm losing him, Vic,' she confessed, feeling suddenly tearful.

'Hey, hey.' Vic, seeing her so downcast, stopped what he was doing and came over. 'This is your birthday, love – H.A.P.P.Y. Stephen will be alright.' He squeezed her round the waist and she gave him an unconvinced smile. A loud fizzing and spluttering caused them both to swivel round smartly, just in time to see the keg explode, spraying a foaming shower of beer all over the newly cleaned windows.

'It's going to smell like a brewery in here now,' complained Peggy when Vic had got the tap closed. She pulled on her rubber gloves again and retrieved the bucket.

'Simon'll never go home,' Vic joked. There was the sound of a key in the door, followed by footsteps in the hall. 'Stephen?' called Peggy. A thump as Stephen slung his bag down. She called again and this time he deigned to appear in the doorway to the living room. 'What?'

'What d'you mean, "what"? How did you get on?'

He shrugged. 'Alright. I'm just going for a walk.'

'You just got in.'

Stephen, ignoring her, went to leave, but Vic was having none of it. 'Oi! Excuse me, but could you manage a few more syllables here? We'd like to know how you did in your examination – if that's alright with you.'

192

Stephen sighed heavily. 'I think it went alright – there's nothing else to say.'

'Did the things you revised come up?' Peggy asked.

'Some did, some didn't.'

'Do you think you passed?'

'I don't know, do I?' he said, sounding hacked off. 'Can I go now?' Without waiting for an answer he left, slamming the front door behind him with such force that a gust of cold air swirled in. Peggy felt herself shiver violently. Vic looked at her unhappy face and made a decision. 'I'm going back to pub to get wine,' he said, putting on his coat. Peggy was left staring at the beer-sodden carpet. She did not feel in a party mood.

Stephen stormed blindly down the road, his head a maelstrom of emotions. Foremost was the thought that he couldn't wait to get away from his home and from Skelthwaite and the small-minded, interfering, parochial world view it represented. The exam, his ticket out, had been difficult, but he had tackled most of the questions. Would it be enough, though, to get him through this time? Even if he did pass, there wasn't any point in applying to a university near Wendy. That was ruined, as he'd told Henry. It had come out after the exam, when they had been discussing their hopes for the future. Stephen wasn't sure why he'd told Henry about his affair with Wendy – perhaps because it didn't matter any more: Wendy had gone, they were both leaving school themselves, the scandal was over. Or perhaps because he needed to talk to someone about what he'd been through. He couldn't talk to his mother any more. Henry was a poor second choice, all the more so because he'd got the hump about being left in the dark for so long.

'I can't believe you didn't tell me. I thought I was your best friend,' he had complained. He let it drop once he realized that Stephen was still suffering, and tried to cheer him up by suggesting their traditional cure-all, taking a four-pack up onto the moors. For Stephen, the thought of drinking cheap lager on a windy hillside had lost whatever appeal it once had. He had made his excuses and left, feeling lonelier than ever.

Now, Stephen made his way to the rec, a place he hadn't been to for years. It had changed a bit – an mini assault course of logs and ropes and ladders and platforms had been constructed on a floor of wood shavings – but the old swings and slides, see-saws and roundabouts were still there, albeit rather battered-looking under their powdery dusting of snow. Seeing them revived memories of being taken to the rec by his mother in the days when Stephen had her all to himself and the only thing he hated her for was not letting him eat any more sweets. He climbed on a swing, standing on the yellow plastic seat, which creaked ominously under his weight. Holding the cold chain links, he started to push, climbing higher and higher, the rhythmical squeak and groan of the old A-frame as evocative of his childhood as the sound of ice-cream vans and the taste of bubble gum. Calmed by the motion, he was enjoying watching the grey sky tipping towards him and the rush of air on his face when someone caught hold of the swing from behind and brought it to a sudden stop. His father's voice said, gruffly, 'I want a word with you.'

Vic squeezed himself with some difficulty onto the swing next to Stephen. 'Sit down,' he ordered. Grumpily, Stephen obeyed. 'You had no right to speak to your mother like that.'

'She had no right to interfere in my life.'

'Of course she had a right – she's your mother. Haven't you punished her enough now?'

'I haven't done a thing.' Stephen kept his eyes fixed on the patch of scuffed grass in front of him.

'How do you think she feels?' Vic said angrily. 'She's spent eighteen years bringing you up and now you turn round and tell her you live in a dump and you can't wait to get away.'

194

'She knows I don't mean it like that.'

'How *do* you mean it, then?' Vic waited for an answer, but Stephen simply hung his head. 'Just remember this "stupid little town" is where you're from and where your family live. I don't give a monkeys what you think about it but I won't have you belittling it in front of your mother and Lucy.' The colour was high in Vic's ruddy cheeks and his pale blue eyes blazed. 'If you don't like it, go – just stop telling us how terrible it is. Like you think you're better than us.'

Stephen rocked his swing backwards and forwards with one foot. 'I never said that.'

'That's what it sounds like from where I'm standing. If you're old enough to sleep with your teacher—'

'Dad!'

'—you're old enough to stop hurting people who care about you.' Vic paused to let this sink in, then he rummaged in his inside pocket, retrieved his wallet and drew out a ten-pound note. 'And buy your mother a decent present,' he added.

Stephen waved the money away. 'I've got one.'

'Then give it to her.' Vic relented a little, feeling sorry for his son. 'Listen,' he said, softening. 'If the worst thing that happens to you in this life is that you were loved too much by your mother . . . that would have been some life.'

Stephen looked at him then properly and Vic saw that he understood. 'There was one thing I wanted to ask you,' he continued, his voice serious. 'You know, about you and . . . teacher.'

'What?'

Vic grinned mischievously. 'What was it like?'

'You understand what's happening, Walter, don't you?' Ruth asked, stroking Walter's cat, which was purring on his lap. She had returned to Walter's dismal flat to explain the outcome of the meeting, in an attempt to make him see that the move would be for the best.

'No,' Walter said, looking apprehensive.

'We're going to find you a nice new place to live,' Ruth said patiently.

Walter became agitated. 'My house?'

Ruth took his hand. She and Simon had been contemporaries of Walter's at school for a while, until the authorities removed him. It was one of the reasons why she felt particularly protective of him: they had grown up together in Skelthwaite, he was one of them, even if he wasn't quite on the same wavelength. 'We're going to find you a new one,' she said soothingly. 'You'll live like a king, Walter. You'll have someone to make your bed and make your meals and your cups of tea. Someone to make sure you don't set fire to yourself. Even someone to look after your key so you'll never be locked out again. Sounds alright, dunt it?'

He did not look convinced. 'Can I go down pub?'

'Of course you can! Nothing else changes, does it? You can go down pub, go and visit St Margaret's—'

'Old people!' Walter brightened.

'—and me and Peggy and Pat will come and visit you, just like we do now. It'll be brilliant, Walter, I promise you,' Ruth said, talking herself into it as much as Walter.

'Can I take cat?'

Ruth stroked the contented animal again, causing its purr to reverberate like a miniature outboard motor. 'Of course you can take cat.'

Happy that Walter had taken her news well, Ruth drove back to the health centre. With all that had been going on, the fight with Simon had slipped to the back of her mind, so when she walked into the nurses' office and found it bursting with what looked like the entire contents of the local florist's she did not immediately make the connection. 'What's happening?' she asked, stunned by the riot of colourful flowers, which occupied every available space. The scent in the warm room was almost overpowering. Patricia appeared from behind a large

196

bouquet of lilies, bright orange pollen speckling her chin. 'I think your Simon's having an affair,' she said, handing Ruth a card. On the card was written, 'Forgive me?'

'I hate it when he grovels,' she said crossly. It was typical of Simon to take even apologizing to excess. One bunch would have been quite enough if he was really sorry. That was the point: had he changed his mind?

'So what's my brother done to put himself int dog-house with you?' Peggy asked, catching the end of the conversation as she breezed in from her lunchbreak, which she had spent attempting to dry out the carpet.

'He doesn't want me to do job – he says I'm putting it before Alfie.'

'Cheeky monkey,' laughed Patricia.

'I'm really upset about it,' Ruth said, unsmiling.

Peggy sniffed a vase of creamy narcissi. 'He's just a bit over-protective.'

'So what would you say if Vic asked you to give up job?' Ruth rounded on her.

'I wouldn't say anything – I'd just cut him off at knees.'

There was a knock at the door and Louise Winters entered, looking taken aback by the hothouse effect. 'Who's the lucky girl?'

'Patricia – she's single,' said Ruth dryly. Peggy took Louise's coat and offered her a chair. 'Sit down, love. We dint expect you back so soon – how did you get on?'

'Good news.' Louise clicked open her briefcase. 'I've found Walter a room in a group home.'

'That was quick!'

'Mrs Pentland's old room at Lodge?' enquired Ruth.

'No, they'd already filled that.'

'Whereabouts is it?' Ruth pressed. Louise hesitated.

'It's not in Skelthwaite, I'm afraid,' she replied. The three district nurses looked at each other askance.

'What d'you mean, "not in Skelthwaite"?' challenged Ruth.

Peggy, looking worried, said, 'It has to be in Skelthwaite – this is the only home he knows.' The others nodded.

Louise looked uncomfortable. 'I'm sorry, Peggy, there's absolutely nothing available locally.'

'Where is it, Louise?' Ruth asked nervously.

'Leeds.'

There was a sharp intake of breath all round as this sunk in. 'It's not what we wanted at all – we can't take Walter out of Skelthwaite,' Peggy insisted.

'It's not about what you want, Peggy.' Louise stood her ground.

'I'm only thinking about Walter.'

Louise sighed wearily. 'He needs sheltered accommodation and we've found him sheltered accommodation. Do you think we wouldn't have found him a place in Skelthwaite if we could have?' she continued, as Peggy tried to interrupt. 'It's a very fine place and I'm sure Walter will be very happy there.'

'No, he won't,' Patricia said stoutly.

Ruth was horrified. 'All the people he cares about are in this town, all his memories – everything.'

'You're not listening to me.' Louise's face hardened. 'If and when a room becomes available in Skelthwaite—'

'When will that be?' Peggy argued.

'You know I don't know that.'

Ruth tried a different tack. 'Why don't we just forget the whole thing? Walter will be alright – we'll just have to pop in a bit more often, that's all.'

'Ruth. You spent the entire morning telling me how much at risk he was.'

'Not "at risk" exactly . . .'

'And we were right,' Peggy said, facing up to the truth. 'He is at risk, and so are his neighbours.' She turned to Ruth. 'Walter has to be looked after.'

'In Leeds?'

'If that's the only option.'

'It is,' Louise confirmed. It was Ruth who posed the question none of them wanted to ask. 'Who's going to tell him?'

After some discussion, Peggy and Ruth both went, feeling equally guilty about the part they had just played in taking Walter away from Skelthwaite. 'It's no good us going in with long faces as if he's facing execution,' Peggy said as she parked the car. 'We've got to make it sound as attractive as possible – stress all the opportunities for him.'

'What opportunities?' Ruth answered dully.

'We'll think of some.' She pressed the bell.

'Peggy!' Walter greeted her with a beaming smile and offered them tea, which they didn't have the heart to refuse, even though it was usually undrinkable. They sat down with it in the living room, perched on the still-damp sofa. 'Now then, Walter Charlton, I want you to listen carefully to me. Alright?' Peggy said firmly. He nodded enthusiastically. 'We know you can't look after yourself properly on your own, don't we, pet?'

'No.'

'That's why everyone's been trying so hard to find you somewhere nice to live where we can keep an eye on you.'

'Because we all care about you, Walter, don't we?' Ruth added.

Walter bounced up and down in the rotting armchair he had rescued from the dump. 'Live like king, go down pub, have tea made, take cat,' he recited. Ruth and Peggy exchanged glances, hating every moment of this. 'That's right. And one day – when a room becomes available – that's exactly what will happen,' Peggy said.

Ruth decided to cut to the chase. 'They didn't have any rooms in Skelthwaite, Walter.'

'But they've found this smashing place for you, Walter,' Peggy went on hurriedly. 'It's in Leeds. You'll make lots of new friends and you'll have all these people running around after you—'

'And we'll come and visit you a lot.'

'Visit? You'll think we live there with you, we'll be round so much!' Ruth and Peggy kept their false smiles up as well as they could, but Walter wasn't fooled by their patter.

'Leeds?' he repeated, looking suspicious.

'Just until we find somewhere closer.'

'I don't like Leeds. Can I stay here?' Walter said, getting up and beginning to pace around the room. He picked up a small suitcase, which he had already packed with his few belongings – clothes, a couple of old photos of his mother, a clock, his badges and some tins of catfood – and began taking things out.

Peggy winced. 'I'm sorry, love, you can't. It won't be so bad, I promise you, and as soon as—'

'You said, live like king, take cat, go down pub,' Walter rounded on Ruth, his face contorted.

Peggy got up and went over to him. 'It's not Ruth's fault, love. Now, we are all going to be very brave about this, aren't we?' At that moment her pager bleeped: Patricia messaging her that they were needed back at the health centre urgently. 'We've got to go,' Peggy said to Ruth. Having a sudden idea, she turned to Walter. 'Listen. I'm having a birthday party tonight just for special friends.'

'Party?'

'Only very special friends, so keep it to yourself, alright? Will you come?' Walter nodded slowly.

'We'll talk about where you're going and how brilliant it's going to be,' Ruth declared. He did not say anything.

'Alright, Walter?' Peggy quizzed him, concerned. He nodded again. 'Good lad.' She patted him on the shoulder.

Outside, wrapping their scarves tightly round their necks to keep the bitter wind out – snow was beginning to fall quite heavily now – Ruth said, 'Do you think he understood?'

'I don't know – who knows what goes on inside his head,' Peggy replied.

What was inside Walter's head was desperation. As he watched them go, a feeling he hadn't had since his mother died, leaving him alone in their run-down old house on the edge of the moors, came back to him. Maybe he would be safe there. He went out into the snow, shutting the door behind him, forgetting both his coat, and his keys, as usual.

# Chapter 15

Peggy, incongruous in best dress and curlers, was blowing up balloons when Lucy asked the question that had been preying on her own mind since the morning. 'Is Stephen coming to party?'

'I don't know.' She tied a knot in the end of the balloon and affixed it to the ceiling in a corner of the living room. 'Your brother moves in mysterious ways these days, dunt he?'

Lucy pondered this as she glued paper chains together. 'Once upon a time he would have done – it would have been his idea and everything.'

'He's had his resits to worry about,' Peggy said, making excuses. She was amazed at her nine-year-old daughter's perceptiveness. She had been thinking the same thing. Maybe that was why she was feeling so flat, Peggy thought. That, and Walter. She hoped he would come. They were going to make a real fuss of him, show him how much they cared, that they weren't going to abandon him to the big, wide world – the big, wide world that her son, on the other hand, couldn't wait to escape to.

'Why does Stephen want to go away from us?' Lucy continued.

'He doesn't,' Peggy lied.

'Yes, he does.'

She went over to Lucy and sat down beside her, explaining, 'He wants to go to university and make something of himself – it's not the same thing at all.'

Lucy had her own opinions about this. 'I don't think he likes us any more.'

'Of course he does.'

'I won't ever go away.' Lucy peered at Peggy from under her pudding-basin fringe, her face serious.

'What – never?' Peggy joked, pulling a mock-horrified expression. Realizing she was being sent up, Lucy gave her a gap-toothed grin, just as Vic came into the room, his trousers undone and his shirt hanging out. 'What have you done to these trousers?' he demanded indignantly.

'I haven't touched them.'

'Well, I haven't – they've shrunk, look at them.' He tugged the two ends of the waistband, which were destined never to meet again. Peggy eyed her husband's beer belly and said in a stage whisper to Lucy, 'We really must stop those trousers going down pub every night.' The two of them exploded with giggles. Vic sucked his stomach in ruefully.

Simon staggered out of the off-licence lugging a crate of champagne for Peggy's party. There was several inches of snow underfoot and he trod carefully as he made his way to the car, his feet sinking into the fresh powder with a satisfying crunch. The thick white blanket of snow had a strangely deadening effect, numbing noise and rendering the town eerily silent, so that he did not notice Walter plodding towards him until he was almost upon him. 'Walter! What are you doing without a coat?' Simon exclaimed. Walter looked back at him, distracted, but did not reply.

'I heard about Leeds,' Simon said, sympathetically, sparking Walter out of his reverie.

'I won't go to Leeds!' he shouted, visibly upset. 'I won't go!'

'Alright, alright. No-one wants you to go, do they? But you don't help yourself walking around int freezing cold like that, do you?' At this, Walter stopped, ready to listen. 'Here's what you do,' Simon continued conspiratorially. 'You go home, you stay in, you keep your head down, alright? You don't burn anything, you don't bother anyone, you just watch telly and play with cat. Can you do that?' Walter nodded, his eyes glued to Simon, his saviour. 'If you can prove you don't need to be looked after, maybe we can get them to change their minds.' Simon loaded the crate into the boot.

'Watch telly with cat?'

'That's it.'

'I can do that,' Walter said happily. Simon, feeling touched by Walter's plight, handed him a bottle of champagne. 'Head down,' he reminded him, as he got in the car. He drove off slowly, leaving Walter staring at the bottle of expensive bubbly. 'Head down,' he repeated. He struck out towards home through the whirling snowflakes, chanting Simon's instruction like a mantra.

'Have you ever thought about giving it up?' Ruth asked, garnishing a plate of neatly cut sandwiches with a sprig of parsley. Peggy was arranging sausage rolls on a platter, her mind elsewhere. 'Giving what up?'

'Nursing.'

Her sister-in-law looked up, surprised. She had forgotten all about Ruth's earlier conversation. 'Of course I have – but in the end the good things always outweigh the bad, don't they?'

Ruth folded her arms and stared out of the kitchen window. 'Take today. All we tried to do was make Walter's life a little bit better but we ended up ruining it instead.'

'We don't know that. Eventually a room will turn up here.'

'But that could be years away,' Ruth fretted. 'Who knows what Walter will be like by then?'

Peggy picked up her platter of sausage rolls, balancing a plate of quiche in the other hand. 'Come on, they'll be hungry.' Seeing Ruth still mooning about by the window, she said, 'You're not serious? About giving up nursing?'

Ruth turned to face her. 'I've got a child now. Maybe

Simon's right – maybe it's time to change my priorities.'

They took the food through to the living room, where the party guests were waiting. 'Here she is! Birthday girl!' cheered Vic, conducting a rousing, if rather tuneless chorus of 'Happy Birthday'. There was much clapping as the assembled company parted to reveal a magnificent birthday cake, complete with single candle. 'Look at that!' Peggy exclaimed, delighted.

'Patricia made it,' Vic said, giving her a kiss. 'I was going to put all the candles on but I only had a couple of days.'

She batted him good-naturedly. 'Watch it, you.'

'Make a wish,' he instructed. He winked at her saucily. 'Nothing too energetic.'

Peggy closed her eyes and thought, *I wish Stephen would come back to me*. Opening them again, she leaned forward and blew the candle out. A thin trail of smoke spiralled up to the ceiling, wafting a promise. It didn't seem much to pin her hopes on.

'Now we've got something to show you,' Vic said, marshalling the rugby team, who had all been invited. 'Ready, Kenny?' Kenny nodded, leading the team in a well-drilled *haka*. Vic stamped energetically, slapping his thighs and forearms and rolling his eyes at Peggy, who watched enthralled. Patricia clutched Peggy's sleeve and whispered, 'Wonderfully primitive, isn't it?' Peggy had to admit that, now they had got their act together, the Skelthwaite Scorpions looked pretty intimidating.

'Our victory over Hoxton – that's our present to you,' Vic panted, beaming confidently.

'You certainly know how to treat a woman, Vic Snow.'

Just then, the door opened and Stephen came in holding a bulky package. 'Happy birthday,' he said, shyly, presenting it to Peggy.

She smiled at him warmly. 'Hello, love. You dint have to get me anything.'

'Yes, he did,' piped up Lucy, who wasn't going to let her brother off the hook that easily.

'What is it?' Peggy felt the lumpy package through the paper.

'Open it and you'll know,' Vic encouraged her.

She ripped the paper off to reveal an abstract wooden sculpture, its surfaces smooth and shiny and rounded. 'Stephen, it's . . . I don't know what to say.' For once, Peggy was lost for words. She stroked the polished grain, allowing her fingers to caress the tactile hollows and planes.

'What is it?' asked Vic, more to the point.

'It's Art, Dad. I did it at school.'

'Oh.' Vic looked at Simon to see if he was any the wiser. Simon, nonplussed, shrugged his shoulders.

Peggy handed it to Ruth. 'Feel that.' Ruth turned it round in her hands, examining it from different angles, noticing the way its form changed. 'It's lovely, Stephen.'

'Come here, you.' Peggy enveloped Stephen in a hug. 'Thank you,' she whispered, holding him close. To receive such a deeply personal, beautifully crafted gift, one that he must have worked on for weeks and weeks, overwhelmed her. It was more than a birthday present, she knew. It was a peace offering.


'No sign of Walter, yet?' Ruth asked, rubbing a clear patch on the fogged-up windowpane and peering out. It was hard to see anything for the driving snow. Peggy glanced at her watch. 'He's probably forgotten and gone down pub. Someone'll point him in right direction.'

'I feel terrible about it, Peg.' Ruth could not stop thinking about how they'd succeeded in banishing Walter from Skelthwaite.

'So do I. But there was nothing else we could do – we both know that.' Peggy, too, looked out and shivered suddenly. It was a raw night. She drew the curtains, leaving a chink in the middle so that Walter could see them.

Outside in the street, Walter watched Peggy's retreating figure and hesitated. The room looked so warm and inviting.

All his friends were in there, eating, drinking and laughing. He wanted desperately to join them but something stopped him. He saw Simon showing off Alfie and remembered his words: 'Go home, stay in.' He had intended doing just that, but when he got there, he found he was locked out again. Walter held up Simon's bottle of champagne and considered his dilemma. 'Keep head down,' he reminded himself, and turned away. Anything not to go to bloody Leeds.

Peggy had been waiting for a chance to get Simon alone, so when she saw him take Alfie into the kitchen to change him, she followed him on the pretext of fetching more glasses. 'You're getting good at that,' she remarked, leaning over his shoulder as he strapped a fresh nappy on.

'There's nothing to it.'

'I always knew you'd make a good dad.' Simon beamed proudly. 'Good dad, terrible husband,' added Peggy, going for the kill.

'Excuse me?' Simon's smile faded. Peggy put down the glasses and fixed him with her formidable big-sister expression. 'Don't make her give up her job, Simon.'

'I never said that! What I said was—'

'She'll do it, you know that, don't you?' Peggy continued, ignoring him. 'If you make her feel guilty about spending time away from Alfie, she'll do it.'

'Maybe it would be for the best.' He bundled Alfie back into his clothes, a defiant look on his face.

'Rubbish! Nursing is what she does, it's what she is – I can't imagine Ruth not being a nurse.'

'You can if you try.'

Peggy put her hands on her hips. 'Do you remember when you took my goldfish out of its bowl?'

'What's that got to do with anything?'

'It died, dint it? And you cried your eyes out, dint you?'

'I was seven years old!' Simon protested.

Peggy softened her voice persuasively. 'Don't make her

208

give up nursing. She was born to be a nurse. She's kind and compassionate and—'

'I never said she wasn't. I just want what's best for Alfie.' He set his mouth stubbornly.

'A happy mother is what's best for Alfie. And for you. She won't be the same woman, you know. She might be in time for a few more meals and she might save you some child-minding money—'

'It's not about money.'

'But she won't be the same old Ruth.' Peggy paused, letting this sink in. 'I quite like her the way she is, don't you?' Simon was silent at this. Peggy left him pondering her words and retreated, forgetting the glasses.

For Simon, the issue of Ruth giving up work had become a matter of principle. When he decided something, he saw it through. Backing down was not in his nature. As far as he was concerned, he was making a completely legitimate point and yet he was the one getting all the flack for it. He had said as much to Vic earlier, when they were at work. Vic's advice was pretty typical: 'Lie on your back, stick your legs in air and let her do what she bloody well likes – she will anyway.' But then Vic had always let Peggy call the shots, Simon told himself. He'd said so Vic's face, but Vic had just laughed when he called him emasculated and retorted, 'Better a live lamb than a dead lion'.

Simon returned to the party, still deep in thought. At one end of the room, people were bopping to a party tape, while at the other, Dick, Terry and Vic were listening intently to Kenny, who was demonstrating an attacking move on the coffee table. 'Blindside wing comes on an angle here, drifts their defence, yeah?' He pushed a lager bottle forward. 'Stephen comes on an angled run here, flips up inside to Dick, who scores under the posts.' They sat back, impressed.

'And then you all wake up,' Simon said scathingly, as he walked past. He went over to Ruth, who was sitting by herself, gazing out at the falling snow. 'One clean baby.'

'Hmmm?'

'What's the matter?' Ruth had obviously been miles away.

'I'm just a bit worried about Walter.'

'Does he have to go to Leeds?' Simon sat down beside her. 'I mean, he's lived here all his life.'

'Do you think I don't know that?' she retorted crossly. Simon realized he had touched a raw nerve. 'Alright, I only asked.'

She sighed heavily. 'We made such a good case for him needing to be looked after – we've left them nowhere else to go.'

'It wasn't your fault.'

'You ask Walter that.' Her voice was bitter. '*If* he ever speaks to any of us again.'

'Of course he will. I spoke to him earlier. He's fine.'

Ruth turned to him, her face serious. 'I've been thinking about what you were saying about me giving up job—'

'Ruth—'

'No.' She put up her hand to silence him. 'You were right. Things *have* changed. Alfie's my life now.'

'You'd give up job for Alfie?'

She nodded. 'I won't tell Peggy now, it'll spoil her party. I'll hand in notice tomorrow.'

'If that's what you want.'

'It's what *you* want, int it?'

Simon took a deep breath. 'I want you to be happy. I don't want you sitting at home fretting about Mrs Wilson's leg or getting Walter's shopping in. I don't want you sitting there looking like Grim Reaper every time I come home because you miss your friends and your patients.'

She eyed him suspiciously. 'You've changed your tune, haven't you?'

'New Man's prerogative.' Simon was a little surprised himself at what he'd just said, but Peggy's words had hit home: he knew, in his heart of hearts, that nursing was Ruth's natural element. It was possible, he conceded, that paternal protectiveness had given him tunnel vision where Alfie was concerned.

'I don't know.' Ruth looked confused.

'So, you'll miss a few meals and put Alfie in a few house fires—'

'It wasn't a house fire!'

'I'm joking, I'm joking.' Simon held Alfie's plump little hand in his and took hold of Ruth's hand with the other. 'Listen. You do what you have to do, that's all I'm saying. Whatever you decide will be good enough for me and him.'

She looked at him, trying to read his eyes, then looked back outside at the dark. 'What shall we do, Alfie?' she asked, jiggling him on her knee. 'What shall we do?'

Despite Peggy's attempts to bribe him with birthday cake, Stephen had fled the party for the sanctuary of his room as soon as he'd given her his piece. He had made it especially for her in art class, knowing that she, of all the family, would appreciate the honed, honey-coloured wood and abstract shape. His mother had always been that much more intuitive. It was a language they shared – which was why her interference in his love life had been such a shock. That she could hurt him like that was a betrayal he was still trying coming to terms with. After his father's talking-to, he had realized that she did it out of love, not spite, which was why he had retrieved the sculpture from his art teacher and given it to her after all. But he still didn't understand her motive. He was mulling this over when there was a soft knock on the door and she came in.

'Not in the mood for partying?'

Stephen shook his head. 'I'm completely bushed after the exam.'

'So, you think it went alright?' she asked tentatively.

'I think so.'

'That's good.' She sat down on the chair at his desk.

Stephen traced the pattern on his duvet with a finger. 'Better not count chickens.'

Peggy did not reply, but Stephen could feel her working up to something. Finally, she said, 'I'm sorry about what happened with you and . . .' Her voice tailed off, as if she couldn't bear to even say it.

'Wendy. That was her name – Wendy,' he supplied.

'Well, I'm sorry. I dint mean to interfere.'

'Yes, you did.' Stephen could feel anger baiting him again.

Peggy tried a different tack. 'You really think you loved her?'

'I don't "think", I know.'

'I know you were very flattered, who wouldn't be? She's very attractive, she's older than you—'

'You're doing it again!' he exploded. 'Don't patronise me. If I say I loved her, I loved her – why can't you just accept it?'

'Because . . .'

'Because what?'

'Because . . . I don't want to,' she faltered. Stephen listened, sensing she was struggling to find the words to express something difficult. 'Because I want you to be that Stephen who brightens up when I come into a room. The one who tells me everything. The one that would be completely lost without me.'

He understood what she was saying – and what it had taken to admit it – and calmed down. 'She made me happy, Mum,' he said.

'Then I'm honestly very sorry. I never meant to hurt you.'

'I know.'

'All I can say is that, if it's meant to happen it will happen, interfering mother or not.'

'No.' He thought of Wendy as he had last seen her, standing by the pool table. He had sought her out and then abandoned her. She must hate him. 'I don't think she feels the same way as me,' he confessed sadly.

★ ★ ★

Relieved that she and Stephen had talked at last, Peggy went downstairs to rejoin her party, silently thanking the angel who had granted her her wish.

'Everything alright, love?' asked Vic, who had seen her disappear upstairs and guessed where she'd been.

'Everything's fine.' Peggy gave him the thumbs up, grinning broadly. 'Is Walter here yet?' She glanced around.

'Haven't seen him.'

'Walter? Is he coming?' Simon pricked up his ears.

'He is, I invited him.'

Simon looked guilty. 'Invited him here? I dint know, did I?'

'Didn't know what?' butted in Ruth.

'I told him to stay at home and keep his head down.'

'Simon.' Ruth sighed.

'I thought it was for best.'

Ruth handed Alfie to him. 'I'll go and get him.'

'I'll come with you,' Peggy said, feeling increasingly concerned.

'We won't be long.' Ruth blew a kiss at Alfie.

'Be as long as you like, love,' Simon replied, cuddling the sleepy baby.

Pulling on scarves and gloves, they headed out into the snow. Vic, who was standing next to Simon, watched them go and observed dryly, 'You put your foot down, then.'

Slithering on the icy pavements in their unsuitable shoes, Peggy and Ruth made their way to Walter's block of flats. 'Nosey,' laughed Peggy, as Ruth strained her neck to see inside a house.

'No, I'm just seeing if Mrs Clarke's got her lights on. She's that worried about her electricity bill she won't even put her lights on, let alone her heating. She won't be told.' Ruth noticed Peggy was smiling to herself. 'What?' she demanded.

'You could no more stop doing this than I could. Have I

ever told you about my goldfish?'

But Ruth wasn't listening. 'Peggy,' she said, her voice thick with fear. She pointed to Walter's front door. A slumped figure, covered with snow, was just visible collapsed under the meagre shelter provided by the lintel. 'Walter?' shouted Ruth, starting to run. They fell on their knees beside him.

'Walter! Walter!' Peggy shook him by the shoulders. There was no response.

Ruth put her face close to his, feeling for breath on her cheek. Nothing. She tipped his head back, opening his airway, and began giving mouth-to-mouth resuscitation. 'Don't you bloody dare, Walter,' she growled, stopping to check for a pulse. She looked up Peggy and shook her head.

Peggy immediately commenced heart massage. Walter's face was blue, his eyelashes crusted with snow. They did not flicker as Peggy pumped at his chest. 'Walter! Come on!' she panted. Ruth took over again, desperately trying to blow life into his lungs, while Peggy took off her coat and threw it over Walter's inert body. They worked in tandem, alternating the cardiopulmonary resuscitation with the artificial ventilation, their hopes fading as Walter failed to respond.

'He's gone, Peg! He's gone,' Ruth wailed, sitting back on her heels. Peggy leaned over him to check for a pulse again and, as she did so, Walter groaned and shuddered, his body kick-started back into life. 'Walter! Walter!' Ruth called, as his eyes opened, uncomprehending.

'Keep him warm – I'll get ambulance.' Peggy leapt to her feet and ran next door to the Crosses.

Ruth took off her own coat and piled it on top of Peggy's, hugging Walter's frozen body to her. 'Come on, Walter. Come on. Stay with me. Please stay with me.' She cradled his head in her arms, repeating over and over again, 'Hang on, Walter. Do you hear me? You bloody hang on.'

# *Chapter 16*

'Poor Walter.' Ruth lay next to Simon in bed, looking up at the ceiling. Outside, an unearthly quiet prevailed, the snow-muffled streets transformed from grim northern town to a crystal-spun wonderland.

'He was lucky.' Simon extended an arm around her, drawing her close.

'Lucky?'

'You saved his life.' Tenderly, he pushed a lock of her hair off her face and kissed her cheek. 'How many people can say they've done that?' Ruth was silent, reliving the long, long minutes she had held Walter's frozen body in her aching arms, willing him not to die. Peggy had brought out more blankets from the Crosses and wrapped one round Ruth's shivering shoulders, but the ambulance, hampered by the weather, had taken an age to get there. Then, watching Walter being lifted onto a stretcher, Ruth wasn't sure if they would ever see him again alive, but Peggy had rung half an hour ago to tell her that the hospital had confirmed Walter was going to be alright. Ruth couldn't get out of her head what a close call Walter had had. If she and Peggy hadn't gone out when they did . . .

Simon shifted uncomfortably beside her, as if he was reading her thoughts. 'I can't believe he dint come to us. Just because I told him to keep his head down. What if he'd died?'

'It wasn't your fault. Peggy's right – it's no-one's fault. In the end he proved us all right.'

Simon felt for her hand and squeezed it. 'You're not going to hand in notice, are you?'

'No,' she said softly, 'I'm not going to do that.'

He raised himself on one elbow and looked at her with new respect. 'I love you, Ruth.'

'I love you, too.'

Peggy had remembered Walter's cat and brought him home with her, tucked into her coat. Lucy, devastated by the news of Walter's accident, had taken on the job of looking after the animal personally and had insisted on taking him up to bed with her. When Peggy went to say goodnight she found her young daughter wide awake, even though it was almost midnight.

'He won't sit on bed, he won't play. He just keeps looking out of window,' she complained.

'He's probably worried about Walter.'

'Will they let Walter come home?'

'He's going to live in Leeds for a while.' Peggy stroked her hair soothingly.

'Why?'

'Because they can look after him properly there.'

'Can't we look after him?'

Peggy sat down on the bed with her. 'We can't be with him every minute, night and day – that's what he needs.'

'He won't like that. He'll hate it.'

'I know he will,' Peggy agreed sadly. 'Come on, now, let's get you to sleep.' She pulled up the duvet and Lucy snuggled down under it. Peggy was just about to switch off the light when Lucy popped her head back up with another question.

'Mum. Why can't things stay the way they are?'

'How d'you mean?'

'Walter's gone. Then Stephen's going to go. I wish everything would just stay the same.'

'So do I, love. So do I,' Peggy said with feeling.

216

Peggy had cause to echo Lucy's sentiments after she and Ruth went to visit Walter the following week. He was a changed man, his normal, sunny disposition and childlike sense of fun gone. Ruth had expected him to be angry with them; what she wasn't prepared for was his look of bewilderment, as if he was permanently disoriented by his new surroundings. 'Why don't we go for a walk, Walter? You can show us round,' Peggy suggested, but Walter had become quite agitated. 'Stay here. Tea time. Stay here.' Clinging to routines seemed to give him a sense of security, with the result that he had rapidly become instituitionalized. In losing his independence – the very thing that made him vulnerable – he had lost something even more significant: part of himself.

'It's as if a light's gone out in him,' Ruth observed afterwards, as they inched their way out of Leeds through congested rush-hour traffic. She blew her nose loudly and Peggy glanced at her, concerned.

'Come on now, Ruth, don't go getting upset.'

'Look what we condemned him to. He's not Walter any more.' Ruth dashed angry tears from her cheeks.

'Yes he is, love, he just needs a bit more time to settle in. It's been a huge upheaval for him – remember he's only just come out of hospital, and that was traumatic enough.'

'Must have been so awful for him to wake up there, all alone. Doctor said he was calling for his mam and asking to go home. Poor lamb.'

Peggy sighed as they just missed another green light. She felt as badly as Ruth did about Walter but was trying to hide it. 'He'll get help there, you know. He'll make new friends. He'll find his feet eventually.'

'Yes, and then he'll become so set in his ways he'll never be able to come back to Skelthwaite.'

'I know,' Peggy admitted. 'But so long as he's happy, that's what counts. And that's a nice little place he's got there. Would have been much worse for him ten years ago. They might have sent him up to Hall.'

Ruth shuddered. 'Merson Hall Asylum. I remember kids talking about it at school. They used to concoct gruesome stories about what the inmates were like.'

'Fear and ignorance,' Peggy said, grimacing, as a car pushed in front of them, 'have a lot to answer for.'


'Will you play rugby at university?' Lucy, her feet tucked under her on the sofa, watched Stephen as he cleaned mud from his rugby boots. Stephen grunted as he prised the caked mud off onto sheets of newspaper, which were spread all over the living-room carpet. 'They don't play rugby down there. Not *real* rugby,' he said disparagingly.

'You won't like that.'

'Then I'll have to find something else to do.'

They were silent for a moment, considering this. For Stephen, who was counting the days, his results were the touchstone to his future: all or nothing. For Lucy, who was also counting the days, marking them off on a calendar she kept under her bed, her brother's results were assuming an equal significance, albeit the opposite of his. 'D'you know what I'd do if I was you?' she asked casually.

'Pass that spanner,' he replied, guessing what was coming. Lucy handed him the stud-tightening spanner, the picture of a helpful little sister. 'I'd stay here,' she continued. 'You could play rugby and see your friends and go to parties and do all the things you like doing – just by staying here.'

'If I haven't passed that's exactly what I'll be doing.'

Lucy brightened at the prospect. 'That'd be good!' She turned round, resting her forearms along the top of the sofa, and stared out of the window, deep in thought. Stephen looked at her back and smiled. He knew she didn't want him to go. Sometimes – just occasionally – he didn't want to go, either. It was so much easier, he thought, to stick with what you knew, the familiar, the safe, the undemanding. Not to dip your toe into that vast, boiling sea of new experiences. If he hadn't had a taste of it – if he hadn't met Wendy, for example – he might have been more content with his lot, but she had opened his eyes to possibilities he'd never dreamed of. Like acting. He had done one other, minor role in a previous school production, but had never taken it seriously until she suggested he audition for *Streetcar*. She had spotted his talent and nurtured it and now he could feel it in himself and the feeling burned there like a flame. Even if there was no hope for the two of them, he couldn't ignore that.

Held up by the traffic in Leeds, and then an accident on the motorway, it was nearly 7.00pm before Ruth arrived home. She found Simon, Alfie tucked under one arm, stirring something on the stove and looking more than a little harassed. 'Dinner or baby?' he asked. Ruth, remembering fleetingly the days when they could put their feet up after work and sink into a large gin and tonic, plonked her bag down on the table and said, 'Baby'. She extracted Alfie and peered into the pot. 'What is it, anyway?' Simon dipped a spoon into the mixture. 'What *was* it,' he corrected her, wincing. 'It's inedible now. I thought you'd be back an hour ago.'

'Leeds was hell.'

'Well, there's worse to come,' he said, scraping the saucepan into the bin. 'Childminder's sick. Her husband brought Alfie back. Says she's in no state to have him tomorrow.'

'Great.' Ruth pulled out a kitchen chair and sat down gratefully. 'Now what do we do? Did she suggest anyone else?'

'Yes, but they're already full up, I checked.'

'Can you take him in with you again?'

Simon pulled a face. 'Be reasonable, Ruth. That was a one-off. I can't be in two places at once and Alfie dunt sleep all day like he used to.'

'Well, I can't, either.'

'Then there's only one thing for it.'

'What?' She looked at him suspiciously.

'You'll have to take day off. Ring Peggy. Tell her to get bank nurse in.'

'Me take day off? Why not you take day off?' Ruth was beginning to lose her temper.

'Because I've got no-one to cover for me.'

'You should have, then. When Stephen turned you down, you should have recruited someone else. It's your own fault. You're a control freak. No-one should be indispensable.'

Simon flushed. 'Quite. And since you're not running a company, I think it has to be you.'

'Give me strength!' Ruth swept out of the kitchen and up to the nursery with Alfie. She had always known juggling a job and a baby would be hard work, but, having made the decision to carry on working, it was sometimes difficult to come to terms with all the compromises that entailed. Simon was trying his best, she reasoned, calming, as she changed Alfie into a clean sleepsuit and got him ready for bed. Previously he'd have just gone off down pub; at least now he was attempting to cook dinner and help her. She would just have to bite the bullet this time and have more back-up lined up in future.

'Ruth!' Simon shouted from the foot of the stairs.

'What?'

'Chicken Korma or Prawn Biryani? I'm ordering now.'

At least meals were easy to compromise on, she reflected. So long as you had a takeaway that delivered.

Peggy had been understanding when Ruth phoned her to explain her predicament, saying, 'Don't worry, pet, we'll bring on substitute,' but the following morning found her panicking when the promised bank nurse had still not appeared by ten o'clock. Patricia, who remained unflappable in a crisis, poured her a cup of coffee and made her sit down, reminding her that the nurse was coming from Bradford, which was bound to take longer. 'How did you get on with taking Gwen Phillips to St Margaret's?' she asked, reaching for the biscuit tin without thinking. 'Did she settle in alright?'

'Bit apprehensive, but too proud to show it,' answered Peggy, sipping her coffee gratefully. She had been up early, helping to move the eighty-year-old widow into the nursing home. Gwen Phillips had been living with her daughter, Jean Alsop, and her family, and Peggy could tell from Jean's guilty expression that the decision to put her increasingly frail mother into a home had been a difficult one.

'It's a good place, there. Good people. A few card games with Arthur and Shirley and the others and she'll be well away,' Patricia said. She picked up a Bourbon, almost put it back, then abandoned any such noble thoughts. Kenny would be going home soon, once the Hoxton match was over, so there wasn't much point in dieting any more, she consoled herself.

'That's what I told her, though I think she's determined not to enjoy herself. She made a point of saying, "You'll not hear me complain".'

'I've heard that one before.' They were both laughing at this when the door bounced open and Ruth came in carrying Alfie, who was bundled up in a padded ski suit and bobble hat.

'Oh-oh, here's trouble.' Patricia took Alfie from her and gave him big smacker. Alfie giggled, delighted at the attention.

'Literally, in my case,' Ruth said, pulling off her gloves. 'I'm sorry to drop you both in it like this, I feel awful about it.'

'We forgive you.' Peggy, too, went over to coo at the baby. 'So what are you doing here, then?'

'I came to drop off this paperwork. I realized this morning I'd taken it home last night after we got back from Leeds.' Ruth dug in her bag and pulled out a manila folder.

'Thanks.' Peggy's mobile went off and she answered it, listening intently. Finally she said, 'Alright, David, I'll be over right away,' and snapped it shut. 'That was Warden at St Margaret's. Gwen's had an accident.'

Patricia looked up. 'Serious?'

'Nasty scald. She spilled a cup of tea. Apparently she's very upset about it and wants to go home.' Peggy started to get her things together.

'I'll come too, if you don't mind,' Ruth said. 'Just to say hello. It's on my way home and I'have been meaning to drop in and see them all ever since Alfie was born.'

Vic stood still, listening to the sound of the rooks cawing in the tall trees surrounding two sides of the rugby pitch. With the match against Hoxton in a few day's time he was like a cat on hot bricks and had persuaded Kenny to come down with him on their lunchbreak to go over their strategy. He breathed in deeply, inhaling the smell of bruised and trodden grass, a smell that always triggered memories of the time his father had first taken him down to the ground. The Skelthwaite Scorpions' Rugby League Club was hallowed turf, then; playing for the club was something every lad in the town aspired to. Vic smiled to himself, recalling the Christmas he received his first pair of rugby boots, aged eight, and the lecture he got from his dad about looking after them: 'They're more than a Christmas present, son. These are a gift for life.' It hadn't made much sense at the time, but later he had understood, and when Stephen was eight he had given him the same present – and the same lecture. It was sad, Vic reflected, that the old ground couldn't conjure up the same magic for Stephen's generation, but the days of its great victories were well and truly over. Well, almost. He closed his eyes and offered up a silent prayer to the spirits of his forebears: 'Please. One little dream'.

Kenny, who had donned a tracksuit, jogged over, his arms full of rugby balls. 'Big day, Saturday, eh, Vic?'

'Big day.' Vic rubbed his hands together nervously.

'Just going to kick a few balls.' Kenny lined them up like a row of giant eggs, setting them carefully on their ends. 'Kenny.' Vic cleared his throat. 'I just wanted to say . . . win or lose, what you've done for this club has been fantastic.'

'Win or *what*, Vic?' Kenny put on a mock-baffled look.

'Win or lose.'

'Sorry, mate, don't know what you're talking about,' Kenny said, walking away. One by one, he slotted the balls through the uprights, increasing Vic's respect for him with every well-aimed kick. Suddenly, he felt very old indeed.

'So what's the opposition like?' Kenny asked later, as they returned to the changing rooms.

'Hoxton Giants? Name should give you a clue.' Vic shrugged. 'Hoxton's next town to Skelthwaite. They like to think they're better than us. Unfortunately, they have been, for past decade anyway. We used to thrash them, though.' He looked at a framed team photo on the wall, now yellowed with age. 'Some of my earliest memories are of this place, you know. Running around here, looking for my dad. All these great, hairy steaming giants looking down at me.' Kenny gave him a gap-toothed grin. 'We were alright in them days, Scorpions,' Vic continued wistfully. 'Some of the mills were still open – we were putting out two, three teams. Won the West Yorkshire League three times int row. Won the cup. Glory days.' He sighed.

'They'll come again, Vic.'

'No. No, they won't. Tide went out on this place long ago.' Vic glanced around the room, at the faded cuttings, fliers, match programmes and memorabilia adorning the walls. Then, stiffening his resolve, he added, 'But that dunt mean we can't have pride in ourselves, does it? All I want is for us to compete, to have a bit of pride.'

'They'll compete. They're a good bunch.' Kenny picked up his holdall, ready to go.

'I hope so,' said Vic as he locked the door behind them. 'It gets under your skin, dunt it? Mediocrity. Expectation of defeat. You get slapped down so many times you think that's how it's meant to be.'

Peggy and Ruth arrived at St Margaret's to find the old folk in subdued mood. Gwen Phillips's agitation over her accident with the hot tea had sent a ripple of disquiet through the lounge and the normally chatty guests were quiet. 'Hello, you lot. Have you met Alfie?' Ruth said, doing her best to cheer them up. It worked instantly and they crowded round, stroking his cheeks, admiring his blue eyes and holding his dimpled hands. 'Hey, one at a time,' she joked, 'You can all have a turn.'

Jane, the care assistant, took Peggy to one side. 'Gwen's through here.' She lead her down a corridor to a neatly furnished bedroom, which Gwen had already added a few home comforts to. Her rocking chair – which had been transported, precariously, on the roof of her daughter's car – was installed in one corner, and she had arranged some family photographs on her chest of drawers, including one of her severe-looking deceased husband.

Jean Alsop had also been called and was already there, holding onto her mother's hand and looking anxiously at her. Gwen Phillips sat motionless on the side of the bed, staring down at her leg, her lips moving soundlessly. Peggy knelt and examined the burn. 'Nothing like starting with a bang, is there?' she said cheerfully. The elderly woman clutched her daughter's sleeve, ignoring Peggy. 'Take me home, Jean.'

'I will, Mum. Just let Peggy finish,' she soothed.

Peggy shared a glance with the warden, David White, who had also come into the room. He lifted his hands helplessly. 'Why don't you give it another go, Gwen?' she said. 'I mean, it were only a cup of tea, weren't it?'

'No,' Jean Alsop intervened. 'I'm taking her home. It were bad idea int first place.'

Peggy, who sensed there was more to Gwen's upset

reaction than met the eye, asked gently, 'Nothing else has happened here, has it, Gwen?'

'I made a mistake, that's all,' she replied.

'It's just not like you. One silly accident and you want to go home?'

'Have you done?' Gwen indicated abruptly that the conversation was closed.

Back in the lounge, Alfie's presence was proving to be a real tonic, bringing the old folk out of themselves and filling the room with delighted laughter as he waved his arms and beamed at them. 'He's lovely, Ruth,' said Shirley, a stout, gregarious white-haired woman, nursing Alfie in her arms. Arthur, St Margaret's flamboyantly dressed resident cardsharp, peered closely. 'He's going to be a rugby player – look at the shoulders on him.' Ruth glowed, her eyes on the baby as he was passed carefully around. 'You must be so proud.' Shirley patted Ruth's arm.

'Just a little bit,' she admitted.

'How's your Simon taking it?'

'He's unbearable,' Ruth whispered conspiratorially. 'He's read a couple of books, sussed out how to change nappies and now he thinks he knows everything.'

'Better than my day. They were like "give me shout when kid's eighteen and I can take it down pub".'

Ruth wagged a finger. 'New man he may be, but I think Simon's still very much looking forward to that part!' They both roared with laughter, causing Peggy, who had just come back into the room with Jean and Gwen, to ask what the joke was. 'We're just comparing notes on husbands and child-rearing. Seems some things never change.'

David White came over to them. 'Before you two go, I wanted to give you these.' He handed over a small box of badges, broaches and stick pins. 'For Walter,' he explained. 'For his collection. We miss him here. The guests had a bit of a whip-round for him, raided their drawers and keepsakes.'

'David!' Ruth was touched. 'What a lovely gift! We'll

make sure he gets them. Thank you very much.'

Gwen, who was impatient to be off, came over with Jean. 'I'm sorry,' she said haltingly to the Warden.

'You've got nothing to be sorry about,' he replied. 'If, in a couple of days, when you've had a think—'

'No,' she interrupted him quickly. 'I'll not be back.'

Arthur ambled over and asked, disappointed, 'You off, Gwen?' but she did not reply or look up as Jean shepherded her out of the room.

'I'm sure she'll be back,' Peggy said reassuringly. She turned to Ruth. 'Come on, then, let's leave these folks in peace. And you ought to be making most of your unexpected day off. Go to park or something.'

Ruth nodded. 'Where's that boy? Where's Alfie?' She looked around. 'Where is he? Who's got Alfie?'

'He was just there. With Martha.' Shirley indicated an empty chair.'

'He's not there now, is he?' Ruth said sharply.

'It's alright. He'll be here somewhere.' Peggy beckoned Jane over. 'Alfie's missing. He were with Martha. Do you know where she's gone?'

'I haven't seen her. She must have wandered off somewhere. She can be a bit absent-minded, sometimes.'

'Well, start looking!' Panic rose in Ruth's voice.

David White, who had been seeing Jean and Gwen to their car, took in the situation at a glance. 'I'll search the rooms. Jane, you do the kitchen, the dining room, the toilets. Peggy, can you have a look in the garden? Ruth, you come with me.'

'Alfie? Alfie?' With every empty room Ruth's heart beat louder and faster, her mind fast-forwarding images she dare not stop to think about. It soon became clear when they met up with the others that neither Alfie nor Martha were on the premises. 'Where's my baby?' Ruth bayed, desperate, as Peggy put a comforting arm around her. 'Where's Alfie?'

# Chapter 17

'Sit down, love.' Peggy guided Ruth to a chair. 'It'll be alright. She's probably just gone for a walk.'

Ruth leapt up again immediately. 'You don't take other people's babies for a walk!' she cried. Jane, who had been hovering nearby, a worried look on her face, said, 'Martha *were* acting a bit strange this morning.'

'Now she tells us!' Ruth exclaimed.

'How d'you mean, "strange"?' asked Peggy.

'She was all upset about Mrs Phillips. Sort of . . . frightened. I found her squashed in corner, like she were trying to hide.'

Peggy didn't know what to make of the information. 'It were only a little burn.'

'I know. That's what I told her.'

David White, who had been searching outbuildings, came back in and shook his head at their look of mute inquiry. 'Right. Get police,' Ruth said, her mind made up.

Peggy laid a hand on her arm. 'Why don't we give her another five minutes? She's probably just—'

'Get police! And Simon! I want Simon!'

At Goddard Paper Products, Simon was having a bad day. They were late with an order, one of the machines had gone down again and his tea was undrinkable. 'Bloody hell.' He put down the stewed tea in disgust.

'What shall I do, boss?' Dick, who had come to report the

227

breakdown, was still waiting for an answer.

'You've sent for engineers?'

'No.' Dick looked surprised.

'Why not?' Simon demanded, exasperated. The phone on his desk started to ring and he waited for Denise to intercept the call. It continued to ring. 'Phone!' he bellowed at the office door.

'Vic phones engineers,' Dick explained patiently.

'Well, where's Vic?'

'Out on his lunch.'

'What about Kenny? Can't he fix it? That's what I'm paying him for.'

'Out with Vic. Putting in some practise kicks.'

'Exactly what I feel like doing,' Simon muttered. The telephone was still ringing. 'Phone!' he shouted again, to no effect. 'I might as well run this bloody place on my own.' He picked up the receiver. 'Goddard Paper Products, Simon speaking,' he said in a sing-song telesales voice. 'How may I help you?' Dick, who was taking his time about leaving, stopped when he saw the colour drain from his boss's face. 'I'm on my way.' Simon slammed down the phone and grabbed his jacket from the coat-stand in the corner.

'Trouble?'

'Alfie's missing.' Simon rifled frantically in his pockets for his car keys.

'They're on your desk,' Dick pointed out helpfully. Simon snatched them up and bolted out of the door, clattering down the stairs and out onto the forecourt. He jumped into his four-wheel-drive Jeep and reversed out with a squeal of tyres. Driving like a maniac, he got to St Margaret's twelve minutes later, halting in the driveway in a flurry of gravel behind a police car. A small knot of people were milling around outside and two officers were interviewing the residents. Simon rushed over to Ruth, who was being comforted by Peggy. 'Alright, love, alright.' He put his arms around her protectively and she buried her head on his chest, unable to speak for the fear clutching at her throat. Peggy caught his eye over Ruth's shoulder. 'We think one of ladies has taken Alfie for a walk,' she said carefully.

The Warden looked agonised. 'I'm very sorry, Mr Goddard.'

'You will be,' Simon said quietly, in a voice filled with menace. One of the police officers came over. 'Mr Goddard? There's no sign of her in the house or in the grounds but she's on foot, she can't have got too far.' He turned to David White. 'Is there any place she likes to go? Any special friend?'

He wrung his hands. 'She dunt go anywhere. She dunt have any friends outside here. We're her friends.'

'It's alright, pet.' Peggy tried to calm him down and focus his mind. 'Where was her home before she came here? You told me once.'

'She came to us after they closed Hall down.'

'Merson Hall?' Simon stared at him, appalled. 'You're telling me a loony's got my child?' He felt Ruth shudder in his arms and held her tighter, stroking her hair.

'She's not a loony, Mr Goddard,' the Warden replied sharply.

'Merson Hall, that's right,' Peggy said, remembering. 'But what about before then?'

'I looked in file – there's nothing before then.'

'Right.' The police officer turned to his colleague and slapped his gloved hands together. 'Let's go and take a look.'

'We'll come with you.' Simon lead Ruth towards the Jeep. Peggy, trying to make a connection between Martha Travis's reported strange behaviour that morning and Gwen Phillips's odd rejection of the nursing home, stopped with David White for a second. 'Was Gwen ever in Merson Hall?'

'Gwen? I don't think so. Why?' He looked puzzled.

'Peggy, are you coming?' Ruth shouted from the car.

'I'll catch you up.' First, she had to pay Gwen Phillips a visit.

The old lady had been reinstalled in her favourite rocking chair, which was by the window, where she could keep watch on the comings and goings outside through the net curtains. She sat stiffly upright, her mouth pursed and her face shuttered, maintaining a dignified facade. 'I'll not go back,' she said determinedly as Peggy entered the room.

'I know you won't.' Jean Alsop was standing guard over her mother, presenting a united front.

'I've not come about that. Well, not exactly.' Peggy hesitated for a second. 'Gwen. Do you know a woman called Martha? She's one of ladies at St Margaret's – you might have seen her this morning in lounge.'

'No.' Gwen Phillips folded her hands in her lap.

'Are you sure, love? It's very important,' Peggy said, leaning forward.

'Never heard of her.' The chair creaked rapidly as she rocked.

Jean Alsop looked surprised at Peggy's questions. 'Who is this woman?'

'We think she's taken Ruth's baby.'

'Taken baby? That's terrible!' She glanced at her mother, her face shocked. Gwen Phillips stopped rocking for an instant. She did not say anything.

'The only thing we can think of that might have upset her is Gwen's accident,' Peggy explained.

'I dint mean to upset anyone.' The elderly woman's severe expression crumpled.

Peggy got up. 'I know you dint, love. It were just a thought.'

'Is there anything we can do?' Jean Alsop asked, her eyes concerned.

'I don't think so.'

'Will you let us know when they find baby?'

She nodded, glancing over at Gwen Phillips. 'If you think of anything . . . anything at all . . .'

'I'm sorry, Peg,' Jean said, showing her out. 'We don't know woman.'

'Dear Wendy. I'm not asking you to forgive me. I just want to explain . . .'

'Dear Wendy. Every day I regret leaving you like that but I had no choice . . .'

'Dear Wendy. I love you. I've never stopped loving you. That's why I did what I did . . .'

'Dear Wendy. I left to let you get on with your life but without you I can't get on with mine . . .'

Stephen screwed up his fourth attempt at writing to Wendy and hurled it at the wastebin in the corner of his room. He missed, and it fell on the floor with his other scrunched up attempts. Tossing his writing pad and pen aside, he fell back on his bed, hands behind his head, fed up with trying to express how he felt on paper. Everything he wrote sounded trite or ridiculous or just plain pathetic. He had tried to put Wendy behind him, chalk the whole thing down to experience, but, now that his resits were over and he had time on his hands, all he did was think about her. Despite telling himself – and everyone else – that the affair was over, something inside his head kept sticking. *We were meant to be together. If I still feel like this, maybe she does. And if she does, then surely we could make it work, wherever we are, whatever we're doing . . .* Then he would imagine Wendy's accusing face and hear her pouring scorn on his naïve utterances or torture himself with visions of Wendy in the pub, her arm around some other, older bloke, laughing with her friends about her schoolboy lover. Stephen sighed and rolled over, swinging his legs over the edge of the bed. Even if she never spoke to him again, he wanted Wendy to understand why he'd run out on her that evening. Above all, he wanted her to know that he still loved her, that he would always love her. Some lines from a Shakespeare sonnet Wendy had taught them at school came back to him:

> 'Let me not to the marriage of true minds
> Admit impediments. Love is not love
> Which alters when it alteration finds,
> Or bends with the remover to remove.
> Oh no! It is an ever-fixed mark . . .'

Stephen went to his English books and looked it up. Shakespeare's Sonnet 116 *was* his message for Wendy:

> '. . . Love's not Time's fool, though rosy lips and
>     cheeks
> Within his bending sickle's compass come;
> Love alters not with his brief hours and weeks,
> But bears it out even to the edge of doom . . .'

He copied it out in full and left it at that. No salutation. No signature. No postscript. Without giving himself time to think about what he was doing, he put it in an envelope, addressed it and hurried off to the post office. As he crossed a busy street, he heard a horn blare and jumped. Looking round, he saw a car swerve around an elderly woman carrying a baby. Her fixed expression was peculiar – she looked almost as if she were in a trance – but, bent on a mission of his own, Stephen did not stop to question it.

Merson Hall was set on exposed high ground above the town, which was covered with a thin crust of frozen snow. Ruth shivered violently in the chill wind whipping off the moors and drew her coat around her. She hardly dared imagine her tiny son outside in this. Simon put a steadying arm around her and they followed the police officers into the derelict building. A loud clatter of wings made her involuntarily flinch as some pigeons, unused to being disturbed, flew up to a broken skylight. Their droppings and feathers littered the floor, which was wet and dirty and scattered with dry leaves and blown rubbish. Puddles had formed in the corridors where tiles had come off the roof and the walls were running with damp, giving the crumbling Victorian asylum a clammy atmosphere that seemed to seep into the bones. Ruth took another, hesitant step, feeling broken glass crunch underfoot, and looked about her. No-one, apart from the pigeons and mice, seemed to have been there for years and it stank of rot and decay. Nature was chewing the place up, bit by bit, reclaiming it for her own. 'Martha! Martha!' David White's voice echoed in the empty entrance hall. The police officers produced powerful torches and flashed them round the walls, illuminating long-forgotten signs and notices, thick with dust. 'Watch your step,' said one policeman, pointing out a fire extinguisher lying on the ground with his torch. 'Let's have a listen,' said the other, raising his hand for silence. They all stood still. The only sound was the continual drip, drip, drip of water. 'Alfie!' Ruth screamed, looking around frantically. 'Alfie!'

'Please, Mrs Goddard, stay here. We'll search the rooms.' The police officers disappeared and they could hear them breaking down doors, their heavy boots thumping overhead.

Ruth shivered again. 'Where's Peggy?' she asked, looking around and realizing she hadn't arrived yet.

'She'll be here, love.'

'It's all my fault.' Ruth bit her lip, trying hard not to cry. 'I shouldn't have left him.'

'It's not your fault.'

'It is. It's my fault.'

Vic and Kenny had returned to the factory to find work had ground to a halt and the staff were standing around talking in hushed voices. 'What's going on here?' Vic asked, jovial.

'Don't tell me all machines have packed up at once.' No-one said anything. He noticed they were giving him sympathetic looks.

'Number three's down again,' Dick volunteered. 'Simon wanted Kenny to see to it.'

'And that's why you've all got long faces, is it? Where is Simon, anyway?'

Dick swallowed. 'He's had to go out. Vic, I'm sorry to tell you this . . . your nephew's missing.'

'Alfie? Where? What's happened?' Vic ran a worried hand through his thin grey hair.

'That's all we know. Simon just ran out.'

'Well, come on then, let's get back to work,' Vic chivvied, taking charge. 'Kenny, lad, have a look at that machine. I'll ring Peg on mobile; see if I can find out anything.' He made his way up to Simon's office, heart thumping. You read about baby snatches in paper, he thought; they didn't happen in Skelthwaite. Everyone knew everyone else, for a start. Their grannies, their children, their family background. It was hard to keep any skeletons in the closet in this town.

An hour and a half later, the police declared the building clear and the search switched to the grounds around the hall. More officers had been drafted in and were systematically combing the area, marking off sections of land with fluorescent orange tape, which tugged and fluttered in the increasingly strong wind. Black thunderclouds were gathering, accentuating the asylum's grim, Gothic look, and the light was fading fast. Simon, trying to convince himself as much as the despairing Ruth, said, 'He's going to be alright. I promise you'.

'No. He's in trouble. I know he is.' Ruth had drawn into herself, staring dully across the bleak moorland, her shoulders hunched. She thought she heard a child's cry carried on the wind, and strained to listen. 'Can you hear that?' She caught Simon's sleeve. One of the police officers came over and cupped an ear. 'There it is again!' she cried, catching the faint, plaintive cry. The officer ran back to the car and retrieved a pair of binoculars. He scanned the horizon slowly. 'I can't see anything.' A bird flew up from the ground some distance away and he refocused the binoculars on it. 'I'm sorry, love, it's just a curlew.'

Peggy's car pulled in, and suddenly Ruth's haggard face was transformed. Peggy, so strong, so dependable in a crisis; Peggy, who always knew what to do. She would make it right. But Peggy, seeing Ruth's look of expectation, merely shook her head. 'No sign of him yet.' Ruth, her last reserves of hope gone, slumped into Simon's arms.

Peggy embraced the two of them, holding the little family together with her warmth and her love. The three of them stood like that for a moment, heads bowed, taking solace from each other. 'If it has to be any of us, take me, not him. Spare my son's life,' Ruth prayed. She was prepared to bargain any sacrifice for Alfie. His small presence had redefined her existence so totally that, at that moment, she felt she would not have the strength to carry on without him.

'He will be alright. He will be alright,' Peggy insisted, as if she knew what Ruth was thinking. Ruth felt wetness on the back of her neck and realized it was raining, great, fat, heavy drops tipping down from the leaden sky. The police radio crackled and one of the officers spoke into it. 'Four-one-two receiving. We need more lights and more people. Get some volunteers up here.' They listened, the awful awareness growing that it would be dark soon, making the hunt harder than ever.

Simon, who was trying to hold himself together for Ruth's sake, could feel his teeth chattering, as much with shock as with the cold. He turned away, trying to hide the hideous thoughts running through his head. *How shall we ever find him in the pitch blackness? How will he survive if he's out in this freezing rain?* He heard Ruth call his name, a quiver in her voice, and turned back to see her face stricken with fear.

He followed her gaze and noticed a commotion among the searchers. A knot of police officers were gathered around Jane, the care assistant, who had come up to the hall with David White. She was looking at something on the ground, her hands to her mouth in a gesture of horror. Simon held his breath. One of the policemen squatted down and started to tug at what appeared to be a heavy iron grating or well cover. Simon put his arm around Ruth and held her tight, but she wrenched free and began stumbling and slipping through the grass and the rain towards the group of people.

'No, Ruth!' Peggy shouted, as they ran after her, but she got there first, in time to see the officer, who was on his knees with his arm down the well, pull out a tiny, nappy-clad baby's body. 'Alfie!' she screamed, lurching forwards, then recoiling in horror. In the policeman's hands lay a lifesize pink plastic doll. Ruth gazed at its hideous eyeless face and torn hair and felt her knees buckle under her. The howl that escaped from her as she collapsed to the ground was the anguished howl of a woman brutally wrenched from her child; a woman crazed with desperation and tortured by fear.

# Chapter 18

As news spread about the search, people from the town began arriving to help, including Vic, Kenny and Dick and several others from the factory, who had all clocked off early as soon as the request for volunteers had been received. It was dark now and arc lights had been set up to illuminate the area, which was humming with activity. A senior police officer hailed the searchers, uniformed and volunteers, gathering them together by a refreshments van. 'Grab yourselves a roll and a hot drink. As soon as you're ready, we'll start on another sector. Any questions? No? Right, let's get cracking.'

Simon, grim-faced, searched next to Vic, relieved to be doing something useful. His fingers were numb with cold and the chill wind was cutting through the thin material of his suit trousers, but he was glad of the discomfort; he wanted to suffer what his little boy was suffering. He could not bear to stand and watch and wait. Aware of Ruth's harrowed face, he had been trying to bear up, but his reserves of strength had been utterly drained. Cocooned in his own despair, Simon knew he could not reach out to her without breaking down himself. Rather than add to her burden, he preferred to search in the freezing rain where no-one could see his tears.

'Drink this.' Peggy, who was looking after Ruth, brought her a coffee from the van.

'I don't want it.'

'You're going to be in a fine state when they find him,

237

aren't you?' she scolded gently. Appealing to Ruth's nurse's instinct worked, reminding her that the last thing Alfie needed was for his mother to be a casualty, too. Ruth took the cup. Her body ached for her baby, her swollen breasts a constant reminder that Alfie should have been fed hours ago. 'He'll be so cold and so hungry,' she moaned. 'How could she do this?

'She's lived in that place all her life. Who knows what that does to you?' Peggy replied.

Ruth turned to her, her face streaming with tears. 'They could put me in there for a million years and I wouldn't do this to another human being.' Peggy folded her in her arms, soothing her like a child. She was refusing to allow herself to think morbid thoughts; instead, she was trying to reconstruct in her mind the events that had lead Martha to abduct Alfie. Something did not add up. 'She dint say anything to you?'

'No, I told you!' Ruth flung at her, her nerves stretched to breaking point. 'I dint even see her.'

'I've known Martha Travis ever since she went to St Margaret's – she's not like this. Something happened to her,' Peggy reflected.

'She took my baby!' Ruth cried wretchedly. 'That's what happened.'

It was more complicated than that, Peggy was sure. She was convinced Gwen Phillips held the key to Martha's disappearance. Maybe Gwen had been holding out on her before? If she was right, Peggy thought, Gwen might be the only person who could save Alfie.

'She told you. She dunt know woman,' Jean Alsop said protectively, when Peggy returned to their house. Her mother sat stone-faced, rocking. A squall of wind blasted a shower of rain against the windowpane, causing her to glance out into the blackness, but she said nothing.

'I know what she told me. Is that true, Gwen?' Peggy addressed her directly.

'Peggy!' Jean was shocked at her forthright intervention. Peggy turned round to her. 'Something upset Martha this morning. Something so bad that she's taken my sister-in-law's child.'

'I know you're worried, but—' Jean began, affronted, but Peggy continued to address Gwen. 'You were desperate to get into St Margaret's, Gwen, weren't you? Not because you wouldn't rather stay here with your family but because you knew it was getting difficult for them.'

'She can stay here as long as she wants.'

Peggy became more brutal. 'Just a little house, int it, Gwen? And you using up one of bedrooms with three growing boys. And you're not getting any younger, are you? You don't want Jean running around after you, do you?'

'Peggy! How dare you!' Jean said furiously. Gwen's rocking became faster. She stared straight ahead, not answering. Peggy upped the ante. 'You don't want to be a burden. You're a proud woman—'

'That's enough!' Jean was not going to have her mother interrogated as if she was a liar or a criminal or a murder suspect.

Peggy ignored her. '—so why would a proud woman like you – a lady that's made up her mind about something – come running home to her daughter just because she spilt a cup of tea on herself?' Still Gwen said nothing, her face a mask. Her impassiveness convinced Peggy that she did know something, something vital. If she really hadn't met Martha before, Peggy reasoned, she would have protested her innocence.

Jean, however, was not going to give Peggy the chance to find out. 'Will you go now, please?' she demanded, white-lipped with anger.

Peggy got up reluctantly, giving it one last shot. 'I don't pretend to know what's going on here,' she said, looking hard into Gwen's hooded eyes. 'But I do know that a little baby is out there in this and if anything should happen to him—'

'I said, go!' Jean propelled her towards the door. Peggy

glanced back over her shoulder at Gwen, hoping that she had penetrated her defences, but the elderly woman did not look up or respond.

'I know it's your brother's child and all, but to come in here shouting and carrying on . . . I'm amazed at you, Peggy Snow. I've got half a mind to complain,' Jean said, shutting the door on her.

Vic straightened his back, stifling a groan. He looked over to where the police cars were parked and saw Ruth standing by herself. Simon, beside him, was still searching the long grass with forced concentration, his bare head sleek with rain. Vic grasped his arm and shouted, 'Go and be with Ruth. Peggy's gone off somewhere.'

'I dunt want her to see me like this.' He dashed an arm across his wet face, trying to hide his red eyes. Vic clapped a firm hand on his back. 'She dunt need you to be brave, she just needs you to hold her. Now go on.' He watched Simon walk over and usher Ruth into the back of the car. The blue flashing lights of the assembled police vehicles illuminated the two of them huddled together, Ruth's head on Simon's shoulder.

On the other side of Vic, Patricia, who had joined the search, slipped in the mud and fell. Kenny extended a burly hand and helped her up. 'This is awful,' she said, shaking water out of her sleeves. 'The rain's getting even heavier.' Her lips trembled. 'I hope to God Martha's taken shelter somewhere. If Alfie's out in this . . .'

Vic swallowed. Now that Simon was out of earshot, there was a question he had to ask. 'How long have we got, Pat? If he is outside, how long can he survive?' She looked at him, her face troubled. 'He can go a little while without food, but if he's wet and cold, hypothermia could set in. And if his body temperature drops and she doesn't warm him up . . .' She couldn't finish the sentence.

'Why would she put him in danger? That's what I dunt

understand. How could a woman do that to a tiny baby?'

Patricia sighed. 'Let alone torment another woman like this.' She glanced over at Ruth in the car. 'It's usually something traumatic or deep-rooted that makes women snatch babies, if they've just lost one themselves or something. But that doesn't add up; Martha's in her late sixties.'

'You dint know she were – well, peculiar?' Vic pressed.

Patricia shook her head. 'She tends to live in her own little world but she's never done anything like this before. Not that David or Jane have heard of. But then, nobody seems to know why she was originally admitted to Merson Hall.' She stared at the stark outline of the derelict asylum and shuddered. 'Oh, Vic,' she whispered. 'That poor little boy.'

Peggy got in her car and slammed the door, angry and frustrated. Jean Alsop could complain to the authorities all she liked; Peggy didn't have time to pussyfoot around with Alfie's life at stake. Not that it had got her anywhere. The sound of raindrops drumming on the roof beat an incessant tattoo, so loud that at first she didn't hear the knocking. She was just about to drive off when Jean Alsop rapped frantically on the passenger-side window. 'Peggy! Peggy! Mum wants you to come back in!' Peggy cut the engine and was out of the car in a flash, following Jean back up the path to the open front door. Panting, she hurried into the living room, not bothering to apologise for her wet footprints on the carpet or her dripping coat. Gwen gestured for her to sit down. She commenced rocking again, slowly this time, staring into space with unfocused eyes.

'It was summer of 1944,' she commenced. 'It were a different world then. Martha was sixteen years old, just a child herself.'

'Who was she?' asked Peggy.

'Who was she?' Gwen echoed bitterly. 'She was my daughter, that's who she was.'

Jean's mouth dropped open in astonishment. 'I've got a sister?'

'Gwen,' Peggy prompted urgently.

'She came into front room that Sunday evening as we were getting ready for church. This ... boy from village was holding her arm as if he were her husband. He stands there int middle of room – bold as brass – and tells us he's going to marry Martha.'

'I've got a sister and you never told me?' Jean could hardly believe her ears. Gwen switched her attention to her, coming back to the present. 'Jean, I never meant—'

'Please. Gwen. Martha,' Peggy insisted, trying to get her to concentrate.

Gwen shut her eyes. 'Martha were pregnant.' She opened them again, finding Jean. 'You remember what your father was like? He were a God-fearing, proud man,' she said, turning to Peggy. 'When they told him she were pregnant, he went berserk. It were absolutely horrible. In the end he threw boy out of house and the boy – Davey, I think she called him – was shouting back, "Don't you worry, Martha, I love you! I'll marry you!" Then father came back inside and took belt to Martha. I tried to stop him but he beat her black and blue.' Jean collapsed in a chair, shaking her head, shocked by her mother's revelations. Gwen held out a trembling hand to her, pleading, 'It were a different world! She had shamed us! Shamed us terribly!'

'What happened to the boy?' asked Jean, composing herself.

'He were killed in Burma a month later. Martha were ... she were devastated. We took her away from village – told everyone we were going to look after a relative in Manchester. In those days there were places you could go to ...' She paused. 'Martha had her baby and no-one were any the wiser.'

'Gwen, Gwen, what have you done?' Peggy said, understanding now why Martha had been so upset and absconded with Alfie.

'What happened to baby?' Jean breathed.

Gwen turned to her, her eyes brimming with tears. 'I'm sorry, pet. I just couldn't tell you.'

'Me?' Jean stared at her mother – the woman she had thought of as her mother – in bewilderment. Gwen, utterly ashamed, nodded. Jean pushed back her chair and fled the room, her hands to her face. Distraught, Gwen called after her in a quavering voice but there was no response.

'Where would she go?' Peggy demanded, standing up, but Gwen wasn't listening. 'He wouldn't let me take her out!'

'Where would Martha go?' Peggy repeated, trying to stay calm.

'When he died I went to see her but I couldn't take her then, could I? She were in right place by then.'

'Gwen! Where would she go?'

'I don't know!' Gwen buried her head in her hands. 'I don't care!'

Peggy stepped forward, putting her face threateningly close. 'You'll not ruin any more lives,' she ground out. 'Now where would she go?'

'I don't know,' wailed Gwen. 'She went straight from our house to that . . . that place.'

'Where was your house?' grilled Peggy, thinking hard.

'In Diggleswade.'

Peggy frowned. 'The reservoir?'

'It used to be village before they flooded valley. That's where we're from.'


'I can't sit here any longer.' Ruth got out of the police car, hardly knowing what she was doing any more. The real world seemed to have receded, to be lapping at the edges of her consciousness over a vast expanse of blackness, so that the figures moving about in front of her in their fluorescent yellow jackets, talking into radios and conferring over maps, seemed almost to exist in another dimension. All Ruth could see was her baby's face: trusting blue eyes peeping up into her own as she nursed him; his smiles of delight when she picked him up; his mouth puckered in sleep when he lay in his cot. She clung to the images like a drowning woman, as if by picturing him in her mind she could keep Alfie alive and safe and herself from being dragged under the waves of panic-stricken madness threatening to engulf her. Simon appeared in front of her and his mouth was moving but Ruth, in her dream-like state, couldn't make out the words. She stared at him, seeing but not seeing, preferring this other place, where she couldn't feel the cold, where her baby snuggled into her arms, soft and fragrant from his bath. She began to croon Alfie's favourite lullaby, swaying gently. Simon, shocked, looked round desperately for Peggy, but she was still nowhere to be seen. 'Ruth!' He took her by the shoulders and shook her hard. 'Ruth! Stay with me! They'll find him.'

'What?' Ruth's eyes were glazed.

He shook her again. 'Don't do that! Don't let go! Stay here with me, darling. We'll get Alfie back.'

She clung to him with a sob and he held her tight, now worried almost as much about her as he was about Alfie.

Nearby, two senior police officers were talking in low voices. Simon overheard one say, 'There's no-one here', and froze as the other one replied, in a resigned voice, 'We'll have to start searching rivers and canals.' Simon closed his eyes and prayed, 'Please, God, no', when another officer came running over, panting. 'Sir! I think we've got some news!'

Peggy, having phoned the police on her mobile, set off for Diggleswade reservoir, driving as fast as she could in the foul weather. The reservoir was in the valley next to Skelthwaite, a mile and a half from the outskirts of town; difficult for a sixty-eight-year-old woman carrying a baby, but not impossible. She peered through the misted-up windscreen, rubbing a clear patch with her hand, trying to see the narrow road as her headlights bumped and dipped on the uneven surface. At last, she recognized the wall by the reservoir and pulled over onto the verge. She got out, turning up her collar against the bitter wind. It took her eyes a while to adjust to the blackness and at first she couldn't make out anything, but gradually shapes became clearer. She walked to a sheep fence a little further along and looked down at the vast body of water. The clouds scudding across the night sky parted momentarily to reveal a pale sliver of moon. In its weak light Peggy saw a sight that made her blood run cold: a figure wading out into the dark water. She cupped her hands and shouted, 'Martha! Martha!', but there was no response. Climbing over the fence, she hurried down through some trees towards the water's edge, tripping and stumbling over exposed roots and fallen branches. Martha continued to wade steadfastly out into the reservoir, her eyes fixed on a distant point as if drawn to it like a magnet. The water had reached mid-thigh level but she seemed oblivious to it. Peggy, reaching the shore, gasped with horror as she spotted a pair of tiny legs dangling limply from Martha's arms. 'Martha, Martha,' she shouted again, trying to sound calm. Martha, now almost waist-deep, stopped and looked around wildly, as if she had just woken up from a trance. 'Davey?' she called, alarmed. 'Davey?' Clearly disorientated, she turned towards Peggy's voice.

'Come here, Martha. Come to me. It's alright.' Peggy held out her hand encouragingly. 'Come on, Martha. Give me baby.' Martha took a hesitant step forwards cradling Alfie, his feet just brushing the surface, but slipped on the slimy bottom and fell backwards, flailing in the freezing water. Peggy plunged into the reservoir, striking out towards Martha, her only thought of saving Alfie. She saw part of his white ski-suit go under as Martha thrashed about, unable to regain her footing, and made a grab for him. Martha, in her panic, had Alfie in a vice-like grip and Peggy struggled to wrest him from her. 'Give me baby! Martha, give me baby!' she screamed, trying desperately to keep his head above the water. For a second, Peggy thought that she, too, was going to overbalance, but she managed to stand firm and prise Alfie from Martha's fingers. Holding him close to her chest, she waded back to the shore. His body was so cold and still, she couldn't tell whether he was alive or dead. Full of dread, she slipped a finger inside the neck of his hood and felt for a pulse.

Ruth and Simon followed the convoy of police cars across the exposed moorland towards Diggleswade, both so taut with anxiety that they did not trust themselves to speak. The cavalcade pulled over onto a grass verge behind Peggy's car and searchers began to spill out, the police officers shining powerful torches through the trees. 'Ruth.' Simon put a restraining hand on her arm. 'Let me go. You stay here.'

'No.' She was out of the Jeep in a flash. 'He's my son. He needs me.'

'Ruth, love.' How could he prepare her for the worst? She had acted so strangely back at the Hall that he didn't know what she would do. 'He's been outside a very long time. And if he's been in the water . . .' Simon swallowed, unable to continue. Suddenly, there was a shout from the shoreline.

'They're over here!' Torch beams picked out Peggy staggering wearily up the slope, one arm cradling Alfie, the other leading Martha. Ruth half-fell over the fence and raced towards them, Simon hot on her heels. 'Alfie, Alfie,' Ruth snatched the baby from Peggy's arms, crooning his name over and over again. His feeble, exhausted cry was the sweetest sound in all the world.

'Is he alright?' Simon asked Peggy, who was dripping wet and shivering.

'He's fine,' she reassured him. Simon took one look at Martha, who was also soaked and trembling, and realized how close his tiny son must have come to drowning. 'You bloody evil bitch! I'll have you locked up,' he shouted, his face contorted with rage.

'No, Simon, not now,' Peggy said sternly, as Martha

cowered behind her. David and Jane came over with blankets to wrap them both in and Simon turned back to Ruth and Alfie, totally overcome. After the terrible visions he had tortured himself with, the sight of their baby alive and well was too much for him. His tears fell unchecked on Alfie's bawling face. 'C'mon love.' Ruth seemed to have regained her strength in an instant. 'Let's get him to doctor, have him checked over. Then we can all go home.'

Alfie had received a chilling but it could have been much worse, the duty doctor, Miss McKenzie, told them, if he hadn't been insulated by his thick ski suit and woolly hat. She advised them to monitor him closely and prescribed lots of warmth, fluids and cuddles. 'You know what to look out for, Ruth. He's a bit dehydrated and he's had a severe shock. He'll need you more than ever. Give him lots of physical contact, reassure him,' she said, showing them out.

Later, tucked up cosily on the sofa in front of a roaring log fire, the lights down low, Ruth admitted, 'I dint know it was possible to be so frightened.' She studied her baby's peaceful face as he fed, sucking drowsily, his eyelids closed. Simon looked at Alfie's hand, which was wrapped tightly round his index finger. 'A few months ago we dint even have him, but now . . . I can't imagine life without him.' He met Ruth's eyes.

She smiled for the first time that day. 'Peg said to take a few days off, and this time I'm going to. Maybe next week, too, till we're quite sure he's better.' Alfie sighed and smacked his lips contentedly. 'Alfie will always come first. My work's my work but it's not my life.' Simon looked at her, surprised. 'I'm not saying I'm giving up – I made decision to carry on and I still want to. But after Walter and now this, I'm going to put a little bit of distance between me and work. Not get quite so involved.'

'I'll give you a week,' Simon said.

# Chapter 19

If she couldn't talk Stephen into staying in Skelthwaite, Lucy was prepared to use sneakier means. She planned her offensive carefully, asking him casually what date his results were due and then waylaying the postman for three days beforehand to be sure of intercepting the vital letter. That Saturday saw her up and dressed and hovering by the window before the rest of the family had even stirred.

'What's up with you this morning? You're not usually an early bird,' Peggy asked, coming downstairs in her dressing gown. Lucy, thinking quickly, said, 'I want to watch cartoons'.

'Better put telly on, then.' Peggy switched on the TV set and disappeared yawning into the kitchen to begin breakfast. Lucy, spotting the postman at the top of the road, checked that the coast was clear and then crept out of the house, closing the door stealthily behind her.

'Not you again!' the postman said cheerily, as Lucy torpedoed him, nearly knocking his bike over.

'Can I have post?' she panted breathlessly.

He smiled at her impatience and rooted in his bag. 'Let's see . . . one for your dad, another for your dad, one for . . . one for Stephen.' He passed them to her, Stephen's letter uppermost. Lucy stared at the official-looking envelope and knew this was it. She was holding Stephen's future – and, as far as she was concerned, her own – in her hands. The postman, a youngish lad who had been a few years above Stephen at

249

school, also guessed what its contents were. 'I bet he's failed,' he joked, noticing Lucy's anxious face. Lucy, hoping he was right, scampered off. Back home, she tucked Stephen's letter in her pocket, arranging the other two envelopes on the mat in the hall. She rapped the letterbox hard, then dived into the living room, waiting with a fast-beating heart as she heard her brother thunder downstairs. There was a pause, then he walked into the room, a disappointed look on his face. 'No news, Luce.' He flung the two envelopes on the table.

'I 'spect they're still thinking about it,' she said innocently, sliding out of the door and charging upstairs to hide her contraband. Once inside the safety of her room, she held up the envelope to the light. It was impossible to read anything. She turned it over in her hands, tempted to open it, then rejected the idea and placed it in her treasure box, which had its own key. She locked it and hung the key round her neck. No-one would find it there.

Stephen wasn't just waiting for a letter from the examining board. He had heard nothing from Wendy in response to his missive and was beginning to feel ridiculous for having sent it. She really would think him a soppy schoolboy, now. If, that was, she had guessed it had come from him. She was probably spoilt for choice, being courted by a coterie of young professionals with big salaries and good prospects and fast cars. He didn't have a hope in hell. Stephen sat down at the table, picking disconsolately at a piece of toast. All of a sudden, his normally voracious appetite had gone. Peggy bustled into the room, bearing a plate piled with bacon, sausages, eggs and grilled tomatoes. 'Big day today, then?' She plonked the food down in front of him. Stephen, assuming she meant his results, merely shook his head. 'Yes it is,' she chided. 'At least, your dad thinks so.'

'Oh. Yeah,' he mumbled, pushing the bacon around his plate.

'Well, look a bit more enthusiastic about it. This means everything to him. I can't get worked up like he does about chasing after a stupid ball on a muddy field, but it's his dream. So support him.' She surveyed Stephen's slow progress with the bacon. 'And eat that. You'll need fuel.'

Stephen sighed. 'The condemned man ate a hearty breakfast.' Lucy reappeared, looking perky, and made a beeline for his plate. 'Can I have your sausage?' Stephen speared it on his fork and passed it over. 'Mmmm. Mum makes the best breakfasts int world.' She beamed up at Peggy. Peggy ruffled her hair. 'What are you after, young lady?'

'Look at her – she's almost a different person.' David White pointed out Martha, who was playing cards with Shirley and Arthur in the lounge and chatting animatedly. Peggy was making a follow-up visit to St Margaret's to check on Martha's progress and was pleased to see that she had made such a swift recovery. The thought of Alfie's narrow escape still sent a shiver down her spine, but, unlike Simon, she couldn't bring herself to blame Martha. Once the whole truth about her had come out, it was clear that the real culprits were Gwen and her late husband.

David White filled in the missing pieces of the jigsaw. 'Put yourself in Martha's shoes. She's been institutionalized for so long that she dunt remember her life before. Then Gwen turns up. The last time Martha saw her mother was more than fifty years ago. The shock was tremendous. Everything came tumbling back.'

'Poor Martha.' Peggy glanced across at her. 'Did you manage to find out what was going on in her head?'

'She said Davey was talking to her. She was convinced he were really there.' The warden looked pensive. 'The mind plays strange tricks . . . she heard the old church bells. They were going back to village to break news about baby before her parents went to evensong.' He shook his head sadly. 'I can't see Gwen coming here now. Jean dunt know what to do for best.'

'Does Martha know who Jean is?' Peggy asked, intrigued.

David White nodded. 'She does. Jean came down later, when we got Martha home. Martha dint need telling – I suppose the resemblance to Davey was there. Jean's visited every day since.'

Martha, hearing her name mentioned, looked up, suddenly apprehensive as she recognized Peggy. Peggy went over and sat down beside her. 'Hello, pet, how are you?'

'Is baby alright? I dint mean to hurt him.'

'He's made a full recovery.' Peggy patted her arm. 'I know it weren't your fault.'

Martha brightened. 'My daughter's coming to see me this afternoon,' she announced proudly. 'And do you know what?'

'What?'

Martha grinned broadly. 'I've got three grandsons!'

Vic had a set routine for match days and he adhered to it religiously. He took charge personally of laundering the shirts, ironing them on the morning to the accompaniment of a bit of upbeat music blasting out on the CD player to get him in the mood. Today was the big grudge match against Hoxton. Vic plumped for his favourite: Chris Rea. Normally, Vic pretended to be hopeless at ironing. The technique, as he and the other lads down the pub had agreed, involved making such a hamfisted job of it that the women would do it for them rather than be shamed by their husband's appearance. With the kit, though, it was different matter altogether. Vic didn't let Peggy come anywhere near that. He enjoyed pushing the hot iron over the green-and-yellow shirts, steaming out the creases and turning the rumpled garments into pristine condition. It was a satisfying feeling, like flattening the opposition before they'd got a foot near the ball. The fact that they would be covered in mud within a minute of kick-off did not perturb him. What mattered was walking out onto the pitch with your head held high, looking the part. It was necessary to have pride, even if you were going to get thrashed. It was all psychological, he supposed.

Lucy, feeling her bedroom floor vibrate with the turned-up bass, peeked round the living-room door and giggled to herself at the sight of her dad, practically bare-bummed, jiggling around in his jockstrap and socks as he ironed. 'We're on the ro-ad. The ro-ad to Hell,' Vic sang loudly and tunelessly and somewhat inappropriately. The team's shirts, bearing the legend, 'Goddard Paper Products', were strewn around the room, draped over the back of chairs and hung on hangers from the picture rail. Lucy stuffed her hand in her mouth to stop herself from bursting out with laughter and ran back upstairs to where Stephen was getting ready. He wasn't his normal jokey self and she felt a pang of guilt for hiding his results. 'Can I walk to match with you?' she asked, hoping to cheer him up.

'I suppose so, Trouble,' he replied, cuffing her round the head in playful, big-brother mode. Lucy, delighted, fought back and they scuffled for a minute on the landing. 'Ow! Get off!' Stephen dumped her unceremoniously on the floor. 'You're getting too good at this,' he said, dusting himself down. 'Just as well I'm going.'

'Or not,' she added hastily, readjusting her hair slide.

'Or not,' he echoed, looking downcast again.

'Would you like a cold drink?'

Stephen blinked at the unexpected offer. 'Ta, Luce. And a couple of biscuits. Since you're asking.'

'You won't get this service at university,' she said, skipping down the stairs.

Half an hour later, Vic having gone on ahead, Stephen and Lucy set off for the Skelthwaite Scorpions Rugby League Club, walking hand-in-hand. 'Did you know circus is coming to town int summer?' she asked, walking quickly to keep abreast of his long strides.

'Circus always comes to town int summer.'

'I know. We're lucky, aren't we?' Stephen said nothing. 'And they're going to build a swimming pool next to library,' Lucy continued, offhand.

'Are they?' This was the first Stephen had heard of it.

'I expect they might. I'm glad I live here, aren't you?'

'Ecstatic,' he replied dryly.

Deborah and Henry approached from the opposite direction and stopped as they met up with them. 'Stephen!' Deborah exclaimed, blushing slightly. She was still holding a candle for him, especially since Henry had told her all about Stephen's mysterious 'older woman'. The fact that he had had an affair with Miss Atkins made him all the more glamorous in Deborah's eyes. Moreover, the news that it had apparently ended gave her renewed hope. She moved apart from Henry slightly, trying to convey that he wasn't her boyfriend. Henry and Deborah had been tagging around together, mainly because Stephen had gone to ground since his resits.

'Alright? What's happening?'

'Nothing – as usual,' Henry said, kicking a pebble.

'Shut up, Henry,' Lucy said sharply, causing the others to look at this outspoken little shrimp in amazement.

'Have you got your results?' Deborah asked.

'Not yet.'

'Gail Samways got hers int post this morning. And Robbie.'

'What did they get?'

'Gail got a "C".'

'And Robbie got another unclassified,' Henry snorted, pulling a stupid face to indicate Robbie's level of intelligence. 'So he won't be going anywhere.'

Deborah, who hadn't taken her eyes off Stephen's face, said, 'You should phone school.'

'I did.'

Lucy blanched suddenly.

'There's no-one there at weekends. Monday morning, I suppose.' He sounded resigned.

Deborah smiled warmly. 'Well, good luck.'

'Come on.' Lucy pulled at Stephen's sleeve. 'We're going to be late.' She started to walk away, dragging her brother along with her. He turned back to the others, amused. 'Are you coming to match?'

'No,' said Henry, who knew that Deborah fancied Stephen and was still working up to asking her out himself.

'Yes,' said Deborah, eager to see her hero in action. Stephen looked from one to the other. 'I'll see you there, then – when you've made up your minds.'


'D'you think he'll be alright, out int cold?' Simon peered anxiously into the pram at Alfie, who was swaddled in several layers of clothing. Alfie beamed back at him and waved his arms excitedly.

'Fresh air'll do him good. He's been cooped up in here these past few days, he needs a change of scene.' Ruth leaned into the pram and pulled Alfie's hat down to protect his ears.

'Are you alright? About going out with him again?'

She straightened up and looked at him. 'We've got to do it some time, Simon,' she said decisively. 'We can't keep him wrapped in cotton wool. Goes without saying I won't be taking him anywhere near work from now on. We've agreed that. But this is just a local rugby match.'

He shrugged on his coat. 'I know. Just don't let go of pram.'

'As if.'

They strolled down towards the ground, admiring the daffodils poking through the grass on the banksides and in peoples' gardens. 'Nice day for it,' Ruth commented, breathing in the crisp air.

'Be even nicer if we win. Which we won't,' Simon replied, negative as ever about the Scorpions' chances.

'What about Kenny. Hasn't he made a difference?'

'He's taught them to do Maori dances. I dunt know about their passing and tackling, though.' Simon was silent for a minute. 'He's going back after this. I reckon if they can't beat Hoxton today, that's it. I'm withdrawing sponsorship. I've already warned Vic.'

'Simon! You can't! Rugby Club's – well, it's a symbol, int it? Of Skelthwaite.'

'Then they can find another sponsor. I can't afford to have my name connected with a bunch of losers.' Terry's car went past and Simon waved automatically.

'It'd create a lot of bad feeling,' Ruth warned.

'I can handle it.'


Vic hung each lovingly pressed shirt up on its peg in the whitewashed changing room and stood back a moment, enjoying a moment of peace before the onslaught. Kenny came into the changing room and clicked his tongue, giving him the thumbs up sign. 'Ready, Vic?

'Ready as I'll ever be.'

'Good man.' He slapped him on the back. There was a clatter of feet the other side of the door and Dick charged in, looking excited. 'They're here, Vic.'

'Right.' Vic squared his shoulders and lead the way outside, to where the Hoxton Giants were disembarking from their coach. 'Alright, lads? Welcome to Skelthwaite. Changing rooms are through bar, then take stairs down to basement.' The team filed past, giving Dick, Kenny and Stephen, who had just arrived, the chance to check them out. A man in a trilby hat and natty jacket got off the coach and came over, arm outstretched. 'Vic!' he shouted loudly, pumping his hand.

'Colin! Long time.' The Hoxton coach, Colin Butler, glanced around disparagingly. 'Lottery money hasn't come through, then?' He noticed Vic's miffed expression and dug him with an elbow. 'Only joking. Little bird told me you're still playing – it's never true?'

'Don't know about playing,' Vic said modestly. 'I'm still staggering up and down pitch.'

256

Colin Butler pointed a mocking finger at him. 'Don't you go having a coronary ont pitch and upsetting my young blokes.'

'I do alright,' Vic replied, stung, as he disappeared inside, calling over his shoulder, 'I'll just get lads settled in.'

Dick, who had been hanging around the doorway with the others, came over looking agitated. 'Vic!'

'What?'

'Did you see who that was?' Dick was seriously rattled.

'Who *what* was?'

'The big lad – one who looked like he'd swallowed a fridge-freezer.'

'What about him?' Vic was still feeling irked by the put-downs about his age.

'That's only Graham bloody Shuttleworth.'

Vic balked. 'It can't be.'

'It is – I promise you!' Dick insisted. 'I've paid good money to watch him play.'

Kenny, nonplussed, noticed the others shaking their heads and muttering and inquired, 'Who is he, Vic?'

'If it's him—'

'It is!' Dick piped up.

Vic took a deep breath. 'Graham Shuttleworth played professional league for Huddersfield up until end of last season. He were good, too.'

A pall of gloom descended on the Scorpions. 'What are we gonna do, Dad?' Stephen asked.

Dick answered for all of them. 'Lose heavily, I should imagine.' He went inside and paid a visit to the Gents. The door opened and a dark shadow fell over him. Dick glanced up – and up – at the gargantuan figure who came over to the urinal next to him. Graham Shuttleworth, who stood at least a head and shoulders taller than Dick, leered nastily back. Dick, intimidated, made a prompt exit, trying, and failing, to keep his cool. He went back into the bar and found Vic having a heated argument with the Hoxton coach about the very man.

'You're turning game into a farce! A professional playing against amateurs.'

'I've told you,' Butler said, 'he's not a professional. He's between clubs.'

'He's a bloody ringer, that's what he is,' shouted Vic, turning red.

Butler looked deliberately at Kenny. 'You'd know all about that, Vic.'

'There's no-one in our team who dunt live int town and work int town.'

'Nor ours, Vic, nor ours. It's not my fault he's decided to live in Hoxton while he looks for another club.' Colin Butler looked distinctly smug. Vic, trying another tack, drew him to one side. 'Come on, Colin. It's no fun for anyone being involved in a slaughter, is it?'

'What can I do?' He spread his hands helplessly. 'It's not our fault you lot can't compete any more.'

'Don't play Shuttleworth.'

'No way.'

Vic lowered his voice. 'You've stuffed us for last ten years anyway – without a ringer.' He cocked his head, thinking up a compromise. 'If we're up at half time – and it's a big "if", you know it is – bring him on then.'

The Hoxton coach wouldn't budge. 'I can't do that, Vic. He's int team – he plays.'

'Do you want a match or do you want a farce?' Vic stormed, fed up with being reasonable.

'I tell you what I'll do,' Butler said cannily. He pushed his trilby to the back of his head. 'You forfeit game, we'll get on coach right now. I'll tell Cup committee Scorpions couldn't fulfil their obligations. I can't say fairer than that. He went off to the bar looking pleased with himself, leaving Vic scratching his head in a quandary. After all they had worked for, to be chewed up and spat out by a professional forward built like a barn door didn't seem fair. Still, Butler was right, he told himself – they did have Kenny, and Kenny could kick

258

any ball in from virtually anywhere. He met Kenny's eye. Kenny nodded. Together, they went back to the changing room where the rest of the Scorpions were sitting around dispiritedly, some of them not even changed. 'Why did Huddersfield get rid of him?' Terry was asking, looking puzzled. 'I thought he was one of their rising stars.'

'I'm trying to remember – there was something,' Dick replied. He smacked his forehead with the flat of his hand. 'What the hell was it?'

'How good can he be?' Stephen said, appealing to the others. 'He can't run round us if we're holding onto his legs, can he?'

'He doesn't run round anyone, Stephen,' Dick said morbidly. 'He runs *through* them – and he dunt pick up pieces after him.' He paced up and down, trying to recall what he'd heard. 'Shuttleworth, Shuttleworth. What was it about that man?'

Vic cleared his throat and the talking died down. 'Is he playing, Vic?' Dick asked expectantly.

'He is.' The team groaned, complaining to each other. Vic rapped on the door for silence. 'And so are we,' he announced defiantly.

# Chapter 20

How could a mother abandon her daughter like that, Peggy mused, as she left St Margaret's. Gwen and Martha's history perturbed her deeply. Times were different then, but even so – to have your own flesh and blood locked away for the crime of loving! And not just physically: Gwen had just as effectively locked away her feelings for Martha. *We expect so much of our kids*, she reflected. *We plan their futures before they can walk or talk and then punish them for not living their lives the way we want them to*. Gwen and Martha were an extreme example but Peggy was uncomfortably aware that she herself was guilty of it, too.

She checked her watch as she walked briskly down the road. The match would be getting underway, she realized, and she had promised Vic she would be there. Besides, she wanted to see Ruth and Alfie again. All the same, a nagging worry remained. What would Jean do about Gwen now? On impulse, she decided to look in on them – the Alsops' house was on her way to the rugby club – to see what they had decided.

'Peggy.' A smartly dressed Jean opened the door. She looked embarrassed. 'I don't know what to say. I feel so bad about what happened. I was completely wrong about Mum – I mean, Gran.' She smiled weakly. 'I still can't get used to calling her that.'

'You weren't to know, love. It must have come as a terrible shock.'

'It was.' Jean beckoned her inside. 'Come in. I haven't got long, I'm afraid; I'm taking the boys to visit Martha.'

'And Gwen?'

'Oh, no. She's stopping here. It's too much for her – she's been a different woman, you know, since it all came out. Very withdrawn. I'm finding it hard to get through to her.'

'Why don't you let me have a try?' Peggy offered.

'Would you?' Jean brightened. 'That would be great.' She paused at the foot of the stairs. 'Come on, boys! Don't forget to bring Martha's present!'

Peggy went into the living room to find Gwen in her rocking chair as before. She was composed, but her face was drawn and wore a haunted air. 'Have they gone?' Gwen asked, without formalities.

The front door slammed shut. 'Yes,' Peggy said.

Gwen looked her in the eye. 'I want you to find me somewhere else to live. Not St Margaret's.' She shuddered and said, almost to herself, 'It's too late for that.'

'It's never too late, Gwen.' Peggy sat down beside her and took her hands. 'You could get to know Martha again.'

'Don't want to.' She rocked petulantly. 'I don't have a daughter. She's been dead to me these past fifty years and now she shames me again.'

'Gwen. Don't cut yourself off from your family. There int anywhere else in Skelthwaite – you'd have to go to Huddersfield, probably.'

'I like my own company. Peace and quiet, that's all I ask now to see my days out. Don't care where it is.'

Peggy sighed. 'Think about it for a little while. I'm sure there's no hurry.'

Gwen set her mouth. 'Jean dunt need me any more, now she's got Her. Sooner I'm gone, the better.'

Vic surveyed the Scorpions as they sat slumped in various attitudes of resignation on the changing-room benches. Simon had had a word in his ear, reminding him about withdrawing sponsorship if they lost again, but he didn't have the heart to tell the lads. They had been knocked for six by Shuttleworth's presence as it was. If they knew the future of the club was at stake they might seize up completely. Right now, they needed to be lifted, motivated, sent out fighting. And that was up to Vic. He drew a deep breath and addressed the dispirited team. 'We've worked hard for this. All those morning runs, all those drills Kenny's put us through, all those tired muscles – all for this moment. Nothing else matters.' He looked around at their faces. 'Terry. Your dad played for this club, dint he?'

'Yes, Vic.'

'And yours, Dick.'

Dick nodded. 'And his father before him.'

'Exactly. There's not one of you who hasn't had a father or grandfather or brother or uncle play for this club. We're just the end of a long line that stretches back a hundred years or more. Think of all the men from this town that have put these shirts on, that have drunk in this pub together, that have sweated and bled out on that pitch. Helping each other, playing for each other, putting their bodies ont line for each other. A hundred years!'

Some of the heads came up at this. They were all listening. Vic, inspired, continued: 'You remember those men when you make a tackle this afternoon. When you run, when you pass, when you kick, when you score! Remember them! Because they are going to be out there with us – hundreds and hundreds of ghosts watching us, willing us on, willing us to be as brave and strong as they were. Let's make them proud, boys. Let's make this whole bloody town proud.'

The team stirred, a ripple of energy running through the room. Vic felt it and stoked it. 'Now, are we going to do this or what?'

'Yes, Vic,' a handful of them murmured.

Vic cupped a hand to his ear. 'I can't hear you!'

'Yes, Vic!' they shouted in unison.

The crowd cheered as the Scorpions came on – there was a good turnout, Vic noticed, pleased – and he felt the hairs stand up on the back of his neck at the thought of the generations of unseen spectators also there, silently rooting for them. Kenny lead the Scorpions in a well-rehearsed *haka*, stomping and slapping and chanting aggressively, which received applause and appreciative whistles from the onlookers. The Hoxton players feigned contempt, waiting impassively for them to finish. Vic overheard Colin Butler remark, sarcastically, 'That's terrifying, that is, int it?' and saw Shuttleworth bare his teeth in what he supposed was a smile.

Ruth, spectating with Simon, Alfie and Lucy, craned her neck, looking up and down the touchline. She recognized Deborah and Henry, the Bevans – Billy looked well, she noticed – Mr and Mrs Byas, Walter's neighbour, Jenny Cross, and her son, Richard. Walter, of course, was conspicuous by his absence. *He'd have loved this*, she thought sadly. Still, by all accounts he had settled in better than expected at Leeds. Louise Winters had visited him and reported that Walter had made new friends and was now quite at home in his sheltered accommodation. Ruth was about to suggest to Patricia, who was also standing with them, that they arrange a visit themselves, but Patricia's eyes were glued to Kenny as he lead the Scorpions in an attacking drive forward, the ball passing along the line in impressively fluid style. 'Come on, boys, come on!' Simon roared, his earlier negativity forgotten.

'I thought you said they were going to get slaughtered?' Patricia said excitedly, clasping her hands together.

'It's early days. Vic's got 'em fired up, though, I'll give him that,' Simon admitted. At that moment, Kenny took a crash ball, powered through a Hoxton tackle and headed for the try-line, the opposition hot on his heels. 'Go, Kenny, go!' Simon shouted, leaping in the air with delight and startling

Alfie as Kenny, quick and determined, put the ball down under the posts. 'He's only bloody scored!' Lucy, too, leapt to her feet, squealing, 'Come on Skelthwaite!' Ruth clapped her gloved hands, casting around for Peggy, who still hadn't turned up. She smiled to herself as Patricia enthused, 'He's good, Kenny, int he?' then pretended not to care. On the pitch, Kenny shook hands with his fellow Skelthwaite players and trotted back with the ball under his arm, his face set and serious. They were definitely competing, but there was a long way to go yet.

Hoxton, taking their turn to attack, showed their mettle with a strong, well-drilled run, but were unprepared for the Scorpions' bold tackling. Dick, his blood up, stopped an opponent in his tracks, causing Simon, never Dick's number one fan, to holler, 'Well tackled, Dick!' from the touchline.

'Are we going to win, Uncle Simon?' Lucy asked.

'Stranger things have happened. Can't think of any off hand, mind,' he replied, keeping his eyes on the game. He groaned as Graham Shuttleworth moved threateningly onto a pass. 'Here we go.' Shuttleworth, brushing aside Scorpion tackles like gnat bites, pounded up the pitch, swerving towards the line. Stephen, playing full back, hovered nervously in front of the uprights, the only man separating the mighty pro and a try. Suddenly, apparently from out of nowhere, Kenny came hammering across, crashing into Shuttleworth with such force that he dislodged the ball from his hands. It bounced towards Stephen who saw his chance and booted it downfield, catching the Hoxton players unawares. He sprinted after it, hacking on again, as the crowd yelled for Skelthwaite. With the opposition closing in, he gave the ball one more kick, dribbling it over the Hoxton try-line and falling on it triumphantly. The supporters went wild, screaming and dancing, particularly Deborah, until she was given a pointed look by Henry. On the pitch, Stephen was being mobbed by his delighted team-mates. 'Good lad.' Vic, absolutely chuffed, embraced his son. Kenny squared up for the conversion, placing the ball down carefully in front of him. His kick sent the ball sailing high and clean between the posts. The Hoxton Giants looked on sourly, shaking their heads, unprepared for such proficient play from the Scorpions. 'Come on, boys! It's a shambles!' Colin Butler said angrily, suddenly envisaging a humiliating defeat. He lowered his voice a little. 'Let the Kiwi know he's in the game, for God's sake.'

'Take him out?' asked one of them, cracking his knuckles.

Colin gave him a meaningful look. 'Just win bloody game.' They all knew what he was saying.


'Alright, Mrs Snow?' Peggy, who was miles away, started and then smiled as she recognized the young lad who delivered the post. 'Hello, love.'

'On your way to match?'

'Yes, I am. My husband and son are both playing.'

'Wish 'em luck from me. Talking of which, how did Stephen get on?'

'How d'you mean?' she asked, baffled.

The postman looked faintly embarrassed. 'He got his results today, dint he? I wasn't being nosey, you just get to know envelopes,' he added hastily.

'I wasn't there when post came,' she replied, instantly concerned. Had Stephen had bad news? Even if he'd failed, he would have let them know. You couldn't hide that sort of thing for ever. 'I'm sure they would have phoned me,' she said, convinced.

The postman looked even more embarrassed. 'I gave envelope to Lucy this morning.'

Peggy, aware of how Lucy felt about Stephen leaving, started to form a suspicion in her mind. 'Thank you very much, love. We'll let you know.' She decided to go back to the house first, to have a thorough search for the letter. So much rested on one, slim envelope. For all of them.

'Come on, boys! Fantastic stuff! Keep 'em going, Vic! Nearly half-time,' Simon shouted, beside himself, as the Scorpions passed the ball sweetly down the line. 'Spin it to Kenny! Spin it!' he added, grinning madly as Kenny took possession. Kenny started to make ground but a Hoxton player managed to grab his legs. Pinioned, but still standing, he looked around for someone to offload the ball to but was knocked flying by two more Hoxton players hitting him from two different directions in a vicious pincer tackle. He hit the floor with a yell of pain and lay doubled up in the mud, clutching his arm. 'Referee!' Simon shouted, outraged at the flagrantly illegal tackle. The Skelthwaite players, realizing what had happened, exploded with fury and began trading blows with the opposition. A fierce scuffle ensued, all the tensions between the two sides coming out, as the crowd screamed its disapproval at Kenny's treatment. Shuttleworth, needled by Stephen's earlier try, faced up to him, jaw jutting. 'Come on, little boy – I'll knock you into next week,' he goaded, advancing.

Stephen, a David to Shuttleworth's Goliath, stood his ground. 'You could try.'

Terry hauled him away before another Skelthwaite player was floored with a serious injury. 'Leave it, Stephen – he's not worth it.'

On the touchline, Simon glanced about for his sister. 'Where's Peggy?'

'Working, I expect,' Ruth said.

'There are men putting it ont line for this town – she should be here,' he demanded, suddenly a passionately loyal supporter. Patricia, watching Kenny anxiously, said nothing. Vic, also concerned about Kenny, who was still on the ground, asked, 'Is it your arm?'

Kenny grimaced with pain but tried to cover his agony. 'It's alright.'

Dick also came over. 'Can you carry on, Kenny?'

'Yeah, no worries.' They helped him to his feet, Kenny

holding on to his arm. Vic, noticing him wince, realized he was trying to tough it out. He gestured urgently to Patricia, who came hurrying across instantly, her face a picture of concern.

'I said I'm alright, Vic.'

Patricia ignored his protests. 'Let me see, Kenny.' He held out his arm. 'Move your fingers.' Kenny could not. 'It's broken,' she said to Vic. 'I'll take him to hospital in my car.'

'I'm sorry, Vic,' Kenny said. The others gathered round, devastated. Without Kenny, their chances of winning had plummeted. Kenny glared at them, daring them to give up hope. As Patricia helped him off, to sympathetic applause, he issued a final brusque instruction through gritted teeth. 'Beat them, lads! Beat them.'

'What's got into them? They were going super. Now they're playing like a load of girls,' Simon said crossly, as the second half got underway with the Scorpions visibly drooping. Hoxton, having despatched Kenny, had their tails up and soon engineered a try for Shuttleworth, who tanked through the Scorpions' defence with ease. Five minutes later, he repeated the performance, swatting Stephen and Terry into the mud to score another effortless try. Simon shook his head despairingly as the conversion flew over the posts. After that, things went from bad to worse. As the attacking Scorpions passed the ball down the line, Dick, clumsy fingered, knocked it forward with his hand, to groans from his colleagues. The referee blew his whistle. 'Knock-on, scrum down! Hoxton ball.'

'Couldn't catch a bloody cold,' Simon said, bitterly disappointed now. The two scrums prepared to engage, Shuttleworth goading Dick, his opposite prop, 'My son's better than you – he's three!'

'Shut your face,' Dick spat back, as the two front rows crunched together like bulls locking horns.

Simon, his loyalty for his team evaporating, said, 'Why did

we have to be born in Skelthwaite, Luce?', causing his young niece to flounce huffily, 'There's nothing wrong with Skelthwaite. Why does everyone keep saying there is?'

'Hang on.' Simon's eyes were fixed on the scrum, which had erupted into a most unsportsmanlike melee. He watched, open-mouthed, as Dick sprinted away, hotly pursued by an enraged Graham Shuttleworth, who was obviously intent on making mincemeat out of him. 'Vic! Get him off me! Get him off me!' Dick shouted, scared, swerving and sidestepping all over the pitch. The two front rows stopped trading insults to observe as Shuttleworth, his quarry within striking distance, pounced, sending Dick sprawling. 'Vic! Vic!' he yelled, as the giant straddled him and started laying into him viciously. Several Hoxton players, realizing their ringer had blown it, hauled him off before he could do serious damage.

'He's a bloody lunatic!' Vic said, appealing to the referee.

Shuttleworth, champing at the bit, was having to be restrained by his team-mates. 'He started it!'

Dick, brushing himself down, remarked, innocently, 'All I said was—', breaking off to leap out of the way as Shuttleworth, snarling, made another attempt to pulverise him. The referee blew his whistle again and held up a red card, to shouts and cheers of approval on and off the pitch. Simon, catching sight of Colin Butler's furious face, wound him up further by saying, 'He's off, mate. Bit of a hot-head, int he?'

'Piss off.' The Hoxton coach stalked away to have words with Shuttleworth, who was having to be frog-marched off the field by his own team. Lucy watched it all with saucer eyes. 'Why is he so angry with Dick?'

'I don't know, Luce. Evens things up a bit, though.'

Encouraged by Shuttleworth's sending off, the Scorpions' game picked up, the exhausted men calling on their last reserves of energy to prevent the away side from scoring any more tries. The match was drawing towards its conclusion, the Hoxton players, five points ahead, happy just to mark time now. Simon looked anxiously at his watch. 'Come on boys! Final minute!' Lucy bit her nails. Even Ruth, who wasn't a big rugby fan, felt her neck muscles tense. A scrummage formed thirty yards from the Hoxton line. Vic knew this was their last chance. Remembering a move they had practised with Kenny, he looked down his line of backs, catching Stephen's eye, and gave him an imperceptible wink. Stephen, understanding Vic's sign, nodded faintly. The two teams locked together again, heads down. Vic put the ball into the scrum and retrieved it at the back. He dummied passing it down the line, successfully fooling the tired Hoxton defence for long enough to pop the ball to Stephen instead, who was steaming through on a short-side run. Stephen tucked it under his arm and ran, streaking down the touchline like a man possessed. 'Go, Stephen, go!' Simon screamed, a cry that was taken up by all the Skelthwaite supporters as he powered towards the try-line. The Hoxton cover was closing in from all sides. Stephen, feeling hot breath on his neck, measured the distance to the line and launched himself at the corner with one last, lung-bursting leap. He landed on top of the ball in the mud just the other side of the line. 'Try!' Simon shouted, beside himself, dancing up and down ecstatically. Lucy joined in, waving her Scorpions' scarf. 'What's all noise about?' Peggy came up to them, looking bemused.

'Where have you been?' her brother remonstrated. 'They're playing out of their skins here.'

'Everything alright?' Ruth inquired anxiously. 'I was beginning to worry.'

'Just trying to sort out a few family problems.'

Ruth raised an eyebrow. 'Home or away?'

Peggy grimaced. 'Both.'

Lucy tugged her sleeve. 'It's been brilliant.'

'Are we winning?'

'One point behind,' Simon said distractedly, watching the Scorpions troop back to the halfway line.

'Last kick,' the referee announced.

'This is it. Make or break.' Simon gripped Ruth's hand.

Ruth nudged Peggy, amused. 'Who takes kicks?' she asked.

'Kenny.'

Peggy surveyed the field. 'Where *is* Kenny?'

'He's in hospital,' Lucy explained with relish.

'Hospital?'

'Broke his wrist,' Ruth hissed. 'Pat took him.'

'Bet she loved being his Florence Nightingale.' They giggled and were shushed angrily by Simon, who was trying to catch the discussion on the pitch.

'Who's taking it, Vic?' Dick was asking.

'Terry?'

'No chance from here,' Terry shook his head. It was the hardest conversion of all, right out on the touchline. 'What about Stephen?' he suggested.

Stephen looked dubious. 'If no-one else wants to – it's a bit out of my range.' He looked around questioningly. Vic, his face set and determined, stepped forward. 'I'll take it.'

Dick's face was doubtful. 'You? You don't kick.'

'I do now.'

Simon stared, amazed, as Vic made a divot in the ground and placed the ball down. 'Vic?'

Peggy, unheeding the drama unfolding on the pitch, put her face near to Lucy's. 'I want a little word with you.'

'Why?'

'I want to talk about a missing letter.'

Lucy backed away nervously.

'Not now, Peg, please,' Simon pleaded.

Peggy wagged an 'I've got your number' finger at her daughter and turned back to the game. Suddenly, she was all attention as she saw her husband lining up the kick. 'Vic's taking it?' she queried, surprised.

'I can't look.' Simon put his hand over his eyes. Peggy caught Vic glancing at her and smiled supportively, knowing the significance of the moment for him.

'Come on, Dad,' Stephen said quietly, willing him on.

'No chance,' Dick, fatalistic, predicted.

Complete silence fell as Vic approached the ball. He delivered an almighty belt, grunting loudly with the brute force of the effort, sending it soaring high into the air. For several long, long seconds, the ball spun slowly, a dark dot against the winter sky, seeming almost to hang there. Every pair of eyes followed its trajectory as the kick, falling long and true, cleared the bar. The referee blew his final whistle and all hell broke loose as the crowd celebrated the Scorpions' narrow win. Simon, ecstatic, kissed Ruth, Peggy and Lucy, while on the pitch, a shellshocked Vic stood staring at the uprights as his team mobbed him. For him, the silent cheers from the legion of unseen watchers were just as sweet.

The victory rally in the pub afterwards was loud and boisterous. 'I can't believe I'm about to say this but . . . first beers are on house!' announced Sally, to hearty shouts of approval.

'I always knew you had it in you, lads.' Simon clapped Stephen on the back. There were groans of disbelief from the other players. 'What?' Simon asked, hurt. Vic put an arm round his shoulder. 'So sponsor's going to cough up for next season, then?'

Simon winked. 'The cheque's in post, Vic.'

'I'm glad to hear it.' Vic raised his glass in a wry toast. He turned to Dick. 'What on earth did you say to Shuttleworth? He went mental.'

Terry, listening, joked, 'I've never seen him move so fast.'

Dick grinned broadly. 'I remembered why he left Huddersfield. Apparently, he caught his wife int club sauna with one of lads from youth team. When he asks her what she's doing, she says she were looking for her contact lens.' The other Scorpions guffawed into their pints. 'I just asked him if his wife had found her lens yet – perfectly civil question.'

Elsewhere in the pub, Lucy, who had been trying to lose

272

herself in the crush, was ambushed by Peggy. 'Right, young lady. Where is it?'

'Where's what?'

'The envelope with Stephen's exam results in.' Peggy fixed her with a steely look. Lucy, knowing the look of old, capitulated. 'I don't want him to go to university,' she whined.

'Where is it, Lucy?' Peggy repeated sternly.

'Nor do you!' Her bottom lip trembled.

Peggy, seeing how upset she really was, softened her approach. 'You're right. I don't want him to go. But I love Stephen—'

'So do I.'

Peggy crouched down beside her. 'And if you love someone, you want them to be happy, don't you? Even if it sometimes makes you sad.' Slowly, Lucy nodded. Peggy took her hand. 'Let's pop and get that letter now, shall we?'

Kenny, his arm in a sling, was greeted with a rousing cheer when he came in half an hour later escorted by Patricia. 'Kenny! Ken-ny! Ken-ny! Ken-ny!' the players chanted, drumming on table tops with their glasses. Kenny, a man of few words, smiled shyly. 'Speech! Speech!' someone called. Kenny looked hesitant. Vic placed a pint glass of orange juice in his good hand and got up on a chair, waving his arms to shush the noisy crowd. 'Kenny, I just wanted to let you know how much we sincerely, unanimously . . . hated you,' he said, to a ripple of knowing laughter. 'We hated you on those early morning runs; we hated you ont training field when you shouted at us; we hated you when you wouldn't drink beer and eat pickled eggs.' There was more laughter at this, particularly from Dick, who brandished said delicacy in the air. Vic became serious. 'But we all know we wouldn't have had a hope in hell this afternoon if it hadn't been for you. Thanks, mate. We hope you have a safe journey home and we want you to know there is a corner of Yorkshire that is forever

Paekakariki.' This was hailed with thunderous applause and much good-natured boozy barracking. Vic gestured to Sally, who produced Kenny's leaving present from behind the bar – a framed Skelthwaite Scorpions shirt, which Vic had ironed meticulously himself. 'Thanks, Vic,' stuttered Kenny, genuinely touched. Vic, with fatherly affection, enveloped him in a bear-hug, accidentally crushing his injured arm. 'Ow!!' Kenny winced, retreating, causing Vic to apologise profusely.

Patricia, who was standing behind him, blinked rapidly and half-turned away. Ruth noticed this and dug in her pocket for a handkerchief. Patricia gave her a watery smile and blew hard, before handing it back. Ruth, remembering Elsa Fowles, pushed it away. 'You keep it.' Patricia eyed Kenny moistly and whispered, 'Thanks.'

Just then Peggy pushed her way through the crowded bar clutching Lucy in one hand and a slim, white envelope in the other. She went over to Stephen, who was drinking and laughing with Deborah and Henry. 'I think this is yours,' she said, holding out the letter. Stephen examined it, reading the postmark. 'Where was it?'

'Ask no questions,' Peggy said pointedly, while Lucy cultivated a butter-wouldn't-melt expression of pure innocence. Vic, who had spotted the exchange, came over. 'What is it?' he asked, concerned.

'His results.'

'Bloody hell,' Vic said emphatically. Some of the others overheard this and looked over curiously. The pub, full of regulars, friends and family, fell quiet as word got around. Stephen stood staring at the envelope as if mesmerised. 'Open it,' Vic urged. Stephen took a deep breath and tore the flap open. He pulled out the enclosed sheet and read it, his face expressionless.

There was a beat. Simon said tentatively, 'There's always job at factory.'

Stephen, the colour returning slowly to his pale cheeks, looked up at his parents' worried faces. 'I passed. I bloody passed.' Once more, the cheering nearly took the pub roof off.

Peggy swallowed a huge lump in her throat and tried not to give in to the tears pricking the back of her eyelids. 'We're so proud of you. Aren't we, Luce?' Lucy nodded bravely as Peggy embraced her son, the tears coming despite her best efforts to stop them. Stephen was still looking stunned. 'I can't believe it,' he croaked.

Peggy sniffled happily. 'Here, take this,' she said on impulse, producing her mobile phone.

'What's that for?'

'I think you need to tell someone good news, don't you?' Stephen looked puzzled for a second, then his face lit up. 'Do you think she'll want to know?' he said, suddenly full of renewed hope.

'I'm sure she will.' Peggy pushed the mobile into his hand. 'You don't just stop loving someone – not if it's real thing.'

Stephen, overwhelmed, took the phone outside where he could hear himself talk. He walked a little way down to the river, which used to feed the old mills, and sat down against a tree, hugging his knees. Swivelling round, he took in the town that had been his only home up until now: the tall, dark stacks of the chimneys; the viaduct with its towering arches; the rows of box-like houses stretching like veins up the sides of the valley. The pub was lit up like a beacon, laughter and roars emanating from it spilling out into the night. He breathed in the smoky air as if it was some kind of elixir, and knew, then, that he would always remember those images, wherever he went. Shakily, he dialled Wendy's number.

Twenty minutes later, Peggy came out and found Stephen staring out across the river, his chin cupped in his hands. 'Alright, love? Did you get through to . . . Wendy?' she inquired, making an effort to say her name.

He nodded.

'Well?'

Stephen turned to her, his face shining, and for a fleeting moment she saw again the little boy she had raised reflected in his expression of unqualified happiness. 'She were really pleased. I'm going down to stay with her for a couple of days.'

'That'll be nice,' she said bravely. 'I told you she knew a good thing when she saw it.'

Stephen was silent for a minute, looking back at the fast-flowing water. 'It was only a dream until just now. Leaving here, leaving everyone I know. No more days like today.'

'You'll have different sorts of days. Exciting ones.'

'Yeah,' he replied, sounding uncertain.

'And if they're not exciting – or they're *too* exciting – then you come back here, don't you? We'll not be going anywhere.'

Stephen smiled at that. Peggy sat down beside him, her knees creaking, and put an arm around him. Tenderly, he laid his head on her shoulder. 'I might have said some stupid things, Mum, about wanting to leave and everything. I dint mean to upset you.'

She pulled him close. 'I know, love. Everyone has to find their place. Some people are lucky and find it in their back garden; some people find it further afield. The only important thing is that you find it.'

'I'll miss you, Mum,' he said, pecking her cheek. She squeezed him again. 'You'd better.'

The celebrations continued to get noisier and wilder, culminating in Vic's decision to stage a blow-by-blow re-enactment of his moment of glory for Kenny's benefit. Stumbling and giggling in the dark, he led Kenny and the remaining Scorpions onto the pitch, watched by Patricia, Lucy and Ruth, who cuddled a sleeping Alfie. Solemnly, Vic placed the ball in the position from where he kicked his historic conversion. 'I'm standing here. Hundreds of people watching—'

'Thoushands,' interrupted Terry.

'—and I can feel the opposition putting evil eye on me but I block it out, concentrating.'

Peggy and Stephen, wandering back to the pub, heard their voices and came over. 'What are they doing now?' Peggy asked.

Ruth snorted with laughter. 'It's an action replay for Kenny.'

'How old are you, Victor Snow?' Peggy called out. Vic continued to mark out his run, ignoring her comment. 'All those players that have been before us – I could feel them watching me, willing me to put it through posts.'

'Come on, Vic.' Simon rubbed his hands together. 'Kick ball and let's get back to pub.'

'Five quid he dunt even reach posts,' pronounced Dick.

Vic tottered unsteadily up to the ball to give it his now-trademark thump, kicked, and promptly fell over in the mud, landing on his backside. The ball, which he had barely made contact with, bobbled a few yards and stopped, to howls of derision and screeches of laughter from his unimpressed team-mates. Vic groaned. 'I think I've pulled something.'

Peggy bustled over to his aid. 'What have you done now, you silly man? Come on, up you get.' Vic, helped to his feet by Peggy and Stephen, instantly made a miraculous recovery, shaking his fist in the air and shouting, 'We won! We bloody won!' As the others joined in his victory chant, Kenny pulled out an instamatic from his pocket. 'Come on, folks – one for the album,' he said, raising the camera with his good hand. They bundled together, joshing and grinning, arms linked and glasses raised. 'Everyone say . . . "contact lenses",' Kenny instructed, taking a picture. Vic staggered up to him and slapped him on the back. 'When you show them that back home, tell them this: we're not big league, we're amateurs – half of us work in bog-paper factory – remember when I told

277

you it weren't Wembley?' Kenny, letting Vic ramble on, gave him a toothy smile. 'Sure do, Vic.'

'But that dunt make any difference to how we *feel* about game. The difference is *why* we play it.' Vic gesticulated extravagantly. 'We play for love of it – and for love of our fellow men.' He swung his arms around Dick and Terry, who both yelled, 'Gerroff, Vic,' and wriggled free.

'What I mean is,' Vic squinted drunkenly at Kenny, 'Dunt matter if you represent your country or your home town. Principle's same. It's all about where your heart is.' He struck his chest dramatically, took a step backwards and overbalanced again. 'Whoops!'

Peggy looked down at her husband sitting in the mud. With his hair standing on end and his expression of injured dignity, Vic made a comical sight. 'His heart's in right place,' she said, hauling him up again. 'Can't say same for his trousers.'

# Heartbeat:
# Constable v. Greengrass

### Nicholas Rhea

## Now a hit TV series

*If ever anything suspicious is reported in the peaceful Yorkshire village of Aidensfield, it's a fair bet that lovable scoundrel, Claude Jeremiah Greengrass, is not far away . . .*

Whether he's trying to squash six sheep into a Ford Anglia, bottling 'holy' water with insanitary results, or running a coconut shy where the coconuts are not all they seem, Claude Jeremiah Greengrass – and his dog, Alfred – always have some dodgy scheme afoot. So it's down to Sergeant Blaketon and P.C. Nick to keep one step ahead of them – without falling over their own feet in the process . . .

A delightful history of the chequered career of Aidensfield's most unregenerate rogue, this new Constable book will delight all fans of the hugely popular HEARTBEAT TV series.

0 7472 5402 8

**HEADLINE**

# Faithful unto Death

## Caroline Graham

When Simone Hollingsworth fails to turn up at bell-ringing practice, her fellow campanologists are unsurprised. Pleasant but dull is the verdict of the Fawcett Green villagers on Simone, who has made countless forays into village activities but stuck at none. Bell-ringing, it seems, is the latest hobby to have fallen by the wayside.

Only her neighbours, the ever-vigilant Brockleys, suspect the worst, for Simone's husband Alan has been behaving very oddly. But even the Brockleys have little inkling of the real reason behind Simone's disappearance. And they certainly have no sense of how her fate is linked to that of their adored only daughter, Brenda. When the discovery of a body draws Chief Inspector Barnaby to the village, it soon becomes apparent that unravelling the painful, tragic connections will stretch the perspicacious Inspector's powers of persuasion to the full.

'The best-written crime novel I've read in ages' Susan Hill, *Good Housekeeping*

'An exemplary crime novel' *Literary Review*

'An uncommonly appealing mystery . . . a real winner' *Publishers Weekly*

'One of those rare books you truly don't want to end . . . satisfies on every level' *San Francisco Chronicle*

0 7472 4970 9

**HEADLINE**